KISS OF FIRE

"When are you going to let me go?" Barbara demanded. "I'll be missed in a few hours if I'm not already." She tried to free herself from his iron grip.

Instead, he drew her closer still. She felt the heat of his skin, then his lips touched her cheek, moving toward her mouth. She gasped in surprise.

He kissed her, his hands firm on her waist. Startled, she stood frozen. She felt strange, light-headed, giddy. An excitement rose in her, a strange expectancy coupled with outrage. How dare he!

Barbara wrenched herself away from him. "Don't touch me again!" she cried. She couldn't stay shut up in this boxcar with him—with a murdering Reb! He was the enemy!

He recaptured her wrists, holding both of them in one sinewy hand, his body pressing against hers.

"No!" she cried, as much to herself as to him.

His lips found hers. Gentle. A lover's kiss.

Her will dissolved. . . .

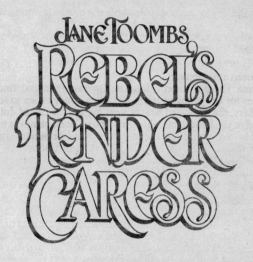

JANE TOOMBS

REBEL'S TENDER CARESS

ZEBRA BOOKS
KENSINGTON PUBLISHING CORP.

ZEBRA BOOKS

are published by

Kensington Publishing Corp.
475 Park Avenue South
New York, NY 10016

First printing: December, 1991

Printed in the United States of America

Chapter 1

Barbara Thackery dabbed with a lace-edged handkerchief at the perspiration beading her forehead and wished she'd worn a lighter gown. The morning's rain had cooled the day for a while, but in the late afternoon the August sun shone hotly down on the Ohio countryside once again.

A thick stand of pines between the country road and the water shut away the refreshing breeze off Lake Erie. Barbara had hoped to be able to visit her friend White Deer at the Chippewa village nestled among those pines, but it had taken her so long to find enough ripe blackberries for a pie that she didn't have time. Already supper would have to be delayed until she got the pie in the oven.

Mother Hargreaves had a finicky appetite but she dearly loved blackberry pie and had asked Barbara to make one. Surely her duty to her ailing and feeble foster mother outweighed her wish to be with the Chippewa medicine woman, but since her father's departure it seemed she had less and less time of her own. She'd begun to treasure each moment she could spend as she wanted to. If only . . .

Barbara glanced along the rutted and muddy road toward the Hargreaves' farm and her thoughts broke off abruptly. The horse tied to the hitching post by the gate—didn't she recognize that horse?

The basket of blackberries swung wildly as, heedless of the mud spattering her gown, she ran up the road toward the two-story farmhouse of tailored stone. Because of the sun reflecting a red glare off the house windows, she couldn't be positive the horse was Mercury, her father's gray, but surely it was. It must be!

She hadn't seen Papa for over a year and there'd been no word from him for almost six months. She knew he was with General Meade's Army of the Potomac and there'd been no newspaper accounts of that army in battle since last October. All the war news was from the western fronts— good news of Union victories.

Barbara felt the ribbons of her gray bonnet loosen and grabbed for them too late. When she stopped to pick up the bonnet she grimaced at its muddy coating. Ruined. Her only decent summer bonnet. Mother Hargreaves would certainly scold her.

Why a bonnet was necessary just to pick berries in the woods was beyond Barbara's understanding. After all, at Mother Hargreaves's insistence she always braided her thick and wavy black hair or pulled it into a chignon to keep it neat and proper. Her father had never insisted on bonnets. Or on braids and chignons, either. He'd enjoyed seeing her hair falling over her shoulders.

Papa! Barbara quickened her pace, then slowed as she neared the horse. He turned his head to watch her approach and she clearly saw that, unlike Mercury, he had a blind off-eye. And he stood shorter than Mercury besides.

Her father could be riding another horse, Barbara assured herself as tears of disappointment pricked her eyes. She blinked and took a deep breath.

Why was she dallying here at the gate when Papa must be waiting inside?

She ran up the steps and burst through the front door into the entryway. There he was in the parlor! The officer's uniform with its dark blue coat and lighter blue trousers, the high black boots . . .

The man turned and Barbara halted abruptly. "Oh," she cried, "I thought . . ." Her words trailed away as she stared into the bearded face of a total stranger standing beside the spooled-leg lamp table.

The astral lamp with its frosted glass shade and dangling lusters had been lit and she could see its glow reflected in his hazel eyes as he looked soberly at her. She glanced at Reverend Hargreaves, who stood next to him, her apprehension growing as she saw the stranger's grimness mirrored on the minister's usually placid face.

"Miss Thackery?" the officer asked.

She nodded.

"I'm Captain Gaines of the Ohio—" He

stopped and looked toward Reverend Hargreaves, "Perhaps you'd better tell her, sir."

Barbara dropped her ruined bonnet and the basket of berries and clutched her hands tightly together under her breasts as she stared numbly at the captain. He licked his lips nervously.

"My dear child," Reverend Hargreaves said, still calling her child even though she'd turned eighteen. "Captain Gaines has brought news of your father." He patted her shoulder.

She wished he wouldn't. He always seemed to be touching her lately and it made her uneasy.

"Is father all right?" she demanded.

"He's alive," the minister went on in his deep, soothing voice, "but I'm afraid he's been taken prisoner by the Confederates."

"That's about the size of it," Captain Gaines said. "Major Thackery is in Libby Prison in Richmond, Virginia."

"But he's a doctor," Barbara protested. "Why would the Rebs take a doctor prisoner? He wasn't fighting them, he was—"

"Miss Thackery, if a man's wearing Union blue he's an enemy to the Rebs."

"What about prisoner exchange?" she asked. "Won't they parole him in return for a Confederate officer?" She turned to Reverend Hargreaves, "There are Rebel officers right here in the Johnson Island Prison. Couldn't you arrange the transfer?"

"I'm afraid your father is in no condition to travel," the captain said. "Besides which, since General Grant took over as commander, he's refusing to trade prisoners. The Confederates are short of men so every exchange helps them more than it benefits the Union."

"Why do you say my father can't travel?" Barbara asked. "Is he wounded?"

"I was told he's gravely ill. The conditions at Libby Prison aren't the best. There's much dysentery as well as malaria."

Barbara held out her hands beseechingly. "Surely they're giving him quinine. And there's medicine for dysentery, paregoric and . . ."

Her words trailed off as the captain reached across and clasped her hands firmly between his.

"The truth is, Miss Thackery, the South is starving. A Confederate dollar's worth no more than a Federal nickel and soon will be worth nothing. Medicine of any kind is scarce. They don't even have enough to treat their own men."

Reverend Hargreaves cleared his throat. Captain Gaines released Barbara's hands and stepped back.

"We must pray that it is God's will for your father to overcome his illness and return to us," the minister said, putting an arm around Barbara's shoulders.

She stood rigid under his arm. "Papa won't die!" she cried. "He won't! He can't!"

The captain shifted from one foot to another, favoring his right leg. "I have a long ride ahead of me," he said. "I regret being the bearer of distressing news and I join you both in your hope for Major Thackery's return." He picked up his cap and gloves from the lamp table.

Barbara tried to gather her wits. "Captain Gaines, may I offer you something?" she faltered. "A cup of tea, perhaps?"

He shook his head. "Thank you, no. I can't tarry. I've other stops to make tonight. War is a hellish business, if you'll excuse my language. When you pray, sir, you might ask the Lord to bring us a quick victory. Good night." He turned and limped to the entryway, letting himself out.

Barbara took a step toward the door but Reverend Hargreaves's arm restrained her.

"No, my dear, the captain can tell us nothing more."

All the tales she'd heard of the Union prison on Johnson Island in Sandusky Bay, where Confederate prisoners were kept, flooded her mind with horror. Maggoty meat. Moldy bread. No heat in the dead of winter and few blankets. Copperhead stories, she'd thought scornfully.

But, if they were true, wouldn't a Confederate prison be even worse? The war had started in '61 and everyone knew the Rebs were starving these three years later, but when President Lincoln had offered them amnesty last Christmas if they'd agree to swear allegiance to the United States, they'd refused.

"Stubbornness and pride prevents the South from surrendering," Reverend Hargreaves had said then, adding, "'Pride goeth before destruction and a haughty spirit before a fall.'"

What was happening to her father in Libby Prison? Tears welled in Barbara's eyes and spilled down her cheeks. She leaned against the minister's shoulder and sobbed. Were her father's jailers giving him any food at all? Did he have blankets for the awful shaking ague of malaria?

"There, there, child," Reverend Hargreaves murmured, putting both arms around her while she wept on his chest. "We must have faith in God's will."

Barbara abandoned herself to her misery and it was some time before she became aware Reverend Hargreaves held her uncomfortably tight against his stocky body. Her sobs broke off as she tried to pull away.

He made a strangled sound and brought his hands down her back to press her even closer, his fingers clutching at her buttocks through her gown.

Shocked into speechlessness, Barbara struggled against him. His white hair was in disarray and his square face, ordinarily so benign, loomed close to her, suffused with blood, mouth agape, completely alien.

"Temptress," he moaned, bringing his lips down on hers.

His wet and slobbery mouth nauseated her. Barbara pushed at his chest, trying to free herself. A spooled sewing stand clattered onto the floor as he staggered back, still holding her to him.

As she twisted her face away, his lips made a damp track as slimy as a snail's across her cheek. She felt her hair come unpinned and fall onto her shoulders, felt his hand stroking it.

"No," she whispered, hardly able to choke the word out.

He pulled her with him across the room toward the green plush couch with its curved arms. She struggled against his hold, kicking at his ankles. He jerked her sideways so she half fell onto the couch, then flung himself on top of her.

One of his hands fumbled at the buttons on the front of her bodice while his weight held her firmly pinned against the seat and, although she twisted and turned, she couldn't rise. He breathed heavily, beads of perspiration standing out on his forehead.

"Let me go!" she cried.

"'Thy breasts are like two fawns, twins of—'"

"Stop!" Barbara implored, horrified to hear him quoting Bible verses. "Please stop."

He yanked at her bodice until a button flew off, then unfastened others, exposing her camisole. His hand squeezed her breast through the cotton of the camisole and his damp lips trailed along her neck as his heavy body pressed her down. Desperate, she began striking him with her clenched fists.

When she felt his hand pulling up her skirts, bile rose in her throat. "What are you doing?" she cried. "You can't!"

He paid no heed, his breath coming in great panting gasps. He seemed possessed by a demon, not the pious minister who'd acted as her foster father. He terrified her.

"Jonas!" The voice was as sharp as a knife.

Reverend Hargreaves slid off the couch so he was kneeling on the floor. Barbara scrambled to her feet, pulling down her skirts and holding

12

together the front of her dress.

"Thank God," she gasped.

Mother Hargreaves, in her bedrobe, stood in the doorway of the parlor, grasping the frame, her face ashen. "Jonas!" she cried again.

He rose slowly to his feet without looking at his wife.

"As for you, miss, go to your room immediately," the thin gray-haired woman said sharply, drawing aside to let Barbara pass.

Cheeks aflame, Barbara fled up the stairs. What a terrible scene for her foster mother to come upon. She shouldn't even be out of bed—hadn't the doctor said so? And to find her husband attempting to—to—well, he'd wanted to lie with Barbara in the way of a husband with a wife. Had tried to force her.

Rape, that was the word her father would use. He'd tried to rape her. Men did that to women. But the Reverend Hargreaves? To her? Barbara's mind reeled with shock.

In her bedroom, airless and stifling, she opened the windows she'd closed against the morning rain, catching a glimpse of herself in the rectangular wood-framed courting mirror—hair tangled, dress in disarray. She turned quickly away and glanced around her room as though it belonged to a stranger—the four-poster bed with its white tester, the cottage chest of drawers with the flowers painted between the pulls, the pine Salem rocker, the floral hooked rug.

The framed sampler Mother Hargreaves insisted she embroider hung by the window. "While

God doth spare, For death prepare," it read.

As she poured water from the pitcher into the basin to wash her burning face, guilt crept through her. Was she somehow at fault? Father had warned her never to wear clothes that tempted men. But surely this old gown of brown cotton was modest enough with its three-quarter sleeves and buttons clear to the throat. She'd not worn a crinoline today to go into the woods and perhaps the worsted material clung to her hips—but not indecently.

Not that her father thought the needs of the body indecent. He'd often told her she mustn't be afraid of what her body told her and when she married she should look forward to enjoying her husband as he would her.

It was the time before marriage he'd warned her of. Had she unwittingly done something to trigger Reverend Hargreaves's conduct? He'd held her while she cried—was that wrong? She'd seen him comforting bereaved parishioners in a similar way. Women in the parish whispered to one another of his handsomeness and his kindly consoling ways.

"How fortunate you are to have such a wonderfully inspiring man as your guardian," one of the ladies had said to her.

Barbara had never brought herself to think of him as a second father, but she certainly had never considered him a man to mistrust or fear.

She dried her face and neck, then buttoned her bodice, shame flaring in her as her fingers found the space where the button had been torn off. Her glance flickered to the framed silhouette of her father's profile on the wall next to her bed. How she wished he were here to talk to.

Tears came to her eyes as she recalled the captain's message. Papa was so far away, needing help himself. If only she were a man she'd enlist, fight her way south to Richmond, and rescue him.

Angry voices drifted up the stairs and she winced. How could Reverend Hargreaves have tried to do such a thing? His wife was rightly furious and anger wouldn't be good for the sick woman. Like as not there'd soon be a coughing spell that would leave Mother Hargreaves spent and breathless.

I must go to her, Barbara told herself. She'll need me. But reluctance kept her motionless.

How can I ever sit at the dinner table with him again? she asked herself. Or kneel beside him in the parlor for morning prayer? Can I ever respect him again? Or trust him? The recollection of his moist lips on her skin made her grimace in distaste and long to wash herself all over again. She felt soiled by his touch. If that was what a husband expected she'd just as soon never marry.

She eyed herself speculatively in the mirror as she brushed her hair and pinned it back into a chignon. Her father had sometimes teased her by saying if only her skin were darker, her high cheekbones would make her look like an Indian. At this moment she fervently wished she *were* an Indian.

Her eyes settled on the thrust of her breasts against the bodice of her gown. Perhaps this brown cotton was too old to be worn, after all. It had fit well enough last year, but now, to her newly critical gaze, it looked too tight, too revealing.

Mother Hargreaves was all but flat on top, no bosom to speak of. Words from the song of Solomon slipped into Barbara's mind: "...my breasts like towers..." She met her brown eyes in the mirror and flushed.

Admitting you had a body wasn't wrong, her father had assured her, but excessive admiration of oneself certainly must be. Besides, she didn't want to be reminded of the minister's hoarse voice as he quoted from Solomon words that were meant to refer to the love of God, not love of the flesh.

She felt ready to explode with her desperation to discuss with someone what had happened. Who? Not Mother Hargreaves! White Deer might understand, but although Barbara loved and trusted the Indian woman, perhaps this was a matter that should stay inside the walls of this house.

If only her father had let her stay in the Chippewa village when he left, she wouldn't now be cowering in her room, wondering what to do. Unfortunately, he'd agreed with Mother Hargreaves when she insisted Barbara must move in with them. Living with Indians was unheard of for a young girl, he'd explained.

"White Deer is a good friend," he'd said, "but her ways are not our ways."

White Deer's husband would never have tried to rape me, Barbara thought. There are no young men left in the Indian village, only the old people.

16

No one there would ever harm me.

White Deer's my true foster mother, Barbara thought, not the woman crying downstairs. She pushed the notion away. Mother Hargreaves couldn't help being ill, couldn't help being weak and fractious.

"Your dear departed mother was my lifelong friend," Mother Hargreaves was fond of saying. "I know she rests easier in heaven with me looking after you."

Barbara sighed. However much she preferred to stay in her room, she must go down and tend to her foster mother. Reverend Hargreaves was helpless with the ailing, although skilled in comforting their relatives. It was quite possible he'd hover about doing nothing until his wife collapsed completely.

Reluctantly, Barbara opened the door. An ominous silence greeted her. She forced her feet toward the stairs, descended, and entered the parlor. To her relief, the minister was nowhere in sight. Mother Hargreaves was slumped against the arm of the green plush couch.

"Are you all right?" Barbara asked, approaching her. "Let me help you back to bed."

The older woman's head snapped up and she glared at Barbara. "Harlot!" she cried. "Jezebel!"

Barbara halted beside the couch, one hand half-extended toward her foster mother. The older woman raised herself enough to strike out at Barbara who retreated, shocked and frightened.

"Thank the Lord your poor mother didn't live to witness this day," Hetty Hargreaves said. "Oh,

17

the trials I must suffer for my charity." She stared at Barbara. "Well, what have you to say?"

"I—I don't know why—"

"There's no need to compound your sin by lying. Jonas told me how you tempted him."

Barbara looked at her in bewilderment.

"I'm aware of your sly ways, miss, don't think I'm not. Reading books not fit to be in a Christian home, consorting with heathens when no decent girl even glances at an Indian."

"Mother Hargreaves, those books are my father's. And White Deer is—"

"Will you be still! How dare you contradict me? Despite your unladylike ways, I never expected you would attempt to entice poor Jonas. Throwing yourself into his arms like a wanton! This is the thanks I get for trying to do my Christian duty."

"But I didn't throw myself at him. He—"

Hetty Hargreaves burst into a fit of coughing, choking as she struggled to speak. "I want you to leave this house. Bag and baggage."

"You don't understand."

"I most certainly do!" The older woman struggled for breath through blue lips.

Upset as the accusations had made her, Barbara felt dismayed by Mother Hargreaves's condition and she held out her hand. "Let me help you to—"

"Don't touch me! I'd rather die than be nursed by the likes of you. Pretending to care for me when all the time you coveted my husband. Get out, I tell you. Out!"

Barbara stared a moment at the gasping, ashen-faced woman, then turned and ran from the parlor, knocking over the berry basket as she passed. She hurried across the entry and through the front door into the blue shadows of the August evening. As she fled down the road, her only clear thought was of White Deer. The Indian woman was the only person in the world she had left to turn to.

She headed away from town, directing her steps toward the Chippewa village. After a few moments she became aware of an unnatural red glow low in the sky above the pines where the Indian camp was situated. Seconds later the acrid smell of burning wood filled her nostrils.

Fire! Where?

Barbara ran faster. If she'd thought to bring a lantern she might have taken the path through the woods but, though there was still enough light to see the road, the gloom under the trees might prevent her from finding the path. She must go the longer way by road or risk getting lost. What was burning? With all the rain this summer it couldn't be a forest fire.

Barbara heard the crackle of flames and the glow in the sky grew brighter. Was the village afire? Her heart thudded with apprehension. A deliberate fire? Even though there'd been ill feeling toward the Chippewas of late, surely none of the men from Sandusky would purposely set the Indian lodges aflame.

The fifteen men and women who lived in the Indian camp were the remnants of once powerful tribes that had roamed Ohio's woods before the white men had settled here. Barbara's father had helped convince the town council that they were harmless and should be allowed to remain where they were.

After her father joined the Army and left, though, there'd been talk again of forcing those "heathen redskins" to move on. Everyone knew Reverend Hargreaves's attempts to bring Christianity to them had been rejected by the small tribe.

Running Otter was the chief but his wife, White Deer, as medicine woman, was the spokesman and true leader. It was she who'd confronted the minister, saying, "I must die as I have always lived. And I will die where I have always lived. We who remain here are the withered stalks of plants who flowered long ago and scattered our children to the winds like seeds. All gods are one. All people are one."

Barbara had heard rumors that the townspeople suspected the Indians of harboring escapees from the Johnson Island Prison and she'd taken White Deer to task about it.

"Your father told me he was leaving his home to seek freedom for all men," was White Deer's answer. "He goes to war for his beliefs. That's as it should be. I understand. But is not a man's spirit the same no matter how he believes? That's what I ask you."

"But the Confederates are the cause of this war," Barbara protested. *"They* enslaved the Negroes. *They* seceded from the United States. You shouldn't protect our enemies."

"Little Snow Bird, you speak with the hot voice of youth. When you're older you'll see how your days are fixed and numbered like the crossing stones in the stream. You'll see that the day and the night are brothers, no matter how different their appearance."

Barbara had given up the argument, knowing White Deer would act on her beliefs no matter what, remembering how Papa had often said that White Deer was a more than a match for any philosopher in the world.

Barbara heard shouts and wailing as she hurried around the last curve in the road and plunged into the pines. When the village came into view she halted abruptly, gasping in horror.

Flames licked skyward. Every lodge was burning.

"White Deer!" Barbara cried in the Chippewa tongue, rushing toward the blazing village. "White Deer, where are you?"

Pine branches tore at her hair so that it tumbled loose onto her shoulders. Smoke stung her eyes and rasped in her throat. Before she reached White Deer's burning lodge, the heat of the fire stopped her. She saw dark forms huddled beneath the trees and ran to them, peering into one face after another until she found Running Otter.

"Where is White Deer?"

He shook his head and she noticed with heartsick dismay that half his hair was burned away.

"Is she all right?" Barbara demanded. "What happened?"

He didn't answer, turning his face from her.

Frantic to discover what had happened to White Deer, Barbara grasped his arm and a piece of

21

charred cloth pulled off in her hand. "Where is she? You must tell me." Her voice shrilled with fright.

"They took her. Your people." He spat out the words. "They torched the lodges. They took White Deer. Seven men. With guns."

"Who were the men?" she persisted. "Where did they take her?"

He pointed toward Lake Erie, invisible beyond the burning lodges. Barbara hesitated only a moment before hurrying toward the lake, chilled by apprehension. She stumbled along the dark path, her eyes still dazzled by the fire.

"Clumsy moose-foot," White Deer had scolded many times. "You're too small to make such a large noise. You must learn to move between the trees as the fox does, without sound so no one hears him pass."

"White Deer?" Barbara called in Chippewa, her voice quavering. Whoever they were—men from town?—they couldn't mean to hurt the old Indian woman. Could they? Oh, please God, no.

"White Deer!" she called again, louder.

An arm snaked about her waist from behind, a hand clamped firmly across her mouth.

"Be quiet," a man's voice warned in English. "Dammit, woman, don't you know what those bastards will do to you?"

Chapter 2

Barbara struggled unsuccessfully to free herself from the stranger's grasp. Since her head reached only to his chin she knew he was tall—and far stronger than she.

"I mean you no harm, do you understand?" he whispered in her ear, his breath warm and disturbing against the skin of her neck. "Listen to me—those idiots ahead of us are capable of anything."

She continued to fight.

"You can't free the old squaw," he insisted. "Not from seven armed men. I'm on your side. I'll let you go if you promise not to yell. Do you understand? Nod, if you do."

He waited, his grip firm, until Barbara nodded her head.

"Help me," she begged in English the instant she was free, keeping her voice low. "We must rescue White Deer."

Strong fingers closed around her wrist. "Who

the hell are you?" he asked.

A match flared. Before it went out, Barbara caught a glimpse of a dark-haired, clean-shaven man dressed in blue trousers and a buckskin shirt. He was lean-faced and handsome, his brown eyes intent on her. Apprehension tingled through her, strangely mixed with another, less identifiable emotion.

"What's your name?" he asked.

"Snow Bird," she said, not realizing she intended to give her Indian name until the words were out. "Who are you?"

After a pause he said, "Call me Ishmael."

Ishmael? The name was familiar. From the Bible—that was it. Ishmael, the wanderer. But she'd heard or read the name somewhere else besides. Though he was dressed like the Chippewas, he was no Indian. Barbara tried to jerk her hand away but he gripped it tighter.

"Where do you come from?" she demanded.

"I was headed for Sandusky when I saw the fire," he said. "Unfortunately, I was too late to be of any use. Do you—did you live in the village?"

"I wish I *had* stayed with White Deer," she cried passionately. "If only my father had known!"

"Shush, not so loud," he warned.

"We're wasting time," she protested. "Whoever you are, you must help me rescue White Deer."

"It's far too late. And if we meet the men—"

"I've no patience with cowards," she snapped. Again she tried to pull away and this time his grip had slackened enough so she freed herself. Turning, she ran toward the lake.

If he comes after me and tries to stop me, I'll kick

24

him, she vowed, the way Papa taught me. No one, no white-livered coward can keep me from reaching White Deer.

Did she see a light ahead? A lantern? Barbara increased her pace, hurrying along the familiar path, hearing the swish of waves on the beach. She was tempted to call White Deer's name but she held her tongue, made cautious by the stranger's warning.

The sound of the waves grew louder, the light dimmer. It was, she saw moments later, a torch thrust into the sand, almost burned away. By its fading glow she made out a crumpled form at the waterline. There was no sign of men with guns.

"Please let it be a log," she whispered, forcing herself forward until she could see clearly. "Dear God!" she gasped, dropping onto her knees, heedless of the wet.

Frantically she pulled at the inert body lying facedown in the water. Shreds of burned cloth came off in her hands and crumbled away. "No," she whimpered. "Oh, no."

Then someone was beside her, lifting White Deer's body, carrying it as she stumbled behind, skirts dripping. A frightful burned stench filled the air.

"I told you it was too late," Ishmael said.

He'd come to help her after all.

When he laid White Deer on the sand near the sputtering torch, Barbara knelt and placed her hand over the Indian's woman's mouth, detecting no sign of breathing. When she touched the face, skin came loose under her fingers. Controlling her urge to retch, she laid her ear against White Deer's

25

chest, desperately listening for a heartbeat.

"She's dead," Ishmael said. "She was dead when they carried her off, dead long before they threw her body into the lake."

There was no heartbeat. White Deer was gone beyond anyone's help. Barbara raised her head, her anguish turning to anger. "How do you know she was dead when they took her?" she demanded.

"There were seven men with guns, as I told you. Two of them pulled her, aflame, from a burning lodge. They rolled her on the ground until the fire was smothered—she was clearly dead by then."

"Oh, dear God, why didn't you stop them? Why didn't Running Otter and the others stop them?"

"They're old men and women—injured and dazed with shock."

"But you're not old. Or injured."

"Nor am I armed," he put in.

"You could have reasoned with the men who took White Deer," she insisted. "They would have listened to a white man. How could you stand aside and do nothing?" Barbara's voice broke on the last word and sobs strangled her.

"Righteous men are the most unreasonable," he said coldly. "Especially those who are certain, as these were, that they're carrying out the Lord's wishes. 'Heathen witch,' they called the poor woman, among other things."

Barbara conquered her tears enough to say scathingly, "And so you let them take her."

"I don't court death to save a dead woman. Don't blame me for what happened here tonight. *I* didn't set the fire that killed White Deer."

Barbara, choking back her sobs, bent over White

26

Deer's body and carefully closed the dead woman's eyes, trying not to recoil from the feel of the charred skin. As she finished, the torch sent up a shower of sparks and went out leaving them in near darkness with only the fading evening glow of the sky over the lake.

"We can't leave her here," she said.

"Hush!" he warned.

Listening, she heard feet on the path. Voices. She couldn't make out words.

"Crawl," he ordered, whispering into her ear. Once again his breath sent a frisson down her spine. He tried to pull her with him. "If we can get behind a dune we might be safe."

"They won't hurt me," she said.

"Don't be a damn fool. Hurry!"

Barbara hesitated, infected by his urgency until she heard guttural Chippewa syllables. It wasn't the armed white men returning. She jerked away from Ishmael and rose to her feet.

"She is here," Barbara called in Chippewa.

Moments later she was surrounded by the Indian survivors of the fire. Keeping her voice as steady as she could, she told them what had happened. "Ask the man with me," she finished. "He saw how they took her. Ask Ishmael."

"There is no man called by that name here," Running Otter said. "You were alone when we came."

She realized then that Ishmael had disappeared into the night. Who was he, this stranger?

"We know what the men from the white man's village did," Running Otter said. "Like old dogs we cowered away from the guns and now we are men no longer. Better to have died fighting. Better to have been killed by an enemy's arrow when we were young. Now there is nothing."

Voices murmured in agreement.

"I'll help you carry White Deer back to the lodges," Barbara said. "I'll see that your wounds are dressed."

"No." Running Otter's voice was final. "She is ours and you are of another people. We will care for our own. You go now."

"I loved her!" Barbara cried. "White Deer loved me, too. Please let me—"

"I have spoken," Running Otter said with the authority of leadership. "White Deer is dead and there is no longer a place for you in our hearts. Go!"

As the Indians edged Barbara away from White Deer's body, she thought her heart would break. In her desperation she tried to call to Ishmael but her throat closed with grief and no sound emerged. The Indians moved off, bearing their dead, and she was left alone. Deserted by everyone. Even the stranger, Ishmael.

At last she started up the path alone, her chest aching with unshed tears, her sodden skirts flapping dismally against her legs. After what seemed like hours, she passed the glowing embers of the village and came to the road leading home.

But it was her home no longer.

Still, she couldn't spend the night in the woods, cold and wet, she must at least change into dry clothes. Then what? Where was she to go? What was she to do? Luckily, she wasn't entirely penniless—she did have money sewn into her red woolen petticoat.

"The Hargreaves are God's workers," her father had said before he left. "You'll be safe and cared for, I shan't have to worry about you." Then he'd counted the gold pieces into her hands. "Nonetheless, it's best to have money that belongs to you alone. This is yours, Barbara, and I won't mention having given it to you. Put the coins away carefully."

She'd always obeyed her father. There was no other man like him. Wise. Compassionate. Tears ran down Barbara's face. Now he was a prisoner in Virginia. Locked in Libby Prison and ill besides, with no medicine and no one but enemies to care for him. She thought of the herbs and powders in her room at the Hargreaves' house.

"Wintergreen for rheumatism, willow bark for fever," White Deer had said as they gathered the plants, using Chippewa words for them. "Bear root for the kidneys, snake root for the lungs."

"I've learned as much medicine from White Deer as I did in medical school," her father had said. "And more practical medicine at that."

Barbara's tears dried. She raised her chin and took a deep breath. If Ishmael could be a wanderer, so could she. She felt a fleeting regret that she'd never see him again but her mind was made up. Mother Hargreaves wanted her gone? Well, she was on her way!

I'll go to my father, she vowed. I'll take the herbs and my money and travel to Richmond and somehow I'll get inside Libby Prison to take care of him.

There was no sign of either of the Hargreaves when Barbara entered the house and slipped quietly up the stairs to her bedroom.

I have a right to my belongings, she assured herself. My father paid for my clothes and the books are his. But her heart beat faster as she shed her wet shoes and skirts and she kept glancing nervously at her closed door.

She chose another of her older gowns, a gray silk, pulling it over just two petticoats, the scarlet wool and a white cotton with some boning in the skirt. Obviously a hoop was impractical when she had no way of knowing how she'd travel to Virginia, but she felt limp skirts would make her look the complete drab.

Unfortunately, the summer bonnet that would best suit the gown had been ruined by the mud of the road. Should she wear her brown one even though it was a winter bonnet? She'd never cared much for its fussy ruffles and the braid and ribbon trim. She must wear a head covering, though, or she'd attract attention. Mother Hargreaves echoed others when she insisted decent women kept their heads covered in public.

Something else her foster mother said popped into Barbara's mind. "No wonder your father calls you by that outlandish Indian name. You're like enough to a chickadee with all the browns and grays he chooses for your gowns. White and pale blues and pinks are far more appropriate for a young girl."

White Deer had given her the name of Snow Bird, as the Chippewas called the chickadee, that

30

winter bird with his black cap, white cheeks, and gray feathers.

A spasm of grief made Barbara clench her fists and close her eyes momentarily. Never again would she gather medicinal leaves and roots with White Deer.

The dried remnants of the plants they'd prepared together lay wrapped in the bottom of the small leather satchel her father had once used for a medical bag. Cramming a dark blue gown and underclothing in on top of the herbs, Barbara glanced longingly at her shelves of books. One volume was all she had room for.

She picked up her Bible but set it back on the shelf. The Bible had been a gift from Reverend Hargreaves and she wanted no reminder of him. One of the Sir Walter Scott romances? No, he wasn't her favorite. Like her father, she preferred American writers. Bryant? Emerson? She shook her head. Hawthorne, Cooper, Dana, Melville?

"Oh!" she exclaimed, jerking *Moby Dick* from the shelf. Opening it, she read the first sentence aloud.

"'Call me Ishmael.'"

No wonder the words had seemed so familiar. Slowly she closed the book. Why had the stranger quoted those lines? Who was he?

He was the most exciting man she'd ever met. And darkly handsome. How strange she'd felt when he had whispered in her ear. . . .

Impatiently she shook her head. She had no time for woolgathering, she must pack and be on her way before the Hargreaves realized she was in the house. Thrusting *Moby Dick* in among her clothes, she shut the bag. She'd worked two of the coins from the hem of her petticoat before putting it on and now she placed them in the reticule, looping it twice over her wrist as Mother Hargreaves had taught her.

She glanced at her father's silhouette, hating to leave it behind. But she had no room and she'd soon be with him if all went well.

I should walk boldly down the stairs, she told herself as she crept down them instead. I did no wrong. Coveting her husband, indeed! Barbara grimaced at the memory of Reverend Hargreaves's feverish hands clutching at her.

He wasn't her father so perhaps she shouldn't have cried on his shoulder—but at the time she hadn't considered it wrong. Were all men so easily tempted?

A saturnine face flashed across her mind, the stranger who called himself Ishmael. Though he'd held her uncomfortably close when he'd waylaid her on the path to the lake, his hands hadn't caused the revulsion she'd felt with the minister. True, Ishmael's grasp had been that of a captor, not a would-be lover. Would she have been repulsed if he'd tried to kiss her?

What was she thinking!

Barbara hurried through the entry and opened the front door, looking back before shutting it behind her. The Hargreaves had sheltered her in good faith and she'd trusted them. What had gone wrong?

It was beyond mending now. She took a deep

breath and set off in the dark along the road to town.

Goodbye to the house where she'd lived for almost three years. Farewell, too, to the countryside where she'd grown up during those happy years before her father joined the Union Army. Grief rose in her breast. White Deer and the Chippewa village had been a part of those years.

Barbara set her chin firmly. She was going to her father, she would nurse him back to health and they'd be happy again. They'd be together. She wouldn't dwell on the night's horror at the Indian camp—men worse than wild beasts burning and murdering the innocent. Despite her resolution, she shuddered as the thought came to her that she might have recognized some of those men if she'd arrived a few minutes earlier.

Would she have seen the face of the blacksmith? The cobbler? The clerk at the general store? Ordinary men with ordinary faces, all of them. Like Reverend Hargreaves? His face was benign enough and she'd believed him to be completely trustworthy. Was it a benevolent mask he wore to fool others? Did all men wear masks to hide a secret foulness within?

No. Her father wasn't like that. He never could be.

The moon edged from behind clouds, gibbous and pale, lending scant light. Although the red glow was gone, a scent of burning lingered on the breeze. Running Otter would be kindling a small fire so the spirit of White Deer could find its way to the Land of Spirits. He'd keep the fire lit for four nights because the journey took that long so her spirit would never be in darkness.

Was that so different from lighting candles over the dead in a church? Did God care about the manner of men's grieving?

Ishmael had heard the men quoting from the Bible about not suffering a witch to live. The Bible didn't mean someone like White Deer—how could anyone think of her as a witch? She was a medicine woman, as much a doctor in her way as Barbara's father was in his. Only the ignorant believed in witches, so her father had told her. If he'd been here he'd have prevented this night's terrible happenings.

Barbara shook herself free of these thoughts, aware that her steps lagged. She must be at the Sandusky station before dawn or miss the next train to Cincinnati.

She'd journeyed there by train with her father on her thirteenth birthday, and she remembered the city as having broad tree-lined streets with rows of substantial, sumptuous houses. She'd been a child, really, admiring the trinkets in the Cincinnati stores, begging her father for a set of painted buttons that depicted bewigged ladies and gentlemen.

"No, Barbara," he'd told her. "My present for you will outlast such gewgaws."

It had been Mrs. Stowe's *Uncle Tom's Cabin*.

"This book might not be great literature," he'd said, "but her melodramatic tale will show the moral evil of slavery to thousands who need a tug at their heartstrings before they'll open their minds."

She'd loved the story.

As she and her father had walked along the Ohio, she'd tried to imagine the river frozen over as Harriet Beecher Stowe must have seen it when she lived in Cincinnati and heard the tales of slaves crossing the ice to freedom.

Barbara sighed and drew her shawl closer around her shoulders. The night was mild enough but her thoughts were chilling. Those happy times were over—her father was gone, the book left behind at the Hargreaves.

Once in Cincinnati, what would she do? Was it possible to cross the Ohio River into Kentucky and make her way to Rebel territory? Or would she be wiser to continue on to the East Coast by train and then try to work her way south from there?

She knew she could get to Washington by rail. There she'd only be across the Potomac River from Virginia, and Richmond couldn't be too far away.

Whether through Kentucky or over the Potomac, somehow she'd get to Richmond. Perhaps by pretending to be a Copperhead, a Southern sympathizer, as too many Ohioans were.

She might even say she was joining her father, that he belonged to the Knights of the Golden Circle and had gone to Virginia to meet with the founder. He'd been a doctor, too, she knew. Any Northerner who belonged to that traitorous organization ought to be welcome in the South. Maybe she ought to use another last name. Barbara what? A Reb-sounding name might be best. Lee? Davis? No, that would be carrying it too far.

She heard a whippoorwill call from the woods to her left, then a farm dog barked to warn his sleeping master of her passing. Her mind gradually blanked with weariness as she plodded on in the dark, only the moon's thin rays lighting her way. When she was startled by the mournful whistle of a locomotive, she stopped, confused for a moment as to where she was. Had she come into town without realizing it?

No, the sound must be from a freight train gathering boxcars from the spur track near the mill on the eastern outskirts. Barbara rounded a curve and saw the big round headlight of the engine. Beside the track, lanterns bobbed about like fireflies and torches flared.

She paused again, staring. Men's voices drifted to her, too faint to hear what they said. What were so many people doing at the mill? It wasn't open at night and surely switching boxcars didn't cause this much commotion.

Her hand flew to her mouth in panic. Had the Hargreaves discovered she' was gone and sent searchers to find her? After a second she smiled grimly. They hadn't had the time, and anyway they had wanted her out of their house. They'd raise no alarm.

She walked toward the waving torches. As she came closer, words became clear.

"Not here."

"Damn Rebs—"

Then a man's voice called out louder than the rest. "Halt! You there on the road. Stop or I'll shoot!"

Barbara stumbled and nearly fell. He meant her!

Chapter 3

Her heart thudding against her ribs at the abrupt and frightening challenge, Barbara tried to gather her wits.

"Who—what do you want?" she managed to call.

"I'll be double damned—a woman!"

In a few minutes she was surrounded by men, their faces made cruel and shadowed by the flaring torchlight. Most carried pistols, two had rifles.

"'Tis the doctor's gal—the one living with the minister and his wife," a man said.

"You seen anything of that Reb prisoner?" another man asked.

"Prisoner?" she echoed. "From Johnson Island?"

"Three of 'em escaped. We got two." The man's laughter was without mirth. "One ain't never gonna fight again. T'other's got hisself a busted leg. We aim to get our hands on the ringleader afore the night's out. A Captain Sandoe." He spat. "You seen anything suspicious? Any strangers?"

"What's she doing out late like this all alone, anyhow?" another man asked, pushing his face so close to hers she could smell his fetid breath. His gaze traveled boldly over her. Hadn't she seen him somewhere in town?

"Well, cat got your tongue?" he demanded.

"I—Reverend Hargreaves took me with him to make an urgent sick call," she said, improvising desperately. "He thought they might need a nurse." She pointed behind her. "At the farm just around the curve. But I wasn't needed and I looked out and saw all the lights here and I—I wondered—"

"Better trot right back," she was advised. "Never can tell what a Reb prisoner might do."

A stranger. An escaped prisoner. Barbara brushed aside her own anxiety about getting to the depot. "What does Captain Sandoe look like?" she asked, afraid she knew already.

"He's tall and kinda thin-faced. Reb with the broke leg admitted they all shaved off their beards, so he won't have one. Got dark hair. The guards up to the prison said he could talk as good as you or me. He didn't sound Southernlike."

Barbara swallowed and ran her tongue over dry lips. "I saw him," she half-whispered.

The man with the fetid breath grabbed her arm and she stared at him, recalling where she'd seen him before. He worked at the town livery stable.

"Where was he?" the man demanded.

Other voices shouted questions.

"Shut up!" the liveryman ordered. "She can't tell us nothing with all the hollering. Now, little lady, you just tell old Bill where you saw the Reb."

Barbara freed her arm. "At the fire. I saw the flames and went to the Indian village to see what was wrong. He was there on the path to the lake. He spoke to me."

"Seems like you been all over tonight," Bill said. "What'd he say to you?"

"He wanted to know who I was. I never dreamed—I mean I didn't know there'd been an escape from the prison or I'd have reported him."

"Them Indians hid out more'n one Reb," a man muttered.

"Copperskinned Copperheads," another said. "They got what they deserved."

"If he was heading for the lake," Bill said, "like as not he's looking for a boat, planning to aim for Canada. We'd best get cracking."

"He sure as hell ain't in any of them empty boxcars," another man said. "I searched every one."

"I hope and pray you catch him," Barbara said. "I just heard that my father—" Her voice broke but she forced herself to go on. "My father's in Libby Prison."

There was a momentary silence.

"Damn shame, the doctor's a good man," Bill said. "We'll get that Reb for you, missy, if it's the last thing we do." He looked her over again, his eyes glinting in the torchlight. "You oughtn't to be out at night alone. Ain't safe for a young lady."

"I—I'll go straight back to the farm," she said, sidling away as he made a move to pat her shoulder.

"Give you a lift on my horse," Bill offered.

Even if she'd wanted to accept she'd never be

able to ride with him, her arms around this bearded man who stared so hard at her, who kept trying to touch her.

"No! Oh, no, thank you. You must hurry and I've just a short walk."

Bill hesitated.

"Besides, Reverend Hargreaves wouldn't approve," she added primly. Without waiting for him to answer, she turned and walked briskly back the way she'd come.

"Let's go, Bill," she heard a man say. "That Reb ain't hereabouts—the gal's safe enough."

The horses trotted past her and she stopped, watching them disappear into the night before she reversed her steps to head for the station once again. She passed the engine hissing on the siding and saw with dismay that the sky was beginning to lighten.

"Ishmael!" she muttered to herself, hurrying past the open maws of empty boxcars. "I hope they capture you, Captain Sandoe, and put you back on Johnson Island where you belong."

If he hadn't escaped, White Deer would still be alive. If he hadn't gone to the Indian village for help, there'd have been no fire.

I wish I'd known, she thought. Why didn't White Deer tell me what she was doing? I'd have convinced her it was wrong. Wrong and dangerous. Somehow, I would have.

Those men searching for the Reb captain acted as though they knew all about the fire. And they had guns. But naturally they'd be armed, it didn't mean they'd set the fire. She pictured the livery owner's bewhiskered face. Was it possible he'd been the one who dragged White Deer's flaming body from her lodge and bore it off to the lake?

He could have been. She'd never know. Barbara bit her lip. Was no one to be trusted?

It was Captain Sandoe, though, who was truly to blame for everything that had happened. Oh, how she despised Confederates! How she hated him!

Had he lied when he told her White Deer died in the fire? Who could believe the word of an escaped Reb? She remembered the feel of White Deer's charred skin under her fingers and shuddered. Catching him wouldn't bring back the Indian woman, but he didn't deserve freedom. Especially when her own father was—

A tall figure darted from the trees and ran across the road directly in front of her, making for the railroad track. Barbara froze. The Reb!

"Help!," she cried as soon as she could find breath. "I've found him! Here! Help!"

The running man stopped, turned, and made for her. Screaming, she raced toward the chugging locomotive. Did no one hear? Couldn't they see what was happening?

Hands grasped her clothes, slowing her. She twisted, struggling until an arm came around her throat and cut off her breath. As she fought for air, she felt him pull her tightly against his body. Golden pinpricks of light danced before her eyes and then she knew no more.

When she regained her senses, she found herself slumped over his shoulder. Before she could force herself into action, he'd dumped her onto a wooden floor. A second later he jumped up beside

41

her. She saw him framed for a moment in the predawn light against an opening, then wood grated on wood and she realized where he'd taken her as the pale light was shut away by him closing the boxcar door.

After struggling to her feet, Barbara stood rubbing her throat for a moment before she groped through the darkness toward the door of the boxcar. Grasping the rough wooden frame, she pulled and the door slid sideways a few reluctant inches. Encouraged, she braced her feet, intending to force the door open just wide enough to slip through.

His hand gripped her arm and yanked her away from the door. She fell against him, her breasts to his chest, her legs to his legs, and she heard him draw in his breath, felt his hold tighten. A faint shout came from outside the partly opened door. He shoved Barbara to one side and pushed the door shut once more. As she edged away Barbara could hear nothing but the sound of her own rapid breathing.

The boxcar shuddered, gave a grinding wrench, first pitching her ahead, then hurling her backward. Losing her balance, she sprawled onto the floor, feeling sawdust beneath her fingers. A whistle shrilled as the engine began to pull the boxcar forward, slowly at first, then faster and faster.

"Let me out!" She hardly recognized the hoarse cry as her own.

"Shout all you like, no one can hear you." His voice, quiet, almost conversational, came from near the door.

"Ishmael!" She put all the scorn and hatred she felt into the word.

"Ah, I was right. You *are* the dark-haired maiden from the Chippewa camp."

She said nothing. Her breathing had slowed though she could still feel the quick beat of her heart. What did he mean to do with her? Nothing pleasant, she was sure.

"Why did you raise that ungodly hue and cry out there?" he asked.

She remained silent. If she could get to the door, she might be able to drop off when the train slowed going through town. Even though this string of boxcars was empty, going up the slight grade would reduce its speed. She'd give it a try—she must outwit this desperate fugitive who'd made her his prisoner.

"Your reticence disappoints me," he said. "I was beginning to look forward to our becoming better acquainted on our journey to Cincinnati. If nothing more, you could have told me of your life among the Indians and I could relate some of my recent adventures vagabonding through Ohio."

"Don't lie to me. I know who you are—Captain Sandoe."

"I feared you might have discovered that. Those louts with the lanterns told you, I expect."

"Louts? Who are you to call names? Reb! Secessionist! And, no doubt, a slaveholder." She paused for breath. "Do you enjoy auctioning off men, women, and children? Do you like to destroy families? Sell loved ones into bondage? Watch your slaves whipped and branded? Does it pleasure you to have your way with their women?"

"You sound like an abolitionist tract. I'm surprised you've read them."

"Of course I have!"

"And believed every word." His tone was cynical.

"They print facts!"

"It strikes me as a waste of education to teach a half-Indian girl to read, simply so she can then be fed twisted truths and outright lies. Tell me, Snow Bird, do you believe all you read? Do you think setting letters into type and printing them will magically produce some sort of revealed truth? Have you ever actually visited the South?"

She struggled with her anger before answering. He thought she was part Indian, that's why he was so surprised she could read. She didn't mind him believing she was a half-breed but he also thought her stupid. How dare he!

"Of course I don't believe all I read," she snapped. "Not all I hear, either—*Ishmael*."

"Touché." He laughed. "My full name is Trevor Ishmael Sandoe, so I do have some claim to honesty. And I have been a wanderer of late. Now you have the advantage, for I know you only as Snow Bird. Have you no other name?"

She hesitated. Perhaps if she told him who she was he'd let her go. Weren't Southern men supposed to be exceptionally chivalrous where ladies were concerned?

"Not that Snow Bird isn't a lovely name for a lovely young woman." His voice had softened and she noticed a drawl she hadn't heard before.

Shamed color rose to her face as she realized she was glad he found her attractive. What did it matter coming from a despised Reb?

"When are you going to let me go?" she demanded. "I'll be missed in a few hours if I'm not already. Those men from town know me. As soon as they hear I'm missing they'll realize what must have happened and they'll telegraph ahead to Cincinnati."

"I doubt anyone will put two and two together so quickly. By the time those gentlemen collect whatever wits they possess, I'll be far from Ohio. I doubt that they know how to do much other than burn and loot and kill defenseless Indians. Besides, will you really be missed soon? A young woman who spends her nights at Indian encampments or else walking the streets?"

She fumed. How dare he criticize her!

"Aren't you a mite confused, Snow Bird? Why did you give me away to those self-appointed vigilantes? They're your enemy, not me. They burned your village, I didn't."

"The village burned because of you," she accused, her voice rising. "Because you were hiding there. Like the other two escaped Rebs would have been if they hadn't been caught. You set fire to those lodges just as surely as though you'd lit and held the torch."

"I've heard some befuddled reasoning in my time," he said angrily, "but you top it all. Reading those abolitionist tracts has addled your wits. What you say is madness. It's all madness."

"I'm not mad!"

"Yes, you are. You, me, this country, the world. Burning, looting, killing, the War pitting brother against brother, fathers fighting sons, thousands

45

dead, bodies left maimed, lives ruined. And what for? To punish a few Southern states that want nothing but the right to go their way in peace. Is that sanity? Is that freedom?''

Momentarily taken aback by his vehemence, Barbara pulled herself together. "You're the one who twists the truth, Captain Sandoe. You're the one who—"

She stopped abruptly when she heard him move, saw his dark outline come closer, closer until his lips touched her cheek, moving on to her mouth.

He kissed her, his hands firm on her waist. Startled, she stood frozen while his tongue parted her lips. She felt strange, light-headed, giddy. An excitement rose in her, a strange expectancy coupled with outrage at him because he dared to touch her and at herself for not ending the uninvited embrace.

Like a sound from another world, she heard the change in the rhythm of the engine's chugging. It was slowing. The hill! They were climbing the hill outside of town.

Barbara wrenched herself away from him and raised her hand. She struck at his face but he stepped aside and she stumbled forward from the force of her futile blow.

"Don't touch me again!" she cried.

"I didn't intend to start a debate," he said calmly.

How dare he be so calm when she quivered with fury?

"I'm tired," he went on and she heard him yawn. "I haven't slept since yesterday morning

46

when they killed poor old Dawson and crippled Langley. Good men, better than me, I expect. Since you've negated the most interesting way to pass the time, I'll try the next solution—sleep."

Her mind was a whirl of confusion, her heart still thudded in her chest from his kiss, and she knew she had no chance to escape while he was between her and the door. She must ignore his insults and concentrate on reaching the door.

"A mite chilly in here, isn't it, Snow Bird? You must be as exhausted as I am. We'd be much warmer if the two of us cuddled together to sleep."

"No! I don't know what you think I am but whatever it is, you're wrong. As wrong as you are about everything else."

"I'll bunk down by the door," he said with a sigh. "And I warn you, I'm a light sleeper."

She listened to Trevor Sandoe settling himself. After a few moments of quiet, she decided she might as well sit down while she waited for her chance. Bracing her back against the side of the car while it clattered and swayed under her, she closed her eyes.

I'll rest until I'm certain he's asleep, she told herself, and then I'll slip past him and somehow get out of this boxcar.

The next she knew, full daylight slitted in through the cracks in the sides of the car and she was stretched out on the floor, her bonnet awry. Sitting up hurriedly, she straightened the bonnet and wondered with dismay how long she'd been sleeping. The train rattled forward. Across from her she made out Trevor's huddled form beside the door.

She rose, stiff from the hardness of the boxcar floor and the early morning chill, wrapping her shawl tightly about her as she crossed the car to stand over him. He groaned, stirring restlessly. He still wore the buckskin shirt and coarse blue trousers. Chippewa clothes, gifts to him from the Indians, she thought bitterly. Gifts some of them had lived to regret.

Trevor shifted and she held her breath but he didn't rouse. There was no way to get past him to the door unless she stepped over him and she was certain he'd wake if she tried that.

Barbara glanced about the empty boxcar, searching for something to help her. There was her satchel, he must have brought it along. What was inside? Clothes, a book, some medicines. Her reticule was still looped over her wrist but its contents were worthless for her purpose.

She frowned. Once he woke she'd never get away—she must devise some plan. Cautiously making her way around the car, balancing herself to offset the lurching of the train, she examined every inch of the floor. Near the front of the car she found several staves, perhaps left over from a smashed barrel. She lifted one, a rough stick the length of her arm, and wondered if it was stout enough to be of use. But there was nothing else to help her.

With the dubious weapon in one hand, she eased back to where Trevor Sandoe lay sleeping. She stared down at him. A strand of black hair curled over his forehead, making him look younger and completely defenseless. Reminding herself he was the enemy, she gritted her teeth, raised the stick over her head, hesitated, and dropped her hand to her side.

He'd have no such compunction, she admonished herself. He's probably murdered Union soldiers by the score. Besides, I won't kill him, only stun him long enough to get away.

But what if she hit him too hard? Struck his temple where the bone was thin? The image of a battered face came to her, bone fragments embedded in bruised and bleeding flesh; she saw the face of a farmer her father had treated after the man had been kicked by a horse.

"All I can do is ease the pain," her father had said. "His brain is damaged beyond any repair I could make."

What if something like that happened when she hit Captain Sandoe? He really hadn't injured her. After all, he could have killed her instead of taking her prisoner. He'd done nothing worse than kiss her since then. She touched the tip of her tongue to her lips as though to taste the memory of the kiss and then shook her head in disapproval.

She couldn't stay shut up in this boxcar with him. With a murdering Reb. White Deer's death was Trevor Sandoe's fault. Barbara brought the stick up again—but it was no use. She still felt it was cruel and cowardly to strike a sleeping, defenseless man.

What would her father say? She could almost hear his voice.

"This is war," he'd tell her. "This man is an enemy of our country. Our enemy."

Catching her lower lip between her teeth and bracing herself against the motion of the train,

Barbara raised the stave over her head for the third time, and, not letting herself think, she swung down at the sleeping man. She closed her eyes as she felt the blow strike home.

Captain Sandoe gave a hoarse cry. Barbara, breathless and frightened, opened her eyes to see him blinking dazedly up at her, his right hand clutching his left shoulder. She swung the stave up again, watching recognition flash into his eyes as he pushed himself to his feet with his back braced against the door. His gaze fastened on the stick.

Before she could swing it, he flung himself at her, knocking the stave away with a sweeping blow of his arm. She heard it clatter onto the floor as she was borne backwards by his rush. She fell, sprawling, her breath knocked out of her. Before she could recover, he was on her.

She twisted and turned, hitting him with her gloved hand until he grasped her wrists, holding them pinioned to the floor of the car.

She fought him, thrusting upward with her knee as her father had taught her to do. He grunted in pain, his grip on her wrists loosening so she was able to free one hand to strike a glancing blow to his ear. He recaptured her wrists, holding both of them in one hand, straddling her hips so her knees thrust up at him to avail.

His free hand found her shoulder, the fingers biting into her flesh. She jerked away and heard the cloth of her bodice tear in his hand.

Panting, she stared up at him, his face dark in the muted light of the boxcar. Far ahead the whistle of the locomotive moaned and the train swung around a curve. Suddenly he lifted her with one arm, the

50

fingers of his other hand pushing aside her torn bodice and untying the ribbons of her camisole.

She felt cool air on her bared breast, then his warm lips, his tongue on her nipple, stirring an unwelcome answering warmth inside her body, awakening something within her, a disturbing excitement she'd never before experienced.

He eased her down, still holding her close, his mouth to her breast. His hand moved, sliding beneath her skirts, on her calf, her thigh, touching her lightly. Through the cotton of her pantalets, his fingers burned like fire.

She wanted him to go on and yet she didn't. She feared what was happening, afraid of her own feelings as much as she feared him. She didn't want to feel anything but hatred for him, her enemy.

"No!" she cried, as much to herself as to him.

His lips found hers. Gentle. A lover's kiss. She felt her will dissolving.

A Reb. He was a Reb! She would not!

Barbara twisted her face away and jerked her wrists free. His only response was to hold her closer, his lips warm at her ear.

"I don't want this," she cried, her voice breaking on the last word. She began to cry. "Let me go," she sobbed.

He released her and stood up.

Barbara sat up, pulling her skirts down and her bodice together, wrapping her shawl closely about herself. As she rose, she watched him warily as he paced back and forth the length of the boxcar, his boots slamming hard onto the wooden floor. Finally he stopped and faced her.

"I've never yet forced a woman to accept me,"

he said. "I don't intend to begin with you, hellcat though you are."

She stared at him, tears drying on her cheeks. Did he mean it?

"If you'll give me your word not to attack me again," he said, "I'll keep my promise to leave you alone. An armed truce."

Give her word to a hated Reb?

Yet what was her alternative? She shivered, feeling colder than she ever had before. How could she have allowed herself to yield even temporarily to his caresses?

"I agree to the truce," she said at last, "but I want you to understand I despise all Rebs, you most of all. Someday, Captain Sandoe, I'll make you wish you'd never touched me. Someday I'll have my revenge."

He smiled one-sidedly. "We'll see, Snow Bird. Something tells me that when that day comes, I'll make you change your mind."

"Never!"

Chapter 4

Deciding Trevor wasn't going to give her the slightest chance of escaping, Barbara retreated to a corner of the boxcar where she sat down, huddling into her shawl although the day was rapidly warming.

He can keep me captive, she told herself, but he can't make me talk to him. I'll ignore him.

Pulling *Moby Dick* from her bag, she opened the book, intending to shut herself away from him by reading, but she got no further than the first sentence before Trevor loomed over her.

"You're a constant surprise, Snow Bird," he drawled, his Southern origins evident in his voice now that he no longer bothered to disguise his speech.

"Stop calling me Snow Bird!" she snapped, her intention of ignoring him forgotten in her annoyance. "I don't care to hear that name from you."

His eyebrows rose. "What do you suggest I call you instead?"

"If you must speak to me, I prefer Miss Thackery." Frost edged her words as she kept her eyes determinedly fixed on the open book.

He remained silent so long she cast a quick glance upward through her lashes. To her discomfort he was staring down at her as though he'd never seen her before.

"Melville, abolitionist tracts . . ." He broke off, shaking his head. "I seem to have made an error in classifying you, Miss Thackery."

Closing the book with a snap, she glared at him. "More than one!"

The corner of his mouth lifted in a wry smile. "I fear you're right. But I refuse to take all the blame. You had your chance to explain, to tell me I'd made a mistake. Why didn't you?" To her consternation, he eased to the floor beside her, propping his back against the side of the box-car.

She eyed him indignantly. "If you were a gentleman you wouldn't have behaved like a brute to any lady, no matter what her origins!"

"A lady, yes. But how was I to know what you were—roaming the woods and tramping the roads after midnight? Where I come from ladies are a bit more circumspect." He raised his hand to stop her when she began an indignant reply. "Suppose you tell me just who you are and what took you on that late night journey?"

"It's none of your business, but I happened to be on my way to catch the early train to Cincinnati."

Trevor chuckled. "And so you did."

She pressed her lips together. He was the most

irritating man she'd ever met. Still, what could one expect from a Reb?

"Do you have family in Cincinnati?" he persisted.

A wave of grief caught her unaware, flooding through her and leaving her devastated. Her only family was her father and he was a helpless prisoner. Tears stung her eyes, a few escaping to roll down her cheeks despite her desperate attempt to recover. A sob caught in her throat.

Trevor muttered something under his breath. "Believe me, I didn't mean to cause you grief," he said.

"You!" she sputtered, her voice ragged with tears. "You're the cause of everything. If it wasn't for the war caused by you and your Rebel comrades-in-arms my father wouldn't be lying sick and helpless in Libby Prison. He's not a fighting man—he's a doctor."

This time she caught his muttered, "Damn!"

She turned to stare at him accusingly. "I was on my way to Richmond when you captured me."

Trevor sighed. "My dear Miss Thackery, in the unlikely event you could have made your way through the battle lines to reach Richmond, what did you imagine you could possibly do for your father once you reached the city?"

"Nurse him! Make him well."

He shook his head. "Chances are you wouldn't even be allowed to see him. But, of course, you'd never have gotten into Virginia anyway."

"I would have. I will." She spoke with determination.

"Did you imagine there was train service all the

way? During a war? Once we reach Cincinnati and head east we'll be lucky to get as far as Baltimore without interference."

"I'm not a fool, Captain Sandoe. And I *will* get to Richmond. To my father. One way or another, interference or not."

Again he studied her far too long, making her shift uncomfortably and reminding her of what an untidy picture she presented. Not that her dishevelment wasn't his fault.

"I presume you have a first name," he said at last.

Taken aback, she answered before she thought, "Barbara."

He smiled. "The wanderer and the stranger. Most appropriate."

"What are you talking about?"

"Until we're in Confederate country, I'm Ishmael. Your name means stranger—didn't you know that? Barbarian comes from the same root."

Barbara blinked. For a moment he'd almost sounded like Papa explaining something to her. it occurred to her, most illogically, that her father would enjoy Trevor. She must be more exhausted than she'd realized. Trevor was as much her father's enemy as he was hers.

"The logical course," Trevor continued, "is for the two of us to join forces."

"Never!"

"Don't be so hasty. Think about this—I may be the only ticket you'll be able to find that can get you through the Confederate lines."

Barbara pondered his words. Was he proposing

56

to help her reach Richmond? It was her turn to study him. His dark gaze held hers. Give the devil his due, the captain was a handsome man, the best-looking she'd ever seen. That must be the reason for her rapid heartbeat and the inexplicable warmth deep inside her. That and the fact she wasn't used to being alone with a man. And certainly not one sitting so close—why, if she reached out she could touch him.

Barbara looked away, drawing her shawl closer about her shoulders. "We're enemies," she said firmly. "Both because of the war and for—for personal reasons."

"It'll take an enemy to see you across enemy lines," he reminded her.

That was very likely true. And she *must* reach Richmond. But could she trust him? Especially considering what had transpired between them? Was any Reb to be trusted, ever? Though it was in his best interests to prevent her from turning him in, how did she know he'd keep his word once they reached Reb territory?

On the other hand, admit it, she knew nothing about how to go about getting through the lines to reach Richmond. She hated to think he had the advantage but, at the moment, he unquestionably did. Might not the best course be to agree for the time being? She could always change her mind later.

"I'll listen to your proposal," she said coolly, "but I make no promises."

"Your silence for my help. You be my ticket to Richmond and I'll be yours as well. Agreed?"

It was what she'd expected. Reluctantly, she nodded.

He thrust out his hand and clasped her hers, saying, "A shake of hands to seal the bargain."

A gentleman's agreement, her father would say, Barbara thought, distracted by the warmth of Trevor's hand and the strange tingly feel his touch sent through her. She drew her hand away hastily.

"You must remember to call me Ishmael," he warned. "Not Captain Sandoe, nor even Captain."

"I can only hope I shall have few occasions to address you." She spoke tartly. "I trust you realize I've agreed to this proposition under duress. I'd much prefer never to see you again."

He grinned. "Poor little Snow Bird, forced to travel another night and day with the big bad Reb."

"I told you not to call me Snow Bird!"

"Ah, but the name fits you. Without that bedraggled brown bonnet, at any rate."

"My bonnet was perfectly respectable when I started on my journey! Being forced into your company has certainly not improved the condition of my wardrobe."

"Or your temper. But it's your own fault for trying to turn me in. If the truth be told, I'd as soon not have you with me. I'm sure someone as well read as you knows that 'he travels the fastest who travels alone.'"

Barbara pointedly fingered the book on her lap. "I'd like to return to my reading, Captain."

"Not Captain. Ishmael."

"But we're alone."

"You need to practice or you'll make a slip when others are about. Ishmael. Say it."

"Ishmael!" She spat the word at him.

He put a hand over his heart. "What pleasure it gives me to hear my name spoke in your dulcet tones, Barbara."

Despite her annoyance, her lips twitched in reluctant amusement. She loathed him, he was forever her enemy but still he fascinated her. She didn't even mind hearing him call her by her first name; his Southern drawl changed the syllables, making them softer and warmer.

Soon after, he left her alone in her corner and she fell asleep over her book. She woke with a start some time later to find the boxcar shuddering and lurching to a stop. Outside, a man's voice called something unintelligible. She staggered to her feet. Were they in Cincinnati?

"I think our car has been switched to a siding and disconnected from the train," Trevor said in a low tone. "Perhaps for loading. We can't risk—" He broke off, cocking his head to listen. A moment later he was at her side, her satchel in his hand. He thrust it at her. "Someone's just outside," he whispered.

Barbara gripped the bag, her mind whirling. This might be her chance to escape and to tell those outside who "Ishmael" really was. On the other hand, she'd given her word she wouldn't. What would her father advise?

"A man's word is his bond," he'd always said. Her bond as well, then. But did that apply when the man the bond had been given to was an enemy? A traitor?

Trevor moved away from her to flatten himself against the side of the car near the door. As something scraped against the outside of the boxcar, he motioned to her to come to him. Hesitantly, she advanced. She was no more than halfway there when the door was shoved open from the outside. A man in a dark blue uniform with a holstered gun at his hip gaped up at her.

"You!" he accused, recovering and pulling himself into the car. "What are you doing here?"

Just as Barbara realized it had been Trevor's intention to use her as a lure to entice the guard into the boxcar, he leaped at the man and hooked an arm around his neck from behind. The guard struggled in vain against the choking hold, finally sagging to his knees. Trevor released him and the man slumped to the floor of the car, lying motionless.

"You—you've killed him!" she cried.

"Be quiet," Trevor snapped, jerking his head toward the open door.

Numbly she watched him remove the guard's pistol from the holster and tuck it into his belt under the loose buckskin shirt. He also took a small pouch from the man's pocket.

"Jump down," Trevor ordered, pushing her toward the open door.

Since she feared it was jump or be tossed out, Barbara obeyed. Trevor was on the ground beside her before she could think what to do next. He grasped her satchel with one hand and took her arm with the other, hustling her along the cinders beside the track.

"Hurry, we have a train to catch," he told her.

"You killed that guard," she accused.

He shook his head. "If I had we wouldn't have to hurry. When he comes to he'll start looking—for you. We'd better be far gone by then."

The truth of his words jolted through Barbara. If she could believe Trevor and the guard was alive, she was the only person the man had actually seen because Trevor had struck from behind. Why she might actually be arrested!

He pulled her with him over two sets of tracks toward the idling engine of a passenger train. The black smoke puffing from the engine's cowled smokestack dispersed quickly in the brisk November breeze. Barbara stared at the pale faces visible in some of the windows of the coaches. How she wished she were one of them, freed from Trevor. Above the coaches she could see the roof of the depot.

"We can't take the chance of buying tickets in the station," Trevor said. "I'm afraid that brown bonnet of yours is all too memorable."

A man wearing dark work clothes opened a door at the end of one of the coaches, jumped to the ground, and walked along the cars toward the engine, poking at the wheels with a metal rod as he passed them.

"Good, we won't have to go around to the platform," Trevor said, urging her toward the open door.

Once there he boosted her onto the step and

climbed up behind her. In the passageway between two coaches, he quickly untied her bonnet, yanked it off her head and jammed it into her satchel.

"That's better," he told her as she put a hand to hair she knew must be tangled and mussed. "Don't worry, you look charming."

She didn't believe him and, hot though it was, arranged her shawl so it covered her head as well as her shoulders.

"Take the first vacant bench you find," he commanded, opening the coach door and holding it for her.

Tense with apprehension, she avoided looking directly at any of the passengers as she hurried along the aisle. Seeing an empty bench on the left-hand side, she slid onto it, moving over to the window to make room for Trevor—no, Ishmael. He eased down next to her. Barbara stared nervously from the window, searching the platform by the station, fearing to see the guard rushing toward the coach.

A mustached man, blond, wearing a well-cut black frock coat with gray trousers intercepted her gaze. He tipped his top hat to her, his brows raised inquiringly. She flushed and looked away, wishing he hadn't noticed her. Why had he? Did she appear that desperate? Though he seemed to be someone she might ask for help, she couldn't forget that Trevor, dangerous even unarmed, now carried a pistol.

Moments later the very same man sauntered into the front of the coach and she held her breath, watching him from the corner of her eye, fearing he'd pause to speak to her or otherwise attract Trevor's attention.

Though rather too thin for his height, the stranger was undeniably well-dressed, his clothes fitting him perfectly. When he passed by without so much as a glance her way and took the seat immediately behind she sighed in relief.

"'Board!" the conductor shouted. "All aboard."

Steam hissed upwards, obscuring the view for a moment as the train pulled from the station. At the front of the car, the conductor began collecting tickets.

Trevor—no, she *must* stop thinking that name—Ishmael—leaned close to her and she saw the money pouch he'd taken from the guard in his hand. "I'm afraid you'll have to pay for your own ticket," he said in a low tone. "There's barely enough here to cover mine."

She drew herself away from him indignantly. Had he expected her to allow him to use stolen money to pay her way to Baltimore?

"Since we're traveling together," he went on, "I'll purchase your ticket from the conductor." He turned his hand palm upward and, after a moment, she understood he was waiting for her to give him her money. She glared at him.

"Don't be difficult," he said. "If I'm caught you know very well I'll fight to stay free. You don't want to be responsible for others getting hurt."

Aware he meant exactly what he said, Barbara bit back her sharp retort and, without another word, dug into her reticule for one of her precious gold coins.

When the conductor reached their seat, she watched in amazement as Trevor, speaking with no trace of a Southern drawl, dealt with the annoyed man. The whisper from behind her took her by surprise.

"Do you need help?" the mustached stranger asked.

God knows she did. But she didn't dare say so. On the other hand she couldn't bear to deny it so she said nothing, praying Trevor hadn't heard.

"Well, sir," a man's voice said from the seat in back of her, "if we're to be fellow travelers, introductions are in order. My name's Hawkins, Gerald Hawkins. I deal in fine china and porcelain."

"Harrison Chambers," another voice, the voice of the mustached man said. He answered reluctantly, Barbara thought, eavesdropping shamelessly.

"I'll make a wager you're from England—right?" Mr. Hawkins said.

"Righto." If anything, Mr. Chambers sounded even more reluctant than before.

"Just visiting the country, are you?"

"I'm a journalist."

"Ah, here to chronicle the War, I've no doubt," Mr. Hawkins observed smugly.

"Something of the sort, yes."

Bit by bit, Mr. Hawkins extracted the information that Harrison Chambers had permission from both Union and Confederate forces to cross the battle lines in his efforts to inform the British public about America's war.

Mr. Chambers *can* help me, Barbara told herself. If I can manage to let him know my predicament, I won't need to count on Trevor's promise to take me to Richmond.

Much as she'd like to see Captain Sandoe unmasked as a Reb, she'd promised not to give away his identity. But that didn't mean she couldn't ask Mr. Chambers to help her escape from him without revealing who the captain really was.

I'll do just that, she vowed, as soon as I get a chance.

Trevor, finished dealing with the conductor, pressed silver coins into her hand. Change from the gold coin she'd given him. He leaned closer. Too close. "Don't even think about it," he whispered into her ear.

The combination of his words—how could he know?—and his warm breath in her ear made her shiver. Since she was already huddled against the window, she couldn't move away from him.

"I overheard the same conversation you did." Trevor's voice was soft and low, almost caressing. His nearness should have revolted her, but instead her insides felt so strangely quivery she had trouble keeping her mind on what he was saying.

"You're staying with me." Her shawl had slipped to the back of her head and his lips brushed her ear as he spoke, making her breath catch.

He drew back slightly and, pitching his voice to carry, said, "I know you're tired. Lean on my shoulder, dear, and try to sleep." His arm slipped around her shoulders, pulling her toward him.

Barbara stiffened, as much against her own

inexplicable inclination to do as he asked as in indignation at his actions. Dear! How dare he call her that?

"Don't be shy," he said. "After all, we're now husband and wife."

Horrified at his words, she tried to push back but he refused to let her go. Rather than struggling and creating a scene, she suffered him to settle her head onto his shoulder. Unwilling as she was, she felt strangely comforted by his warmth and by the protective arm encircling her.

He's deliberately creating a picture of a married couple, she told herself, for Mr. Chambers's benefit. He's doing it to spike my guns. How I hate him!

Under her ear she could hear his heart beat, steady and soothing, reminding her of her childhood, resting on her father's lap with her head against his chest. But he wasn't her father.

I won't stay like this, I'll move, she told herself. In a few minutes. When he isn't expecting it.

Her emotions seesawed one way and the other until, before she realized what was happening, her eyelids drooped shut. . . .

Trevor looked down at the sleeping woman in his arms, his lips curving into a reluctant smile. She'd fought him every inch of the way only to be overtaken by sleep. No wonder, she must be as exhausted as he was. Just the same, she'd be furious when she woke.

Her shawl had fallen from her head, leaving her

dark hair shining against the drab buckskin of his shirt. She smelled of soap and of herself, a clean, enticing fragrance. Long, black lashes hid her expressive brown eyes, their darkness emphasizing the creamy tones of her skin. Did she know how lovely she was?

Her soft curves pressing against him were definitely unsettling, tempting him, reminding him of how he'd held her in the boxcar. True, she'd fought him and he could hardly blame her— he'd been a rash fool—but for a second or two he would have sworn she'd responded to his kiss.

He wished he had the time to explore that response, to be the man to teach her the delights of lovemaking. But even if the time could be found, she'd still see him as the enemy. Damn the War!

He knew he should keep alert. Though safe for the time being, danger could arise at any moment. From Chambers, that British journalist in the seat behind, for instance. He'd swear the man had whispered something to Barbara while he was buying tickets. Had she somehow alerted Chambers? For the life of him he couldn't figure out how she could have.

At the moment, the man was engrossed in a newspaper. Or pretending to be. Perhaps the husband and wife comment had persuaded him to keep out of what could be a domestic dispute.

Trevor found it strange how Barbara's warmth and her nearness soothed and comforted him. It would do no harm to rest his cheek on the top of her head for a few minutes. Not that he'd close his eyes. . . .

He awoke to gunshots and men shouting. Struggling to focus his groggy mind, he thought for a moment he was in the field, fighting. Then the train gave a mighty lurch, grinding to a stop and all but catapulting him from the seat.

Barbara, still in his arms, cried out. A woman up ahead screamed. Some man called out orders. Guns cracked, both small arms and rifle fire. He disentangled himself from her and reached for his pistol just as soldiers in gray uniforms burst into the coach.

A Rebel raid! About to congratulate himself on his luck, he held. He didn't have any identification; these soldiers would never believe him. Their leader might—if he could stay alive that long. Since waving a Colt at them might be sure death, he took his hand off the gun and concentrated on looking harmless as he did his best to block Barbara from their view.

The soldiers took over the coach, acting with amazing efficiency. A guard was set at the front and back while the six other armed men herded the passengers out of the train, bench by bench. When it was his turn to be ushered up the aisle, Trevor noticed the wolf shoulder patch they all wore.

Meachum's Raiders. His heart sank. Bold and successful as Meachum had been, those who knew him more than casually shook their heads when his name was mentioned. Mad Dog Meachum, they called him behind his back.

"Plumb crazy and mean along with it," Lieutenant Logan had told Trevor at the Johnson Island prison. "I ought to know; I rode with

Meachum for nine damn long months. Until word of Meachum's peculiarities filtered back to General Lee. Lee demoted Meachum to major and threatened him with a court martial. When Meachum continued to defy Lee, the General repudiated the Raiders, denying them official status in the Confederate Army. That was enough for me, I left his outfit for a regular cavalry unit.

"But I never forgot riding with Meachum. Or those raids of his where he separated men captives from the women. He killed off the men one by one, slow and nasty. Makes me sick to remember. The women—" Logan grimaced. "God forbid he should ever get his hands on a young woman of your acquaintance. Any woman under fifty, Yankee or Reb, who he captures just disappears. No one ever sees her again."

Trevor met Barbara's frightened gaze, tensing with the realization he couldn't take on an entire cavalry troop. He was helpless. If he could convince Meachum to accept him as a fellow Confederate, he might survive. But what about her?

Dammit, she didn't belong to Meachum—if she was anyone's, she was his. Now what the hell was he going to do about it?

What *could* he do about it?

Chapter 5

Barbara shrank away from the gray-clad arm extended to help her down from the coach and jumped to the ground unassisted. She looked behind her for Trevor and was jolted to find he was nowhere in sight. Only then did she realize every passenger standing near her was a woman. The Reb raiders had separated the women from the men. Why?

A beardless Reb, so young she wondered if he was even capable of growing whiskers, urged her and the five other women toward the rear of the train, away from the gunfire at the front.

"My husband!" a blond woman of about thirty cried, stopping to look around. "Where's my husband?"

Their guard prodded her back with the muzzle of his rifle and she began to weep. Barbara glared at him and put an arm around the woman. Another Reb, one with a red beard, hurried up and grabbed the blonde's arm, yanking her away from

70

Barbara and propelling her along.

"You'd best come quick if you know what's good for you," he advised, his tone suggesting he'd as soon shoot them as not.

By the time the group reached the last car, there were ten women in all. The two Rebs stopped and lined them up. Redbeard walked from one to the other, peering into their faces. Like someone intent on buying a horse, Barbara thought, anger mixing with her fear. Will he check our teeth next?

"Not her," he said jerking his thumb at the third woman past Barbara. "She's too old."

"Back in the coach, ma'am," the beardless man ordered, forcing the woman to climb into the end car.

The remaining nine women were herded over a ditch and into the woods where those with hoops under their skirts—all except Barbara—were told to shed the hoops in order to be able to straddle the horses that were tethered to the trees.

A small dark-haired woman burst into tears. "My baby," she wailed. "You're going to kill my baby."

Redbeard grasped her arm and hauled up her skirts until everyone saw her bulging stomach. "She's in the family way, all right," he muttered, dropping the skirts, releasing her and giving her a shove toward the train. "Go on back," he told her gruffly. "Meachum ain't got no use for you."

As Barbara watched the woman stumble away she wondered apprehensively what Meachum planned to do with the rest of them. General Meachum's border raids had terrorized Ohio in the early years of the war and dreadful rumors had circulated about his cunning and cruelty.

They couldn't still be in Ohio. Judging by the sun it was well past midday—they must be in West Virginia. West Virginia, a new state carved from Virginia just last year, wasn't a part of the Confederacy; it was a border state and supposedly neutral.

Seeing Redbeard boost the blond woman onto a horse, Barbara decided that was one indignity she refused to suffer. Choosing a bay mare tethered near a stump, she hiked up her skirts, climbed onto the stump, and mounted by herself.

With Beardless in the lead and Redbeard bringing up the rear, Barbara and the other women rode away from the train through the woods, climbing ever higher into the hills. Some of the women wept and at least one prayed. Barbara did neither. Tears would do no earthly good, and she'd been taught by her father to believe that God helped those who helped themselves. At the moment she saw no way to help either herself or any of the other women. It didn't seem as though God intended to help, at least not at the moment.

What had happened to Trevor? Much as she disliked him, she certainly preferred him to General Meachum's Rebs. She found herself hoping he was all right and shook her head. Likely enough he hadn't been harmed—after all, he was a Reb, too.

But why had Meachum separated the men from the women? And why had he singled out younger

72

women who weren't pregnant? What was going to happen to her and her companions? She shivered, both from her thoughts and the gloom under the trees. Where were they going?

When she was younger, Barbara had often ridden astride in divided skirts, but the groans and complaints she heard from the other women persuaded her that none of them was used to a man's saddle. She wasn't too comfortable herself with her skirts hiked up as they had to be to sit astride.

Near dusk, when she was close to joining in the chorus of moans, she smelled smoke. Some minutes later she saw the gleam of a campfire and caught her breath. Though she was aching and exhausted, she feared what they had to face would be far worse than a horseback ride.

When they halted, in her haste to avoid being lifted off the bay mare by a loathsome Reb, she slid to the ground and almost fell when her knees buckled. Despite her aches and pains she forced herself to stand up and helped the blond woman when they were ordered to walk toward the fire and line up behind a fallen log.

A man with a thin mustache and black hair skimming the collar of his gray uniform jacket strode from the darkness under the trees to confront them. Like the other Rebs, he wore cavalry boots. Barbara took note of the gold stars on his shoulders and tensed. How gaunt and pale his face was, his black eyes glittering feverishly as his gaze traveled over the women.

"When I point at you, you will tell me your first

name," he said softly. Something about his voice and the way he looked reminded Barbara of a snake.

Too fearful to argue, Barbara and the other women obeyed him. As they did, Barbara tried to memorize their names. The blonde beside her was Emiline.

"Oh, please," Emiline begged General Meachum, "please tell me what you've done with my husband."

"Was he an Englishman?" the general asked.

Emiline shook her head.

General Meachum smiled. "Since an Englishman was the only one I allowed to go free, I expect we must have shot your husband with the rest of the men."

Barbara gasped at his words, biting her lip to prevent her cry of protest. Trevor dead? No!

"After all," the general continued, "you knew perfectly well Union soldiers were concealed in the baggage car. That was no passenger train you rode, it was a troop train. Therefore, the men deserved to die and I consider you women legitimate spoils of war."

"We didn't know!" Emiline wailed above the shocked murmurs and sobs of the other women. "How could we know?" Her voice rose to a shriek. "Paul! Oh dear God, Paul!"

Barbara caught her as she crumpled and eased her to the ground. Crouching beside Emiline, she glared at the general, both horrified and outraged.

"I thought Southern men prided themselves on being gentlemen," she said hotly.

The general's cold black eyes fixed on her. "Oh, but I am a gentleman in my own way, my dear Barbara. As you will discover." He turned his back and walked away into the darkness, leaving Redbeard and Beardless to guard the women.

"You might as well sit on that log till the vittles come along," Redbeard told them, leaning on his rifle.

Barbara paid him little heed, intent on reviving Emiline.

"Is she all right?" a buxom, thirtyish woman named Amelia asked, kneeling beside Barbara.

"I think she's coming around," Barbara assured her.

"Poor thing. I'm a widow myself—my Oscar died fighting at Gettysburg." Amelia glanced at the guards and lowered her voice. "How could General Meachum be so cruel? I've heard the most awful tales about him and now I suspect the stories were true. I don't mind telling you I'm scared to death."

Before Barbara could respond, Emiline stirred, moaning. Her eyes opened and she stared up at Barbara, her bewilderment changing to grief as she took in her surroundings. Barbara helped her to sit up, then, assisted by Amelia, to stand and walk the few steps to the log so she wouldn't be sitting on the damp ground.

Somewhat to Barbara's surprise, Emiline didn't begin to weep again, instead she stared numbly into the gathering darkness. Like the other women's skirts, hers drooped sadly without the hoops meant to hold them in a circle. They all looked as bedraggled as Barbara felt.

"What's going to happen to us?" a slim woman named Irene asked in a half-whisper. She wore expensive clothes, including a stylish plum hat decorated with artificial fruits and flowers.

Zoe burst into tears. "I can't bear any more," she sobbed. "That horrible man shot my brother and now he's taken us captive. We'll never come out of this alive."

Irene put an arm around her shoulders. "The beast killed my uncle, too," she said.

"But we're still alive," Lorraine said.

Lorraine's older sister, Edna, shook her head. "That may turn out to be no consolation." She glanced sideways at the guards and huddled into herself.

Thin-faced Wilma who hadn't uttered a word up until now, said, "I'd rather die than have one of those brutes lay hands on me."

Barbara wished with all her heart she was still Trevor's captive. Though he was a Reb and had treated her none too kindly, she'd felt fairly safe with him. But Trevor was dead. Tears pricked her eyes at the thought. No matter what he'd done, what he was, he didn't deserve to die. He'd been so vital, so alive. She remembered his heart beating under her ear and sighed, feeling strangely bereft—almost as if she'd lost a loved one.

All the time they'd been talking, she'd noticed Redbeard ogling Emiline, who was what Barbara had heard described as a fine figure of a woman. His avid gaze reminded her unpleasantly of Reverend Hargreaves's look back in Sandusky

76

when he'd tried to rape her.

Was rape in store for all of them? She clenched her fists, wishing she had some kind of a weapon.

When the crackle of leaves crunched under boots warned of others approaching, Barbara grasped Emiline's hand, squeezing it tightly as she held her breath.

Four men approached, two carrying food, the others a tent and blankets. While the women ate stew from a single bucket, sharing one spoon, the men set up the tent behind the log and dumped the blankets inside.

Later, Barbara decided it was too small a tent for eight to share, but the women huddled close together under the blankets without complaints, grateful to be left alone. Listening to the muted sobs, Barbara didn't expect to so much as close her eyes, but when she woke it was to a gray morning.

The sky remained overcast as, shivering in the cool wind slipping through the trees, they ate hard bread washed down with tea. White Deer would say she smelled a weather change, Barbara thought and swallowed against the lump in her throat when she was reminded of what had happened to the Chippewa woman. There was no comparison between her feelings for White Deer and for Trevor, of course, but she *had* lost them both. She could only hope her father still lived.

The women were blindfolded with scarves before they mounted the horses. Cracking a whip, Redbeard threatened that they'd be beaten if they removed them. Riding blind turned the already dreadful journey into a nightmare. Up and up they went, then through what Barbara thought must be a rocky defile or perhaps even a tunnel because the clatter of hooves on rocks echoed all around her.

Eventually they left the rocks and began to descend so steep an incline it felt as though she would slip over the horse's head, the blindfold making it doubly difficult to stay in the saddle. Just when Barbara thought she could bear no more, it began to rain.

When at last Redbeard called a halt, she was thoroughly soaked. Rough hands grasped her around the waist, set her on the ground and yanked off the blindfold. Barbara stared in shock at a white columned mansion of three stories with multiple outbuildings behind and to either side. Surrounding fields were ripe for the harvest.

A plantation. General Meachum's? It must be.

"Civilization, thank God," Irene said.

Though she was relieved to see they wouldn't be forced to sleep in the rain tonight, Barbara wasn't ready to thank God, not yet. Not as long as she was a captive.

Redbeard led the eight women to a square wooden outbuilding, unlocked the door, and forced them to file inside ahead of him. In the dim interior, with the only light coming from four windows set high in the walls near the roof, Barbara gaped at the iron bars running across the room from floor to ceiling.

While Beardless guarded the outer door, Redbeard unlocked a metal door set into the bars. "Inside, all of you," he ordered.

They had no choice but to obey. Barbara's heart sank when the iron door clanged behind them and Redbeard turned the key in the lock. Like the others, she glanced around the cell. Ten canvas cots, with blankets. Ten doorless commodes with tin pitchers and basins on their tops and a pail on a shelf underneath for a slop jar. Skimpy muslin towels hung on a rack, one to each commode.

"All the comforts of home." Irene's voice dripped with sarcasm as she lifted a blanket from one of the cots and wrapped it around her.

About to do the same, Barbara noticed that Emiline stood inside the barred door, her shoulders slumped as she gazed blankly into space. Fearing Emiline was past caring for herself, Barbara led her to a cot, eased her wet outer garments off, wrapped her in a blanket and persuaded her to lie down.

By the time the outer door opened again, Barbara, blanket-wrapped like the rest of the women, was resting on a cot. She sat up hurriedly, clutching the blanket around her.

A slim, attractive dark-haired young woman entered, followed by two Negro men carrying baskets which they set on a bench running along the wall. The only other furnishing outside the cell was a range in the corner with kindling and small logs stacked beside it. The woman lit a lantern hanging on the wall, then sauntered over to the bars, her gaze touching them all.

"Eight," she drawled.

Barbara got off the cot and walked toward her.

The woman eyed her with interest. "What's your name?" she asked.

"Barbara."

"I'm Tibba. How old are you?"

"Eighteen."

"Me, too."

Close up, Barbara noticed Tibba's light brown skin and realized she was part Negro. "What's going to happen to us?" she asked Tibba.

Tibba shrugged. "I don't have anything to do with that. Except for the clothes. But that's later. I brought food—ham, cheese, and bread." She looked at the two men who'd come in with her. "Tobias, see if the stove needs more wood and then set the kettle on to boil."

Barbara leaned against the bars. "Please," she said, "won't you tell us why we've been taken prisoner?"

"You'll find out soon enough," Tibba said. "After the Choosing." Again she turned away. "Nat, lay out eight napkins and divide up the food."

Since the men obeyed her without question it was obvious Tibba had authority. She focused her attention on Barbara once more, her amber eyes pitying. "Won't anything happen till tomorrow, so y'all just eat and rest tonight."

Try as they might, neither Barbara nor any of the other women were able to pry another word from Tibba. Once the kettle boiled, Tibba made tea and poured it into eight individual tin cups which, like the napkin-wrapped food, were slipped through the bars by Tobias and Nat.

Then all three of them left.

They ate in the dark since Tibba had snuffed the lantern before leaving. Some of the women talked to one another in low and tremulous voices, but no one speculated out loud what Tibba could have meant by the Choosing. The girl had given the word such emphasis that Barbara believed it must be a ceremony or rite of some kind. Were all of them to be chosen, or just one? And for what purpose?

"You notice how that Tibba bossed those two slaves around," Amelia said. "I wouldn't have her working for me. You can't trust those high yellow girls, they get above themselves."

Above themselves? Was that another way of saying Tibba didn't know her place? Barbara wondered. Some of the townspeople back home had said the same about White Deer and she'd been a kind and knowledgeable woman. Though it was too soon for Barbara to decide what Tibba was like, she had no intention of condemning anyone because of skin color.

"How can you all carry on as though nothing's wrong?" Zoe demanded, her voice quivering. "You know very well we're prisoners, locked in a jail. We should be on our knees, praying for deliverance."

No one disagreed.

At dawn, Barbara was startled from a troubled sleep when she heard a key turn in the outside lock. By the time the door opened, she was sitting on the bed, her blanket wrapped around her. Tibba entered, followed by Tobias and Nat. She directed one to rekindle the fire in the stove and the other to portion out the food—hominy mush in a wooden bowl with molasses and milk poured over it.

Evidently General Meachum didn't mean to let them starve.

After they'd eaten, the men left. Once the door was closed behind them, Tibba approached the bars and called, "Come over here if you please, Miss Barbara."

When Barbara obeyed, Tibba handed her a small cake of soap with a lemony fragrance. "This soap has to do for all of you," Tibba warned. "You're to strip naked, wash, and then put on a white shift." She gestured toward a pile of garments on the bench. "Nothing else."

"I'll do no such thing!" Amelia announced, and the others chimed in.

Tibba raised her voice. "The order comes from General Meachum, not from me. Either you do as he says or Tobias and Nat will return and force you to obey. By that I mean one will hold you while the other undresses and washes you."

Amelia gasped in outrage. Before she or any of them could speak, Tibba went on. "No use to argue. I'll count to ten and then call in the men. One, two . . ."

"Hand me the shifts," Barbara said, realizing they had no choice. "I'll pass them out."

Embarrassed by having to undress and wash in front of others, she did both as rapidly as possible. The shift, she found, reached only to her knees, was open in the front and tied by only two ribbons, one at the throat, the other at the waist. As she

82

handed the soap to Amelia, she shivered, not from cold but from apprehension.

"Can't I wrap a blanket around myself?" she asked Tibba.

Tibba nodded. "For now. But you have to take it off before the Choosing."

A shudder shook Barbara at her words. The Choosing sounded more ominous each time the words were spoken.

"She's not undressing." Tibba pointed at Emiline who sat on her cot staring at the floor.

"Don't call the men," Barbara said hurriedly. "She's not well. We'll help her get ready."

When they were all wearing nothing but a shift with a blanket draped over it, Tibba opened the outer door and called Tobias and Nat back inside. Then she unlocked the metal door.

"Come out, one at a time," she ordered, "but leave your blanket on your cot. Miss Barbara first."

Barbara took a deep breath, dropped the blanket and, hiding her terror as best she could, marched through the cell door. One by one, the other women followed, Amelia pushing Emiline ahead of her. Tibba lined them up in front of the bars while Tobias guarded the outer door, and Nat, standing protectively by Tibba, looked on, grinning.

Never had Barbara felt so humiliated. The scanty cover of the shift was a mockery, hardly better than nothing. Apprehension over what would happen next made her bite her lip as she crossed her arms over her breasts.

"Ready," Tibba said to Tobias. He stepped

aside and flung open the outer door.

Three gray-clad men entered, General Meachum first, then Redbeard and Beardless.

"Well, gentlemen," the general said when they were inside, "these are the ones you saved from the culling." His gaze traveled from one woman to another. "A fair exhibition, wouldn't you say?"

"Yes, sir," the soldiers responded in unison, ogling the women.

"With at least one, perhaps two prize specimens," the general continued. He walked slowly along the line of women, stopping in front of Emiline, who gave no indication she noticed him. With a quick flick of his fingers, he untied both ribbons and flipped open her shift to reveal her nakedness. "Very nice, yes," he said softly. "She may do."

The general moved on to consider Alice but Emiline didn't move, making no effort to cover herself. Redbeard stared at her so avidly that spittle formed in the corners of his mouth. Unable to bear the men leering at Emiline's exposed body, Barbara slipped from her place at the end of the line, skirted the general, reached Emiline, and retied her shift.

She turned to find herself face to face with General Meachum. "Were you told to move, my dear?" he asked, his voice as cold and sharp as a steel knife.

"She's too grief-stricken to help herself," Barbara said indignantly. "Have you no decency?"

The general's thin smile was bone-chilling. "I give the orders, Barbara. As you'll come to

84

understand." He looked her up and down and turned away abruptly, nodding to Tibba.

"Barbara," he said. Without a backward glance, he stalked away, opened the door, and left the jail.

"Please go back inside the bars, Miss Barbara," Tibba told her.

Barbara hesitated, looking at Emiline, loathe to leave her unprotected.

"Do you need Nat's escort?" Tibba asked.

Seeing she had to obey, Barbara retreated inside the cell and wrapped herself in the blanket again, not wanting to know what else was happening, but unable to keep from watching.

Redbeard sauntered to Emiline, tilted her face up and gazed into her eyes. "Picked this one from the first," he said. "She ain't going to give no trouble, no trouble at all." He grinned at Beardless. "That's how I like 'em."

Barbara wasn't sure but she thought she saw Tibba shudder.

"Gimme her clothes, I'll take her along now," Redbeard told Tibba.

Barbara clenched her fist as she watched Nat fetch Emiline's things from the cell, bundle them and hand the bundle to Redbeard.

Unable to bear it in silence, Barbara called to Redbeard. "She's not in her right mind. Please don't—don't hurt her."

Redbeard, a hand gripping Emiline's arm, shot her a crooked grin. "Ain't her mind I'm interested in, miss."

Once he'd taken Emiline from the jail, Beardless walked along the line of remaining women, chose the weeping Zoe, got her clothes from Nat, and left with her.

"What happens to the rest of us?" Amelia demanded.

"You get shared among the men," Tibba said. "All except Miss Barbara. She goes to the house. For *him.*"

Barbara swallowed. Why had General Meachum chosen her? She supposed she should be grateful she wouldn't meet the terrible fate of Amelia and the remaining four women, but the man frightened her. She found him both terrifying and repulsive.

I won't go to him willingly, she vowed. He's my enemy. A man as despicable as he is would be my enemy even if he wasn't a Reb. I'll never give up. I'll fight him every inch of the way.

It never once occurred to her that her rebellious spirit might have been the very reason he'd picked her.

Chapter 6

After Tobias and Nat led the five weeping, frightened women from the jail, Barbara was left alone with Tibba.

"You can get dressed if you want," Tibba told her.

Barbara hurriedly donned her wrinkled and soiled clothes. No matter what might be in store for her at General Meachum's house, she was grateful that she wouldn't be forced, like the others, to parade around in a skimpy shift.

"Will I see my friends again?" she asked Tibba as she draped her shawl over her head and shoulders.

Tibba frowned. "They all were your friends?"

"After what we went through together, I feel each and every one of those women is my friend."

"Whether you see them again or not depends." Tibba opened the cell door and motioned for her to come out.

"Depends on what?"

"On who survives."

Jolted by the words, Barbara followed Tibba in silence as they left the jail. Was it her friends who might not survive or was it her? How long would any of them live? Somehow she must escape!

Barbara glanced around. A mild, damp breeze ruffled the leaves on the sycamores they passed and a few yellow ones spun to the ground, reminding her that September had begun. Though the rain had stopped, sodden gray clouds hung low over the valley, obscuring the tops of the surrounding mountains. Even supposing she found a way to sneak away from the house, how could she escape from this mountain-ringed valley?

"Thinking of running off?" Tibba asked. "Don't bother. There's no way to get out of the valley except through the pass and that's guarded day and night."

Barbara's heart sank.

"Besides," Tibba added, "*he* doesn't take kindly to anyone who tries to escape."

No need to ask who "he" was. Barbara raised her chin. Impossible or not, she refused to give up.

Tibba led her to the side of the white-columned house and along a stone-paved path through a rose garden. A few overblown roses still bloomed on the thorny stems, spilling both petals and perfume. The many windows of the house stared like prying eyes, making Barbara wonder apprehensively if the general was watching her approach through one of them.

Tibba opened a French door and stepped aside for Barbara to precede her. She found herself in a music room dominated by a rosewood grand piano and a gilded harp.

"Do you play?" Tibba asked.

Barbara shook her head. "I have no real musical talent."

Tibba's fingers touched the harp caressingly as they passed, piquing Barbara's curiosity. "Are you a harpist?" she asked.

To her surprise Tibba put her finger to her lips and that was the only answer she got.

The music room fronted on a large foyer with an intricate parquet floor that was polished to a fare-thee-well. A buxom Negro woman with a feather duster in her hand peered curiously from a room across the foyer as they walked under an ornate brass and crystal chandelier and started up a long, curved staircase.

Bucolic scenes painted in oil and framed in gold decorated the staircase walls, but Tibba whisked Barbara along so fast she had no time to do more than get an impression of what she passed.

Two corridors led away from the sitting room at the head of the stairs. They took the left. Barbara counted four closed doors before Tibba stopped and opened the fifth.

"This is your room," she said. Walking to a built-in closet, she opened that door. "These are your clothes. They'll all fit—or close enough."

"How is that possible?" Barbara asked, staring at the colorful array of gowns.

"He always chooses a woman smaller than he is, a slender woman."

Barbara swallowed, moistening a throat gone suddenly dry before she was able to ask, "Where are they now, those other women?"

"I'll show you some time. If you still want to

89

know after—" Tibba broke off and jerked a bell pull. "I'll have Yola bring hot water and then I'll help you dress."

"I *am* dressed," Barbara said. No matter how bedraggled her gown was, at least it was hers and hers alone. She didn't want to wear clothes abandoned by other "chosen" women who were God knows where now.

"You have to put on a dress from the closet. It's not my order, it's his. My advice is don't fight about things that don't matter."

As Barbara pondered these words, a Negro girl of about twelve appeared in the open doorway with a pitcher. "Water's good 'n hot, Miss Tibba," she said, flicking a glance at Barbara.

"Thank you, Yola." Tibba waited until the girl set the pitcher on the commode and left before saying, "Would you like me to decide on a gown for you to wear?"

Barbara had no way of knowing whether Tibba's advice could be trusted but she decided not to go on arguing about changing her clothes. "If you would, please," she said. "I won't need your help to dress—I'm quite used to dressing myself."

Tibba shrugged. *"He* wants me to be your maid so I will be whether you need me or not."

Barbara waited until Tibba lifted a green and gold gown from the closet, laid it across the tester bed, and turned to face her. Gazing directly at Tibba, she asked, "How long have you been taking orders from General Meachum?"

Something that might have been anger flickered in the depths of Tibba's yellow eyes. "Since the day I was born." There was an edge to the words that suggested she wasn't entirely happy about it.

Was it possible Tibba might help her escape? Barbara wondered as she submitted with some embarrassment to being assisted to change clothes. What was Tibba's status in the general's household? It wasn't likely she was an ordinary slave since Yola had called her "Miss" and the Negro men had obeyed her. Perhaps she wasn't a slave at all.

Afraid Tibba would take her clothes away, Barbara managed to drop her red petticoat with the gold coins sewn into the hem onto the floor, then surreptitiously kick it far enough under the bed so the dust ruffle hid it.

"Didn't you have a maid at home?" Tibba asked.

Barbara shook her head. "It wasn't necessary."

"But you must have had servants."

"My foster parents paid a woman to come in and do the laundry and the heavy cleaning twice a week, otherwise, no." Her father had always had a housekeeper but, under the present circumstances, it was too painful to think of, let alone speak of, the old, happy days at home with her father.

"What happens to me next?" she asked Tibba, determined not to be put off.

"Yola will serve you lunch in your room and then you may rest until dinner at seven. Dinner with him."

Barbara took a deep breath to give herself courage to go on. "And after dinner?"

Tibba looked away and didn't answer immediately. "Why do you think he chose you?" she asked finally.

91

"I imagine he expects to—to force me to lie with him. It would have to be by force because I'm not willing. Never!" Despite herself, Barbara failed to keep her voice from quivering.

Tibba caught her full lower lip between her teeth and grimaced. "He picked you 'cause he saw you were a fighter," she said. "It'd be better if you weren't."

"Are you suggesting I don't try to fight him off?"

Tibba nodded. "Otherwise you might not last the night."

Barbara bit back a gasp, shaken by Tibba's words. What kind of a monster was General Meachum? Based on what she'd seen and heard so far he was cruel and unfeeling. A man who battened on the misery and humiliation of others. Someone who enjoyed inflicting pain.

"Tibba—" she began.

"I can't tell you any more," Tibba insisted. "No use to ask me; I've said too much already."

Before Barbara could try to reason with her, Tibba hurried to the door and slipped through it. The click of a key in the lock told Barbara she was locked in.

First she retrieved the red petticoat and, for safekeeping, thrust it deep into a riding boot in the closet. Then she toured the room searching for a weapon but found nothing she could use. Looking from the windows, she noted the steep drop to the ground and saw a Negro man raking leaves from the lawn below. Even if she managed to reach the ground unhurt, he'd see and capture her. No doubt others also watched to make certain she didn't try to escape through the windows.

Terror clogged her throat and thrummed along her nerves. Not only pain and humiliation awaited her tonight but, if Tibba could be believed, possible death as well. She paced from one end of the room to the other, back and forth, back and forth. She must escape! But how?

What would her father advise?

Thinking of him calmed her slightly. Papa would tell her to use her wits. "If you believe there's no way out of a dilemma," he'd often said, "then your expectation is likely to be fulfilled. But as long as you keep searching for a solution you stand a chance."

When Yola brought her a tray at noon, Barbara examined the eating implements in the hope she'd find a knife or even a fork that might double as a weapon but all they'd given her was a spoon. Though she had little appetite, she forced herself to eat to keep up her strength.

Later, she propped the back of a chair under the doorknob to be certain no one could enter without alerting her, removed the soft kid shoes Tibba had insisted she wear and stretched out on the bed. Tibba had promised to bring back her sturdy ankle boots after they'd been cleaned and polished but would she? Barbara sighed. She could trust no one. Meanwhile, she must try to rest in order to be at her strongest for what was yet to come. But how could she possibly relax?

She wondered what had become of her satchel with her belongings. In it had been White Deer's herbal medicines that she'd hoped to bring to her father. And her copy of *Moby Dick*.

"'Call me Ishmael,'" she murmured.

Trevor Ishmael Sandoe. The man who called himself Ishmael was dead. His face formed behind her closed lids—dark hair, warm brown eyes, his mouth curved to one side in a half-smile. How warm his hands had been when they held hers, how steady and reassuring the beat of his heart. . . .

She was alone and surrounded by greenery. Tall evergreen shrubbery grew to either side of her, blocking her view while forming an aisle. A maze, she was lost in a maze and must find her way out before it was too late. If she took a wrong turn she might penetrate to the center of the maze, the lair of a dreadful beast.

Her heart beat fast as she came to the first choice of passageways—to the right or to the left. A disembodied whisper told her to choose the right. She did.

Again and again the whisper guided her as she hurried along the evergreen corridors; she trusted the whisper because she had no choice. The blue sky above darkened and shadows joined her, racing ahead, following menacingly behind, but she didn't despair for soon she'd be free of the maze, soon she'd be safe.

At last she rounded a final corner and stopped dead in horror. She'd come to the center. She was doomed.

"Welcome to my home," a voice whispered. She stared into the cruel obsidian eyes of a monster, half beast, half man.

"No!" she cried. "No!"

"I'll save you!" a voice called. A man swept past

*her to stand between her and the monster, his
sword raised on high.*

Trevor! She breathed a sigh of relief.

*The monster sprang at him and Trevor's sword
slashed down, down. The monster opened his
mouth and a fiery blast obscured man and sword.
When the smoke cleared nothing was left of
Trevor.*

*The monster smiled, showing sharp, jagged
teeth. "You can't escape me," he whispered and
took a step toward her.*

"Trevor!" she screamed.

But Trevor was gone forever. . . .

Barbara awoke panic-stricken. She sat up,
hugging herself, looking frantically around.

Even in the dim light she saw she was alone in
the room. The room in General Meachum's house.
It had all been a bad dream, for what comfort that
was. She wished she could be sure what faced her
wouldn't be a worse nightmare.

The click of a key warned her someone was
unlocking the door. "Who's there?" she called, her
voice shaking.

"Tibba."

Relieved, Barbara rose and moved the chair so
Tibba could enter.

"It's time to get you ready for dinner," Tibba
announced.

Despite Barbara's protests, Tibba chose yet
another gown from the closet—a rose velvet with a
low neckline—and insisted Barbara put it on.

As she helped her into the steel hoops that went
with the gown, Tibba said, "I think maybe you're
the one I've been waiting for."

"Waiting for?" Barbara echoed. "What do you mean?"

Tibba leaned closer. "I want to get away from here as much as you do," she said in a half-whisper. "I hate him."

Barbara recovered quickly from her surprise. "But you said escape was impossible." She kept her voice low.

"As long as he's alive, it is. But if he was dead . . ."

Barbara stared at her. "You'd kill him? How?"

"Shoot him. With your help. I've had it figured out for a long time but I couldn't trust any of the women he chose until you came along. You've got nerve. I need a gun and the only way I can steal his Colt is when he's with you tonight 'cause that's the only time he's off guard."

"I'm willing to help," Barbara told her. As far as she was concerned a monster like General Meachum didn't deserve to live.

"I knew you would be. What I'll do is hide in this closet while you're at dinner with him because once he's in this room he not only locks the door but padlocks it from the inside. But I can't act till he takes off his holster. He'll do that after he ties you up."

"Ties me up?" Barbara's voice rose and Tibba put a warning finger to her lips.

"So don't struggle too much," Tibba advised, "'cause you'll only get hurt worse and it'll take longer for him to get to the tying."

Barbara twisted her hands together, sickened and scared by the picture Tibba's words painted.

"When he takes off the holster you have to let

96

me know somehow," Tibba went on.

Barbara thought a minute. "How about if I call out, 'Ishmael, Ishmael'?"

"Ishmael, like from the Bible?"

Barbara nodded. "Won't everyone come running when they hear the shot?"

Tibba shook her head. "They'll think he's doing the shooting, that it's part of his pleasure. No one ever interferes when he's with a woman. Once he's dead we'll creep out and ride to the pass. The guards will let me through and you with me."

"Are you sure?"

"Of course. They won't dare question my word any more than the slaves do." Tibba seemed far more certain than Barbara was that they'd be able to get away with no trouble. But either she placed her trust in Tibba's plan or she had no chance at all.

She caught Tibba's hand. "I'm frightened," she said, "but I'll do my part."

Tibba squeezed her hand. "I know you will. Otherwise I wouldn't have told you my plan. Now let's finish getting you ready for dinner."

Glancing at her image in the pier glass, Barbara's eyes widened. The vivid rose color and the elegance of the gown made her look like a stranger. For an instant she was back in the boxcar with Trevor, listening to him tell her what her name meant.

"You look like you're off in a dream," Tibba said. "You got some man you favor?"

Barbara spoke without thinking. "He's dead."

"His work?"

Meaning General Meachum. Barbara nodded,

reminded anew of the general's murderous cruelty. She met her own gaze in the mirror, vowing to do her best to bring an end to his crimes.

"You look a sight better in rose than you did in that drab gray dress you were wearing," Tibba said.

Barbara stared at her exposed upper breasts and plucked at the jet beads decorating the bodice of her gown, fervently wishing the neckline were higher. "I'm not used to such fancy clothes. Or baring my—my shoulders like this. Isn't there a shawl in the closet I can wear?"

"He wouldn't want you to cover up. I did the best I could for you—most of the evening gowns would show even more of your bosom than this one." Tibba rummaged in the closet and brought out dainty slippers with leather soles and rose velvet uppers to match the gown.

As she slid her feet into the shoes, Barbara couldn't help wondering what had happened to the woman who'd worn these slippers before her.

Tibba ushered her to the door, pausing before opening it to whisper, "Ishmael."

Clutching the word to her for comfort, Barbara walked along the corridor and began to descend the stairs. It was an unpleasant shock to see the general, still in uniform, waiting for her in the foyer, at the foot of the staircase.

The chandelier held candles rather than oil lamps, their flickering lending his face an even more sinister cast than she recalled. Trying desperately to show no emotion whatsoever, she made her way slowly down the steps. When, at the bottom, he held out his hand, she forced herself to give him hers, suppressing a shudder when he brushed its back with his lips.

"How lovely you are, my dear," he said, offering her his arm.

She placed her hand gingerly on his coat sleeve and he led her to the dining room. Though she tried to fix her attention on the furnishings to calm herself, her heart wasn't in it. At most she received only an impression of well-polished cherrywood furniture with curved legs and plush burgundy upholstery before he was pulling out a chair to seat her at the long table. Though she'd have greatly preferred to be at the far end, away from him, he placed her next to him, at his right.

"How rosy your skin looks when you wear that color," he told her.

From the corner of her eye she could see him gazing avidly at her décolletage. She clenched her hands together under the table, making no reply.

He didn't appear to notice. While she toyed with course after course, making the barest pretense of eating, he spoke of various victorious campaigns, relating bloody details that made her want to cover her ears with her hands to avoid hearing. The Negro servants who served them were careful not to so much as glance at either the general or her.

The meal seemed interminable but the apprehensive Barbara, fearful of what would happen afterwards, wished it would last even longer than it did.

At last he poured the after-dinner brandy and offered her a glass.

"I don't drink spirits," she repeated, as she had each time a different wine was poured for her during the meal.

"A pity," he said. "Perhaps you'll change your mind later."

When he finished his brandy, he rose from the table and pulled out her chair. "I believe, my dear, that it's time to retire."

His words struck terror into her very soul and she felt her legs tremble as she rose. Again he offered his arm and she placed a reluctant hand on his sleeve. As he led her to the stairs and along the corridor to her room, she fought her fear, reminding herself that she wouldn't really be alone with him, that Tibba was hidden in the closet.

Unless Tibba had been lying to her. But why would she? Barbara tried to shore up her confidence in Tibba and their plan for escape but when he unlocked and opened the door, Barbara's knees almost gave way.

Her steps faltered when she entered the room and saw the white silk nightgown laid across the turned-down covers of the bed. One small astral lamp burned low on a stand near the window, making shadows shift in the corners. If only she could hide in those shadows.

"Ah," General Meachum said, nodding in approval. "Everything seems to be in order. I'll make myself comfortable while you change into your nightclothes."

Barbara stood rooted to the spot, unable to make herself move while he slipped a padlock through the brass hasp on the inside of the door and clicked it shut. What if Tibba wasn't in the closet? What then?

"Shy, my dear?" he asked. "Shall I assist you?"

"No!" She flung her refusal at him. He smiled and leaned a hip against the writing table, his cold obsidian gaze never leaving her.

Since there was no way to avoid undressing, Barbara retreated to the far side of the bed before slipping off her shoes. She had to struggle to reach the buttons at the back of the dress but she finally managed. As quickly as she could, she pulled the gown over her head, terrified he'd approach while she couldn't see what he was doing.

Temporarily relieved to discover he hadn't, she did her best to blank her mind while she discarded the several petticoats, then attacked the fastenings of the hoops and removed them. Now she was down to her drawers, stockings, and chemise. Postponing the inevitable, she bent and pulled up a leg of the drawers to take off one lisle stocking, then the other.

Standing straight, she reached for the night-gown, intending to slip it over her head and finish undressing under its flimsy cover.

"No, my dear," he said.

She froze.

"You will take everything off before you touch that nightdress," he insisted, taking a step toward her.

Barbara swallowed. His eyes had changed and their avid glitter frightened her so acutely that her shaking fingers fumbled when she tried to untie the ribbons on the chemise. She tore a ribbon off in her anxiety to get the underwear removed and the gown on before he came any closer.

She finally pulled the nightdress over her head and faced him defiantly, hoping he couldn't tell how scared and humiliated she felt.

He sauntered to the opposite side of the bed, reached under the pillow and took out four long thin strips of white material. It took her a moment to realize she was looking at silken cords. As Tibba had warned, he meant to tie her so she'd be helpless!

Before she could prevent the word from escaping, she cried, "No!"

He smiled again and started around the bed. Unable to prevent herself, she retreated until her back was up against the wall. Why, oh why had she boxed herself into this corner?

The general grasped her arm and when she struggled to free herself he twisted it cruelly, backhanding her hard across the face. Gasping with pain and shock, she forced herself to take several deep breaths. What else had Tibba said? That if she fought he'd hurt her and the longer it took him to subdue and tie her the longer it would take to put their plan into action.

Calling up all the strength she possessed, Barbara made herself stop resisting though it went against her every instinct.

The general shook her. "No more fight?" he asked. "You fooled me, Barbara—I thought you'd show a bit more spirit."

She hung her head, rage and frustration thrumming through her. How she hated him! It was torture to remain limp and spineless when she ached to pound him with her fists, to kick and scratch, to bite if she had to.

The general lifted her and flung her onto the bed. He yanked one, then the other of her arms over her head and tied her wrists to separate bedposts. Her loathing must have shown in her eyes because he laughed.

"If looks could kill that would be the end of me," he said. "I'm glad to see some spark remains, Barbara. It promises to make the night more interesting."

Next he tied each one of her ankles to the lower bedposts. Helpless, she glared at him, deliberately fueling her anger to ward off terror.

He reached into a pocket and took out what looked like an ivory case. But then he flicked it and a bright steel blade sprang out.

A knife! Dread stopped her breath as he leaned over her. He grasped her nightgown at the neck and raised the knife, slitting the garment from top to bottom. With the blade, he flipped back the material so her body was fully exposed.

"Ah," he said. "Quite lovely, yes."

As she lay rigid with apprehension of what was to come next, he stepped back, lay the knife on the nightstand and reached for the belt holding his holster and gun in place.

Barbara moistened her dry lips with her tongue and tried to clear her throat of the lump of fear clogging it. When she saw him drop the holster onto the floor she tried to cry out but only a whisper emerged.

"Ishmael!" she finally managed to croak. "Ishmael!" The general shrugged. "I'm afraid that's not my name, Barbara."

She stared past him at the closet door, willing it to open.

The door stayed closed.

Chapter 7

Barbara gazed with horror at the general as he leaned over her. He smelled of brandy but nothing else, as though he were scentless, like a snake. Bile churned in her stomach and burned the back of her throat at the thought of his mouth touching hers. Unable to move otherwise, she averted her face.

She heard a scraping sound, then a gun roared. Trembling, half-deafened by the noise, Barbara turned her head to look. Tibba, dressed in a black gown, stood near the open closet door, the gun in her hand pointed at the general's chest.

"Give me that!" the general ordered. "You don't know the first thing about guns."

Tibba scowled at him. "The next time I pull the trigger you'll see how much I know. Back away from the bed. Now."

Slowly the general obeyed. Keeping her eye on him, Tibba hurried to the nightstand, grabbed the knife, slit the silk tie holding Barbara's left wrist, then shoved the ivory hilt of the knife into Barbara's free hand.

As quickly as she could, Barbara cut herself free and sprang from the bed. She lifted a dressing robe off the back of the rocking chair and slipped it on.

"I mean to kill you," Tibba told the general, her voice thick with hatred. He laughed, though Barbara noticed he watched Tibba warily. "You may have learned to fire my Colt," he said, "but you'll never be able to shoot me. Come, stop this nonsense and give me that gun." He took a step toward her.

"Don't come near me!" Tibba cried, edging backward. "I'll shoot. I swear I will."

Barbara stood by, careful not to get in the way but uncertain of what she ought to do—if anything. She held her breath as the tension between Tibba and the general coiled tighter and tighter.

He took another step forward and held out his hand. "The Colt, Tibba."

"No!"

Barbara was dismayed to see that Tibba's hand had begun to shake so badly that the muzzle of the gun wavered back and forth. What could she do to help?

The general flicked a glance at her before concentrating on Tibba again. "It takes a killer to recognize a killer," he said. "You'll never be one, Tibba girl." He inched toward her as he spoke.

Again Tibba backed away. As she did so, the general took two quick strides, grabbed her wrist, wrenched the Colt away from her and struck her hard across the side of her head with the barrel. Tibba stumbled sideways, fell to her knees, and toppled over onto the floor. The general pointed the Colt at her and Barbara gasped.

But he didn't pull the trigger. "You need a taste of the whip, girl," he told the unmoving Tibba, prodding her with his foot.

Shifting his gaze to Barbara, he smiled. "Did you think to escape from me, my dear? No woman has ever bested me and none ever will." He reached for her wrist.

The sudden clanging of a bell outside the house startled them both, the sound loud and clear and urgent. The general held for a moment, then scooped his holster from the floor and strode to the door, unlocked the padlock and pocketed it. He left the room without another word, locking the door behind him while the bell continued to sound an alarm.

Barbara dropped to her knees beside Tibba who moaned and opened her eyes. "The bell," she whispered, struggling to sit up with Barbara's help.

"He's gone," Barbara said.

Tibba felt her already swollen face gingerly. "The bastard," she muttered. "I should've shot him stone dead. Now he's going to whip me, just like I was nothing but a slave." Tears gathered in her eyes and rolled down her cheeks. "I'm not a slave any more than my mama was," she cried brokenly. "I'm his daughter."

Barbara rocked back on her heels. General Meachum was Tibba's father? The relationship accounted for Tibba's status in the household. "No wonder you couldn't bring yourself to kill him," she said.

Still weeping, Tibba managed to get to her feet. Barbara rose and put an arm around her to steady her. "What was that bell?" she asked.

"The guards gave the alarm." The fact seemed to cheer Tibba; she pulled away and began mopping her wet face. "I hope the Yankees finally found his damn secret valley and are attacking."

Was it possible? The off chance they might escape in the confusion galvanized Barbara. Whatever developed, she meant to be ready. Hurrying to the closet, she began rummaging through the clothes, finally coming across a plum colored riding costume. Making certain to retrieve and put on her red petticoat, she dressed in the habit.

Tibba, who was looking out the window, turned to say, "I see a few men with lanterns—nothing else."

"I wish we could get out of this room," Barbara said.

Tibba pulled a key from her pocket. "He doesn't know I've got a master key that fits every lock in the house." She started for the door.

About to follow her, Barbara paused. "Did you pick up the knife?"

Tibba shook her head. "Last I saw it, I gave it to you."

Had the general taken the knife or was it somewhere amidst the bedclothes? Barbara ran to the bed and flung the rumpled covers all the way down to the foot. As she did so, the knife slipped free. She grasped the ivory handle, folded the blade inside and slid the knife into a pocket of her riding jacket before joining Tibba in the corridor.

They'd almost reached the head of the stairs when Barbara heard the front door open. She grasped Tibba's arm. They both paused to listen.

"Come into the library, Captain," General Meachum said, "and we'll discuss this message over a brandy. I regret any discomfort you might have suffered at the hands of my guards. I do not encourage visitors. Of course, an emissary from General Lee is always welcome."

Creeping backward for fear of discovery, Barbara didn't hear the captain's response, if he made one.

A door closed below. "They've gone in the library," Tibba whispered. "General Lee turned the Raiders out of the Confederate Army two years ago and took away my father's commission. He's been waiting all that time for General Lee to beg him for help."

The Rebs must be getting desperate, Barbara thought, if they were willing to welcome an evil man like General Meachum back into their ranks.

Tibba sighed. "I was hoping it was a Union raid so we could try to escape. This won't help us in any way. What with the alarm and all, his men'll be on the alert. We'd be stopped before we even got on a horse."

Barbara took a deep breath and her fingers clutched the knife in her pocket. "I'm *not* going back in that bedroom."

Tibba looked at her, thought for a few moments, and nodded. "He won't bother you again tonight, not with the emissary here. Probably not me, either, but I'm afraid to take the risk of staying in my own room. What we'll do is lock your door in case he happens to check, and then we'll find another place for both of us to sleep."

"Sleep! I won't be able to so much as close my eyes."

Tibba caught her hand. "Come on. I know just where we'll go."

By the light of a lamp Tibba took from one of the bedrooms, they crept down the back stairs to a room behind the kitchen containing four cots. "When he has a celebration for the men," Tibba said, "a couple of the field hands come in to help and they sleep here overnight."

Like the other door, this one locked with Tibba's key. Barbara tensed when she heard the click that meant they were shut inside.

"I hate being locked in!" she said.

"At least the window's closer to the ground than the one upstairs," Tibba pointed out as she sat on one of the cots. "Better choose your cot 'cause I got to snuff the lamp so the men outside won't get curious. And we'd best not talk, just in case."

Despite her anxiety, eventually Barbara did doze off, sleeping fitfully until dawn grayed the window. She glanced at the next cot but Tibba wasn't there. Barbara sat up hastily and, with relief, saw Tibba, standing by the door, listening.

"Oona's in the kitchen fixing breakfast," Tibba said. "She was a friend of my mother's. She'll give us something to eat and then—"

"And then what?" Barbara asked when Tibba didn't go on.

Tibba's smile was lopsided because of her swollen face and the skin of her left cheek and temple was bruised dark. "Then we'll try to stay away from him as long as we can."

Barbara didn't think that would be very long. "There must be another way out of this valley besides the pass," she said. "I know my horse forded a stream once we came down from the hills. Where does that stream go? Water doesn't run uphill so the stream must cut through the rock somewhere. Could that be a way out?"

"The stream goes through a tunnel in the rock. But—"

"Isn't there a possibility we can escape through the tunnel?"

"You didn't let me finish. He's got a grate blocking the tunnel mouth."

"Grates can be moved," Barbara persisted.

Tibba shook her head. "Not this one."

"Have you ever tried?"

"No, but—"

"I want to see it. Can you take me there?"

"Go outside?" Tibba frowned, considering. "I reckon we could. Outside's as safe as anywhere. He'll be occupied with that emissary and no one else is likely to bother us. Not that it'll do any good to look at the tunnel, but I'll show it to you if you want. But we'll eat first."

Barbara half expected to find the general waiting on the other side of the door when Tibba opened it. He wasn't there, nor was he anywhere in the kitchen.

110

Oona was a large woman with warm brown skin who wore a blue and white handkerchief tied over her head. Her eyes widened when she saw them emerge from the room but she said nothing. When Tibba asked, she readied two plates of hot biscuits and gravy with a slice of ham on each and set them on the kitchen table. Tibba pulled up two chairs, they sat down to eat, and Barbara, finding she'd regained the appetite she'd thought lost forever, ate faster than she ever had before.

The sun had risen by the time they slipped through the kitchen door. Barbara took a deep breath of the fresh morning air, imagining she felt a touch of fall in it. Her relief at being free, even if it was to be only for a brief few hours, made her feel giddy.

As they walked away from the house, she noticed a few slaves working in the fields but the men only glanced their way. Though Barbara kept expecting someone in authority to shout at them, ordering their return to the house, when it didn't happen she relaxed a little.

The sun glittered on water and Barbara pointed. "Is that a lake?"

"His latest improvement was to dam the stream to make that lake. He calls this his kingdom. But it wasn't his until he stole it from another man. You see that pine grove to the right?"

Barbara nodded.

"The Layton cemetery's in back of it. They're all dead, the Laytons. Like my mama. She's buried there, too. And the other ladies."

111

"What other ladies?" Even though she was afraid she knew, Barbara couldn't stop the question.

"The Northern ladies who shared my father's bed. Like you, not by choice. My mama didn't have a choice, either. Her name was Lorena and she was a free woman, not a slave, from New Orleans. A proud and beautiful woman. Until *he* got a hold of her—he had to marry her to get her." Tibba's eyes flashed and her fists clenched. "How I wish I'd shot him!"

"I'm sorry you didn't but I understand why you couldn't. I don't know that *I* could shoot a man, and he *is* your father."

Tibba gripped Barbara's hand. "I'm afraid you'll be sorrier yet. I like you and I'm sorry I failed us. Now I can't stop what's going to happen to you—or to me. He'll have his revenge sooner or later. He's the king of this valley."

Barbara grimaced. The general was the king of nothing but evil as far as she was concerned. Would she soon lie buried in that cemetery? No, never!

"Look!" Tibba pointed.

A woman ran across a field, her unbound blond hair streaming behind her and the short white shift she wore fluttering in the wind.

"Emiline!" Barbara cried.

Far behind, two men pursued Emiline, one a Negro, the other Redbeard. Barbara took an impulsive step forward and Tibba caught her wrist. "No! You can't help her. Whatever you try

112

to do, she'll be caught. Don't call attention to yourself or you'll be locked up even sooner."

Barbara bit her lip. She knew Tibba was right and yet. . . . "I have to know what's going to happen to Emiline," she insisted.

Tibba sighed. "All right. You wanted to see the tunnel anyway and she's headed that way. But we have to be careful."

"Hearing that her husband had been shot affected Emiline's mind," Barbara said. "How can anyone bear to take advantage of someone in her condition?"

"He picks men as much like him as he can find. And then he makes them worse. I hate him, hate him, hate him!"

They reached the stream that overflowed from the lake and walked along its banks until they neared a wall of sheer, dark rock, obviously unscalable. Tibba led her up a narrow path cut into the rock, a path that ended suddenly. She pointed. "The tunnel's down there."

Looking straight down, Barbara saw the stream flowing and she followed the moving water with her gaze toward a heavy iron grate that covered the tunnel's dark opening. A white cloth was caught across the lower end of the grate, rippling in the water. Barbara leaned over to get a better look. No, not a cloth. It was—oh, God, it was . . .

Barbara clapped her hand over her mouth to muffle her scream when she noticed two men hurrying along the bank of the stream toward the grate.

"Emiline," she breathed.

"She must have jumped from here," Tibba said in a shocked whisper.

Watching the Negro and Redbeard lift the limp body from the water, Barbara knew Emiline must be dead. She blinked back tears.

"Let's get out of here." Tibba's whisper was urgent.

When they were almost to the house, Tibba spoke again. "I told you it was impossible to escape through the tunnel."

Barbara clenched her teeth. The grate was obviously far too heavy for her to move, even with Tibba's help, but she would not give up! She wouldn't have her name carved into a marble headstone in that cemetery and she wouldn't die like poor Emiline either. "We've got to get away," she told Tibba.

"I know, but how?" A moment later, Tibba jerked her sideways, all but dragging her inside a potting shed not far from the rose garden. As they hid behind the partially open door, Barbara heard the general's voice.

". . . the rose garden. Natrually this isn't the best season for roses, as I'm sure you're aware, Captain."

She peered through the crack near the hinges just in time to catch a glimpse of the general's back. The man with him, General Lee's emissary, turned back to glance at the house and Barbara saw his face.

The next she knew, she found herself lying on a

114

dirt floor with Tibba's anxious face above her.

"Thank the Lord you're all right," Tibba said.

Barbara moistened her dry lips. "What—what happened?"

"Right after they went by you fainted."

The general. And the emissary. The captain. Captain Sandoe Trevor. Which was impossible. Barbara closed her eyes. I'm going mad, she thought.

"Barbara!" Tibba shook her shoulder.

Barbara opened her eyes and cautiously sat up. "Did you see him?" she asked.

"Who?"

"Captain Sandoe."

"Is that his name? I didn't hear it. Yes, I saw him."

Barbara swallowed. "Describe him."

"Tall. Dark hair, brown eyes. Handsome. Looked like he was starting to grow a beard."

The description was right but it could fit any number of men. I must be wrong, Barbara told herself.

"Why are you asking me all this?" Tibba demanded.

Barbara clutched her arm. "I must see the captain again. Right away."

"Do you know him?"

Oh, dear God, I hope so. "I can't be sure until I get another look at him," she told Tibba.

"Is that why you fainted? 'Cause you thought you recognized him?"

"The general said he killed all the men from the

115

train except for an Englishman. Trevor isn't English. So he must be dead. How can he be here? Maybe I'm going crazy."

Tibba shook her head. "Not you. Who is this Captain Sandoe?"

"Someone who might help me." Barbara spoke uncertainly, her mind roiling with confusion. If Trevor had escaped death and was now General Lee's emissary, would he jeopardize his mission to rescue her?

"I hope you're right," Tibba said. "But we don't dare go running after him. As it is, I'm afraid the men chasing your friend saw us and will tell the general. You'll have to wait until this emissary returns to the house."

Barbara saw the sense in Tibba's words and she tried to curb her eagerness to know for sure if she'd really seen Trevor or had merely mistaken another man for him. But she feared if she waited she might not have the chance to find out. "What if he doesn't come back?"

"He will. I heard my father tell him they'd have fresh-caught fish from the lake for lunch."

Anything might happen by then. Taking both of Tibba's hands in hers, Barbara gazed earnestly into her eyes. "Promise me that if I'm not able to see him you'll find out if his name is Captain Sandoe and, if it is, you'll tell him that Barbara Thackery's a prisoner in the general's house."

"I promise." When Barbara would have released Tibba's hands, Tibba tightened her grip. "Please," she said, "if he *can* help you, don't leave me behind."

116

"Never!"

They slipped in through the kitchen door. Oona, standing at the kitchen range stirring the contents of a pot, hardly glanced at them. As Tibba passed her, she muttered, "Trouble," and jerked her head toward the front of the house.

Tibba hurried to the back stairs and had started up them when Beardless burst into the kitchen. Barbara, behind Tibba, seeing she was too late to escape discovery, closed the stair door and leaned against it.

"You're to come with me, miss," Beardless said. "General's orders."

Unsure whether he'd seen Tibba or not, Barbara didn't move, hoping to give Tibba time to hide. "Where are you taking me?" she demanded.

Beardless advanced toward her. "You're going back to your room. 'Tis my job to see you stay there."

Afraid if she delayed any longer, he'd drag her away, Barbara allowed herself to be taken up the back stairs, breathing a sigh of relief when she saw no sign of Tibba.

Beardless not only locked her in but, from the sound, Barbara decided he'd pulled up a chair outside the door and was no doubt sitting in it. Thus guarded, she was truly imprisoned in this hateful room. If only she had the padlock to secure the inner side of the door so she could keep the general from entering.

Where was Tibba? Could she elude capture long enough to pass Barbara's message along to Trevor?

If it was Trevor.

She crossed to the window but there was no sign of either the general or Trevor. I couldn't have mistaken him, she told herself.

Maybe not, but will Trevor help you? And, even if he wants to, can he? Think about it. What can a lone man do when he, like you, is trapped within this nest of evil? Barbara sighed and turned away from the window.

The only one who'd escaped so far was poor Emiline and Barbara shuddered as she recalled how. She fingered the ivory case of the knife in her pocket and wondered if she'd be able to use it against the general when the time came. She tried to picture herself plunging the blade into his back and grimaced.

Stop being squeamish, she warned herself grimly.

But, like her father, she was a healer, not a killer.

She paced about the room until exhaustion caught up with her. Unable to so much as touch the bed, much less lie on it, she finally sat in the rosewood rocker and closed her eyes.

Evil. She was surrounded by evil, evil that couldn't be forgiven. Barbara remembered Reverend Hargreaves preaching about the power of forgiveness, but she also remembered White Deer telling her that the Chippewa tongue had no word comparable to forgive. Perhaps White Deer understood evil better than the minister. Surely a man as evil as General Meachum deserved to die.

She hadn't expected to be fed, but at midday her door was unlocked and Beardless handed her a tray

118

with food that she could only bring herself to nibble at. After that she was left to herself until dusk when he passed her another tray of food and removed the first.

Barbara managed to eat a slice of bread and the apple compote. What would happen, she wondered, if I began screaming and refused to stop? She toyed with the idea, discarding it when she decided that even if Trevor heard her she'd be no nearer escape. The general would make some excuse to the captain and send one of his men to tie and gag her.

Where was Tibba? A prisoner, as she was? Or had Tibba eluded capture? If she had, was it possible Barbara's message had been passed to the captain?

The moon had risen by the time Barbara heard the scrape of the key in the lock again. She sprang from the rocker and faced the door, heart hammering in her chest, one hand in her jacket pocket. When she saw who it was, she bit back a moan of despair.

"Did you think I'd forgotten you?" General Meachum asked.

Chapter 8

General Meachum pulled the padlock from his pocket. As she stared in dismay at him, the accumulation of anger and fear and loathing inside Barbara burst forth.

"You!" she cried. "How can you call yourself a human being after the way you hounded that poor woman to her death today? I swear you're a true minion of Satan rather than a man. Some demon from hell's depths has taken over your soul and drives you deeper and deeper into a morass of evil. That woman deserved to live; you do not."

For the first time since she'd met him, General Meachum seemed taken aback.

"I assure you I am my own master," he said after a moment. "And the woman sought her own death—it was none of my doing."

"You may deceive yourself but you won't deceive me." She pointed her finger at him, words coming to her from the Bible: "'Ye are of your father the devil . . . he was a murderer from the beginning . . .' "

"Stop that!" He dropped the padlock and advanced on her, his face contorted into a frightening mask of rage. Grasping her by the shoulders, he shook her until her teeth rattled. "I am a man! Do you hear? A man." He stopped shaking her, his fingers digging into her shoulders painfully. "You speak lies."

"The devil is the father of lies," she gasped out. "It's you who belong to him, not me."

His pale face turned an ugly reddish purple, veins writhed hideously on his forehead. His fingers slid up to fasten around her throat, cutting off her breath. As she clawed at his hands, struggling in vain to free herself, black specks clouded her vision and then darkness closed in around her. . . .

Barbara roused to find herself sprawled on her back atop the bed with the general poised over her. Groggy from his near fatal choking, she tried in vain to clear her mind. Confused and terrified, she fastened on the only word that came to her.

"Ishmael!" she cried hoarsely. "Help me, Ishmael!"

"If you mean Tibba," the general said, "she's locked in the jail. She won't rescue you this time." He yanked a pillow over her face and pressed down, stifling her cries.

Using what little strength remained in her, she managed to turn her head to the side in a desperate attempt to draw in air. Her ears rang, blood

121

pounded in her head, she was aware of nothing but her own struggle to breathe.

Suddenly the pressure on the pillow eased. As Barbara weakly pushed it to one side, she realized belatedly that all the noise wasn't in her head, that what she heard was wood splintering.

Just as she managed to sit up, the bedroom door burst from its hinges and a man rushed into the room, pistol in hand. He whirled, crouching, aiming the gun at the general who had his Colt half drawn.

Trevor!

"Pull that gun and I'll kill you," Trevor snarled. He flicked a glance at Barbara. "Get behind me, Snow Bird."

Barbara slid off the bed and stumbled to his side, her mind in a jumble. As Trevor thrust her in back of him she noticed that the general had dropped the Colt back into its holster.

"I should kill you in cold blood, Meachum," Trevor said, "like you ordered me killed. I damn well will if you provoke me. Walk ahead of me and keep your hands above your head."

Barbara had recovered enough to snatch her riding hat and her gloves from the dressing table before following Trevor from the room. She still had trouble believing he was actually alive and here in front of her.

Trevor eased up behind Meachum, removed the Colt, and gripped it by the barrel, still holding his own gun to the general's back. "Into the next room, Meachum," he ordered.

As the general hesitated in the doorway, Trevor

swung the Colt hard, its heavy metal handle slamming across the back of Meachum's head. The general fell heavily across the threshold. Trevor slid the Colt into his own holster, shoved the unconscious general all the way into the room, crouched and removed a ring of keys from Meachum's pocket, then locked the general inside.

"Now," he said, grasping Barbara's arm and propelling her toward the stairs, "let's get the hell out of here."

"We have to rescue Tibba," she said. "I promised."

"There's no time."

"One of those keys you took must unlock the jail. If Tibba hadn't helped me . . ." Barbara broke off, shuddering. "I intend to keep my promise."

Trevor muttered what sounded like a curse. "We can't spare more than a minute or two. Tibba, if you insist. But no one else."

Her heart heavy with the knowledge that five other women must stay behind to suffer, but realizing it would be impossible to locate them easily, she ran with Trevor across the grounds toward the jail. A thick layer of clouds covered the moon and stars, making it difficult to see where they were going. The darkness, though, would aid their escape.

Barbara brightened when they found not only Tibba locked in the cell but also Wilma, Amelia, Edna, Lorraine, Irene and Zoe. As she tried to explain, Trevor looked askance at all of them, cutting short the women's exclamations.

"No time for talking," he said curtly. "Keep

quiet and follow my orders without question or we'll never make it to the other side of the mountains."

Barbara, like the others, followed him in silence for what seemed like miles. When he finally stopped and lit a match, she saw to her surprise that he'd led them to the grate that covered the mouth of the tunnel that the stream flowed into. What now?

Using the tiny flare of the match flame, Trevor searched among the rocks, apparently for something he'd hidden there earlier. When the match winked out he lit another, muttered "Thank God," snuffed the flame, and then fumbled in the darkness with whatever he'd retrieved.

Barbara longed to ask him how he expected to remove the grate but she didn't speak. The time for questions would come after they escaped. If they did.

Still, she trusted Trevor's ingenuity. He'd already escaped from Johnson Island Prison in Sandusky—less than a handful of Rebs ever had. And he'd not only survived General Meachum's attempt to have him shot, he'd also found a way into the very heart of Meachum's kingdom.

"Everyone get down on your face behind this boulder," he ordered in a sharp whisper. "Down flat. See they obey, Snow Bird."

"All down," she whispered.

After a moment or two he flung himself next to her. "No one moves until I say—" His words were cut off by a brilliant yellow flash accompanied by a tremendous rattling roar. Small rocks and gravel pelted down onto the women but no one cried out. An acrid stench filled Barbara's nostrils, making her realize what had happened.

He'd dynamited the grate!

"Up," Trevor ordered. "Form a queue like before, each holding to the one in front. Ready?" He grabbed Barbara's hands and hooked her fingers onto his belt. Without waiting for agreement, he added, "Let's go."

He led them through the dark into the cold and shallow water of the stream where they climbed over the rocky debris from the blast and plunged into the deeper darkness of the tunnel.

Barbara freed one of her hands to hoist her skirts above the water and felt fortunate to be wearing riding boots high enough to keep her feet dry. But as time passed and they splashed on and on, the echo from rocky walls telling her they were still underground, she began to wonder how long the tunnel was. Did Trevor know?

She forced herself to remain silent. If she asked and he didn't know, all she'd accomplish would be to undermine the other women's trust in him. Even if he did know, it wouldn't make their passage any shorter.

"What's that noise?" Tibba's call came from near the end of the line, echoing off the walls. Accompanying her words was a rushing sound.

"Damn!" Trevor broke into a run, all but dragging Barbara off her feet. "Meachum must have gotten to the sluice gate of the dam and raised it. He's flooding the tunnel. Hurry!"

The woman behind Barbara—Zoe, she was

almost sure—screamed and let go of the back of Barbara's jacket. There was no time to wait for Zoe to grab hold again, not with Trevor pulling her so fast she could barely keep up. The thought of being trapped and drowned in the tunnel terrified Barbara as the roar of water grew louder. Closer.

Behind her other women screamed, their cries cut off abruptly. And then the wall of water swirled around and over her, tearing loose her grip on Trevor, tumbling her off her feet to be swept along helplessly. She held her breath, struggling to reach the surface of the flood waters to find air, but the force of the current was greater than her own strength.

Just as she felt her lungs about to burst her head broke through the water and she gulped in a great gasp of air before she was sucked under again and flung violently against something hard. Without conscious thought, she grabbed what she'd struck—a rock—and pulled herself up. And found air once more.

After what seemed an eon of dragging herself up onto the rock, Barbara discovered she was perched above the water. For long moments she hugged the rock as she drew in deep, gasping breaths. Eventually she realized there was light. Moonlight. And in the light she could see pine trees. She was free of the tunnel!

Her triumph faded as quickly as it had come. Where were the others? She sat up. "Trevor!" she called over the rushing, splashing flood. "Tibba!"

No one answered.

Barbara shivered, chilled as much by the fear she

might be the only survivor as she was by the night wind blowing against her wet clothes. Hardly aware of what she was doing, she began wringing water from her skirts. Trevor couldn't have drowned; she refused to believe it. She'd search until she found him.

Struggling to her feet, she climbed carefully from the rock onto the crumbling bank and began to make her way downstream through the pine forest, hugging herself against the cold, her sodden skirts flopping against her boots.

"Trevor!" she called again and again, pitching her voice above the roar of the torrent.

Finally, numb with cold, she could only stumble along, her teeth chattering so hard she could scarcely say his name. When a hand gripped her arm and swung her around she was too exhausted to scream.

"I've been calling your name," Trevor's voice said in her ear. "Didn't you hear me?"

She'd heard nothing but the flood waters and the echo of her own voice. Barbara clung to him, unable to let go. He held her close.

"We'll be all right," he murmured. "I've found shelter."

"Are the others with you?" she asked.

"I haven't seen any sign of them."

Keeping one arm around her, he led the way. Barbara was past noticing her surroundings, but she did catch a whiff of burning wood before the welcome glow of flames beckoned. Only after he'd brought her to the fire and released her did she realize they were no longer in the woods. She glanced around at rocky walls.

"A cave," she whispered as much to herself as to Trevor.

"Complete with firewood and blankets," he said, handing her one of the blankets as he spoke. She started to drape it over her shoulders but he stopped her. "No. Take off those wet clothes first or you'll never get warm."

She stared at him. He'd already stripped off his uniform jacket and was starting on his shirt. Much as she disliked the idea of disrobing in front of him, common sense told her he was right. She hesitated briefly, then turned her back to him, set the blanket aside and unbuttoned her riding skirt.

Barbara stopped when she'd removed everything except her chemise. Though it, too, was wet, she left the chemise on, wrapped the blanket around her and turned cautiously toward Trevor. To her relief he had a blanket thrown over his shoulders and crossed in front of him.

"I've dragged a log in to sit on," he told her, gesturing to the opposite side of the fire.

As she eased down onto the log, Barbara noticed pine boughs stacked behind it, their clean fragrance permeating the cave. But at the moment her only real interest was to warm herself.

About the time her teeth stopped chattering, her mind began to function and she looked more closely at the gray blanket draped around her, conscious now of its musty smell. She looked sideways at Trevor, seated on the log next to her. "Who left the blankets here?"

He shrugged. "Renegades is my guess."

128

Barbara tensed, shifting closer as she glanced past him into the darkness outside the cave.

Apparently sensing her alarm, he shook his head. "The blankets are old, the firewood was dry as the desert—no one's been here for a long time. Lucky for us that the human scent kept animals from using the cave for a den."

"Lucky," she echoed.

He slid over and freeing an arm from his blanket, draped it over her shoulders. "Very lucky." His arm tightened around her. "For a while there I was afraid I'd lost you."

"I knew you couldn't have drowned," she told him, watching the flames dance in his brown eyes. "Not you."

He smiled and touched her cheek with the fingers of his other hand. "Ah, Snow Bird, even bedraggled you're beautiful."

She drew in her breath, enthralled by his words and warmed by his touch. No longer did she mind him using her Indian name; now she felt it created a bond between them.

"You called for me in his house," Trevor said, so close to her she could feel the soft caress of his breath on her face. "You called for Ishmael."

"And you rescued me."

His grip tightened. "Did he—hurt you?"

"He hit me once."

"But did he—that is—" Trevor paused.

Belatedly, Barbara understood what he was trying to ask. "I—I wasn't—" she stammered. "He—he didn't—" Again she broke off, wondering why it was so difficult to say the word her

129

father would use. The terrible, violent word for what General Meachum had meant to do to her. But the correct word, nonetheless. Gathering her courage she tried again. "I wasn't—raped."

Trevor held her away from him and gazed into her eyes. "Thank God," he said fervently. "It took me so long to find my way into that foul den of his. I could only hope—" He didn't finish.

"The general said he'd shot you."

"I knew he'd kill the men—I had a friend in the prison camp who rode with Meachum and told me some god-awful particulars. So when we were separated from the women and herded from the train, I kept my eyes open for the slightest chance. The Yanks from the baggage car were still firing and some of the shots were coming our way. One got a Raider next to me clean through the head.

"Figuring this was my only possible escape, I staggered and clutched my chest, pretending to be hit, too, fell and rolled down the embankment into the ditch beside the dead Raider. The hardest part was not moving while at any moment I expected to feel a bullet slam into me from one of Meachum's men making sure I was dead."

Trevor released her and held his hands out to the fire, looking into the flames as he went on. "After they forced the other men into the woods, I dragged the dead Raider behind a tree, changed clothes with him, grabbed a horse, and got the hell out of there, wishing there was some way to bring you with me." He shook his head. "I knew I couldn't. Somehow I had to outsmart Meachum. It's my belief that General Lee would rather lose the war then accept Meachum back into the Confederate Army, but I was pretty sure that Meachum had never given up hoping Lee would apologize and beg for his help."

"It was clever of you to arrive as Lee's emissary," Barbara told him. "*I* even believed you were."

"Meachum's a wily opponent. In the end he nearly did for us."

Reminded once more of the other women, Barbara half-rose. "Shouldn't we go out and search for Tibba and the rest?"

"I did search. You were the only survivor I came across between here and the end of the tunnel. In the morning we'll be traveling downstream and perhaps—" He broke off. "Don't be too hopeful; I'm afraid those behind us had even less of a chance in the flood waters than we did."

Tears filled her eyes. "If it weren't for Tibba—" Sobs took her words away.

Trevor enfolded her in his arms, drawing her close and murmuring soothing words as she wept. After a time she became aware her wet cheek rested not against the blanket but against his bare chest. He smelled of woodsmoke and of himself, a remembered scent that dried her tears and sent her pulses scudding. She was safe in Trevor's arms— or was she?

If she drew back would he let her go? Somehow she thought he would. But she didn't want to be released, she wanted to remain nestled here, feeling his warmth deep within her, savoring the heretofore unknown pleasure of flesh against flesh.

He comforts me, she told herself, trying to block the knowledge that comfort didn't make the breath catch in the throat or cause the heart to pound. Nor did comfort ignite this new and strange yearning she felt, a need to press even closer to him.

"Snow Bird," he murmured, his lips touching her ear and sending a tingly, shivery sensation through her that had nothing to do with cold or fear.

The realization that she was about to turn her head so his lips could find hers jolted Barbara. "I—I'm all right now," she whispered, pulling away.

He let her go and immediately she felt bereft. "Are you warm enough?" he asked.

She nodded.

"Pine boughs make a fair mattress," he said, rising from the log. "These I cut should be green enough not to flare up from a spark—I'll pull them closer to the fire so we can get some rest."

Watching him rearrange the boughs, she realized they'd be lying side by side on the fragrant mattress. Instead of being shocked or outraged, a thrill shot through her.

He's still a Reb, she warned herself. He may have rescued you but he's still your enemy. Don't forget his beliefs are different. He forces his fellow men to be his slaves and his compatriots have imprisoned your father.

Was she then to lie on the cold stone floor of the cave? Already she could feel the chill of the stone through the soles of her bare feet. "Can't we separate the boughs?" she asked.

132

He glanced at her, one eyebrow raised. "There's hardly enough. Don't you trust me?"

Barbara flushed. Trevor had risked his life—and come very near losing it—to save her from General Meachum. Trevor might be a Reb but he'd more than proved he was trustworthy. "Never mind," she muttered.

When he'd smoothed the boughs to his satisfaction, Trevor bowed slightly, gesturing for her to be the first to lie down. "Feet toward the fire," he advised.

She edged toward the makeshift bed and stretched out gingerly, her blanket clutched tightly about her. When Trevor lay beside her, she turned her back to him. This is merely a practical arrangement, she told herself firmly. After all he's already done for me, Trevor shouldn't be expected to spend half the night cutting boughs to make two separate mattresses.

Anyway, she was already dreadfully compromised after spending a night with him in that boxcar. Her father might understand, but she feared no one else would. Of course, no one would have to know. Once morning came she and Trevor would make their way to the nearest village and sooner or later she'd be on her way to Richmond. He'd go his way and they'd never meet again.

The thought made her sigh.

"What's wrong?" Trevor asked.

"I was thinking about my father in Libby Prison." While not strictly true, it wasn't exactly a lie—her father's precarious situation was never far from her mind. "He's a doctor, not a soldier. It's shameful to keep him behind bars."

"*I* didn't put him there. In my opinion it would make more sense to assign a Yankee doctor to treat the wounded rather than imprisoning him."

She turned to face Trevor. "War brings out the worst in men."

"Don't judge us all by Meachum. War can bring out the best in men as well."

In the darkness, lit only by the flickering light of the fire, Trevor's face was shadowed and unfamiliar. And far too close to hers. His nearness made her forget what she'd been about to say. He inched closer yet and his lips brushed hers lightly, lingeringly, in a kiss that warmed her clear through to the soles of her feet.

He made no attempt to touch her otherwise; nothing prevented her from turning away from him. But turning away meant ending the kiss and she couldn't bring herself to do that. Not yet. For a moment or two she meant to savor the new and exciting sensations springing to life inside her.

Without willing it, her hand slid from under the blanket and found the nape of his neck, her fingers tangling in the soft silk of his hair. He shifted position, raising his head so that she had to turn onto her back to avoid breaking the kiss. The tip of his tongue caressed her lips, easing between them, parting them gently, slipping inside.

How strange and wonderful he tasted! Her excitement increased, making her ache deep within, less an aching than a driving need for something she'd never known, something only

134

this man could give her. She didn't know what it was, but he must.

"Ishmael?" She whispered the name against his lips.

Trevor's heart slammed against his ribs when he heard her plea. She was so delightfully, so maddeningly innocent that she didn't even know what she was asking for. He knew. And he damn well wanted the same. In fact, he couldn't recall ever wanting a woman more. But he also knew he should stop, here and now, while he still could.

He would stop. In just a minute or two. After a few more sips of her sweetness.

Her blanket had fallen back, revealing the swell of her breasts under her thin batiste chemise. Before he was fully aware of what he meant to do, he'd covered one breast with his hand. Her tiny enticing moan inflamed him as much as the luscious softness under his fingers.

He had to taste her. The tiny buttons at the neck of the chemise yielded to his impatient fumbling, and he trailed kisses down her throat to her bare chest. When he took her nipple into his mouth she arched to him, offering herself, offering more than she understood.

How different from in the boxcar, when she'd fought him every inch of the way. He'd been on fire for her then, but thank God he'd retained enough sense to stop. He was no Meachum; he'd never in his life taken a woman by force and never would.

But this wouldn't be rape—she was as passion-driven as he. He ached with need for her—why shouldn't he take what she so eagerly offered?

Because, dammit, she didn't have the slightest notion what was going to happen to her. He'd be taking advantage of her innocence, not as violent and misguided as rape, but still wrong. Wasn't it? After all, he had no intention of marrying this girl.

His hand slid over the curve of her hip and he drew in his breath when his fingers encountered the bare flesh of her thigh. He had to touch her, had to discover and caress the warmth that awaited him.

Once he touched her there and found her moist welcome, he couldn't make himself stop. She moaned in what he realized was pleasure, her arms held him to her, she pressed against him ardently, expectantly, making him throb with desire.

Raising himself above her, he vowed he'd be gentle, he wouldn't hurt her, he'd take care to bring her the pleasure she begged for. . . .

No! With a muffled curse, Trevor broke free, grabbed his blanket, sprang up from the pine boughs and strode to the mouth of the cave.

He hadn't saved her from Meachum only to take by stealth what Meachum would have taken by force. She deserved better. He'd always believed himself to be an honorable man, and honorable men didn't deprive lovely young ladies of their innocence. He didn't even have the excuse of being in love with her—he merely wanted her.

One hell of a lot. But then, she was extremely desirable—what man wouldn't want her?

She needed protection against unscrupulous

men. Luckily the Meachums in this world were few, but the same couldn't be said about men who'd take advantage of her innocence. He must convince her to forget this nonsense of rescuing her father from Libby Prison—an impossible task in any case. Surely she had a home back in Sandusky where she'd be safe. Somehow, he must persuade her to return.

She couldn't continue on alone to Richmond. Nor could she go to Richmond with him. He was no protection for her; he couldn't trust himself where she was concerned. It was all he could do not to turn around right now, walk back to the pine boughs and lie with her again. She fitted into his arm as though meant for him and him alone. The taste of her was still on his lips, he could almost feel her soft warmth under his fingers.

She'd wanted him; she'd welcome him back. God knows he longed for her. . . .

So why was he being such a damn fool as to stand here and freeze his balls off in this cold darkness?

Chapter 9

Light slanting in through the cave opening
woke Barbara from a deep sleep. For a long
moment she stared at the rocky ceiling in bewilderment, trying to remember where she was and why.
The scrape of leather against rock made her sit up
abruptly. She cast an apprehensive glance all
around.

The form of a man, tall and broad-shouldered,
was silhouetted against the light streaming into
the cave. She tensed, clutching the blanket closer.

"Time we pushed on, Barbara," Trevor said.

At the sound of his voice memory flooded
through her, making her flush in angry humiliation. Averting her eyes, she rose and plucked her
red petticoat from the rocky floor. Keeping the
blanket about her as best she could, she dressed in
her still damp clothes and stamped her feet into the
stiffening boots. Smoothing her unbound hair as
much as possible without a brush, she took a deep
breath and turned to face Trevor.

He was nowhere in sight. After last night, wasn't it a bit late to play the gentleman and step out while she dressed? She'd never forgive him for what happened. Never. She doubted that she'd be able to forgive herself, either.

Her father had told her never to be ashamed of her body and its feelings, but he'd been referring to marriage. To a wife's love for a husband. Trevor was certainly not her husband and as for love— how could she possibly love a Reb?

Yet she'd not only permitted Trevor to kiss and caress her but had even encouraged him. In short, she'd behaved like the wanton he'd originally believed her to be. Though she wasn't certain of the details, she was aware there was more to lovemaking than she'd experienced last night, and she supposed she ought to be grateful Trevor had stopped short of the final indignity.

He'd stopped. That was the rub. *She* should have been the one to protest, to push him away. Would she have, even if he'd tried to—? To what? She wasn't exactly sure what more he might have done. The very thought of it caused her insides to flutter alarmingly, the thrilling sensation much the same as when he'd held her close.

Barbara bit her lip. Why hadn't she been repelled by Trevor's touch as she had been when Reverend Hargreaves forced his caresses on her? Why hadn't she been terrified as she'd been when General Meachum laid hands on her? She'd resisted Trevor spiritedly enough in the boxcar— what had changed between them that made her welcome his kiss?

She raised her chin. She'd certainly never allow him to kiss her again.

"Coming in," Trevor called. "All right?"

"Yes," she said crisply.

He crossed to the pine boughs and picked up the folded blankets. "We'd better take these along; we may need them." Glancing at her, he added, "I'm glad you were able to sleep."

"The makeshift mattress was quite comfortable," she said coolly. Actually, she'd hadn't fallen asleep for some time after he'd left her alone. His abrupt rejection had brought tears, tears dried by anger before she'd suffered the embarrassment of having him hear her weep.

They walked downstream with Trevor in the lead, constantly on the lookout for the other women. Barbara called one name, then another. There was no response.

Trevor was courteous to a fault, holding aside branches for her and assisting her over the rough terrain. She wished she could refuse his help, but the riding boots, stiffened by their dunking, were not the easiest footgear for hiking in the wilderness. By noon her feet hurt almost beyond bearing. She was also hungrier than she could ever recall being.

The fate of the other women preyed on her mind and she longed to talk about them, especially Tibba. But not to Trevor. She refused to share anything with him. He made no attempt to converse with her, either.

Much as she hated to, she was about to admit she couldn't take another step when he halted in a small clearing, tersely announcing a short rest period. Barbara promptly eased herself to the ground, thankful to be off her feet, and leaned back against the trunk of a hickory. Looking up through a gap in its leafy branches, she saw a hawk spiraling high above.

Trevor apparently followed her glance because he said, "If we could only sprout wings and fly over these endless mountains. Do you have any idea how many mountainous miles lie between us and Virginia?" He went on without waiting for an answer. "Almost the entire width of the Alleghenies." He sighed. "What I wouldn't give for an observation balloon. Or even a decent pair of boots. That Raider's feet were smaller than mine."

It took her a moment to understand he was complaining that his feet were sore from ill-fitting boots.

"On the other hand," Trevor continued, "he's dead and I'm alive. But it's difficult to appreciate that at the moment. Especially when I'm starving. I keep imagining I smell something savory cooking."

Because Barbara had been thinking the same thing, she raised her head and sniffed the air. Surely more than the damp odor of forest duff and the ubiquitous pine scent rode the November wind.

"Salt pork and beans," she said, as much to herself as to him.

"So the smell *is* real. Salt pork and beans it is. Army rations."

Her eyes widened. "Meachum's Raiders?"

141

"Not here. This is Yankee territory these days. More likely to be Union troops." He glanced at his gray uniform. "I'm taking no chances of stepping into a nest of Yanks. But they're not your enemies." He gave her an appraising look. "Yes, that would be best."

She bristled. "What would be best? To turn me over to the Union Army?"

"What choice do you have? We've no supplies, no mounts. Alone, I can forage for myself, but with you holding me back, I'm limited."

She glared at him. "You want me to be sent back to Ohio, don't you? After you promised to see I made it to Richmond."

He shot her an exasperated glance. "Dammit, Barbara, be practical. Even if you manage to reach Richmond—"

"Don't lecture me!" She sprang to her feet. "I won't listen. There's nothing you can say that will make me give up trying to get to my father."

"Calm yourself and try to be reasonable. I think you'll agree these are perilous times for a woman and doubly dangerous for a woman alone. What can I do for you as things stand? I don't have so much as a crust of bread to offer and we're in what to me is enemy territory. I'll scout ahead, but I'm willing to bet what little I possess that those are Yanks cooking that salt pork. Your friends. They'll help you where I can't."

"Union soldiers won't help me get to Richmond and you know it."

"I damn well can't help you, either!" He took a

step toward her and she eyed him defiantly.

They both froze when they heard a man's voice calling to someone. Though the sound was too faint to make out the words, it told them someone was within shouting distance.

"Stay here," Trevor ordered and melted into the woods.

Quelling her impulse to run after him—her feet just weren't up to the challenge—Barbara sought cover. Finding a log admist a tangle of brush, she sat on it, wanting to be hidden from whoever might come until she'd made certain the man wasn't one of Meachum's Raiders. No matter what Trevor said, she wasn't entirely convinced they were near a federal outpost.

Would Trevor return once he'd scouted the camp? He hadn't said so. If he did find Union soldiers it wasn't likely he'd come back to her. She swallowed, feeling a sudden lump in her throat. How could he leave her forever without so much as a goodbye?

He gave me his word he'd help me, she thought forlornly, and now he's deserting me.

She listened for the sound of voices or the crackle of dried leaves under men's boots but heard only the sough of the wind in the boughs above her. Hours seemed to pass. She was trying to decide whether to remain where she was or to look for the camp herself when a blue jay's raucous cry erupted nearby. She tensed, knowing that jays gave the alarm when intruders entered their territory. It could be an animal that had alerted the bird but she suspected it was a man. Or men. She peered apprehensively through the thin cover she hid behind.

"Damn jay! He'll get me caught yet," Trevor grumbled. "Barbara? Where are you?"

He'd come back! She was so relieved she jumped up from the log, pushed through the brush, and ran to him. Without thinking what she was doing, she flung her arms around him. "I thought you'd left me," she cried.

For a short and wonderful moment, he held her close to him. Then he put her firmly aside. "I'd never abandon you in the woods. It's a Yankee camp, as I suspected, and I'll guide you closer before I go. You'll be safe there."

She didn't want to be safe; she wanted to stay with him. Only because he was her hope of getting to Richmond, she told herself.

"Don't look at me like that," he said. "We both know I must travel alone."

Barbara realized it was futile to argue. He meant what he said and wouldn't be swayed. But she had no intention of giving up. She'd merely tackle the problem from another direction.

Trevor took her hand. "We'll say goodbye here. Once we're nearer the camp we can't risk talking. I've scouted thoroughly and have both their sentries spotted. One's near the horses. What I plan to do is leave you close to him. While he's distracted by your arrival, I'll get my chance to make off with a horse."

She could ruin his plan; she could give him away. Wasn't he a Reb, an enemy? But she knew

144

she wouldn't. Taking a deep breath, she pressed his hand and released it, saying, "God go with you, Trevor."

He smiled crookedly. "Last night you called me Ishmael."

She felt her face flame and started to turn away but he caught her by the shoulders. "I'll never forget you, Snow Bird," he said softly and bent his head to kiss her hard but briefly.

She touched her fingers to her lips as he led her through the woods, wishing it was possible to preserve a kiss in the same way one preserved fruit, so the kiss could be stored away to be savored later, in a season of no kisses. At the same time she wondered how much farther she could manage to walk in the boots. At last Trevor halted and put a finger to his lips.

Pointing, he whispered, "Go straight that way. The moment I'm out of sight start calling for help." Without another word he was gone, vanishing into the woods.

Barbara stumbled on, her heart heavy. Dutifully she cried, "Help, oh, help me! Help me, please!"

Minutes later she heard someone crashing through the brush in front of her, then a red-faced youth in a blue uniform burst into view, rifle at the ready. He stopped when he caught sight of her and lowered the muzzle of his gun.

"Thank God!" she cried, hurrying up to him. "Thank God I'm saved."

"I reckon you are, miss, right enough," the soldier told her. "Be you another of them near-drowned ladies?"

145

She stared at him. "Yes! How did you know?"

"We got three more of you back to camp and we buried four dead 'uns."

There were other survivors! She caught at his arm. "Who? Who's alive?"

"I don't rightly know their names. You'll see 'em soon enough, miss, 'cause I got to take you into protective custody."

She dropped her hand and took a step backward. "Protective custody? Whatever for?"

"Been a lot of spying going on; can't take no chances. Leastways, that's what Major Lifkin says. Please to come along with me, miss."

Barbara didn't care for the sound of *protective custody* but, in her eagerness to see the other survivors, she refused to worry about it for the moment. Camp noises—men whistling, male voices calling to one another, the rhythmic chip of an axe as someone cut firewood—speeded her pace despite her aching feet. Who had survived; who had died?

Pale canvas tents bloomed like huge gray-white mushrooms in a small clearing. The sentry guided her toward them, past a wagon with ropes and hoses trailing from it to a large pile of what looked like tan cloth on the ground nearby. Soldiers swarming around the wagon stopped when she went by to gawk at her as though they'd never before seen a woman.

The sentry led her among the tents. As they approached one set somewhat apart from the others, Barbara's heart leaped for joy when she saw the girl lounging in front of the tent, chatting with what must be a guard.

"Tibba!" she cried and ran toward her friend.

Tibba shrieked her name and met her halfway. They hugged one another until both were breathless.

"I knew you couldn't be dead," Tibba told her. "Not you."

"I was so afraid you'd drowned," Barbara said.

"He'd say I was too ornery to drown." She tugged at Barbara's hand. "Come on, the others are in the tent. Wilma's still down—we pumped a lot of water out of her—but Amelia's feeling pretty good, considering."

In the tent, after hugging Amelia, Barbara dropped on her knees beside the cot where Wilma lay. "How are you?" she asked.

Wilma mustered a weak smile. "Other than surprised I'm alive, you mean? I wouldn't be if it weren't for Tibba. How she pulled me from that flood I'll never know."

Tibba grinned at her. "Got my hand caught in your belt so I didn't have any choice." Sobering quickly, she turned to Barbara and dropped her voice. "Amelia said we'd best not mention the captain, him being a Reb. So we haven't. Told them all about the general, though, and where he is." Her mouth hardened and her eyes flashed. "The Yanks hate him almost as much as I do. He won't escape this time."

Amelia shook her head. "I hope not because such a monster shouldn't be allowed to exist. I can never forgive him for the horrors he forced us to endure. Though I thought at the time that death

147

would be preferable, I survived. God must have some purpose yet for me to fulfill."

"*My* goal is to dance on General Meachum's grave." Wilma's voice was grim.

"Poor Zoe, Irene, Lorraine, and Edna," Amelia said, wiping away a tear. "And Emiline, too. May they rest in peace."

Barbara bowed her head, silently echoing the prayer.

Later, Tibba took Barbara aside to whipser, "What happened to the captain? I know they didn't find his body."

"He's alive." Barbara pitched her voice as low as Tibba's. "Heading south."

Tibba nodded. "I'm glad he didn't drown. Now, about the major. I figure he's going to interview you like he did us. We mostly told the truth, except I gave them my mama's last name. You're the only one who knows what it really is."

Barbara pressed her hand. "As far as I'm concerned La Harpe *is* your real name."

When she was called before the camp commander, Barbara related the story of her father's imprisonment and how she'd been traveling to Baltimore when Meachum's Raiders attacked the train. She left Trevor completely out of her tale.

"We'll see to it you're sent back to Ohio as soon as possible, Miss Thackery," Major Lifkin said. "Meanwhile, for your protection and ours, you'll be sequestered here."

"But my father—"

"I'm sorry. Going to him is out of the question. Had you reached Baltimore, you'd have discovered for yourself how impossible it is to travel on to Richmond. We're fighting a war, Miss Thackery, and in war everything and everyone suffers."

Deciding it was better for her plans if she didn't antagonize the major, Barbara bit back a sharp retort. With her father ill in Libby Prison she hardly needed to be reminded about suffering.

"I realize an army camp must find four women an inconvenience," she said as pleasantly as she could. "We're grateful for your help."

Major Lifkin smiled stiffly. "It's no more than our duty."

While she'd been talking, Barbara had scanned the map of the area pinned to a post behind the major, finally locating the camp at a spot not far from the Virginia border. Her heart sank as she saw the great mountain range between her and Richmond. Trevor had been right. But she'd still get there. Somehow.

When the major dismissed her, one of his aides escorted her back to the woman's tent where she cornered Tibba.

"I plan to escape," she whispered. "Will you help me?"

Tibba didn't hesitate. "I'll do better. I'll come with you."

"It might be dangerous."

Tibba shrugged. "Can't be any more dangerous than living with *him*. And I sure don't belong here. Amelia and Wilma, they got homes they'll be going to; I've got nowhere to go except with you."

149

Barbara didn't argue further. She'd certainly welcome Tibba's company.

"We'll need two horses, then," she said.

"And two uniforms."

Barbara stared at her. "Uniforms?"

"Every soldier in the camp stares at us—didn't you notice? We can't get away dressed like women. I saw a wagon unloading clothes and blankets into the supply tent this morning. Maybe I can persuade Charlie to bring me two jackets and two pair of trousers." Tibba plucked at her black skirt. "After all, my gown *is* a mess. And so is yours. I'll tell him we need clothes to wear while we launder ours."

"Who's Charlie?"

"Our guard. He's from a farm somewhere in New York. Sweet but dumb." She flashed Barbara a saucy grin and eased through the flap of the tent.

Barbara couldn't help but overhear Tibba's shameless flirting with Charlie. Rather than being shocked, she admired Tibba's performance. Because her father had taught her to be frank and open, flirting wasn't a skill Barbara had ever mastered. If it could be mastered. Perhaps a girl had to be born with the knack.

Tibba's wiles proved successful; Charlie managed to slip two sets of uniforms into their tent. Barbara, taller than Tibba, tucked the bottoms of her too-long trousers into the top of her riding boots but Tibba was forced to roll up the bottoms of hers several turns.

The too-big jackets were a blessing since the bagginess more or less concealed their breasts.

Still, when they'd piled up and hidden their hair as best they could under the army caps, Barbara eyed the voluptuous Tibba critically and shook her head. "You don't look like any man I ever saw. I imagine I don't, either."

She'd told Amelia and Wilma of their escape plans and now turned to them. "What do you think?" she asked.

"Barbara might pass," Amelia said doubtfully. "Tibba, never."

"At dusk no one will notice the difference," Tibba said confidently. "You just wait."

"I wish you luck," Wilma said.

The day grew overcast in the late afternoon, thick white clouds moving up the sky to blot out the sun and create an early twilight while the evening meal at the camp was being prepared.

Barbara decided they might be less noticeable when other soldiers were walking freely about the camp than later, after taps had sounded. "Whatever we do," she cautioned Tibba, "we mustn't look sneaky. Hold your head up and stride along like a man."

"I don't think I'm made right for striding but I'll do my best."

Since the horses were tethered near the stream running close to camp, Barbara carried the water pail from their tent in the hope that it was customary to see soldiers going to fetch water. They didn't dare bring along any of their belongings, not even a blanket, in case someone might grow suspicious. Because she couldn't leave it behind, Barbara had put on her red petticoat under the trousers and rolled it up to her waist, a bulge hidden by the jacket.

More than once Barbara had to slow her pace so Tibba could keep up, each time becoming more and more nervous. They *had* to get away on their first try. If they were caught there'd be little or no chance of escaping again.

"You're going too fast," Tibba muttered. "You'll attract attention." A moment later she caught Barbara's arm. "Oh, God, here comes the major."

Quickly, Barbara shook herself free, hoping no one had noticed Tibba's very feminine action. "Turn to the left," she murmured, "and slip behind that wagon. We can't take the chance of passing him."

Their maneuver disturbed one of the camp pets, a dog chewing a bone by one of the tents. He snarled at them and then began to bark when their feet tangled in the ropes trailing over the ground from the wagon. They freed themselves and hurried past the pile of cloth on the ground. Barbara couldn't imagine what its purpose was, but that wasn't important, only getting away was.

When they finally approached the horses, she was perspiring despite the evening's chill. The worst should be over, she told herself. All that's left is to find mounts.

Without warning, a voice spoke from her left. "I hope to hell you brought some grub. Me belly button's touching me backbone."

A sentry! Barbara thought frantically. Pitching her voice as deep as she could, she said, "Get your own damn grub. I'm your relief."

The words sounded all wrong in her own ears and she went rigid with apprehension, certain the sentry could tell she was a woman. When all he did was curse and stomp off she couldn't move for a moment or two. By that time Tibba was running toward the horses.

They circled around and chose two horses from those tethered farthest from the camp. Their presence made all the horses uneasy, causing much snorting and stamping of hooves. Grabbing a saddle each, they hurriedly slung on and buckled the gear, then mounted and swung away from the camp. In the gathering darkness Barbara could only hope they were heading southeast.

As they rode, Barbara kept listening for any hue and cry that would signal pursuit. Reassured when she heard nothing, she relaxed a little. "We're away free and clear, Tibba," she said, relieved.

The words were scarcely out of her mouth when her horse veered abruptly to the right. Belatedly she noticed the dark rider looming ahead of them.

"Just where in hell do you think you're going?" the man demanded.

Chapter 10

Barbara fought to control her startled horse, hearing Tibba's gasp as the rider barred their path, preventing escape.

When she was certain of her mount, she took a deep and angry breath. She'd recognized the man's voice and she meant to give him a piece of her mind. But he spoke first.

"Must you always interfere with my plans?" Trevor growled.

"I told you I was going to Richmond and I am," she snapped. "Let us pass."

"Don't be an idiot. You'd be lost in five minutes. Besides, it's dangerous to travel at night in the mountains."

"Captain Sandoe?" Tibba quavered. "Is that you?"

"I'm afraid so, Tibba." His voice gentled when he answered her, annoying Barbara even more.

"I thought you'd be miles from here," Barbara said. "Why are you lurking this near the camp?"

"Because I mean to make off with the damn balloon, of course. Now, thanks to your harebrained scheme, my chances are shot."

"Balloon?" she echoed. "I didn't see any balloon."

"It's deflated at the moment. I've been waiting for them to fill it."

The wagon with the ropes, the pile of cloth on the ground—was that a balloon? Barbara realized it must be. How he thought one man could steal the balloon from a camp full of Union soldiers, she had no idea but it seemed a foolhardy notion.

"Since you've changed your plans, why not consider guiding us through the mountains?" she said.

"They'd catch us as soon as it was light," he told her. "Like they'd have captured you if I hadn't stopped you. No, we'll have to try for the balloon, though God knows how. The entire camp will be in an uproar when they discover you're missing."

"With luck that won't be until later tomorrow," Barbara said. "Tibba and I stuffed towels in our dresses and left them covered with blankets on our cots, like we were sleeping. Amelia and Wilma will pretend we're in the tent as long as they can."

Trevor didn't speak for a long moment. "If you left your dresses behind," he said finally, "what are you wearing now?"

"Yankee uniforms," Tibba told him. "Caps and all."

"Ah." Trevor sounded pleased. "This may not be such a calamity as I thought. I doubt if anyone will think to count the horses tonight. They'll

155

start inflating the balloon just before dawn—I may have a chance, after all."

"*We* may have a chance," Barbara said firmly. "You, me, and Tibba."

"Have you ever been up in a balloon?" he asked.

"No," Barbara and Tibba answered together.

"This could prove to be dangerous," he warned. "A disaster."

Barbara tried to recall what she knew of balloons. Only the little her father had told her.

"A balloon is fashioned from silk that's varnished to close the pores," Father had said, "and this material forms a thin envelope to hold either hot air or hydrogen gas. You've learned that hydrogen is lighter than air and so you can understand why the hydrogen-filled envelope lifts from the ground to float like a great bubble into the sky. If hot air is used, the balloon also rises because that's what hot air does. But hydrogen is more efficient—if more expensive."

"What will they use to inflate the balloon," she asked Trevor. "Hot air or hydrogen gas?"

"Your knowledge constantly surprises me," he told her. "Hydrogen, without a doubt—Confederate Army observation balloons use hydrogen and there's no reason to believe the Yanks won't. The wagon probably holds the gasometer."

"You saw that balloon when you first scouted the camp," Barbara accused. "Yet you didn't tell me."

He sighed. "I wanted you safe in that camp, not dangling in a basket from a balloon that, for all I know, may not make it over the mountains."

"I'm going with you," Barbara said, speaking more positively than she felt. While the idea of floating over the mountains was appealing, it was also frightening.

"If she goes, I go," Tibba said.

"You may change your minds in the morning once you see how small the riding basket is. And don't forget the balloon's not yet ours—the Yanks still have it."

Once they'd dismounted, Tibba offered Trevor the wedge of cheese she'd secreted inside her jacket and he fell on it hungrily. Since they'd brought no other supplies, Barbara and Tibba spent the night huddled together under one of the two old blankets from the cave while Trevor, after hiding the horses some distance away, kept guard wrapped in the other. In the grayness of predawn he woke them.

"Your uniform looks to be the larger so you'll change clothes with me," he told Barbara. "If I'm to get anywhere near the balloon I'll have to be wearing a friendly uniform."

The Union Army jacket and trousers fit Trevor fairly well. Barbara wished she could say the same for the threadbare and dirty Reb outfit she had to wear. She helped him transfer the captain's bars to the blue jacket and handed him her cap in exchange for his hat. As he buckled on the holstered Colt she decided he looked very handsome in Union blue.

But then she'd liked his appearance from the beginning. Not that looks had anything to do with a man's character. Trevor might be handsome and brave but, like all Rebs, his beliefs concerning slavery were unconscionable. It galled her every time she remembered that the South had precipitated this war by their refusal to admit that human beings were not property to be bought and sold. The Rebs even blamed the North for forcing them into war!

She scowled at Trevor.

"Do I look that bad?" he asked.

"*I* can't tell you from any other Yank," Tibba put in.

"There's no way to help what's missing—insignia, regimental patches, and the like," he said, his eyes on Barbara.

This was no time to tell him exactly what was missing from his miserably wrong-headed Reb principles and practices. Not when he needed encouragement.

"You have a talent for making people believe in what you say," she told him. "They're sure to accept you."

He smiled crookedly. "That talent got me into this mess in the first place."

Barbara didn't understand what he meant but he gave her no time to ask.

"I want you both to stay at the edge of this clearing," he said. "Don't come after me because I won't be able to help you if you do. When you see the balloon, run out and try to grab one of the trailing ropes. I hope to be able to set down here long enough to haul you into the basket. I promise I will if I possibly can." He gazed into Barbara's eyes. "I promise," he repeated.

158

She could only trust he meant *this* promise.

He saluted her, turned on his heel, and strode off in the direction of the camp. As she watched him disappear among the trees, Barbara wished she could somehow see what was going to happen when he reached the camp. She eyed a tall sugar maple's broad limbs speculatively. When she was a child she'd excelled at tree-climbing. . . .

Sometime later, minus her boots and standing in the crown of the tree on a branch that gave slightly under her weight, Barbara peered over the woods at the camp. A few pines partially blocked her view but she could see the wagon and the balloon.

"They're already inflating it," she told Tibba who had climbed no farther than the lowest limb, claiming she didn't like heights. "It's beginning to look like a balloon instead of a jumble of cloth. I can't make out Trevor yet, though."

"I never saw a balloon in my life," Tibba said from below. "Never expected to ride in one, either."

"Actually you ride in a basket that hangs by ropes below the balloon."

"Don't tell me too much; I'm already scared. Don't even like being up this tree, to tell the truth."

"There's Trevor! He's with what look like Union officers. At least they haven't taken him prisoner yet."

"He fooled the general, didn't he? Nobody ever fooled *him* before that I know of. Not and lived."

Barbara wished she could hear what was being

159

said at the camp. It looked to her like Trevor had begun to give orders, gesturing to the men holding the ropes attached to the rapidly expanding balloon.

"I can see the passenger basket now," she told Tibba, not adding that it did look small, as Trevor had warned. Its size could be an illusion, though, given the distance between her and the camp and also the fact that the balloon, rising above the basket, was so much more vast.

After what seemed an interminable time, the varnished silk envelope of the balloon grew taut. Trevor climbed into the basket and pulled something, she wasn't sure what, from the ropes above him, eased it over the side, and dropped it to the ground. He walked around inside the basket waving to the men holding the ropes.

Suddenly he grabbed several objects from the ropes and flung them all at once to the ground. The balloon rose, jerking the ropes from the men's hands except for one man who held on and was lifted off his feet into the air. He let go and sprawled onto the ground. The balloon bobbed through the air, the basket barely clearing the tents, then, rising, drifted toward them.

"Climb down now!" Barbara called to Tibba as she slid from one branch to another, ignoring the scrapes in her hurry to get to the ground.

They rushed into the clearing as the balloon, treetop high floated nearer and nearer. Too high, Barbara thought in dismay. We'll never get aboard.

"Look out below," Trevor's voice called.

Barbara heard a hiss, as of gas escaping, and the basket lowered until it skimmed the ground. Grabbing Tibba's hand, Barbara raced to it. Trevor reached a hand to each of them and hauled them half over the side. Barbara wriggled over the rest of the way and dropped into the basket, Tibba landing next to her an instant later.

"Get on your feet and start throwing out sand bags until I say stop," Trevor ordered, reaching for a bag in the overhead ropes as he spoke. "Hurry!"

They obeyed. Breathless moments later the basket brushed against the treetops and then the balloon floated free. Up and up it sailed. To Barbara's astonishment the ground seemed to be leaving her rather than she leaving the ground.

Trevor threw off the unattached ropes and let down a rope that was toggled onto a hoop above the basket. "The trail rope," he explained. "It'll help to slow us when we land."

"Thank God you've handled balloons before," she said.

He smiled slightly but said nothing.

She glanced up at the open neck of the giant balloon above them and remembered her father saying that gas expanded in the lighter air of the atmosphere so as the balloon rose the gas needed a way to escape. This must be what he meant.

Tibba, who'd been too timid at first to look down finally peered tentatively over the side. "Everything's moving down there," she said in amazement, "but it doesn't seem like we're moving at all. I don't feel any wind."

"We drift with the wind," Trevor said, "at the

161

same speed, that's why."

After a time, Barbara realized how quiet it was, the only sound the creak of the lines against the basket. And it was a small basket, with barely room for the three of them.

"It's an observation balloon," Trevor said as though sensing her thought. "Meant for one man whose job is to spy on the enemy's movements. I convinced Major Lifkin that General Sheridan was in urgent need of this balloon to use against General Early's forces in the Shenandoah Valley and that he'd sent me to fetch it for him."

"I'm surprised the major believed you," Barbara said.

"Why shouldn't he? Everyone knows Sheridan's in the Valley fighting Early's troops and could well use an observation balloon. The major never stopped to wonder how Sheridan knew he had the balloon and I gave him scant time for any second thoughts. I got the balloon up and out as fast as I could."

A light, gauzy vapor swept around the balloon, chilling the air. It took Barbara a moment to realize they were floating in the midst of a cloud.

"It's going to get colder," Trevor advised. "The higher we go, the colder it gets, and since we have to clear the mountain peaks we have to keep going up. I wish we could have brought the blankets."

"You can't see any peaks," Tibba complained, huddling again in the bottom of the basket. "You can't see anything."

"Don't worry," Trevor said. "We're still rising so we'll be out of the clouds soon."

As he finished speaking they floated up into the sunlight. Glancing over the side, Barbara saw only cloud layers below them—the earth had disappeared. She hugged herself against the cold, thinking it was as though they'd entered a world of air and sun where nothing else existed.

"Marvelous!" she exclaimed.

"You're not frightened?" Trevor asked.

She shook her head. What she felt was exhilaration. Belatedly recalling that her father had mentioned the lowered oxygen level at high altitudes, she wondered if perhaps her light-hearted, almost joyous sensation could be light-headedness from the thinner air. She cast away the thought, preferring to believe she was moved by the wonder of being so high above the earth.

"This must be how birds feel when they fly," she told Trevor. "Gloriously free. I'll never put a bird in a cage again."

His smile warmed her; his eyes told her that he shared her sense of wonder.

"If birds like flying so much," Tibba muttered from the bottom of the basket, "why do they spend half their time on the ground? I wish *I* was on the ground."

Tibba's words broke the almost mystic communication Barbara had sensed flowing between herself and Trevor.

The balloon drifted in the sun. Though it hardly seemed to be moving, Trevor assured them that they were traveling east at a speed he estimated would get them across the Alleghenies before sundown. Occasionally he tugged gently on a rope and Barbara would hear the hiss of gas escaping.

"The sun's heat causes the hydrogen to expand," he said, "so I have to let some of it out through the escape valve at the top. Otherwise we'd rise so high we wouldn't be able to breathe the air."

Tibba covered her ears, protesting, "I don't want to know."

Some time later, though she had no sensation of dropping, Barbara found the balloon basket once again surrounded by the misty chill of a cloud with nothing to be seen except grayness. It was a relief when the basket popped into clean air once again. Now they were under the clouds where no sun shone.

Looking over the side, Barbara puzzled over silver ribbons winding through patches of green and brown until she realized she was seeing rivers curving through the mountainous terrain.

"On the nose, by God!" Trevor cried, pointing. "There she is—the Shenandoah Valley." He pulled the release valve rope, letting out more and more gas.

The details below grew larger and clearer until what had been only a mass of green to Barbara became a pine grove on a hillside. She could see tiny houses and, beyond the valley, another ridge of mountains.

"I've got to set her down fast," Trevor warned, "or we risk landing in the Blue Ridge Mountains across the valley." He reached up and opened a red bag that was attached to the hoop above the basket and took out a red rope. Holding the rope in his hands, he ordered Tibba to her feet.

"Both of you be ready to grab the lines and climb onto the basket rim the instant I tell you," he said.

"I can't look," Tibba mumbled as Barbara helped her up and made her hold onto the lines so she'd be ready.

"You don't have to look, just do what Trevor says," Barbara told her, thinking it was just as well Tibba wasn't peering over the side because now the ground below was flying past them faster and faster. It didn't seem possible they could ever stop.

Trevor yanked on the red rope. A ripping noise came from the silk envelope above them and the balloon began to cave in on itself. "On the rim!" Trevor shouted, pulling loose the grappling hook stowed outside the basket and flinging it down.

Barbara shoved Tibba up and, holding to the lines, climbed onto the rim herself, staring down with fascination at the ground rushing up at them. Then the basket hit, bouncing wildly as it was dragged along. They stopped jarringly when the hook caught somewhere behind them. Before Barbara could collect her wits, the silk envelope collapsed over the basket, shrouding them all.

Moments later Trevor caught her hand, pulled her free of the collapsed balloon, then rescued Tibba.

"I'm never going up in one of those things again," Tibba announced, holding on to Barbara's arm. "Never!"

"I'll admit the landing was a bit rough," Trevor said, looking around. "Since I didn't want to take any chance of overshooting the valley, I pulled the rip cord to let all the gas out at once." He smiled crookedly. "I didn't tell you before we went up but this was only my second time aloft. The first time was with an army observer."

The woman stared at him. "I thought you were a balloon expert," Barbara said.

"No. That's one of the reasons I wanted to leave you behind. The observer explained everything he did and I'm a good listener, but I was far from sure we'd arrive in one piece, if we got here at all. Still, we made it and there's the Valley Pike." He pointed.

Barbara looked past a yellow-stubbled field to where a mule-drawn wagon was drawn up alongside a macadamized road, its driver gaping at them and the downed balloon.

"The Pike will take us a good part of the way to Richmond." Trevor turned and strode toward the wagon.

"I never expected to come down alive," Tibba said. "I reckon Captain Sandoe can do most anything. Are you going to marry him?"

Barbara stared at her in consternation. "Marry him! Where did you get such a ridiculous idea? He's a Reb!"

"What's that got to do with it?"

"He—he's my enemy," Barbara sputtered. "I couldn't possibly love—much less marry—a Reb."

"Don't the Bible say 'Love thine enemy'?"

"Well, yes, but—oh, Tibba, you don't understand. I can never forgive the Rebs for imprisoning my father. Nor can I ever agree that slavery is a

Christian practice. You certainly don't believe in slavery, do you?"

Tibba shook her head. "The general made slaves out of everybody, not just Negroes. Even his men did everything he ordered. Though he tried his best to break my spirit, I was the only one who ever defied him and lived. If I hadn't gotten away he would've killed me in the end. Would've killed you, too. We both owe the captain a great debt."

"Yes, we do. But—"

"Captain Sandoe must be mighty fond of you. Otherwise, why would he risk his life to rescue you?"

"Maybe because he knew it was his fault General Meachum captured me to begin with."

Tibba raised her eyebrows but before she could comment, Trevor came trotting back across the field, the wagon driver walking behind him.

"We've got a ride as far as New Market," Trevor said, "and the promise of beds for the night. All he wants in return is the balloon."

Trevor and the driver, a lanky older man by the name of Bernard Yates, folded the deflated balloon and stowed it in the empty wagon bed. Trevor rode on the seat with the driver while Tibba and Barbara made themselves as comfortable as possible atop the varnished silk of the balloon.

"Yessir," Mr. Yates said as soon as he clucked the mule into motion, "soon's I saw that there balloon, I says 'that's one of ours.' Then you come running crost the field all dressed in Yankee blue and I says, 'he ain't none of ours.' Goes to show a man can be wrong, yessir. Soon's I heard you talk I knowed you was a down-home boy. Course, some of *them* joined up with the wrong army, don't see how they could do it, no sir." He turned to look at Barbara and Tibba. "Never in my life did I see women dressed in army uniforms. Not even a Nigra gal like that high-yeller one there."

"I told you—" Trevor began.

"You did and all. Can't say I took to your story right off, purty strange, it was. But once I saw them women dressed like that, I came to heel, yessir, I did. Stands to reason they sure wouldn't outfit theirselves thataway less'n they had to. I swear it's against God and nature to see women in pants— Ma'll find 'em some decent clothes."

"That will be very kind of Mrs. Yates," Barbara said. She might not believe it was against God or nature to wear men's clothes, but it would be a relief to get out of the ill-fitting and dirty Reb uniform.

True, the Yates were enemies but she was in no position to refuse a badly-needed gift.

The wide pike was fairly level but nevertheless the wagon jounced along, making Barbara regret having to give up the smoothness of the balloon ride. She wondered just how Trevor had explained their odd arrival and peculiar dress to Mr. Yates.

"The fields are all burned," Tibba whispered.

Sharp-eared Mr. Yates heard her. "Sheridan's work," he said. "The Yanks can't beat us so they mean to starve us. Ain't hardly none of us got enough food to last the winter. Can't complain—I still got my house and my barn."

Barbara bit her lip as she looked at ravaged fields and the blackened ruins of homes. Except for the Reb prison on Johnson Island and the men away fighting, the war hadn't really touched Sandusky. Certainly everyone had enough to eat. She'd never really thought it through before, but obviously life was far more precarious for those unfortunate enough to live where battles were being fought.

After a time Barbara saw a church spire in the distance. New Market? Before reaching the settlement, Mr. Yates turned off onto a narrow and rutted dirt road. They passed an apple orchard and a pond where one white duck paddled forlornly, then he turned the mule into a driveway that was no more than a track. A two-story frame farmhouse with peeling white paint stood behind a screen of tall pines with a large gray barn in back.

"Ma!" Mr. Yates yelled as he halted the mule. "We got company."

A short, plump woman appeared at the side door, wiping her hands on her apron. Trevor lifted Barbara, then Tibba down from the wagon.

"I'll just drive old Penny to the barn and unhitch her," Mr. Yates said. "Ma'll take good care of y'all."

Before the bustling Mrs. Yates reached them, Trevor leaned down and whispered to Barbara. "To avoid complications, I told him Tibba was your maid."

Since there was nothing Barbara could do about it, she merely nodded before greeting Mrs. Yates.

"I'm Miss Barbara Thackery," she told the plump woman, "and this is Captain Sandoe and

169

Tibba. I'm sorry that we look so bedraggled but we've just been rescued from desperate circumstances and had to leave our clothes behind."

Mrs. Yates's unsmiling gaze shifted from one to the other of them. Trevor stepped forward.

"I may be wearing blue, ma'am," he said in the broadest drawl Barbara had yet heard from him, "but my heart's true to the Rebel cause as Mr. Yates will explain to you."

Mrs. Yates's expression cleared. "He said you were company and you're welcome to our house. Shame on me for making you all stand out here. Come in, do."

"Thank you, but first I'll see if I can give your husband a hand," Trevor said.

The kitchen was filled with such delicious cooking odors that Barbara's mouth watered. The plump woman led her and Tibba through the kitchen, down a hall into a small entry, and then up a staircase. She opened a door and gestured to Barbara to go inside.

The bedroom wasn't large and there was a slight musty odor as though no one had slept in the room for a long time.

"Send your maid down to bring you up some hot water," Mrs. Yates said. "You're lucky to have her. Our three Nigras went off, following Sheridan's army. Left us flat, they did, the ungrateful wretches. About clothes—if you don't mind gowns twenty years out-of-date, I've kept my mother's good dresses and underthings stored in a trunk in the attic and you're welcome to help yourself to what you need. You and Tibba, too. She can't go

170

round like that; it's a disgrace."

As soon as Mrs. Yates left the room, Barbara said, "I'm sorry, Tibba, but for some reason Captain Sandoe told Mr. Yates you were my maid and it seems that his wife assumed the same thing."

Tibba shrugged. "I don't like the way Mr. and Mrs. Yates talk about me as though I wasn't there but I don't mind pretending about being your maid. We're friends, aren't we? I'll get the water while you help her with the clothes from the trunk."

Barbara hugged her. "We'll always be friends."

Tibba pulled away and started for the door where she stopped to look back over her shoulder and grin. "Even if I decide I really am a Reb?"

After an ample evening meal of stewed chicken with biscuits and apple pie, Tibba offered to help Mrs. Yates wash the dishes. Barbara said she'd help, too, but Mrs. Yates wouldn't hear of it, saying, "Tibba and I will manage quite nicely, thank you. You sit in the parlor and keep the men company."

Mr. Yates excused himself to do the evening chores, leaving Barbara alone in the parlor with Trevor—she perched on the edge of a round-seated, lyre-back chair, he leaning against the fireplace mantel.

"The trousers were a novelty," he said, smiling, "but I've decided I prefer you in a dress."

Barbara fingered the tobacco brown taffeta of the full-skirted, high-necked gown she wore. Bands of shirring decorated the bodice and the

171

sleeves. The cuffs were ecru lace to match the collar. It fit her fairly well, much better than the uniforms.

"It's far from stylish but I rather like the gown," she said, determined to ignore his words. "I do appreciate Mrs. Yates's generosity."

He cocked his head to study her. "Someday I'd like to see you wear flame-red," he said. "In that color no man could resist you."

Barbara flushed. "I'm more interested in discussing how soon we'll get to Richmond than I am in the color of future gowns."

"Ah, but I'm not." Trevor pushed away from the mantel, stalked to her chair, reached down for her hands, and pulled her to her feet. "I can't resist you no matter what you wear."

His gaze held hers; she couldn't look away. Her breath caught, her pulses pounded as his head lowered. He brushed her lips with his and almost immediately raised his head. With dismay she heard her tiny murmur of protest because the kiss ended so soon.

"I want more, Snow Bird," he said, running his forefinger down her cheek. "You don't yet know how much more."

If his longing was as intense as hers, she did know. Forgetting the vow she'd made two short days ago, she raised on her tiptoes and touched her lips to his. He groaned, wrapped his arms around her, and pulled her close, deepening the kiss until she wondered if she'd die of pleasure.

Still holding her, he pulled back slightly. "Snow Bird, listen to me." His warm breath was like a caress. "You don't realize what you do to me. If I kiss you again I'm afraid I won't stop. I'm afraid I'll carry you up those stairs to my room, strip you out of that gown, and make love to you all night."

Fire shot through her at his words. How desperately she wanted to be swept into his arms and carried off for the night. Carried off by Trevor forever.

By an enemy Reb.

Barbara tore herself free, ran up the stairs into her room, shut her door, and leaned against it, drained of strength. Never before had any man affected her the way Trevor did. When he touched her she couldn't even trust her own will. The only solution was never to be alone with him between here and Richmond. Once there, she wouldn't have to see him again and her worries about how to resist him would be over.

Wouldn't they?

Chapter 11

Barbara tried to tamp down her rising excitement as she stared at the wooden signpost: Richmond 5 miles. It had taken a week on the road but they were almost to the Confederate capital.

After they'd spent the night at his house, Mr. Yates had driven them into New Market and found a wagoner willing to take them farther down the pike to Harrisonburg. Then came days of walking, sometimes hiding from Union troops because Trevor once again wore a Reb uniform, before they'd gotten three more wagon rides, this last one into Richmond itself.

She could hardly wait to make her way to Libby Prison. To her father.

"We'll get off here, if you don't mind, Mr. Moxley," Trevor said to the driver, surprising Barbara.

Mr. Moxley obediently halted his ancient swaybacked horse and Trevor jumped down from the wagon.

"But we're not to Richmond yet," she protested.

Trevor gestured to a tree-lined lane leading off the main road. At the lane's end Barbara glimpsed a large white house.

"Fairlawn—the Reynolds plantation," he said. "You and Tibba will be staying here."

Deciding she wouldn't argue with him in front of Mr. Moxley, she reluctantly allowed Trevor to help her from the wagon. As he lifted Tibba down, Barbara thanked the driver for his help.

"'T'aint nothing much, miss," Mr. Moxley said. "Glad to lend a hand to y'all. These days we share what we can. I'm mighty lucky old Prince here don't look as strong as he is, otherwise the Yanks or the Rebs, one or t'other'd taken him. I wish y'all luck, too." He waved, clucked to the horse, and the wagon jolted into motion once more.

"You didn't tell me we wouldn't be going into the city." Barbara's voice was tart.

Trevor half smiled. "This way we only argue once. It's the best arrangement for you. Francine—Miss Reynolds—will be more than happy to have you stay at Fairlawn."

Barbara found herself unaccountably disturbed that Trevor had called Miss Reynolds by her first name. Evidently he knew the woman well.

"I suppose I'm to be Barbara's maid in the Reynolds' house like I was at the Yates'," Tibba said.

"If you like, I'll try to explain the unusual circumstances to the family," Trevor said.

Tibba shook her head. "From what I've seen of Virginia folks, I'd say they wouldn't take to me at all. It'll be easier for Barbara and for me if I just go

175

on pretending to be her servant—then they'll ignore me. Are you going to be staying at Fairlawn, too, Captain?"

Barbara waited eagerly for his answer to a question she'd been reluctant to ask.

"No, I've my own quarters in town. Naturally the two of you couldn't stay there."

"You live in town." Barbara spoke flatly, her words laden with anger. "You neglected to mention your home was in Richmond. What else haven't you bothered to tell me?"

Trevor shrugged. "I've said from the beginning you'd be better off going back to Sandusky. I well knew that if I ever let slip that I lived in Richmond I'd never be rid of you."

Barbara drew herself up. "Rid of me!"

He eyed her levelly. "You'll have to admit your journey's been perilous. I was only trying to save you discomfort, danger, and—"

"I've half a mind to bid you goodbye and walk into Richmond alone," she snapped.

Trevor raised his eyebrows. "Think of poor Tibba. Is that fair to her?"

Tibba, glancing from one to the other, said nothing and the silence grew.

"Well," Trevor said at last, "are you coming or not?"

Knowing it wouldn't be right to ask Tibba to follow her blindly into a city where neither of them knew a soul, Barbara nodded reluctantly. Like it or not, she was linked to Trevor for the time being. At least until she found a way to contact her father. But his words festered within her mind. *Never be rid of you.*

Did he imagine she *wanted* to be with him? That it was her choice? He was her ticket to Richmond and to Libby Prison, that was all. Then *she'd* be rid of *him*.

The three of them walked along the lane under the interlacing branches of huge old oak trees. As they came closer to the house at the end, Barbara realized it was a mansion even larger than General Meachum's. She glanced at the dusty brown gown she wore, a gown that had once belonged to Mrs. Yates's mother, and raised her chin. What she looked like couldn't be helped.

Trevor, in his threadbare gray uniform, might be as travel-stained as she and Tibba but since he was a soldier it didn't matter. She'd become so accustomed to the beard he'd grown that she hardly recalled his appearance without it. In truth she thought the beard made him seem more dashing. Not that she'd ever tell him.

"The way we're dressed, might be they'll turn us away from the front door," Tibba said, echoing Barbara's thoughts.

"Francine and I have known each other since we were children," Trevor assured her. "Any friends of mine will be friends of hers."

A circular drive swept around to the front of the house with an offshoot to the porte cochere. Determined not to hang back, Barbara matched Trevor's pace as he strode up the broad stone steps between large white pillars. He lifted the brass knocker and let it fall on the strikeplate once, twice.

A white-haired Negro man opened the door and stood gaping at them.

"Obed, don't you recognize me?" Trevor demanded.

Obed blinked, then broke into a grin. "Massa Sandoe! You is a sight for these old eyes. Come right in, sir, right in."

Trevor ushered Barbara and Tibba ahead of him into a wide foyer where a polished hardwood floor gleamed in the sunlight streaming in through the long windows on either side of the front door.

"I'd like to see Miss Francine," Trevor said.

Obed's grin grew wider. "She gonna be mighty happy to see you, mighty happy. I done hear her say your name just this morning. Y'all seat yourself in the parlor while I be getting her."

As Obed started up the long, curving staircase, Trevor led the way to a spacious room to the left of the foyer. The burgundy velvet draperies were drawn against the sunlight but even in the dimness Barbara noticed that the beautiful floral carpet was threadbare in places.

She perched uneasily on a damask settee, gesturing to Tibba to sit beside her. Trevor crossed the room and flung open the draperies.

"I hate a dark room," he said. "It always reminds me—" He broke off to gaze intently at the wall over Barbara's head.

She twisted around to look. Two large unfaded rectangles on the cream and rose wallpaper told her that paintings once hung on this wall.

Trevor glanced about the room and swore under his breath. Barbara wasn't sure what upset him but to her eye the parlor did seem rather sparsely furnished. Had he expected to see pieces of furniture that weren't here?

"The War brings hard times to everyone," he muttered.

Then Barbara understood. The Reynolds' must have been forced to sell some of their possessions. Now, in the brighter light, she could see several holes in the damask upholstery of the settee. Yes, hard times.

"Did you see it when we passed?" Tibba whispered to her.

Barbara blinked. "See what?"

"In the music room. A harp." Tibba's amber eyes shone. "I hope we stay here, I truly do."

"Trevor!" a woman's voice, high and musical, called from the foyer. "Trevor, is it really you?"

A moment later a young, attractive blond woman, her blue silk skirts rustling over a wide hoop, rushed into the parlor, flung herself into Trevor's arms, and kissed him enthusiastically.

Barbara stiffened. Good friends, indeed!

Trevor held her away from him, smiling down at her. "I'm glad to be home again, Francine."

Barbara rose, Tibba following suit, and waited. After what seemed forever, he released Francine and turned toward them.

"This is Miss Barbara Thackery," he said, "and Tibba. They're in desperate need of a place to stay and I've assured them our Virginia hospitality is the finest in the country."

Francine smiled and held out a hand to Barbara. "Welcome to Fairlawn, Miss Thackery."

179

As Barbara murmured a polite response, she noticed Francine's ice blue eyes assessing her and finding her wanting.

"You're not from hereabouts," Francine remarked.

"I live in Ohio."

Francine glanced at Tibba and raised her eyebrows.

"Tibba is a free woman of color," Barbara said tartly, "not a slave."

"But I assume she *is* your maid."

Barbara was upset enough to deny it but, before she found the right words, Tibba, standing to one side of her, dipped in an extravagant curtsy and said to Francine, "Yes, Miss Reynolds, that is correct."

Francine sent her a sharp look.

Trevor, looking amused, said to Francine, "If propriety would permit, I'd put Miss Thackery up temporarily at my townhouse. But—"

Francine cut him off. "Naturally that's quite impossible. My father and I will be happy to have her as our guest."

"How is the colonel?" Trevor asked.

A shadow darkened Francine's face. "He has his bad days. Still, I'm fortunate the Lord has spared him thus far."

"I didn't realize your father wasn't well," Barbara said, feeling a shaft of sympathy for the first time. "I hope my staying here won't be too much of a burden."

"No, no." Francine smiled. "Actually, you'll be a diversion. Perhaps we'll even have a party here at

Fairlawn in your honor—it's been forever since the last one. And, of course, everyone will be just dying to talk to Trevor. Including myself." She tucked her hand under his arm and glanced sideways into his face. "It's been so lonesome without you."

He patted her hand. "I can't promise I'll be staying in Richmond long but I always look forward to a Fairlawn party."

Francine's face took on a dreamy expression. "We'll have music and dance until dawn like we did before the war—everyone I know will be thrilled to unpack their ball gowns. We'll have games with silly prizes and we'll all laugh—it'll be marvelous fun. I can hardly wait to begin planning."

Putting what Mr. Yates and Mr. Moxley had said about the scarcity of supplies together with the evidence of financial problems she'd noticed in the parlor, Barbara wondered if a party was wise. Since it wasn't her place to mention this, she merely smiled politely.

Francine's brow furrowed. "Oh, dear, I forgot about Junius. You recall him, Trevor?"

"The fiddling footman? He was a very talented performer."

"He's no longer with us." Francine shook her head. "Junius used to think himself above the field hands but then he turned around and ran off with five of them to join the Yanks. How can they be so ungrateful?" She sighed. "Junius used to play at every Fairlawn ball—it won't be the same without him. Still, there's always the piano. Perhaps Miss

Thackery will be kind enough to demonstrate her skills for us at the party."

"I fear playing the piano is not one of my skills," Barbara said.

"I'm so sorry. I do hope I didn't embarrass you by asking."

"Not at all." Barbara spoke so coolly that Trevor shot her a puzzled glance which she ignored. He might not understand what Francine was trying to do but Barbara was uneasily aware her hostess meant to show her up one way or another.

"Shame on me," Francine said, "keeping you standing here talking when you must be terribly fatigued." She crossed to a bellpull and tugged on it. When a young Negro girl appeared in the archway, Francine told her, "Show Miss Thackery to the gold room, Lyla."

"If you don't mind," Barbara put in, "I'd prefer to have Tibba sleep in my room."

Francine waved a hand. "As you wish. Lyla will bring in a cot."

"Thank you." Barbara nodded to Trevor. "Goodbye, Captain Sandoe. I appreciate—"

"Miss Thackery," he said, bowing slightly, "I believe a more appropriate farewell is 'Au revoir' for we surely will meet again." He gazed solemnly at her but the gleam in his eyes betrayed his amusement at her attempt to formally dismiss him.

She made no response as she swept past him, following Lyla toward the stairs. What was there to say with Francine hanging onto his arm as though she never meant to let him go?

Once Lyla left them alone the gold room, Tibba, after looking around critically, said, "They're sure not as rich as they used to be."

Though the spooled cherry furniture shone from polishing, Barbara noted that the gold window curtains were faded where the sun had bleached them. The gold and ivory rug, too, had a worn spot near the bed.

"That Francine," Tibba went on, "with all her cooing at the captain and her kissing and hanging on him—she means to get him one way or another. Are you going to let her?"

"I have nothing to say in the matter." Barbara spoke firmly, hoping her unhappiness didn't show. "Obviously they're very good friends."

"*She'd* like us to think they're more than friends."

"It's none of my affair if they are."

Tibba's expression told Barbara she didn't believe her but all Tibba said was, "We've got to find you a ball gown before this party. To do that I reckon I'll have to get better acquainted with the house servants. And don't try to put on about how you don't care how you look. I know better."

Barbara admitted to herself that she did care. Standing beside pretty Francine in her fashionable blue and rose gown, she'd felt plain and dowdy. A chickadee next to a darting, colorful humming-bird. How could any man prefer her to Francine?

If she were truthful, by any man she meant Trevor. Barbara shook her head. Trevor was nothing to her. She neither wanted nor had any claim to him. It should make no difference whatsoever who Trevor paid attention to. Or who he kissed.

Why, then, did it?

"I'm not going to worry about a ball gown," she said, as much to herself as to Tibba. "My reason for being here is to see my father and I mean to concentrate my efforts on that and that alone."

Lyla served Barbara and Tibba an evening meal in their room, saying that Miss Francine was going out for dinner and that the old colonel wasn't feeling up to coming downstairs to dine.

Hearing this, Barbara decided that Francine must be with Trevor. She listened to Tibba chattering away to Lyla with half an ear as she wondered whether their hostess and Trevor were dining with friends or alone. Afterward, would he find a private spot where he could take Francine into his arms and kiss her? Would he whisper to her how wonderful she was?

Barbara bit her lip as she imagined them embracing. Anger rescued her from the threat of tears. How dare Trevor make love to her as he had when all the time he had someone waiting for him here in Richmond? How dare he be brazen enough to bring her to Fairlawn, to Francine's house? Or hadn't it even occurred to him how cruel that was?

He might not be as bad as General Meachum but he was no better than Reverend Hargreaves.

"Men," she muttered.

Both Lyla and Tibba turned to look at her and a moment later Lyla slipped out the door.

"The colonel would like for them to marry," Tibba told her, "but the captain hasn't asked Francine. Yet."

Barbara stared at her. "I didn't hear Lyla say anything like that."

"Lyla's not the only one I've talked to. And, listen, the colonel's not always in his right mind. No one dares cross him when he's taken bad—everyone's afraid of him then. So we'd best be careful."

Barbara dismissed the warning—what did Colonel Reynolds have to do with her? She hadn't so much as met the man.

"Do they think he will?" she asked.

"Will what?"

"Ask Francine to marry him."

"Oh, the captain. Some do, some don't." Tibba grinned at her. "As long as you're around, I'm pretty sure he won't—but I thought you didn't care."

"I was simply curious, that's all."

"After we eat would you come down to the music room with me?" Tibba asked. "I don't like to go alone, not in this house."

About to ask why she wanted to visit the music room, Barbara remembered Tibba's interest in the harp and nodded her agreement.

The music room was dark but there was enough light from the sconces on the walls of the foyer to dimly illuminate the harp. It stood on a dais to the right of the grand piano, covered with a white dust cover. Barbara watched as Tibba carefully lifted off the cloth. As she had in the general's house, Tibba stroked the harp's gilded frame gently, her face rapt. After a time she reached a finger to one of the strings and plucked it gently, releasing a single golden note that fluttered into the air like a bird escaping from a cage.

When the last faint trace of the note had disappeared, Tibba sighed and replaced the cover. "Francine wouldn't like me touching the harp any more than *he* did." She gazed intently at Barbara. "But I had to. I couldn't help myself."

Recalling that Tibba's mother played the harp, Barbara pressed her hand in understanding. In silence, they walked together from the music room across the foyer to the stairs. It wasn't until they were halfway up that Barbara noticed the white-haired man in a dressing gown standing at the top of the staircase. She touched Tibba's arm and they both halted.

"The colonel," Tibba whispered.

"She's in there, isn't she?" Colonel Reynolds said and raised his arm.

Barbara gasped. He brandished a sword!

"Answer me!" he shouted.

Only after swallowing several times did Barbara manage to speak. "Colonel Reynolds, we're guests in your home, guests of your daughter." She couldn't help her shaking voice.

Where were the servants? Surely someone was supposed to be looking after the colonel.

He paid not the slightest attention to what she'd said. "You came from that room, I saw you. And she's still inside, isn't she?"

"Do you mean your daughter?" Barbara asked.

"You know very well who I mean." He swung the sword through the air. Dammit, woman, is she there?"

"Don't cross him," Tibba whispered.

186

"There was no one else in the music room," Barbara said.

"You lie!" He started down the steps, stopping a short distance above them. "No one ever touches Cynthia's harp except her. She must be there."

Frightened, not knowing what to do or say, Barbara huddled close to Tibba, feeling her take a deep breath and let it out.

"Colonel, sir, it's my fault," Tibba quavered. "I played that note on the harp. It was wrong, I know, but I touched the string because it reminded me of when my mother used to play long ago. She's dead now, sir, and the sound of a harp is all I have left of her. I'm sorry I've upset you."

He glared at Tibba for one long, breathless moment and then the sword dropped from his hand, clattering down the steps. The colonel made no effort to retrieve it. Instead, he sank down onto one of the steps, buried his face in his hands and began to weep.

Barbara hesitated until Tibba moved on up the stairs. She followed slowly, gingerly picking up the sword by its hilt. Tibba sat beside the colonel and put an arm around his shoulders. "Everything's all right," she murmured.

Seeing dark faces peering from the top of the stairs, Barbara edged past Tibba and the colonel and handed the sword to old Obed. "Put this away, please," she begged.

With Tibba's help, the Negro man and woman attending the colonel got him up the steps. Barbara followed them along the hall to his suite in the other wing of the house from the gold room.

187

Obed tagged after her, still carrying the sword.

"Massa, he gonna sleep now," Obed said. "He always do afterwards. He don't never hurt no ladies, not no way." Obed lifted the sword so the hall lamps gleamed on its curved steel blade.

Barbara shuddered. "He certainly frightened us."

"Seem like no matter where we hide this old sword," Obed said, "the massa, he always do find it."

Determined not to be threatened with this particular weapon again, Barbara said, "Give the sword to me and *I'll* hide it."

Obed hesitated, obviously taken aback, but when she held out her hand he relinquished the sword. Not waiting for Tibba, Barbara turned and marched to her room where she thrust the sword under the mattress of the Jenny Lind bed. Unfortunately, there was no key in the lock on the bedroom door. Even with the sword safely hidden, sleep would be impossible behind an unlocked door.

As soon as Tibba returned and they'd both placed their footgear in the hall to be polished, Barbara propped a chair under the doorknob before preparing to retire. A servant—probably Lyla—had turned down the covers and left a white cotton nightgown folded on the pillow. Similar nightwear lay on Tibba's cot. A gracious gesture on Francine's part.

"There's no harm in that old man," Tibba said as she undressed. "He was just searching for his wife. Cynthia Reynolds has been dead for ten years but sometimes his memory goes awry and he

188

forgets. No one would tell me the whole story but I learned enough to suspect Cynthia was unfaithful and the colonel killed her lover when he found them together in the music room."

"No wonder it preys on his mind."

"Francine is her mother all over again, I'm told. In disposition as well as looks. The men flock around her but so far she hasn't married. Been waiting for the captain to return, so I hear."

Barbara shrugged, determinedly squashing sprouting tendrils of jealousy. If Trevor married Francine, it was nothing to her, nothing at all. She donned the nightgown and slipped into bed, telling herself she wouldn't allow her thoughts to dwell on Trevor, neither tonight nor in the days to come. She didn't need his help any longer. Tomorrow she'd find her own way into Richmond.

Exhausted by the journey and the evening's alarm, both she and Tibba slept well that night. In the morning they awoke to a knock on the bedroom door.

"I'll move the chair," Tibba said, yawning as she slid off the cot.

Lyla, garments piled over her arm, slipped into the room as soon as Tibba opened the door. "I brung clothes for you, miss," she said. "Tibba, too." She opened the wardrobe and hung some of what she carried inside, putting other garments into the drawers of a chiffonier. Last of all Lyla set two pairs of cloth-soled house slippers neatly onto the floor and began gathering up their discarded clothes.

"Gonna be taking these to clean," she said.

"Please leave the red petticoat," Barbara said before Lyla laid a hand on it. "I'll take care of washing the petticoat myself."

When Lyla left, Tibba sorted through the gowns in the wardrobe. "No hoops for us, I see. I didn't expect them but she might have sent them for you; all but one of these dresses are made to be worn with crinolines."

"I really don't mind. It'll be wonderful to have clean clothes to wear."

Barbara padded barefoot to the wardrobe. Four gowns hung inside, one plum, one dove gray, one mustard, and one black. As she fingered the black, Tibba reached for it.

"That one's meant for me—it's made like those the house servants wear." Tibba held it up to herself. "Nothing fancy but at least it's short enough not to drag under my feet." She glanced at Barbara. "I reckon I shouldn't complain about what's freely given."

Barbara chose the plum, a three-tiered, high-necked dress that would have been improved by the addition of a crinoline but, since whoever the gown had been made for was shorter than Barbara, the fit without a hoop was adequate. One of the two petticoats she'd been given was stiffened with horsehair so the effect, if not fashionable, was neat and ladylike. She wouldn't shame her father by her appearance.

Opening the door to retrieve her boots, Barbara found they hadn't yet been returned so she was forced to put on the house slippers. She'd see to getting the boots back after breakfast since the cloth-soled slippers would wear through in less than an hour if worn outside the house.

Francine was waiting for her in the dining room.

"Father won't be with us this morning," Francine said after greeting her. "I hope you'll be able to meet him later today."

Deciding not to mention she'd met him last night, Barbara smiled politely. "I hope so, too, but I'm planning to go into the city this morning."

"Oh, I'm terribly sorry," Francine said, "but we haven't a horse at the moment. The army only left us the one and I'm afraid I loaned him to Captain Sandoe."

"I don't mind walking."

Francine glanced at her feet. "You can't very well walk in those flimsy slippers."

"My boots are sound enough, I believe. I *must* go."

"I had no idea. If I'd known I wouldn't have sent your boots to the cobbler to be resoled. And I fear my feet are so tiny you could never fit into any of my shoes." Francine lifted her skirt to show dainty ankle boots. Boots far too small for Barbara. As she knew Tibba's shoes were.

Barbara bit her lip. "My father's in Libby Prison," she said. "Somehow I have to get to Richmond."

"Not today, I'm afraid," Francine said. "It's a pity but it can't be helped."

Something in her voice didn't ring quite true to Barbara. She eyed Francine critically. The cold blue eyes meeting hers gave nothing away but wasn't there a suspicion of a smile on those curved and rosy lips? Why would Francine smile at a guest's discomfiture? On the other hand, why would Francine care whether she went into the city or not? Unless someone had told her to prevent Barbara from going.

"It's *his* doing, isn't it?" Barbara blurted out. "Trevor's."

Francine's eyebrows raised. "I assure you that your boots *are* at the cobblers. They were in desperate need of repair."

Barbara dismissed her words with a wave of a hand. "I'm not accusing you of lying. But he put you up to this. He's tried to prevent me from reaching my father from the very first." She glared at Francine. "I won't be made a prisoner!"

"A prisoner? Heavens, what an accusation." Francine put a hand over her heart. "Do I look like a jail-keeper?"

"Admit it, this is Trevor's idea."

Francine's eyes narrowed. "Oh very well then, he did ask me to see that you waited until he was free to escort you into the city. 'She's impulsive,' he said. 'Alone, she'll manage to get herself into real trouble, creating a headache for all of us.' He explained the agonies he's already gone through in order to rescue you from perils of your own making. Don't you think you've tried dear Trevor's patience far enough?"

Chapter 12

Barbara paced angrily up and down in the bedroom. "I won't be ordered about," she insisted to Tibba. "A problem, am I? Well, Captain Sandoe needn't concern himself with my welfare one minute longer. I not only don't need his help—I refuse it!"

"Since you have no way to get into the city without him, just how are you going to avoid accepting aid from the captain?" Tibba asked.

Barbara whirled to face her. "With a little assistance from you, that's how. I can't go around begging from the servants—like as not they wouldn't give me what I need even if I did. But you ought to be able to find me something sturdy to put on my feet."

"If I should bring you shoes and you decide to go, you'd best take me with you. Proper Southern ladies don't walk in the city streets by themselves."

"I'm not a Southern lady. I come from Ohio and I intend to behave the same as I would in Sandusky. I'll go alone." Seeing Tibba's hurt expression, Barbara added, "It's not that I don't like your company—you know you're my best friend. But this is my own personal venture. Please don't worry about me—I can take care of myself."

Shaking her head, Tibba left the room. As soon as she was gone, Barbara lifted up her skirts and, with a small pair of nail scissors from the vanity table, unpicked the stitches holding two of the gold coins in the hem of her red petticoat and hid them in a pocket of the plum gown. It wasn't that she didn't trust Tibba, for she did, but it was best that no one knew she had this money.

The gold had been given to her by her father and she meant to use the coins for no other purpose than to free him. Meanwhile, she'd wait here in the room. She might be beholden to Francine for her hospitality but it was difficult to forgive her hostess for plotting with Trevor to keep her confined at Fairlawn. She didn't wish to see Francine or speak to her any more than absolutely necessary.

Time passed and Tibba didn't return. "You must learn patience," White Deer had often advised. "Patience outwaits the deer and the fish so they may be taken for food, patience sews the finest moccasins and brews the best medicine."

But Barbara found patience difficult to practice when she thought of her father lying ill in Libby Prison. How dare Trevor and Francine conspire to keep her from him? Where was Tibba? What in heaven's name could be keeping her?

When at last the door opened and Tibba stepped into the room carrying a bundle wrapped in white cloth, Barbara's nerves were stretched to the breaking point. Only her affection for Tibba prevented her from grabbing the bundle and dumping out the contents. She clutched her hands together while Tibba laid the bundle on the bed, carefully folded back the cloth and removed first a lavender bonnet, then a pair of dull black boots.

Tibba held the bonnet aloft. "Lyla found this for me to give to you—it's an old one Francine doesn't wear anymore. And here's gloves to match."

Barbara hadn't even thought of a bonnet or gloves—of course she'd need them. But the boots were the most important. When she picked them off the bed to examine, she found a pair of heavy gray wool stockings stuffed inside one.

"The boots might be a tad large," Tibba said. "That's why the colonel gave me the socks."

Barbara stared at her. "The colonel!"

Tibba grinned. "Don't worry, he's on our side. I didn't plan to tell him but when he overheard me asking Lyla about shoes he sent her off and made me come into his suite. 'What's this all about, girl?' he says. 'Come, spit out the truth, I can spot a lie a mile away.'

"It was plain to see his mind was clear as a bell so I decided to trust him with your story. I didn't mention that his daughter and the captain had schemed to keep you stranded in the house, I simply said your boots were being repaired and my shoes and Francine's were too small to fit you."

"I don't know if that was wise," Barbara said.

Tibba shrugged. "He was very sympathetic. After he thought about it a bit, he went into his bedroom, opened the door to a closet and unlocked something inside. I didn't dare leave the sitting room to see what it was in case he'd be angry. He came back carrying those boots, all covered with dust they were.''

"They're old," Barbara put in, "but sound enough. I think they're men's boots, though they look too small to be the colonel's—he's a big man.''

"What he said was, 'I trust these boots will take the wearer on her way to do good instead of ill.' I must have looked puzzled 'cause he smiled sort of sad. 'I'm sure your mistress is a good woman,' he goes on. 'The man who last wore these was as rotten at heart as a weevil-infested cotton boll. Take the boots: It's past time for me to forget. Forget, yes, forgive—never.' Then he rummaged in a drawer for the socks and pulls a pillowcase from his bed to hide the boots and socks in. I thanked him and was going out the door when the colonel says, 'He was a small man, you know, both in stature and in spirit.' His voice sounded so strange I was afraid his mind had started slipping again so I hurried off as fast as I could.''

Barbara stared at the boots she held, thinking of the story Tibba had told her last night about the colonel's wife betraying him and how he'd killed her lover. Had the boots belonged to that man? But why would the colonel keep a dead man's boots all these years? She grimaced and abruptly set the boots on the floor.

"So you think the same as me," Tibba said, pushing at one of the boots with her toe.

Barbara took a deep breath and let it out slowly. "What does it matter who they once belonged to? I need to get to Richmond and boots are boots. With the heavy socks these ought to fit me well enough."

But long after she'd successfully slipped from the house and made her way to the road leading into the city, she couldn't get it out of her mind whose boots she was walking in. Only when a woman's voice hailed her from a wagon rattling past, asking if she wanted a ride, did Barbara forget about what she was wearing and turn her thoughts to what lay ahead.

As the wagon rattled toward Richmond, Barbara soon discovered from the driver, Mr. Olmstead, that the main part of the city lay across the James River, as did her destination. Through the trees she caught glimpses of church spires and, occasionally, the mast of a ship. Mrs. Olmstead chattered away and Barbara answered her questions absently-mindedly, her thoughts busy with what she'd do when she finally reached the prison. Surely they'd let her in.

The five-mile journey seemed to take forever but finally the wagon, on its way to the docks along the other side of the James, reached Mayo's Toll Bridge. With nervous eagerness Barbara eyed the dingy buildings across the river, mostly brick, with dilapidated frame survivors from an earlier era.

The bridge was jammed with carts, wagons, and horses, slowing them to a turtle's pace and, during the crossing, she did her best not to fidget impatiently. Once on the opposite side, Mr. Olmstead pulled left onto a narrow street alongside the river and stopped.

"Yonder's where you want to go," he said, pointing. "'Tis that big brick building—Libby Prison used to be a warehouse and ship chandlery in the old days."

"Do be careful," his wife admonished as Barbara climbed down from the wagon. "A young girl alone is always at risk and this war has brought parlous times."

Barbara thanked the Olmsteads, crossed the street, dodging between carts and wagons, and walked toward the prison. A Confederate flag whipped in the wind above the roof of the four-story building and armed guards stood beside tents pitched to one side. Since she could see no obvious way into the building, she hesitated, wondering if she should approach one of the guards.

Before she'd made up her mind, she noticed a roughly dressed man watching her from the river side of the street and a shiver of apprehension coursed along her spine. Deciding she dare not linger any longer, she started toward the guard but paused, startled, when a man with a marked British accent called from a side street.

"Pardon me, madam—are you the young lady from the train?"

The mention of the train made her realize he must be speaking to her. Despite her reservations, Barbara turned to look at a tall well-dressed man in a frock coat. After a moment she recognized him as the English journalist with the blond mustache who'd sat behind her on the train from Cincinnati. The one who'd offered to help her. She even remembered his name. Harrison Chambers. What on earth was he doing here at Libby Prison?

"I say," he went on, coming toward her, "you *are*, aren't you. I do hope I'm not intruding."

"No," she said holding out her hand, "not at all. I'm pleased to see you reached Richmond unharmed, Mr. Chambers."

He pressed her fingers. "You do have the advantage, Mrs.—?"

"*Miss* Thackery," she said crisply.

"I beg your pardon. I assumed—"

"Captain Sandoe is not my husband. At the time you and I met on the train, he had just escaped from the Union prison near Sandusky and had taken me hostage."

"And then General Meachum took us all prisoner. Luck was with me, for he had no quarrel with England and so let me go my way. But what a dreadful time you've suffered through, Miss Thackery, and how fortunate you were able to free yourself from both captors. Perhaps sometimes I might persuade you to relate your story to me—if you wouldn't mind my writing it for my readers back home in England."

Barbara brushed his words aside. Her story was of no importance; it was her father who concerned her. Hadn't Mr. Chambers said something to his seatmate on the train about having passes to get him through both Reb and Union lines? Did that mean he could also get into Libby Prison?

Without preamble she said, "I must get into Libby Prison to see my father. Can you help me?"

His hand came up to tug at his mustache. "I'm terribly sorry but since they've refused me entrance, I'd be of no use to you, much as I'd like to be. I'm afraid they're allowing no one but

Confederates into the prison at present."

Barbara bit her lip. "But I must see my father, I must!"

Mr. Chambers studied her with concerned blue eyes. "You've come so far under such dreadful circumstances," he said sympathetically. "I sincerely regret my uselessness in the matter. What I can do, little enough as it is, would be to put you in touch with a Richmond woman, a Miss Elizabeth Van Lew, who is permitted to visit the Union prisoners to allay their suffering. I can't be certain but it's possible she might be able to speak to your father and pass a message along from you to him."

Barbara gazed up at him imploringly. "Please do introduce me to Miss Van Lew as soon as possible. It would be a great relief just to know how my father is."

"We'll call on her now, if you like," he said, and offered his arm.

With one last backward glance at the formidable brick prison, Barbara set off with Mr. Chambers.

Van Lew mansion was some five blocks from the river, all uphill and in a far more attractive setting. From the window of the parlor where, a short while later, they were having tea with Miss Van Lew's mother, Barbara could see terraced gardens with neatly trimmed boxwood hedges and a lovely little summer house beyond which was a view of the James River. The parlor, with its silk-brocaded walls and teardrop crystal chandeliers showed no sign of the deterioration she'd noticed at Fairlawn.

"Jenny Lind sang in this very parlor," old Mrs. Van Lew said as she set her cup back into its saucer. "Ah, those were the glory days."

Barbara smiled politely but her attention was focused on the parlor entrance, for she'd heard the front door open and close. Elizabeth Van Lew had arrived home.

Miss Van Lew was introduced to Barbara and greeted her cordially. "So pleasant to see you again, Mr. Chambers," she said to him.

"Doubly so for me," he told her. "Any visit with you is a pleasure. Today, though, I've come for help. I've brought Miss Thackery here in the hope you might be able to help her. It seems her father is a prisoner at Libby."

"Thackery," Elizabeth Van Lew repeated before Barbara could speak. "I thought the name was familiar. Is your father a doctor, my dear?

Barbara nodded.

"Dr. Thackery is a remarkable man; you have good reason to be proud of your father. Ill as he's been, he's done his best to treat his suffering comrades at Libby."

Barbara clasped her hands tightly together. "Please tell me how he was the last time you saw him."

"Why, my dear, that was only yesterday," Miss Van Lew sighed. "I wish I could give you better news but the truth is Dr. Thackery is a sick man. If he hadn't been so ill they would have shipped him to Georgia when they moved most of the other Union prisoners."

"Is there any way I might get into the prison to see him?"

Miss Van Lew shook her head, gazing at Barbara sympathetically. "The Confederacy has no chance of winning this war, as you may know. Jeff Davis has come to realize the truth, though he won't admit it. Perhaps because his army nears defeat, he's tightened regulations in the city. I'm one of the few civilians still allowed to visit the Union prisoners at Libby and any day now I expect to be turned away and warned not to return."

Barbara blinked back tears. Crying wouldn't help her cause. "Would you consider giving my father a message from me?"

"Of course, my dear."

"Tell him that I'm here in Richmond and that I'm determined to find a way to get him out of that terrible place."

Later, as Barbara walked away from the Van Lew house with Mr. Chambers, he said, "I must say I admire your courage, Miss Thackery. Please do allow me to escort you to your hotel."

"Thank you, but I'm staying five miles outside the city at Fairlawn, the Reynolds plantation."

"Well then, I shall see you to your carriage."

Disturbed as she was about her father, Barbara smiled at the thought of the Olmstead's old wagon being described as a carriage.

"I shall assume your smile is an affirmative," he said.

"Mr. Chambers, you're very kind but I have no carriage. I was walking into Richmond when I was fortunate enough to be offered a ride in a wagon."

He stared at her, pulling at his mustache. "That won't do, not at all. I can't allow you to trudge five miles unescorted. Certainly not. I'll find some sort of conveyance." He glanced around but there were no carriages of any kind in the street.

"Perhaps you should return to the Van Lews and wait there while I—" he began.

"That won't be necessary." She waved a hand at the substantial homes lining the street. "This is obviously a respectable neighborhood and there—" she nodded her head toward a small square of greenery at the corner—"is a bench for me to sit on while I wait for your return."

He looked at her dubiously. "I really would prefer—"

"Mr. Chambers, I have no intention of going back to bother the Van Lews. Though I appreciate your efforts to help me, I'm quite capable of taking care of myself. I'll wait on the bench."

Seated on the white-painted iron bench, Barbara watched him stride away toward the center of the city. He carried himself well, his clothes were impeccable, and his manners delightful. How helpful he'd been! She was most happy to have run across him so unexpectedly.

She arranged her skirt carefully to cover all except the toes of the men's boots she wore and hoped the Van Lews hadn't noticed what she had on her feet. Not that it really mattered but she still felt a bit peculiar about these particular boots.

She was so lost in ruminating over the betrayal of Colonel Reynolds and its consequences that she didn't at first notice the man standing to her left, half-hidden by the shrubbery.

"Oh!" Barbara started to rise, trying to stifle her exclamation too late.

"Don't mean you no harm, miss," the man said. "Look, I won't come no closer."

She swallowed, staring at him. Wasn't he the

same ruffian she'd seen by the prison? Glancing quickly around, she found no one else in sight. Should she run? But if she did, he might be faster.

"I maybe can help you, that's what," he said. "Otherwise I wouldn't've followed you." True to his word, he stayed where he was. "I seen you there at the prison. Looked mighty sad, you did. Got a husband in there?"

Though she'd meant not to say a word, Barbara blurted out, "My father!"

He nodded. "You'll be wanting to get him out."

"Yes, oh, yes."

"Friend of mine's a guard at Libby. He's in sore need of money."

Barbara tried to gather her wits. Was this ruffian actually offering to help her? Be careful, she warned herself.

"I might be able to raise some money," she said cautiously. "But what proof do I have you can free my father?"

"Yeah, well, you got to trust me. Look, I ain't talked to my friend yet, I got to do that afore we make any plans. Where you staying?"

Telling him seemed harmless enough. "At Fairlawn."

"I know the place. What I'll do is get a message to you there, where to meet us and all. Fifty dollars in gold'll take care of my friend. You pay half ahead of time and the rest when your pa's freed. That's fair enough."

"I don't know. What I mean is, I don't know you—or your friend."

"Yeah, like I don't know you or your pa. What

204

difference does that make? You want to get your pa out or not?"

"Yes, of course I do!"

"So, I'll send a message. What's your pa's name?"

"Thackery. Dr. Thackery. But you can't send a message addressed to me, it would be remarked on at Fairlawn."

"Got to have some name on it."

"Tibba," she said. "Say it's for Tibba."

He smiled, revealing a missing tooth in front, touched the brim of his cap, and melted into the shrubbery. Only then did she notice the clop-clop and rattle of an approaching carriage.

Though the hack Mr. Chambers had rented featured a somewhat rickety carriage and a snail-paced, gaunt-ribbed horse, Barbara felt she was riding back to Fairlawn in style. When they pulled up under the porte cochere she was so grateful she impulsively invited the journalist in.

A frowning Francine met her at the entrance. The frown was replaced by a polite smile when Francine realized Barbara wasn't alone.

"This is my friend, Mr. Chambers," Barbara said. "Mr. Chambers, Miss Reynolds, my hostess."

"Ah, the reigning belle of the city, if I'm not mistaken," he said, bowing over Francine's hand. "It's an honor to meet you."

Either Harrison or his British mannerisms charmed Francine since she almost immediately invited him to dinner and also to the party to be held three nights later.

"Thank you but, with regret, I must decline for

tonight," he told Francine, "for I have a previous engagement. But I shall be delighted to attend the party."

After he left, Francine eyed Barbara up and down as though reevaluating her. "I wasn't aware you had any friends in Richmond," she said.

"As luck would have it, Mr. Chambers just happened to be in the city," Barbara returned, determined not to give any hint of where she'd met him or how short their acquaintance really was.

"I wasn't expecting you to go into Richmond today."

Barbara looked her in the eye. "As I recall, I told you I meant to."

Francine's eyes narrowed. "I can see why Trevor warned me about you. It's plain you'll do as you like no matter what tribulation your deviousness may cause others. Very well. But remember, I take no responsibility for your welfare unless you remain at Fairlawn."

"I'm sorry if I've distressed you, Miss Reynolds." Barbara's tone was formal; she disliked being thought of as devious. "I do appreciate all you've done for me and for Tibba." The sentiment was true enough. The very clothes on her back were a gift from Francine. "My worry over my father has perhaps led me to a breach of good manners."

Francine inclined her head, accepting the apology. "My father tells me your maid plays the harp. Is this true?"

Barbara blinked, not only because of the abrupt change of subject but because of what was said. Tibba was certainly fascinated by harps and her mother had played—but did she? And why had the colonel mentioned it to begin with?

"I'll ask Tibba," she said.

"Please do. If she's sufficiently talented, I'd like her to play during the party."

It was on the tip of Barbara's tongue to ask if harp music might not upset the colonel but at the last moment she recalled that she wasn't even supposed to have met him, much less know his likes and dislikes.

"I trust you'll excuse me," Francine said. "I must change for dinner. My father will be joining us and the captain tonight. At eight."

Captain? She must mean Captain Sandoe. Doing her best to ignore the expectant leap of her heart at the thought of seeing Trevor, Barbara said, "I look forward to meeting Colonel Reynolds."

After a half hour of indecision in her bedroom, Barbara decided the mustard gown, because of its scoop neck, was the only appropriate dress to wear to dinner even though she wasn't taken with the color.

"Lyla found me some bits of ribbon," Tibba said. "I think there's one that color. I could tie up your hair, if you like."

Once the gown was on and Tibba had coaxed the back of her hair into a cascade of waves held in place by the ribbon, Tibba announced, "Some can wear bright colors. You're one of them."

Barbara, looking at herself in the mirror was surprised at what she saw. She'd thought mustard far too strong a color but she had to admit Tibba was right.

"I hear the captain's coming to dinner," Tibba said, smiling.

"I suppose he'll be angry with me." Barbara hesitated before going on. She hadn't yet told anyone about the stranger who'd approached her with the offer to free her father but Tibba would have to know because if the man did send a message, it would come to her. Taking a deep breath, she plunged into the story.

"I'm not sure yet that I can trust him," she finished.

"I don't like the sound of it," Tibba said. "First you meet that Englishman, supposedly by chance, and then some ruffian just happens to appear with his offer. How can you be sure of either of them?"

Barbara shook her head. "It's absurd to think that meeting Mr. Chambers was anything but fortuitous. As for the other man and his friend— what if I refuse to deal with them and he and his friend actually can free my father?" Barbara bit her lip. "Don't you see I must take the chance they can help because it may be the only chance my father has?"

Tibba shook her head. "I undestand how you feel but it still seems a frightful risk. And where will you get the money?"

"I—have it."

Tibba's eyes widened. Before she could ask any more questions, Barbara said, "The colonel told Francine you play the harp. Is that true?"

Tibba's hands flew to her mouth. "The colonel said that? How did he know?"

"Then you do play."

"My mama taught me. But after she died, *he* hit

208

me if I so much as touched her harp. I used to play in secret when he was gone and bribe the servants not to tell. What I can't understand is how the colonel knew I could play."

"You told him. Last night."

"But he wasn't in his right mind. And I only plucked one string, just one single note, that's all."

Barbara shrugged. She had no other explanation. "Anyway, Francine wants you to play for the party."

"Won't the colonel mind?"

"Francine didn't seem to think so."

Tibba grasped Barbara's hands and swung her round and round, her face transformed by joy. "Nothing could make me happier than to play. Nothing!"

When Barbara began to descend the stairs for dinner and looked down to see Trevor standing in the foyer looking up at her, she suddenly felt exactly the way Tibba had looked a few minutes before. Transformed by joy at the sight of him. While she was still endeavoring to mask her emotions, he leaped up the steps, grasped her arm, turned her, and pulled her with him to the top where he propelled her into the first room they came to—an unoccupied bedroom—and shut the door behind them.

"You went into Richmond today," he accused.

"I—yes," she stammered, trying to cope with the rush of sensation his touch evoked.

He gripped her shoulders. "Francine gave you my message, that you were to wait for me to take you there. Why didn't you?"

209

Annoyance steadied her. "You have no right to give me orders. I went because I wanted to learn what I could about my father and see him if possible."

"I assume you learned seeing him was impossible."

"Yes."

"You also met that British journalist from the train, the one who was so eager to help you." Trevor gave her a little shake. "*He* can't help you. You ought to have more sense."

She met his angry gaze defiantly. "What have you done to aid my father? Nothing! Through Mr. Chambers's efforts I learned today that my father's very ill. I have to find a way to free him or he might—might—" The word stuck in her throat and tears stung her eyes.

"Oh God, Snow Bird, what am I going to do about you?" he demanded, pulling her to him.

His mouth covered hers without tenderness, possessive, possessing, in a kiss that wiped every thought from her mind. She was in Trevor's arms and, for the moment, nothing else mattered.

Chapter 13

Trevor sat in Fairlawn's library with Colonel Reynolds over after-dinner brandy, half-listening to the colonel reminisce about his cadet days with General Lee at the Military Academy at West Point. Though the brandy was excellent, the last of fine old French stock, Trevor tasted the sweet fire of Barbara's lips rather than the wine. Letting her escape from his arms had been damn near impossible.

She had him at his wit's end. How could a man be expected to serve the Confederate States in this desperate struggle for the Southern cause and look after such an unpredictable woman at the same time?

He'd been given his orders and would do his best to carry them out but he couldn't simply sail off and leave her in Richmond at the mercy of that damned British journalist, Chambers. He had little use for foreign scribblers nosing around, always safely behind the lines, in the pay of newspapers and journals catering to their subscribers' appetite for gory battle stories.

Help her, hell. Chambers would be about as much use to Barbara as one of those pug-nosed lap dogs. All the bastard wanted to do was to help himself. To her. Trevor clenched his fists. The way he saw it, she was his and no one else's.

Unfortunately, she didn't seem to see it that way. And, under the circumstances, he had no right to claim her.

"I gave her the boots, you know," the colonel said. "Kept 'em all these years, high time to get rid of 'em."

His words snapped Trevor to attention, confusing him as he tried to make sense of them. "Gave who the boots, sir?" he finally asked.

"Gave 'em to that pretty little high yellow gal—for her mistress. Smart as a whip, that Nigra. If I could buy her, I would, but she claims she's freeborn."

Realizing he must mean Tibba, Trevor said, "She's telling you the truth. Tibba's never been a slave. But I don't quite understand about the boots."

"Your Yankee gal wore the boots to go into the city. A tad large for her, I expect, for all she's tall—though he was undersized for a man. You know I shot him, of course."

With difficulty Trevor refrained from gaping at the colonel. Was he referring to the old scandal about Cynthia Reynolds and Gerald Renfrew?

"Folks whisper about it but no one has ever dared accuse me directly," the colonel went on. "Don't have the nerve. In any case, old Obed and I buried him where he won't be found till judgment day. But Cynthia—ah, she knew I'd shot him and she couldn't forgive me. She never told a soul what I'd done but the knowledge killed her." He gazed somberly down at his feet. "I didn't know she'd found his boots and hid them until I went through her things after she died."

Trevor shifted in his seat, uncomfortable with being the recipient of Colonel Reynolds's confession. Rumors were one thing, admission another. Also, it bothered him that Barbara had worn a dead man's boots.

"Keeping a secret can affect the mind, you know," the colonel announced. "Came clear to me after that little yellow gal plucked at Cynthia's harp. The sound made me slip a cog like I've been doing more and more of late and I played the fool with my granddaddy's old sword—dull as one of Father Youst's sermons it is—but I'm ashamed to say I put those two innocent gals in fear of their lives. Tibba, though, had the courage to face me down and then the heart to comfort me when I wept. She set my mind back into order, thank God."

He took a long draught of the brandy. "I can see you don't want to hear this but I had to tell someone. I chose you for three reasons. One, your father was my best friend. No better soldier ever died for our cause than Preston Sandoe. Two, like me, you're a devious kind of chap or you wouldn't be successful in what you're doing for our cause. Three, it's your right to know that Francine's another Cynthia. She's my daughter and I love her dearly but blood will tell, boy, don't let any damn fool try to convince you otherwise."

"I—I'm rather at a loss for words, sir." Trevor felt that was a gross understatement—the colonel had him reeling. For one thing he'd had no idea the old man knew his real army role. Secondly, he'd believed the colonel's dearest wish was to see him marry Francine.

Not that he'd planned to in the near future, if ever. Marriage wasn't for men who had to take the chances he did. So far he'd been lucky—he'd happened to be riding with a regular Confederate calvary unit when the Yanks captured him and so he'd been able to pass himself off as one of the unit officers. If the Yanks had fathomed his true purpose, he'd have been gallow's fodder long ago.

Should he happen to survive the war and, by some catastrophic trick of fate, change his mind and decide to marry, Trevor supposed Francine was as good a choice as any. But the very idea of marriage made him feel like a hobbled horse. He couldn't imagine volunteering to chain himself to any woman. Even though his desire for Barbara was so intense he couldn't be near her without wanting her, his need didn't make him desperate enough to consider marrying her.

"Well, sir," the colonel challenged, "you've heard the truth. Do you intend to turn me in?"

Trevor shook his head. The Renfrews were all dead and buried now—what good would come of disinterring an old scandal? As for punishment—hadn't the colonel done that to himself?

Colonel Reynolds smiled. "Then I'm free to offer my services, such as they are, to my old academy brother-in-arms, Bobby Lee. I'm still a dead shot and not too decrepit to lead men into battle. At this moment the South needs every man she can get—as you know, of course. Hence your mission. I wish you every success in freeing those gallant men for our cause." He raised his glass. "Here's to the Confederate flag—long may she wave."

As Trevor drained his glass, the colonel's words about freeing men triggered an idea, a possible way to earn Barbara's undying gratitude—and, therefore, her help. After all, she was not only a native of Sandusky but a loyal Union supporter. No one would ever suspect her.

"Sir," he said, "before I take it up with my commanding officer, I'd like your opinion on this plan I've just now conceived . . ."

After three days with no message from the man who'd approached her near the Van Lews, Barbara decided his plan, if he'd really had one, must have fallen through. That evening, as she dressed for the ball, her heart was heavy with worry over her father.

She watched listlessly in the mirror while Tibba, after arranging her hair so it fell in smooth waves from a center part, fastened a red silk rose above her left ear and stood back to admire the effect.

"Red's your color, it truly is," Tibba announced.

A memory came to Barbara of Trevor telling her he'd like someday to see her in a crimson gown and she smiled. The dress she wore was pale pink with a red lace overskirt, a combination achieved by

Lyla's talent for discovering old gowns that had been packed away and Tibba's heroic efforts with a needle.

"Don't you think the neck's a trifle low?" Barbara asked, fingering the deep-cut decolletage uncertainly.

"You know as well as I do it's the fashion. Besides, you've got pretty shoulders and your—"

Not wishing to hear Tibba describe more intimate parts of her body, Barbara said hastily, "The gown's lovely, thanks to you. I never expected to be so well-dressed for this party."

"It's too bad you have no jewelry. A ruby pendant would be perfect. On the other hand, I expect they'll all be wearing jewels so you'll stand out because you're not."

Barbara didn't want to stand out, she merely wished to be dressed acceptably. No, that wasn't exactly true—oh, admit it, she wanted to be dressed attractively enough so Trevor would look at her admiringly. Was she? Standing up, she turned this way and that in front of the pier glass.

"The captain's sure to find you beautiful," Tibba insisted, "'cause you are."

Barbara flushed, wishing Tibba wasn't so good at reading her thoughts.

"You're well-turned-out yourself," Barbara said, to change the subject. It was true. Tibba had attained a certain elegance by attaching a white satin collar and cuffs to her black servant's gown and trimming her white satin apron with scrolls of black braid.

Tibba shrugged. "I have no need to impress anyone with my appearance, it's my playing that worries me. When I touch the harp, I only hope the colonel isn't disappointed. The others don't matter. Except for the colonel—and maybe the captain—I can't say I care much for Virginians."

Barbara clasped her hand. "When my father's free, I'd like you to come back to Ohio with us."

"Sometimes I wonder if I'll fit in anywhere." Tibba sighed. "I hated living in *his* valley, in *his* house, but at least I was somebody there. When people spoke they didn't act as though I was invisible." She squeezed Barbara's hand and released it. "I can play at being your maid 'cause you're my friend, but I hate being a servant."

"After we leave this house you won't have to pretend ever again," Barbara promised.

Tibba left the room first since she was supposed to be playing the harp when the guests arrived. Barbara waited, her door ajar, until the faint sound of voices rising from the first floor told her the party was getting under way. As she descended the stairs, several people in the foyer, all strangers, glanced up at her.

Francine's high, melodic laugh drifted from the parlor, acompanied by the rippling notes of the harp coming from the music room. As she reached the foyer, Barbara steeled herself to face Fairlawn's guests, enemies she must be polite to. She glanced toward the music room and paused. Wasn't that lanky figure lounging in the doorway Harrison Chambers?

Glad to see a familiar face, she walked toward him. Though she didn't recognize the music Tibba was playing, the sound was lovely. Apparently Mr. Chambers thought so, too, for he stared at Tibba as though transfixed. So intent was he that Barbara decided to wait until Tibba finished her piece before speaking to him.

A moment later, Francine glided past her, gtreen skirts aswish, and tapped Harrison's arm playfully with her fan.

"I declare, sir," Francine said to him, "you'll not get out of our games by hiding. Do come into the parlor."

Mr. Chambers turned away from the door. "I do beg your pardon," he said. "I was so enchanted by the harp I quite forgot my manners. You're fortunate to have so talented a servant."

"Tibba doesn't belong to Fairlawn," Barbara put in. "Or to anyone. She's freeborn."

Mr. Chambers glanced over his shoulder at Tibba. "I say, how unusual." He smiled at Barbara. "Delightful to see you again, Miss Thackery."

Francine tucked her hand under his arm, leading him toward the parlor. "You must join us, too," she said to Barbara. "The games are simple enough, after all."

Barbara had no trouble reading between the lines—simple enough for an ignorant Yank. She squared her shoulders and followed them into the parlor. Perhaps she was ignorant but she was determined to do her best to prove Francine wrong.

A sliding door had been opened, turning two rooms into one and the large double parlor was full of guests. Barbara scanned them, recognizing only the colonel. Apparently Trevor either couldn't come or hadn't yet arrived. She tried to deny her disappointment, telling herself she wished he were there only because he'd be someone she knew amidst all these strangers.

Colonel Reynolds caught her eye and she edged through the crowd toward him. As she came near him she heard one of the two older men he was talking to, a man with one eye covered by a patch, say, "Now that Hood's on the prowl he'll chase that damn Sherman out of Georgia once and for all, see if he don't." The man gestured with his half-filled glass.

Barbara stopped, listening.

"May your wish come true," the colonel said. "What I'm afraid of is that Sherman will catch Bobby Lee by the rear while Grant grips Lee's head."

"Lee's too wily to be trapped," the man with the eye patch insisted.

The colonel shrugged. "I don't doubt there are a few kicks left in the old war horse yet—but Lee can't turn the tide without more men." He glanced up, saw Barbara, and motioned her over.

"Miss Thackery, Major Alexander and Major Welks," the colonel said. "Gentlemen, Miss Thackery is our guest."

Barbara couldn't help be disarmed by the gallantry of the men as, in turn, they bowed over her hand.

"With your daughter as Snow White and Miss Thackery as Rose Red, I'd say Fairlawn has cornered the market on belles," Major Welks observed, his uncovered brown eye frankly admiring.

One of the house servants came by with a tray of

stemmed glasses filled with golden liquid. "Sherry, Miss Thackery?" Major Alexander offered, plucking a glass from the tray and holding it out to her. To be polite she took the glass from him, smiling her thanks.

She touched the rim of the glass to her lips as she tried to think of an appropriate subject to mention—what did one discuss with enemies in the middle of a war?

"I find Virginia weather quite warm for mid-September," she said at last.

"Finest weather in the country," Major Alexander boomed. "None better. Evidently you're not from these parts."

Barbara shook her head, reluctant to go into any details of where she came from. Making it evident she was on the side of Generals Sherman and Grant wouldn't make polite conversation. With relief she noticed two large bosomed ladies bearing down on them and, moments later, the colonel introduced her to Mrs. Alexander and Mrs. Welks.

"Such a charming gown, Miss Thackery," Mrs. Welks said, examining her through a lorgnette. "I fear we've slipped behind the times here in Richmond. Is lace becoming fashionable once more?"

Barbara had no idea but was saved from answering by Francine's arrival.

"Time to pair for *tableaux vivants*," she said, smiling. "Do you care to play 'living pictures,' Miss Thackery?"

She doesn't give me credit for being able to translate the French, Barbara thought. Aloud, she said, "I'll be happy to be included."

"Papa, I thought you might like to be Miss Thackery's partner," Francine went on.

"My pleasure," the colonel said, "but will Miss Thackery feel the same?" He turned to Barbara. "I'm devilishly poor at these things."

"I'd be delighted to have you as a partner," Barbara said, glad to be paired with someone she knew.

Francine quickly organized everyone into a circle with the women seated and the men standing behind them. Somewhat to Barbara's surprise, there were as many men as women, most of the men in uniform. Francine, she saw, had picked Harrison Chambers as her partner and the two of them were the first to enter the circle.

The object of the game, she knew, was for the pair in the center to enact a tableau depicting a story, song, poem, or play. The audience then had to guess what it was. Whichever pair first gave the correct answer became the next in the center. After every pair had its chance to enact a tableau, the winner became the pair who'd most often entered the circle.

Though Barbara knew from watching how the game was played, she'd never actually been a participant because the Hargreaves had ruled such games frivolous and a waste of her time. She was almost certain Francine and Harrison were depicting Sir Walter Scott's *Rob Roy* but it took her a few minutes to become confident enough to say so and by then the Alexanders had guessed correctly.

This pair presented Shakespeare's *Romeo and Juliet* and Barbara's voice was drowned in the chorus as the right answer rang out from all around the circle.

The next pair's act was harder to pin down. The man was obviously pantomiming using a bow and arrow—was he one of Cooper's Indian heroes? No, everything so far had been English—he must be Robin Hood. Or wait, what was the woman doing with her hand, wasn't she setting something imaginary on top of her head?

"William Tell," Barbara cried.

From behind her, a man's voice echoed her words. Surely that wasn't the colonel. She turned to look. The colonel no longer stood behind her chair; instead, Trevor smiled down at her. "The colonel appointed me his deputy," he said.

Barbara told herself the rapid beat of her heart was due solely to her surprise. Since they were clearly the winners, they'd be next in the circle, so she rose. Though she and the colonel had chosen what to enact, she hadn't had a chance to consult with Trevor.

"Ishmael," he whispered to her as he offered his arm.

Once inside the circle he stretched out on the floor, making swimming motions. Barbara thought a moment, then walked a few steps with one leg stiff, stopped and, with both hands curved to form circles, placed one hand in back of the other, raised them in front of one eye and peered through them at Trevor. Setting aside the imaginary telescope, she lifted her arm and cast an invisible harpoon toward Trevor.

Major Welks was the first to guess *Moby Dick*. At the end of the game, Trevor and Barbara were one ahead of Francine and Harrison Chambers.

"No fair," Francine said, shaking her finger at Trevor. "It was naughty of you to take Papa's place." She slipped her hand under his arm, gazing up at him from under her lashes. "I may never forgive you."

Watching Trevor smile at her, Barbara suppressed a sigh. In her ruffled gown of new leaf green with her blond hair gleaming, Francine looked every inch what Harrison had called her earlier—the belle of Richmond.

Annoyed by her rush of jealousy—why should she care who Trevor preferred?—she turned away and, encountering Harrison's gaze, mustered a smile for him.

"Would it be appropriate for you to introduce me to the harpist?" he asked. "I've never met a freeborn Negro woman. If Negro is the proper word. Obviously she has white blood."

"Tibba—that is, Miss Meachum—is my friend," Barbara told him. "I'm sure she'd enjoy meeting you."

Harrison offered her his arm and, as they strolled toward the music room he said, "Meachum is a rather unusual name. Is it possible that pretty little harpist can be related to General Meachum?"

Too late Barbara remembered Tibba's decision to go by her mother's name of La Harpe. After a moment's thought, she said, "Tibba's his daughter, but she prefers not to be reminded of it."

"Thank you for telling me. I shan't say a word."

They found Tibba standing by the piano examining sheets of music.

"Oh," she said when she saw Barbara. "Were you sent to ask me to play again? I thought I was free until refreshments were served."

Barbara shook her head. "This is Mr. Harrison Chambers, the English journalist I mentioned to you. Mr. Chambers, Miss Meachum."

"Charmed," Harrison said, lifting Tibba's hand to his lips.

"In this house, as well as everywhere else in Virginia, I'm just plain Tibba," she said tartly.

Barbara noted with interest that Harrison seemed reluctant to release her hand. Was that why Tibba's face was so flushed?

"I've rarely heard a more talented harpist," he said, "and I've never seen a more comely one."

Tibba withdrew her hand from his and smiled up at him. "Thank you."

"If you must be Tibba to me, then I must be Harrison to you," he said. "It's only fair."

Barbara chuckled at the thought of Francine's face should she ever hear Tibba calling him by his first name.

Tibba glanced at her and her eyes widened. "I almost forgot," she said. Taking a folded paper from her pocket, she handed it to Barbara.

Not wishing to open the note in front of Harrison, Barbara excused herself and made for the stairs. This had to be a message from the man who'd offered to help free her father and the only safe place to read it was in her room.

The scrawled writing and the misspelled words made it difficult to decipher but Barbara finally understood that tomorrow at noon she was to meet the man and his friend at the given address in the city—near Libby Prison—and pay them the first half of the money. She was then to wait there until they came back with her father before paying the rest of the fifty dollars.

"We want gold, not paper," the note reminded her.

To free her father she'd gladly give every penny she possessed.

Since she had no pocket in her gown, she lifted the lid of a potpourri jar and slipped the note inside. The faint scent of dried roses perfumed the air as she left the room to return to the party.

The last of the roses in the Hargreaves' side garden had been blooming when she'd closed the door of their house for the final time. She remembered their scent following her down the dark road. The overblown roses in General Meachum's garden had briefly sweetened the air before shedding their petals onto the muddy ground. Now, in September it was too late for roses, even in the warmth of Virginia, and only the ghost of their perfume lingered in the potpourri.

She was as eager to leave Fairlawn as she'd been to depart from the Hargreaves' house and Meachum's mansion. With her father and Tibba, she'd travel north until they'd left the Confederates States behind and never return.

She'd never see Trevor Sandoe again.

He was waiting for her at the bottom of the stairs. Without saying a word, he took her arm and propelled her along a side hall until they reached the library door. He guided her inside.

No fire warmed the room but on a long table an argand lamp turned low cast a dim light, making shadows dance in the corners.

"I'll meet with you here late tomorrow," Trevor said, his dark eyes intent on hers.

"But I—" she began.

"You will *be* here for that meeting. Do you understand?"

About to snap that she wasn't his to command and that, in any case, she wouldn't be here, Barbara caught the words back at the last moment. Best not to tell him she'd be gone. If he discovered what she meant to do tomorrow he'd certainly stop her; she didn't dare raise any questions in his mind. Yet she disliked lying.

"If you insist," she temporized, "how can I refuse?"

Trevor frowned, as if not satisfied with her answer, but she maintained a stubborn silence.

"I must go," he said at last. "I took time I could ill afford to come here tonight."

"I see you've found a new uniform," she said, not adding that she thought its trim fit suited him very well.

"An officer can hardly go around looking more ragged than his men. General Lee always manages to have a clean uniform on hand no matter how hard he's driven."

She didn't give a fig how General Lee dressed, the only soldier who concerned her at the moment was standing so close that only inches separated them.

"Will you kiss me good night?" His voice, low and husky, sent a thrill of anticipation shimmering along her nerves.

She should say no; she would say no. He had no

right to smile so intimately at Francine and then ask *her* such a question. But the word refused to come. Instead, she leaned closer to him.

After all, this will be the last time I see him, she told herself. Once my father is free, I won't return here. I'll send for Tibba and have her join us in Richmond. What harm is there in a farewell kiss?

Trevor lowered his head until their lips almost met. She reached up and cradled his face between her hands, memorizing the feel of his skin and the soft beard under her fingers. Raising on tiptoe, she brushed her lips across his. Though she'd meant it to be a brief, light caress, she found herself lingering, reluctant to end the kiss.

Her arms wound around his neck, she pressed herself close to him. He pulled her even closer, deepening the kiss until the delicious fire of his tongue against hers melted her bones like wax.

She fit into his arms so sweetly. Never before had a woman set him aflame so quickly, so completely. His need for her burned through him like a fire out of control, all-consuming. Nothing mattered but the feel of her softness against him and her passionate response to his kiss.

She was his. *His.* Her breathless moans as he trailed kisses down her throat to where her gown revealed the beginning rise of her breasts told him she wanted more, that she wanted him as much as he wanted her.

His for the taking.

"Ishmael," she murmured.

227

"Ah, Snow Bird," he whispered, "you make my heart sing."

His for the taking, but not at Fairlawn. Not tonight. He meant to have her; he would have her. But at a time and place of his choosing. A private place, where there'd be no interruptions and enough time to make love slowly, to enjoy every second of each kiss, each caress. To savor their lovemaking.

If she'd still have him after he revealed his plan tomorrow afternoon, a plan he had no doubt his superior would approve in the morning. She'd go along with his plan because she had no choice, but he feared she'd despise him for forcing her into it.

Even though he foresaw that after tomorrow the right time and the right place might be further away than he wished, might, in fact, never come to be, Trevor sighed and released her.

And cursed himself for being so hellishly honorable. Unfortunately, he couldn't help it—a Sandoe male imbibed honor with his mother's milk.

But honor was little comfort for the throbbing demand pounding through him, the overwhelming desire to hold her and never let her go.

The truth was he needed this damn Yankee in more ways than one. It was his bad luck that the ways very likely would prove mutually exclusive.

Chapter 14

After Trevor left the house, Barbara started to return to her room but was intercepted by Colonel Reynolds who gallantly offered to escort her into the dining room where a late-night supper was being served. She didn't feel she should refuse.

It was over an hour later before she could politely excuse herself and slip upstairs. As she entered her bedroom, she noticed the scent of roses still lingered, seemingly stronger than ever. Frowning, she hurried to the potpourri jar and lifted the lid. She sighed with relief when she found the note still nestled among the dried rose petals. Removing it, she hid the folded paper in a pocket of the gown she meant to wear tomorrow.

Extricating all but two of the gold coins from the hem of the red petticoat took but a few moments. She divided the money and tied it into two handkerchiefs, sliding them under her pillow before preparing herself for bed.

Once in her nightgown she realized she was far

too restless to fall asleep. Because she was so excited about being reunited with her father she knew she might well find herself still awake at dawn. Propped on her pillows, she lifted a small volume of English poetry from the bedside table, turned to John Donne and read:

Stay, O sweet, and do not rise!
The light that shines comes from thine eyes;
The day breaks not: it is my heart.
Because that you and I must part. . . .

She stopped reading and stared into the distance. Her dearest wish was to be with her father again, but in gaining him she'd lose Trevor. When she left Richmond, she and Trevor would be parting forever. The kiss in the library had truly been their last.

The two of us were never meant to be together, she told herself firmly. How could I ever find happiness with a man who upholds the inhuman values of the Confederacy? I couldn't possibly marry a Reb.

Not that he'd asked her to marry him. Or ever would ask her. Francine was a far more appropriate choice for Trevor's bride and, no doubt, he was well aware of that.

Had he ever kissed Francine in the same way he'd kissed her? Barbara's stomach knotted as the poison of jealousy seeped through her. Unable to bear the thought of him holding Francine in his arms and caressing her, she gritted her teeth, the book slipping from her grasp as her hands clenched. It thudded to the floor just as Tibba opened the door.

"I purely loved playing that harp," Tibba said. "I don't recall ever being so tired and happy both at the same time."

Determinedly, Barbara wrenched her thoughts away from Trevor. "Tomorrow's going to be the happiest day in *my* life," she said. "I'll be reunited with my father."

Tibba sank down on her cot and stared worriedly at Barbara. "That's what was in the note?"

Barbara nodded. "I'm to meet him in the city. I can't bring you with me when I go but as soon as he's free of that horrid prison, I'll send for you to come to us and we'll all travel north together."

"Are you sure it's safe for you to go into Richmond alone? If you're meeting that man who asked for money, how do you know you can trust him? You'd best have me with you."

"I must go by myself," Barbara said, recalling the instructions in the note.

Tibba shook her head, her expression dubious. "Where are you meeting this man?"

"Near the prison. Don't worry so. I can take care of myself."

"You still got *his* knife?"

General Meachum's knife was the only thing that had survived all Barbara's changes of costume since she'd escaped from the valley. She'd hidden it in the back of the wardrobe drawer on arrival here. "Are you saying you expect me to carry that knife with me tomorrow?"

Tibba's nod was emphatic.

"I don't think I could bring myself to use a knife to—to hurt anyone," Barbara said, remembering how, in desperation, she'd planned to defend herself against the general with that very same knife and had wondered if she could.

"Promise me you'll take it. I'll feel better knowing you have the knife with you."

To end the discussion, Barbara agreed.

After Tibba was in bed and the lamp extinguished, Barbara tossed and turned for some time, unable to sleep. She thought Tibba had dozed off so was a bit startled when she suddenly asked a question.

"Do you like him?"

"Like who?"

"Harrison." Tibba whispered his name.

"Why, yes, he's most pleasant. He certainly admired your musical ability." Barbara smiled in the darkness. "And you, too."

"Men say pretty words but they don't always mean them." Tibba sounded wistful.

Barbara wished she could assure Tibba of Harrison's sincerity but she knew him too slightly to be certain he was sincere. Besides, hadn't she heard him praise Francine's attractiveness as well as Tibba's?

"I can't believe all his interest was in the harp," she said finally.

"He said he'd like to meet me sometime—in the city. I told him it wasn't possible." Tibba sighed. "I wish I could have said yes but I know what he's after. He wants to get me into his bed. Men, that's all they want and once they get it you don't matter to them anymore. Or worse, they treat you mean and hurt you like *he* did to my mother.''

Pain twisted Barbara's heart. Was that all Trevor had ever wanted from her? She hated to believe it was true.

''Like as not Harrison and I will never meet again,'' Tibba said and sighed again. ''I could hardly keep from staring at him: he's the handsomest man I've ever seen.''

Tibba's words jolted Barbara from her misery. Harrison handsome? Tibba must view him with a far different eye than she did. In her opinion Harrison couldn't hold a candle to Trevor. But then no man she knew could. . . .

Shortly before noon, Barbara stood in front of an old and grimy brick building not far from Libby Prison. Comparing the metal numbers nailed to the door with the address on the note, she nodded. This was her destination. There was no sign of the man who'd written the note so she climbed the steps and reached for the rust-stained iron ball and hand that served as a door knocker. She'd barely touched it when the door swung open.

Barbara waited but when no one appeared she realized the door must have been left slightly ajar. For her? The uncurtained windows on either side of the door stared at her, giving no clues, and she noticed that one of the streaked and dirty panes was cracked. Hesitantly, she entered the open door and stopped in the dim and dusty entryway. The inside smelled of emptiness and decay. She didn't like the smell or the looks of the place.

To her right a corridor ran into the depths of the building with closed doors at intervals. To her left a stairway rose to the next floor. What now?

"Up here," a man's voice called from the top of the steps.

Barbara swallowed, belatedly wishing Tibba had come with her. "Who—who are you?" she asked.

"Ain't you Dr. Thackery's daughter?"

"Yes. Yes, I am."

"Then come on up. I ain't got all day."

"Why can't you come down?"

"Others come in and outta this place—it ain't safe anywheres near the door. You gonna stand there arguing or you gonna do business? The quicker you pay me, the quicker your pa gets out of Libby."

Still uneasy, she reached into the small leather pouch Tibba had found for her and took out the knife, leaving only one of the handkerchiefs containing the coins. The rest of the money was in her pocket. She lifted her skirts slightly to climb the stairs, the fabric concealing the folded knife in her hand.

The man who'd accosted her near the Van Lews stood in the gloom at the top of the stairs. He stepped aside when she reached the top and jerked his thumb toward an open door. "In there."

Barbara glanced into a dark box of a room with a single curtainless window facing a brick wall.

234

Unless a filthy mattress on the floor could be counted, the room was unfurnished. She halted on the threshold.

"I prefer to give you the money here," she said, doing her best to sound firm as she offered him the leather pouch.

He glanced along the hall and she followed his gaze. All the other rooms had closed doors. He looked more unsavory than she recalled and she wished he wasn't between her and the stairs.

"I tell you it ain't safe out in the open," he insisted.

"I'm not going into that room."

"You got all the money in here?" he asked, taking the pouch from her.

"Half. We agreed on half now, the rest when you bring my father to me."

"Yeah. You can wait in the room."

"No!"

Without warning, he grabbed her upper arm and propelled her into the room. When he kicked the door shut, she saw with dismay a second man had been hidden behind it, a man with a crooked nose whose appearance was even more disreputable than the first man's. Though she tried to tell herself he must be the guard who was to free her father, she wasn't convinced because she no longer believed they ever meant to help her.

Fearful, Barbara thrust her hands behind her back, frantically trying to open the clasp knife.

"We want all the money," the first man said. "Now."

235

Why wouldn't the knife open? "We agreed—" she began.

Crooked Nose advanced on her, his pale eyes glittering in a heavily bearded face. Frightened by his menacing mien and sickened by his fetid breath, she retreated.

"My pal ain't got much patience," the first man warned. "Give him the rest of the money or you're gonna get hurt."

At last the knife sprang open, freeing one of her hands. She jammed that hand into her pocket, grabbed the other handkerchief-wrapped coins and flung them at Crooked Nose, hoping to distract him so she could slip past and run for the door.

He dashed her hopes by catching the handkerchief in midair and tossing it to the first man. "Where you got the rest of your money hid?" he demanded.

"I—I don't have any more."

Crooked Nose grinned, showing broken teeth. "Gals like to hide money in their clothes. Bet I'm gonna find yours afore we get to the skin." He lunged at her.

So terrified she hardly knew what she was doing, Barbara brought the knife from behind her back and jabbed it at him. The blade sank into his side just under his arm.

Crooked Nose howled with pain, reeling away from her. Barbara rushed toward the door. The other man barred her path.

"You little bitch," he snarled, flinging her onto the dirty mattress. "You ain't going nowhere." He

236

swung around to look at Crooked Nose who was hunched over by the window, trying to pull out the knife. "How bad you hurt?" he asked.

Horrified, she watched Crooked Nose yank the knife free. "Don't know yet," he muttered, glaring at Barbara. Knife in hand, he started toward her.

She screamed, scuttling across the mattress until her back was against the wall, her eyes never leaving the blood-stained blade held by Crooked Nose.

"Wait," the first man urged. "Let's have some fun with her first."

Crooked Nose paid no attention. He reached the mattress and Barbara screamed again and again when he lunged at her. She flung herself to one side, hitting her head so hard against a shelf sticking out from the wall that her surroundings blurred. She collapsed, sprawling half off the mattress, sure that this was the end.

A man shouted—or was it many men shouting? The door slammed into the wall beside her. With an effort, Barbara raised her head and tried to focus. The room whirled. She blinked, unsure of what she saw. The room seemed to be full of men in gray. Soldiers. And the captain kneeling beside her—surely that couldn't be Trevor.

"Are you all right?" he asked.

It *was* Trevor! Barbara burst into tears.

He lifted her into his arms and after that time seemed to stand still. She didn't return to complete awareness until she found herself lying not on a filthy mattress in a dingy room but on the clean coverlet of a brass bed with a strange man

237

leaning over and peering into her eyes.

"Oh!" she cried, startled.

He straightened. "I'm Dr. Longview," he said soothingly. "Captain Trevor asked me to make certain you weren't seriously injured."

She noticed then that the doctor was wearing a gray uniform. Tears misted her vision as she was reminded that Dr. Thackery, in his blue uniform, was still in Libby Prison.

"You have quite a lump on your head," Dr. Longview said. "No doubt that's what's causing the pain."

Her head did ache but her heartache was far worse. "That awful man lied to me from the first," she mumbled, speaking more to herself than to anyone else. "I should have listened to Tibba's warning."

"Yes, you should have." Trevor's voice, tinged with anger, came from the foot of the bed. "But you never seem to listen to anyone. Or only to the wrong people. How could you have placed your trust in such obvious lowlifes?"

"I don't believe her head injury is serious," Dr. Longview said to him. "To be certain, keep her in bed until tomorrow." The doctor gave her a reassuring smile and left the room.

She was alone with Trevor. An angry Trevor.

"What's the matter with you?" he demanded, still standing at the foot of the bed. "Don't you realize you could have been killed? The only reason you're still alive is because last night Francine found that note where you'd hidden it and she read it. Because she never dreamed you'd be so foolish as to actually go, she didn't notify me immediately. You're lucky I got there with my men in time. Damn lucky."

Barbara closed her eyes, trying to come to terms with what he'd said. No wonder the rose scent had been so strong last night when she came up to bed. Francine had crept into her room and, guided by the smell of roses, found the note, read it, and put it back in the jar. Under the circumstances she had to be grateful for the trespass, even though she was almost sure Francine's motive had been to get her into trouble rather than to save her life.

When Trevor next spoke he was much closer and his voice was gentler. "Are you in pain?"

She opened her eyes to see him pulling up a chair beside the bed. "A slight headache," she said. "Where am I?"

He sat in the chair. "At my place. Where I should have brought you to begin with. And set a guard at your door to keep you from slipping away and creating problems."

"Tibba will worry."

"I've already sent for her. I'm taking no more chances. You're both staying here until we set sail."

Barbara stared at him. "I don't understand."

He looked at her impassively. "We're going to make a trade, you and I. Your father's freedom in exchange for your aid in my mission."

She struggled to sit up. He reached out as though to help her, then drew his hand back, letting her push the pillows into place herself until she was propped against the headboard.

"You told me you couldn't get my father out of Libby Prison," she said.

"I've spoken to those in authority. They agree to free him if you agree to cooperate with me."

Her mind whirled. Cooperate. Mission. She didn't like the sound of those words. But she'd do anything to assure her father's freedom.

Even betray her country?

No, she couldn't.

But her father's life was at stake. What should she do? Before she made any decision she needed all the facts.

"What do you mean by cooperate?" she asked.

"You'd help me reach my goal by doing exactly what I tell you to do and say."

Barbara narrowed her eyes. "What is your goal?"

He looked at her a long time before replying. "Freeing the Johnson Island prisoners."

She gasped, shocked.

Trevor smiled wryly. "You, of all people, should be sympathetic."

"My father is a doctor, not a soldier. He should never have been jailed in the first place. Those Rebs on Johnson Island are soldiers, one and all."

"And we need them, one and all."

Barbara remembered being told about General Grant's cancelling of all prisoner exchanges for that very reason—because the Confederacy was desperate for men while the Union was not.

"It would be a traitor's act for me to help you," she said slowly.

"It's a fair exchange." His words were clipped.

Her father's life for her own betrayal. Impossible to refuse. But once she gave her word she'd be committed—a Thackery never broke her word. She bit her lip. Was it worse to betray your country or break your word?

What would her father advise?

Barbara shook her head. This was one time she couldn't depend on what he'd say because she was certain he'd tell her to refuse outright and leave him in prison. She'd never agree to that.

"Does that head shake mean you're rejecting my offer?" Trevor asked.

"I wish I could refuse," she said bitterly, "but I can't. Not with my father's life in danger."

He smiled, reached for her hand and clasped it in his. "To seal the bargain," he said.

She drew her hand away, a new emotion churning inside her. Hate. She despised Trevor for forcing her into this distasteful agreement. Gazing at his triumphant smile, she vowed then and there to do everything she could to give him the comeuppance he deserved.

"Why the scowl?" he demanded. "You journeyed all the way to Richmond under perilous circumstances in an attempt to get your father released from prison. You risked your life more than once—this last time needlessly, but we'll ignore that. Now that I've handed you the key to setting him free you should be happy."

"I *am* happy he'll be freed."

"You don't show it." He rose from the chair. "Perhaps you'll feel better after a rest." He started to turn away, paused, and added, "If you need

241

anything, please let me know."

"I'd rather not remain in your house," she muttered.

"That's not negotiable." Impatience tinged his words. "You will stay here until we leave Richmond together and that's the end of any discussion about it." He reached into his pocket, took out her two handkerchiefs still wrapped around the gold coins and thunked them onto the bedside stand. "I believe these are yours," he said before striding from the room.

Barbara was still seething when Tibba arrived with their belongings stuffed into two carpetbags.

"I took what we'd been given," Tibba announced, as she set the bags onto the floor, "and it's no use to tell me I shouldn't have because I already did. We need the clothes."

"I don't like to use anything Francine gave me," Barbara said crossly.

"None of it came from her wardrobe except maybe the lavender bonnet. Lyla found what we've been wearing in trunks in the attic." She sat on the edge of the bed and laid her palm on Barbara's forehead. "No fever, thank the Lord."

"I bumped my head, that's all." Barbara grasped Tibba's hand, holding it tightly. "I—I stabbed one of the men. I had to. Oh, Tibba, it was so horrible. They were going to—to—" Her words trailed off as she began to sob.

Tibba held out her arms and Barbara wept on her shoulder. After a time Barbara eased away and fumbled a handkerchief from the pocket of her gown.

"I've been such a fool," she said.

"I feared that man who wrote the note was up to no good," Tibba said.

"Not only him. I've been a fool about Trevor, too. I should have known he didn't care a whit for me, that he only wanted to use me for his own nefarious purposes."

Tibba's eyes widened. "What's he done now?"

"He's making me sail with him to Bermuda where we'll board an English ship for Canada. Then, while he meets with vile Copperheads in Canada, I'll travel alone—or with you, rather—to Ohio where I'll be forced into becoming a traitor to the Union."

"I don't understand. How can he force you to be a traitor?"

Barbara told her. When she finished, Tibba shrugged.

"What's wrong with freeing those poor soldiers?" she asked. "All they did was fight for their cause."

"Their cause isn't mine!" Barbara cried. "The Rebs believe in slavery. One man owning another is wrong and you know it as well as I do. We went to war with the Rebs to free the slaves and anything I do to help the Confederate cause betrays my beliefs."

"He said we were at war because the North wouldn't let us go our own way."

"General Meachum owns slaves. His way—the South's way—means keeping those men and women and their children forever after as slaves. You said yourself most Virginia people behave as

243

though you're invisible and we both know that's because your mother was a Negro and Virginians think of anyone with Negro blood as a slave. Think how terrible it must be to be born a slave and always be treated as though you weren't quite human."

Tibba hugged herself. "I hope it's different in Ohio."

Barbara thought of how White Deer's village had been burned and the medicine woman killed. She remembered how some of the townspeople hated the Indians. Tibba wasn't an Indian but she was a different color. How well would they accept her? Barbara didn't know.

Trying her best to be honest and yet hold out hope, she said, "People where I come from, in northern Ohio, mostly never owned slaves. It's bound to be better than here in Virginia."

Tibba said nothing. After a few moments she rose from the bed and began unpacking the carpetbag. "I'm glad about your father. I know how worried you've been about him," she said as she shook out the gowns before hanging them in the wardrobe. "And I expect it'll be exciting to sail the ocean. I've never been on a ship. What's it like?"

Barbara was forced to admit she had only been in rowboats and canoes. "Just on Lake Erie, not the ocean." Despite her despair, her spirits lifted a little as she pictured a ship, white sails afurl, scudding before the wind.

"The captain must have given us his bed-room," Tibba observed after opening the wardrobe, "'cause his clothes are still here. I'll just push them aside—there'll be room enough."

A frisson shot along Barbara's spine. At this very moment she was lying on Trevor's bed!

"'Course he never told me I'd be sharing this room with you," Tibba went on, turning to look at Barbara. "Maybe *he* plans to."

Barbara sat bolt upright, ignoring the pounding in her head. "Never!" she cried.

Someone knocked and Tibba hurried to open the door. When she saw Trevor standing on the threshold Barbara flushed with anger. "This is your room," she said accusingly.

He ambled inside and handed something to Tibba, Barbara couldn't see what. "So it is," he said. "You're in my house, my room, my bed."

She swung her legs over the edge of the bed. "I'd prefer another room."

"Don't you dare get up," he warned. "Not until tomorrow. What's wrong with this room?" When she didn't answer immediately his expression changed to wry amusement.

"Are you afraid you're inconveniencing me by putting me out of my bed? Or are you worried that perhaps I won't be inconvenienced because I have no intention of sleeping elsewhere?"

"I—you—" she sputtered, furious.

Trevor laughed. "The only person you'll be sharing my bed with is Tibba—if you don't mind."

Barbara knew her face must be a ripe apple red. No man had ever made her angrier than Trevor Sandoe. "I expected that would be the arrange-

245

ment." Her words were coated in ice.

Trevor was still chuckling. "But you weren't sure, admit it."

She refused to.

Trevor strode to the bed, grasped her ankles and swung them back onto the coverlet, then pressed her shoulders until she was forced into lie down once again. "Be a good girl and rest like the doctor ordered. I won't be bothering you again until tomorrow." He stood looking down at her. "But maybe I should leave you a little something to remember me by."

Before she knew what he meant to do he bent, brushed his lips quickly over hers, turned and was gone, leaving her angry not only at him but at her own wild inner response to his all-too-brief kiss.

How was it possible to hate someone and long for his touch at the same time?

Chapter 15

Barbara stood with Tibba on the deck of the *Sir Walter*, a Confederate blockade runner out of Wilmington, North Carolina. The night sky was overcast, the moon hidden. There was no sound except the creaking of the ship, the whistle of the wind and the slap of the waves against the hull as the *Sir Walter* eased from the harbor into the open sea.

"A perfect night for slipping past the blasted Yanks," the ship's captain, a man named Prevorst, had told Trevor just before they weighed anchor.

By listening to everything said in her presence and by means of a few carefully worded questions, Barbara had learned that Wilmington was now the only seaport left open to the Rebs. The Union not only controlled all the rest of the Southern ports but also patrolled the waters off Wilmington, sinking every blockade runner they spotted.

The gray-painted *Sir Walter* wasn't the splendid many-rigged ship Barbara had envisioned. A long and narrow shallow-draft vessel with two short pole masts and two smokestacks that could be telescoped into stubs, she'd been built low and fast to outrun Union gunboats. Everything about her, including her gray color, was designed to make her inconspicuous.

"It's so dark; there's not even one lantern lit," Tibba complained to Barbara.

"You know why," Barbara reminded her. "The *Sir Walter*'s like a Rebel fox being hunted by Union hounds. We may never reach Bermuda if the gunboats spot us."

"Will we get there even if they don't? It's beyond my understanding how Captain Prevorst can be sure where he's going—if I can't see my hand in front of my face then he's as much in the dark as me."

Barbara didn't know any more about seafaring than Tibba, but Trevor had assured her the captain was an experienced blockade runner. She was trying to think of some way to reassure Tibba when a starburst of light blossomed low in the sky. A rumbling explosion made her gasp and grip the rail.

Tibba clutched her arm. "They found us!" she cried.

"Not yet." Trevor spoke from behind them. "That's a shell from the Fort Fisher battery. Odds are they're firing at a Yankee gunboat but that doesn't mean the Yanks have seen us. All the same, you two had best go inside the cabin."

"We won't have any idea what's happening," Barbara protested.

"Don't argue. Until we're in the clear the

248

captain has enough to worry about without two women on deck."

Though she hated the idea of being cooped up inside, Barbara realized she and Tibba might well be in the way and so she kept quiet, allowing Trevor to lead them to the tiny cabin she shared with Tibba, a cabin built directly onto the deck because of the vessel's shallow draft. Once inside, she groped about in the darkness—they'd been warned not to light the lantern—until she located the lower bunk. She sat on it, Tibba joined her, and they huddled together.

"I keep telling myself anything's better than being back with *him* in that valley," Tibba said, "but I can't say this is much better."

Aware that Tibba needed reassurance, Barbara made an effort to overcome her own fear. "I don't like waiting in the dark any more than you do but, remember, Captain Prevorst has survived so far. He must be as wily as a fox to stay afloat as long as he has."

"Not all foxes get away—not every time." Tibba sighed. "I wish now I'd told Harrison I'd meet him in Richmond—just so I'd know about being with a man before I die."

"We're not going to die!"

"With all my heart I hope you're right. But don't *you* ever wonder what it's like to lie with a man?"

"No." Even as she spoke, Barbara knew she wasn't telling the entire truth. Not with *a* man, no. But where Trevor was concerned she felt far more than curiosity, she longed to be loved by him in the way a man loved a woman. Her longing would never be fulfilled. Never. Because she refused to allow herself to be embraced by a hated enemy. Ever.

"We may as well try to get some rest," she said, wishing to set aside the uncomfortable subject of lovemaking. Recalling Tibba's fear of heights she added, "I'll take the upper bunk."

"How can I close my eyes when I don't know if I'll ever get to open them again?" Tibba asked plaintively. "But maybe you're right about lying down. Being asea's making me queasy."

The ship *was* rolling and pitching more than she had earlier, Barbara thought. She'd watched boats tossed by Lake Erie's waves during a storm and wondered how it must feel to be aboard. It looked as though she was about to find out.

Was a storm brewing? Or were the ocean's waters always rougher than the lake's? She shook her head. Whatever the answer, there was nothing she could do about it and so she climbed into the upper bunk, holding fast to avoid being thrown to the floor.

She hadn't removed anything except her hat, her gloves, and her boots. Stretching out on the hard mattress, she laid her woolen shawl over her and then pulled the single blanket up to ward off the damp chill, her head resting on a large and spongy but firm pillow.

On deck, the salt tang of the night air had been refreshing but, though the wind seeped through the cracks in the on-deck cabin, inside everything smelled of mold. Barbara closed her eyes, willing herself to ignore the smell, the rising whine of the wind, and the danger from Union gunboats.

Trevor's face sprang into her mind, his eyes glowing as they had that night in the cave when they'd lain in each other's arms in the firelight with only the thin fabric of her chemise between them. He'd caressed her so intimately, so wonderfully, in secret places where no man had touched her before, evoking a wild and wanton urgency within that made her forget everything except her need for him.

Just recalling that night brought back the desire, making her ache deep inside, making her desperate for the unforgettable sensation of his body pressed hard against hers, the heat of his lips on hers, the sweet caress of his hands. How was she to put him from her heart when the mere thought of him evoked this overwhelming longing?

Her reverie ended abruptly when the ship rolled sharply, almost flinging her from the bunk. Rain slapped against the cabin roof. Fumbling in the dark, she discovered a leather strap attached to the side of the bunk. After she found a hook on the opposite side, she strapped herself in, listening in dismay to the increasing tumult outside the cabin. An ocean storm! What were they called? Hurricanes, that was the word.

"Dear Lord, save us," Tibba moaned from below.

Silently, Barbara echoed the words. Had they outrun the Union gunboats only to become the victims of a hurricane?

As the storm grew worse, Barbara gave up trying to rest. Finally admitting she was too terrified to be alone, she climbed down and eased onto the lower bunk next to Tibba, who promptly flung her arms around Barbara and began to cry. Comforting Tibba helped to partially ease her own fear.

"I've been trying to remember all the prayers my mama taught me," Tibba said after a time. She spoke directly into Barbara's ear to be heard over the shriek of the wind and the wild rush of the waves against the ship's hulls. "*He* never prayed. I always reckoned it was because he thought he was God himself. Or maybe the devil."

"My father told me that becoming a doctor had made his faith in God stronger," Barbara said. "He realized the best he could do was help God heal."

"You're lucky to have a father like that."

More of Barbara's fear seeped away as she thought about her childhood days and how happy she and her father had been. She *was* lucky. Whatever happened, she'd made the right decision when she agreed to Trevor's plan. On the first of October, the day they'd left Richmond for Wilmington, he'd given her his word that her father had been freed and was receiving proper medical care.

Trevor might be a Reb and her enemy, she might hate him, but she believed he'd kept his part of their bargain. With the ship in the midst of this hurricane, she might not have to worry about keeping hers. But Papa was safe. Free.

Comforted by the knowledge and by the realization she wasn't alone, she grasped Tibba's hand. "I never expected to find a such a good friend as you," she said.

"I didn't reckon to ever *have* a friend," Tibba replied. "I'm glad we're together."

Barbara had no idea how much later it was when the cabin door was flung open and Trevor splashed inside holding a lantern. "All right in here?" he shouted over the roar of the storm as he struggled to close the door.

"Yes," Barbara answered. "Is it a hurricane?"

He nodded, holding onto the frame of the upper bunk as he peered down at them. "We're off course but Captain Prevorst thinks the ship can weather the storm."

Barbara stared at the water sloshing over the cabin floor and hoped the captain was right.

Trevor followed her glance. "That's from waves breaking over the gunwales. The hull's sound enough and every man aboard is a seasoned sailor who knows what to do." He smiled one-sidedly. "Except me. I've read lines where poets compared ships to horses but it's obvious a cavalryman's not much use on a ship. In fact, the captain ordered me inside this cabin before I was washed overboard. I hope you don't mind."

"We're not using the upper bunk," Tibba said.

Barbara masked her relief at having him near her by saying, "We must obey the captain's order."

Trevor raised an eyebrow at her but didn't comment. He removed the cabin's unlit lantern from a wall holder and set the lighted lantern in its place, then pulled himself onto the top bunk.

"You'll have to strap yourself in," she called up to him.

Whether it was having a light in the darkness or whether it was because Trevor was with them, Barbara's apprehension ebbed to the point where she dozed off, only to jerk awake time and again when the ship gave a particularly violent shudder. Tibba, snuggled next to her, slept more soundly. Above them, Trevor turned and shifted.

Finally the lantern winked out and, in the darkness, Barbara slept for a time. She woke to see dim gray light seeping into the cabin, hardly relieving the gloom. Outside, the storm continued to batter the ship. When she sat up she noticed water still sloshing over the floor.

She'd half-expected the hurricane to have passed over. Lake Erie's storms, while often vicious, rarely lasted more than a few hours.

Tibba stirred and opened her eyes. After a moment she said, "I thought I was having a bad dream but I reckon it's real enough."

"We're still afloat," Barbara pointed out. With the coming of the light, gloomy as it was, her spirits had risen. Wondering if Trevor was awake, she eased herself up to look, keeping a tight grip on the frame.

The upper bunk was vacant. He had left the cabin while she was sleeping. Disappointed, Barbara dropped back onto the lower bunk.

The day dragged on. Twice Trevor brought bread, cheese, and water to share with them but left after he ate, warning them not to set foot on deck if they valued their lives. Given the fury of the storm, Barbara didn't need his warning. Neither she nor Tibba had any intention of leaving the cabin. They passed the time by telling one another of their childhoods and once again Barbara blessed her good fortune in being the daughter of a wonderful man like her father.

The day never brightened. As the grudging light

was fading into true darkness, a grinding roar startled Barbara. The ship bucked and shuddered in what she was certain had to be death throes. She and Tibba clung to one another in panic, not knowing what to do.

The cabin door slammed open and Trevor called to them, "Stay where you are. We're grounded on a reef—no way to get off. The captain believes the storm's easing and he thinks we're near shore but there's no chance of getting there until the sea calms. The cabin's as safe a place as any for now." He forced the door shut again.

Barbara wished he'd given her a chance to ask how badly the ship had been damaged when she ran aground. If the ship broke apart, they'd be at the sea's mercy.

"He didn't say what shore," Tibba said. "Is it Bermuda?"

"I don't know. The captain said last night we were off course. This reef may be near one of the other islands in the Caribbean Sea." Though Barbara had located Bermuda on a map as soon as she knew where they were going, she was too apprehensive to be able to recall what islands were close to Bermuda. Or if any *were* close.

A reddish light flared briefly through the two tiny windows of the cabin. After a few moments of wondering what had happened now, Barbara remembered that lake boats carried distress rockets to shoot off in an emergency so other boats might come to their aid. She told Tibba about the rockets.

"Maybe the captain's hoping for help from the shore," she finished.

"In this storm?" Tibba asked. "If we can't get to

shore, how can anyone on shore get to us?''

Barbara had no answer. She fished her boots from the storage net attached to the wall, tugged them on, and sloshed over to peer through the slit of a window. In the near darkness, she thought she saw the glimmer of a far-off light but it disappeared before she could be certain. She hadn't yet gone back to the bunk when Trevor burst into the room, a coil of rope in his hand.

He grabbed one of the pillows from the bunk, tore off the cover and thrust it at Barbara. ''Hold this to your chest,'' he ordered, ''and I'll lash it on. The pillows are cork so they'll float.''

''What's happening?'' Barbara's voice quavered.

''Ship's breaking up, it's every man for himself. Take your boots off, they'll weigh you down.'' He cut the rope and touched her cheek briefly with the back of his hand before turning away.

''Quick, Tibba, grab your pillow and come here,'' he snapped.

''What about you?'' Barbara cried.

''I'm a good swimmer,'' he said as he tied the only other pillow to Tibba. ''After the rocket went up we saw a light from the shore. I'll show you the direction when we get on deck.''

Barbara was a fair swimmer herself, but she doubted if even the strongest of swimmers would have a chance in such stormy waters. They were doomed, cork pillows or not.

As Trevor herded them from the cabin they climbed the quivering deck, now angled upward. Barbara noticed a great chunk of rock had smashed through the hull near the bow, impaling the ship.

The wind whipped her hair over her face as she

peered into the darkness toward where she thought she'd seen the light in the same direction Trevor was pointing. It took her a moment or two to realize that, though waves splashed over the gunwales, the rain had stopped. She could see no light in the darkness.

"Hang onto the mast and wait here," Trevor told them, hooking first Barbara's, then Tibba's arm around the small pole mast. "I'll be back as soon as possible." He strode away.

Barbara, who'd gone past terror to numbness, was hardly aware of the water pouring at intervals over the sides of the ship, drenching her and tugging at her ankles as it ran down the sloping deck toward the stern. She heard Tibba moaning, heard the cries of sailors, invisible in the darkness, heard the splash of the water, and tasted the salt on her tongue but nothing had any meaning to her. Only Trevor tugged weakly at her thoughts— where was he? Was he all right?

The numbness lasted until a wall of water deluged her. Tibba's cut-off shriek rang in her ears and Barbara grabbed for her friend with her free hand only to feel the fabric of Tibba's gown torn away from her fingers. She screamed Tibba's name and let go of the mast, groping for her friend. The water caught her, sweeping her up, tumbling her over and over, choking her until she had the sense to hold her breath.

Eventually her head bobbed free and she gasped in air, coughing up the water she'd swallowed. Confused and frightened, with no idea where she was, she tried to understand what had happened. Even in the darkness one fact became rapidly clear—she was no longer aboard what remained of the *Sir Walter*. The second thing she understood was that she was floating in the sea with the aid of the cork pillow.

With no idea of where the shore was, all she could do was keep her head above the water and allow the waves to carry her wherever they would.

Much later, almost beyond hope, Barbara felt her feet, then her knees, drag along a hard surface. It took her a long time to realize she was touching bottom—and that a light glowed ahead in the darkness. She was all but beyond feeling relief. With great effort she dragged herself erect and began wading through the surf, her eyes fixed on the light.

When the water reached her ankles, she tripped over something and fell headlong. About to crawl free of the object, she belatedly realized it was a human body. The long hair and the skirts she felt under her fingers told her it was a woman.

"Tibba!" she cried.

There was no response.

With her last ounce of strength, she got her hands under Tibba's armpits and dragged the limp body free of the water. Kneeling beside her, Barbara frantically tried to find the pulse under Tibba's jaw but could not.

"No," she mumbled, tears running down her face, "you can't be dead. No, I won't let you die."

Trying desperately to remember what her father had said about drownings, Barbara turned Tibba onto her face, her head turned to one side, and began pressing the palms of her hands against Tibba's back as hard as she could.

"Live!" she begged. "Live, Tibba, live!"

Yellow light illuminated Tibba's cheek, showed the trickle of water oozing from her mouth. In Barbara's overwrought state, she didn't understand someone had arrived with a lantern until he spoke.

"Allow me, mademoiselle."

Barbara gaped up at the man who promptly knelt beside her and set the lantern onto the sand.

"Dr. Phillipe Dusharme," he said, nodding. Then he shoved her gently aside, flipped Tibba onto her back and bent over her.

Barbara sat back on her heels, staring uncomprehendingly as Dr. Dusharme put his mouth to Tibba's. What was he doing? Her mind, working sluggishly, finally worked out that he must be breathing into Tibba's water-clogged lungs.

When at last Tibba coughed, Barbara thought it was the most wonderful sound she'd ever heard.

"She's alive," Barbara babbled. "Alive! Tibba's alive!"

"Barbara!"

She swung around, unsure where the call came from. Then she saw him stumbling toward her and staggered to her feet, crying his name. "Trevor!"

He collapsed before she reached him.

"It seems I have yet another patient, *n'est-ce pas?*" Dr. Dusharme said from behind her. Putting a whistle to his lips, he blew three times, the shrill sound carrying easily above the roar of the surf.

A few minutes later the Negroes came, twelve men, marching with the stiff gait of soldiers. They stopped in front of the doctor, waiting, their faces devoid of expression. Speaking French, the doctor gave them orders, telling them, or so she thought, to carry the man and the two women to the house.

"I can walk," she protested weakly.

To no avail. She was lifted by Dr. Dusharme onto a seat made by the crossed hands of two of the Negroes and they bore her off. She clung to their arms to avoid falling, admitting to herself that she was grateful to be carried. Before they reached the house, though, she couldn't help but notice how cold their dark skin was.

Of course, the night was cool. In her drenched clothes, she was shivering.

The Negro men carrying her stopped at the front door of a low, rambling house covered with flowering vines.

"Those of you carrying the man and the women may enter," Dr. Dusharme told them. He spoke slowly and distinctly, otherwise Barbara, with her limited French, wouldn't have been able to translate his words.

Minutes later, following their master's orders, the men carrying Barbara deposited her on her feet beside a four-poster bed draped with mosquito netting. They turned and left while she was thanking them. Almost immediately a woman with light brown skin glided into the room. Unlike the men, her dark eyes shone with curiosity.

Though she also spoke French, Barbara understood that her name was Yvette and she'd been told to obey Barbara's every request.

"Where am I?" Barbara asked. "Is this the island of Bermuda?"

"No, no, you are in Jamaica," Yvette said as she handed Barbara a towel to dry her hair.

While Yvette helped her take off the wet clothes and slip into a white nightgown, Barbara tried in vain to recall exactly where in the Caribbean the island of Jamaica was.

"Tonight you sleep," Yvette advised, "tomorrow a bath."

"My friends?" Barbara asked, searching for the right French words. "The man, the woman—where are they?"

"Others attend to them."

"I must make certain they're all right."

"Yes, after the doctor finishes with them. While you wait, I bring you refreshment."

Barbara wanted to protest, wanted to march out the door and search for Trevor and Tibba but exhaustion had caught up with her. Marching was completely beyond her, staggering was about all she'd be able to manage. And she didn't want to be in the doctor's way. When Yvette brought in a steaming cup on a wooden tray, Barbara sipped at the liquid eagerly, believing it was tea. Instead, it was a fruit drink of a kind unfamiliar to her and she started to set the cup aside.

"The doctor wishes you to drink the tisane," Yvette said. "It will help you."

Barbara took up the cup again, reluctant to disobey the man who'd proved to be their Good Samaritan. The liquid was too sweet for her taste but she swallowed most of it obediently.

"Lie back on the bed," Yvette urged, "and I will see if the doctor is finished treating your friends." As she spoke, she pulled down the bed covers.

261

Perhaps if she rested for a few minutes and gave the tisane time to work, she'd feel stronger, Barbara thought. She stretched out on the bed and closed her eyes. . . .

She flitted from branch to branch of a tree, fluffing her feathers when she lit for a moment. It bothered her that the tree wasn't a pine but of some variety she didn't recognize with green leaves the size of dinner plates and wine-dark flowers far larger than her tiny body, even with her wings outstretched.

Sensing something approaching, she flew to the top of the tree and watched a doe trot between the vast, dark trunks of the strange forest trees. The doe wasn't the usual brown, she was pure white. She stopped and her pink eyes stared up at Barbara.

"I see you, Snow Bird," the doe said. "You must be careful for things are not what they seem."

Before her eyes, the deer changed into a fox, his black-tipped red brush held high. "Bird of winter, listen," he said. "There are worse fates than drowning." The fox vanished as though he'd never existed.

The shadow of an eagle startled her, sending her fluttering to a lower branch, close to the trunk. The eagle drifted closer and spiralled above the exotic tree.

"I would never harm, you, little one," the eagle said, his white head shining in the sun. "But beware. Not all are like me."

Wishing she flew with him, she watched the eagle's powerful wings carry him higher and higher until she could no longer see even a speck in the blue of the sky. Made uneasy by the warnings and by the too-sweet perfume of the blossoms, she tried to decide what to do.

"Fly!" a hawk called to her. "Fly away before it's too late!"

She looked to see where he was but a ring of the purple-red flowers now surrounded her, reaching malevolent tendrils to bind her. Once she was helpless, the largest of the flowers drew her toward its malignant maw. She struggled in vain to free herself, hearing the swoop of the hawk's wings as he flew into the tree, hearing his scream of rage when he attacked the devouring blossom.

"You can't have her," the hawk cried. "She's mine! Mine. Mine!"

Barbara awoke with a start, the hawk's cry still echoing in her head. To her amazement the sun was shining; she'd slept the night through. A warm, perfumed breeze blew in through the louvered windows, dispelling the remnants of the nightmare. But as her head began to clear, anxiety sprang anew.

What had happened to Trevor and Tibba while she slept?

Chapter 16

Barbara pushed the mosquito netting aside and eased herself from the bed. When she stood on her feet, a momentary wave of dizziness surprised her and she gripped the bedpost until her vertigo passed. Even then she didn't feel herself—not ill exactly, but logy and thickheaded with a touch of nausea.

She was reminded of the time she'd sprained her ankle as a child and her father had given her laudanum to ease the pain. She'd disliked the aftereffects of the drug so much that she'd told him she'd rather suffer the pain than take another dose.

At the washstand, she rinsed her face with water, hoping to clear her head a bit, then looked around the room. Her clothes were nowhere in sight—even her red petticoat with the two gold coins sewn into the hem was gone.

In the wardrobe she found a white dressing robe, pulled it over the cotton nightgown, padded across the room and opened the door. Before she did anything else, she must find Trevor and Tibba. Where were they? Somewhere in the house, of course, she had no reason for her uneasiness.

She stood in a corridor facing a closed door opposite hers. Another set of closed doors was just along the hall. What now? Barbara thought a moment, wishing her mind were clearer. Finally she took a deep breath, opened her mouth and called, "Trevor! Tibba!"

Nothing happened for several moments. She was getting ready to call again when the door across from hers opened and she saw Tibba. At the same time, Yvette appeared at the entrance to the corridor.

Paying no attention to the maid, Barbara rushed to Tibba and flung her arms around her. "Are you all right?" she asked.

Tibba leaned against her. "I feel as weak as coffee made from used grounds. The doctor said I was as good as drowned. He told me he brought me back from the dead."

Though Dr. Dusharme's statement was more or less true, a shiver ran along Barbara's spine. *Brought back from the dead.* The words chilled her, adding to her unease.

"The doctor says you both should be resting," Yvette scolded as she came up to them.

"Where's Trevor?" Barbara asked, ignoring Yvette's advice. "Captain Sandoe." She searched for the correct French words. "The man who was with us. I must see him."

"He's sleeping," Yvette said. "As you should be."

"Take me to him," Barbara demanded.

"In good time. First—"

"Now!" Barbara pulled away from Tibba. "I will see him *now*."

"The doctor will not like—"

"I don't care. I demand to see Trevor."

Yvette raised her eyebrows. "If you insist. But she—" Yvette pointed at Tibba—"must rest."

"I'll wait for you in my room," Tibba told Barbara.

Yvette led Barbara from the corridor across a large, bright entry and along another hall where she opened the third door to the left and gestured for Barbara to enter.

Trevor lay on a canopied bed much like the one in Barbara's room. She ran to him, pushed the netting aside and sat on the edge of the bed. He didn't move. She put the back of her hand to his cheek to check for fever, eyeing the bandage around his head with apprehension. His skin was warm but not hot.

"Trevor?" she said.

A muscle in his face twitched but he didn't open his eyes.

"Trevor!"

He didn't rouse. Alarmed, Barbara looked around at Yvette, still standing in the doorway. "What's the matter with him?"

Yvette stared at her blankly and, realizing she'd spoken in English, Barbara repeated her question in French.

"You must ask the doctor," Yvette said. "He told me the patient was not to be disturbed but you

266

insisted—" She broke off and shrugged.

Biting her lip, Barbara stared at Trevor, trying to recall everything she knew about injuries to the head. He seemed to be in a stupor. Most likely he'd suffered a concussion. Her father had once mentioned that the longer the stupor lasted, the more serious the injury to the brain.

"You must come away and allow the patient to rest," Yvette said. "For his sake. Dr. Dusharme will be most upset that you're disturbing the captain."

Though she hated to leave Trevor, Barbara was aware she could do nothing to help him. She touched his cheek again and this time he mumbled something unintelligible.

"What?" she bent over him, ear to his mouth. "This is Barbara, Trevor. What did you say?"

"Help," he mumbled. Or at least that's what she thought the word was, she couldn't be sure.

She waited, hoping he'd open his eyes but he didn't. Nor did he say anything else, even when she called his name.

After a few minutes, Barbara decided she must get dressed and find the doctor. She told Trevor she was leaving and would return soon but there was no sign he'd taken in her words. When she reached the door she looked back but he hadn't moved.

A tin bath half-filled with warm water was in her bedroom when she walked in. Politely declining Yvette's help, Barbara quickly bathed and washed the salt water from her hair. Clean underclothes and a fresh gown awaited her after she'd climbed from the tub and dried herself. Since

267

she had nothing else to wear, she donned the clothes—a short shift, a single petticoat, and a high-waisted ankle-length white-on-white embroidered gown with a low neck and short sleeves. It was much like the gown Yvette wore, obviously meant for the island's warm weather.

"Where are my clothes?" Barbara asked as she slipped a pair of flat-soled leather sandals onto her bare feet.

"I will return them when they are clean," Yvette assured her. Barbara could only hope the two gold coins would still be in the hem when she got the red petticoat back. It was all she had.

Before they'd left Richmond, she'd handed Trevor the money he'd recovered from the two thieves who'd stolen it from her, asking him to give it to her father. Later, Trevor had assured her the gold had reached Dr. Thackery.

Remembering her manners, she said, after a moment's search for the right words, "It is kind of the doctor to take us in." How she wished she were more fluent in French! "Does everyone in Jamaica speak French?" she asked Yvette.

"No. Most are English. The doctor and I, we are not; we come from Haiti."

Haiti. Barbara thought she recognized the name of another Caribbean island but she wished she'd studied the map more carefully. "The men last night," she said, "the ones who carried us to this house—they are from Haiti, too?"

To Barbara's surprise, Yvette shuddered. "I don't like to speak of them," she muttered.

Her attitude recalled Barbara's own uneasy

feelings about the men. "They seemed like well-trained troops," she said tentatively.

Yvette shook her head, refusing to discuss the matter further. "The woman, Tibba," she said. "Tibba is your maid?"

"No. Tibba is my friend. She's not a slave; she's a free woman of color. I don't require the services of a maid."

Yvette was obviously taken aback. "Ah, but you must accept *my* assistance. Otherwise the doctor will be annoyed."

Barbara shrugged. Though she couldn't put her finger on the reason, something about Yvette, or the house, or the doctor—perhaps all three—disturbed her. For one thing, she was all but convinced she'd been dosed with laudanum in last night's tisane and she couldn't help but wonder if Tibba and Trevor had also been given the drug.

Well meant as the laudanum might have been, Barbara preferred to know when she was given medicine. Wary of volunteering more information than she had to, she decided not to reveal her suspicions for the time being. Except, possibly, to Tibba.

Tibba was not in her room when Barbara went to find her.

"She washed and dressed earlier," Yvette said reprovingly. "She's having breakfast with the doctor. I will take you to them."

Since she was eager to question Dr. Dusharme about Trevor's condition, Barbara followed Yvette willingly, passing through louvered doors into a courtyard where a table was set under a tall, spreading tree with large and glossy dark green leaves. Unfamiliar orange-red fruits hung temptingly from the branches. She noticed many colorful birds fluttering among the leaves, but the greater part of her attention was on Tibba and the doctor who sat side by side at the table. As she approached she heard the doctor laugh.

"You are most refreshing, mademoiselle," Dr. Dusharme said to Tibba. "It's not often I meet a belle so enchanting as you. I've had interesting objects wash onto my shores following a hurricane but never before such a fascinating jewel."

Barbara raised her eyebrows at his extravagant compliments. Not that her friend wasn't pretty, because she was. Tibba was also intelligent, but from the moon-calf way she was gazing into his eyes, her wits seemed to have deserted her.

"Bonjour," Barbara said briskly.

Dr. Dusharme rose to his feet, smiling. "Ah, mademoiselle, good morning. Do join us." As he seated her he added, "I find myself overwhelmed that you two lovely American ladies speak French. Nevertheless, I prefer to speak English with you so I may better my command of the tongue."

"Your English is far better than my French," Barbara told him. "I do thank you for your hospitality as well as your medical skills. I've recovered from my near drowning and it seems Tibba has, too. But Captain Sandoe—how badly is he hurt?"

The doctor sighed. "The captain has, I fear, a most serious head injury."

270

"Is his brain concussed?"

Dr. Dusharme looked astonished. "Is it possible you know something of medicine?"

"I've learned a few things from my father—he's a doctor. How serious is Trevor's—uh, Captain Sandoe's—concussion?"

"It is too soon to tell. As you must know, any injury to the brain is sometimes fatal."

Barbara drew in her breath, her hands flying to her mouth as she half-rose from her seat, determined to hurry back to Trevor immediately.

"No, no," the doctor said, pressing her gently back into the chair. "You must remain here. I didn't intend to alarm you. The captain's condition won't change in the next hour or so, perhaps not for the next day or two. I insist you relax and eat with us." He clapped his hands and a black-garbed Negro woman standing in the tree's shadow stepped forward, startling Barbara.

"Mimba, you will serve the lady."

Of the sliced fresh fruits on the serving platter Mimba proferred, Barbara recognized only pineapple. She hesitated.

"Try the mango," Tibba suggested, pointing to a reddish-orange fruit. "It's delicious."

What Barbara really wanted to do was return to Trevor's side, but she decided she had to make some pretense of eating to satisfy the doctor.

"The captain, he is your fiancé, *n'est ce pas?*" Dr. Dusharme asked.

"No, nothing like that," Barbara said hastily. "Only a—a friend." Which wasn't exactly the

271

truth but the relationship, besides being none of the doctor's business, was too complicated to explain.

"Still, one senses you are *trés* fond of the young man. Naturally, I will do what I can for him."

Though his words were harmless enough, something in the doctor's manner set Barbara's teeth on edge. She glanced at Tibba and frowned when she saw her friend gazing raptly at him.

"I understand you come from Haiti," Barbara said.

The doctor hesitated an instant before replying and she thought she saw an annoyed glint in his dark eyes. "That is true. Do you know the island of Haiti?"

"Not any better than I do Jamaica." Barbara wasn't certain why she felt she had to reply cautiously, why she felt it important to convey as little information as possible.

To avoid his probing look, she tried the mango, found it tasty, and finished the slice, along with two slices of pineapple. She was dabbing juice from her lips with a napkin when something popped above her head and a small yellow kernel fell onto the table.

"Good, good," Dr. Dusharme said. "The akee are ripe." He gestured at the red fruit on the overhanging branches.

Several of them, Barbara saw, had burst open, revealing yellow kernels attached to black seeds.

"Akees are poisonous, you know," the doctor went on, "until they are perfectly ripe. Then they're delicious if properly prepared. But one must wait until they break open of their own accord or risk possible death."

Barbara barely controlled her shiver, her appetite completely gone. Jamaica was proving to be full of unexpected perils.

"If you've finished eating," the doctor said, "I will show you the grounds."

"Thank you, I'd enjoy seeing them but I must go to the captain first." Barbara spoke firmly. "I'd like you to come with me, Tibba, if you will, please."

Tibba blinked at her, shot a sidelong glance at the doctor and then nodded somewhat reluctantly. "If you wish."

When they left, Barbara had the feeling she was all but dragging Tibba from the doctor's side.

"You behave as though that man has mesmerized you," she scolded when they were out of earshot.

Tibba stared at her indignantly. "I find him charming."

"Obviously. I thought you didn't trust men."

"Dr. Dusharme is a gentleman," Tibba replied coolly.

"So is Harrison Chambers, as I recall."

For a moment Tibba looked confused. "Harrison. I'd all but forgotten about him. How strange. I confess I do feel rather odd—like I'm floating."

Barbara said nothing more but as soon as they were shut in Tibba's room, she put her hands on her friend's shoulders and stared not into her eyes but at them. Tibba's pupils, she saw, were much

273

smaller than they should be in a room where the light was shut away by curtains pulled across the windows.

In darkness, the pupils of the eyes widened to take in as much light as possible—Tibba's did not. Opium, Barbara remembered, was one of the drugs that constricted the pupil of the eye. And laudanum was derived from opium.

"Did you have a fruit drink last night?" she asked Tibba.

Tibba frowned. "I'm not sure. What happened last night is all blurred in my mind. I think someone might have given me something to drink. And Yvette did bring me a fruit drink before breakfast that was very refreshing. Why do you ask?"

Barbara couldn't decide what to say. The doctor had no reason to dose Tibba with laudanum again, yet he must have because it was hard to believe Yvette would act on her own. Why would he do such a thing?

She didn't dare mention any of her suspicions to Tibba, given her friend's present condition. Under the influence of the drug she might well tell everything she knew if she were questioned. And it didn't help that she seemed to be unduly fascinated by the doctor. Barbara wouldn't put it past him to actually *be* mesmerizing Tibba.

"Would you do me a favor?" she asked Tibba.

"You know I will."

Barbara chose her words with care. "Before you drink anything Yvette hands you, please wait for me to join you."

Tibba waved a hand. "I'll do that."

"If I'm not around, come and find me."

Tibba smiled. "I know where you'll be. With the captain."

Much as Barbara longed to share her worries with someone, she knew she couldn't trust Tibba—neither to talk to nor to be of any assistance. She'd have to do what she could alone.

"We'll both go and see Trevor now," she told Tibba.

"You don't want me along," Tibba protested. "I'd rather lie down."

Barbara wasn't about to let Tibba out of her sight any more than she could help. "You can rest when we return." Taking her friend's arm, she started for Trevor's room.

In the second corridor she counted three doors down, opened that door and stopped short, gaping. Not only was the bed empty, it was freshly made up, as though no one had ever used it.

Had she counted the doors wrong? Releasing Tibba, Barbara flung open each door along the corridor, one by one. All the rooms were empty. At the corridor's end she tried the knob of the last door and found it locked.

"Trevor!" she cried, banging on the wood. "Trevor, are you in there?"

"Is doctor's rooms." Mimba spoke from behind her. "Just fe him."

Barbara whirled. "Where's Trevor? The sick man." She pointed toward the room he'd occupied earlier. "The man who was in there."

Mimba cast a look over her shoulder. "Is him

275

gone," she mumbled.

Barbara hung on to the few shreds of patience she possessed. "I know he's gone. Where?"

Mimba put a finger to her lips and gestured with her head, indicating that Barbara should follow her. Grabbing the confused Tibba's hand and pulling her along, Barbara trailed Mimba back to the third room. Mimba shut them inside, then scooted across the room to French doors, opened them, stepped outside, and ducked into a mass of greenery, disappearing from view.

"I'm so tired," Tibba complained, her steps lagging. "I can't walk any farther."

Barbara sat her in a cane-seated rocker near the open French doors, cautioning her to stay there, and hurried after Mimba. She found the black woman waiting for her in a tiny clearing within a ring of flowering bushes. Mimba motioned her closer, then put her mouth to Barbara's ear.

"Is bad fe talk, that house. Bad fe live. Is doctor make dead walk, make dead work. Is doctor take me man fe him grave, make me man's spirit wander in darkness. Is me tell master, him good man, send me 'long to this bad house fe work, give me chance fe get me man back in him grave where him belong. Is rest him spirit, then. Is doctor make captain-man same like my man. Haiti folk say zombie. Jamaica, me, us say walking dead."

Barbara pulled away to stare at her, trying to make sense of the story.

"Is you see dead walk come darkness," Mimba warned. "Is you see them once already before—them carry you here."

She must mean the marching men! Barbara swallowed. Impossible as she knew it was for the dead to walk, she couldn't deny there'd been something eerie about last night's blank-faced army of Negro men. Dr. Dusharme must have put them in some kind of trance, sapping their will, perhaps with drugs, so that they became mindless, able only to obey him.

Zombies. The very word raised the hair on her nape. And Mimba had said the doctor meant to make Trevor one of what she called the walking dead. Never!

She grasped Mimba's arm. "Where did they take the captain?"

"Is carry him fe sea caves." Mimba pointed. "Darkness come, is me show the way. Us go then. Is me fetch salt."

"Salt?"

"Put salt on them tongue, walking dead fall down. Is us give my man Cuffee salt, him zombie no more. Him dead already once, dead for really then. Him at rest."

Barbara shuddered, frightened. What was Dr. Dusharme planning to do to Trevor? He must be stopped! "Can't we go now?" she demanded.

Mimba shook her head. "Doctor see, him stop us. Is bad happen then."

Barbara could well believe bad would happen if Dr. Dusharme discovered her with Mimba. At the same time she was worried sick about Trevor and found it hard to have to wait until nightfall.

"Doctor, him tell you captain-man dead," Mimba warned. "Is me see when them carry captain-man off. Him breathe, him mumble, him try fe fight. Is us save him come darkness."

Dear God, I hope so, Barbara thought desperately, terrified of what might happen to Trevor in the hours before they arrived.

"Is you go back in house," Mimba advised. "No talk. When darkness come, me come."

As soon as she stepped through the French doors Barbara noticed Tibba wasn't in the rocker where she'd left her. Tibba wasn't in the room, nor in the corridor. Hoping against hope Tibba had wandered away to her own room, Barbara hurried there.

She flung open the door to Tibba's room and gasped with relief when she saw her friend curled up on the bed. Running to her side, she laid a hand on Tibba's shoulder.

"Wake up!" she said urgently.

Tibba opened her eyes and gazed so blankly that a chill ran along Barbara's spine.

"Tibba?" she whispered. "Say something, Tibba."

There was no reply.

Barbara shook her friend's shoulder. "Tibba, what's wrong?"

"She's exhausted, that's all." The doctor spoke from the open doorway. "She needs rest. It takes time to recover from drowning."

"You mean almost drowning." Despite her determination not to show fear, Barbara's voice quavered. She rose and faced him. "Trevor's not in his room. Where is he?"

"My dear child, I was on my way to find you

278

when I heard you speaking to your friend. I regret to tell you—" He broke off, entered the room and crossed to her.

Barbara stiffened, preparing herself for the words Mimba had warned her she'd hear.

Dr. Dusharme laid a gentle hand on her shoulder. She looked up at the concerned expression on his thin aristocratic face and for a moment she wondered how what Mimba had told her could possibly be true. Then she glanced at his eyes. No sympathy lay in their dark and glittering depths.

"I fear the captain is gone," the doctor said softly. "I regret that my efforts to save him were to no avail."

Braced though she was, the words shocked her. Barbara drew in her breath and tears sprang to her eyes. She eased from under his hand and sat on Tibba's bed, her head bowed.

Trevor's not dead, she told herself over and over. He's alive. Not dead. Alive. But tremors she couldn't control shook her.

"You must come with me," Dr. Dusharme said, repeating the words when she didn't respond. How soft his voice was, how seductive, reaching through her apprehension to tug at her, urging her to do his bidding, to come with him.

Beside her, Tibba stirred and started to sit up.

"No, Tibba," the doctor said. "I'm speaking to Barbara. You must rest."

Tibba immediately lay back down.

Barbara swallowed, now convinced Tibba was completely under his control. Whatever she did, she mustn't leave Tibba. Summoning all her will,

Barbara made herself stretch out alongside Tibba. Holding a handkerchief to her eyes, she said, "I'll stay here and rest with my friend." She hoped he'd believe the quiver in her voice was from grief instead of fear. "Tibba's the only one who can understand how I feel."

Though she didn't look at him, Barbara knew he still stood beside the bed gazing down at her. She managed to imitate a sob, dabbing at her eyes with the handkerchief. If he insisted on her leaving she vowed he'd have to drag her off.

She hardly dared believe her luck when she heard him walk away. A moment later the door closed. Risking a peek, she saw he was really gone. Limp with relief, she didn't care whether he'd been taken in by her performance or had decided not to force obedience—what mattered was he'd left her alone with Tibba. Before he returned, she had to find a way to rouse Tibba from the trance she seemed to be in.

When no amount of talking or shaking altered Tibba's blank stare, Barbara steeled herself. Muttering that she was sorry to hurt her, she slapped her friend hard. Tibba's head snapped to one side but she remained oblivious.

Barbara sighed in despair, unable to think of any way to undo whatever Dr. Dusharme had done to Tibba. What would happen tonight? Would she have to leave Tibba here at his mercy while she followed Mimba to the sea caves? Barbara was pacing up and down the room, trying to come up with some other solution, when someone knocked at the door.

"Who is it?" she demanded.

Though she hadn't invited her to enter, Yvette opened the door. "I've brought you lunch," she said and gestured behind, her stepping aside while Mimba pushed a wheeled cart into the room.

Barbara stared at the steaming dishes, fighting not to show her suspicion of their contents. Who knew what drugs might be in the food?

"Island dish called rundown, missy," Mimba said reassuringly. "Salt fish and akee."

Barbara remembered the persimmonlike fruits she'd seen on the large tree in the courtyard. She also recalled all too well what the doctor had said about akees. Mimba seemed to be telling her the food was safe to eat but how could she be certain?

Concealing her fears as best she could, Barbara said, "Thank you. I'll serve Tibba and myself."

Mimba nodded and departed but Yvette lingered until inspiration struck Barbara. "Won't you join us for lunch?" she asked Yvette.

"No, no, I have eaten," Yvette said. "I only wish to make certain Tibba drinks the cordial the doctor has prepared for her." Yvette reached for a glass on the cart as she spoke.

Barbara pulled the cart toward the bed, putting the glass out of Yvette's reach, saying, "I'll be happy to see that Tibba takes what she's supposed to."

Yvette hesitated. "I must see to this personally."

Barbara feigned surprise. "Am I, Tibba's best friend, not to be trusted to do what's best for her?"

"I do not mean to accuse you of—"

"Then please allow us some privacy." Barbara's tone was imperious.

Reluctantly, Yvette left. Barbara immediately pushed the cart to the French doors that opened to the outside, dumped the contents of the plates and glasses into the shrubbery and replaced the dishes on the cart. As she was about to reclose the French doors she heard the drums.

The deep throbbing rhythm seem to surround her, seeping into her pores until it reached the very marrow of her bones, frightening and beckoning her at the same time. A high-pitched melody from some flute-like instrument rose above the drumbeats, a summoning song that made her want to follow the tune to its source.

Barbara gritted her teeth against the urge and again started to swing the doors shut. A hand fell over hers, stopping her. Tibba's.

"I'm coming," Tibba said, looking not at her but through the French doors toward the sound of the drums and the flute. "I hear and I obey."

Chapter 17

Barbara caught Tibba's arm, pulled her back into the room and closed the French doors. Though her friend didn't fight, her face turned toward the sound of the drums and the flute. Barbara had no idea who was making the music or where it came from, but she knew Dr. Dusharme was responsible and she was determined to prevent Tibba from answering the flute's summons.

How could she stop her friend? Remembering there were no outside doors in her room, she grasped Tibba's hand firmly and all but dragged her out of the room into her own. Now, at least, there was only the one door. The song of the flute was fainter here but the throb of the drums was disturbing, causing her to think in circles. And all the while Tibba kept trying to pull away.

"I must go," Tibba said, over and over.

Barbara sat her on the bed, holding her there by putting an arm around her. "No, you must *not* go. He means you harm."

"He calls me. I must go."

A desperate inspiration struck Barbara. Though in her drugged state Tibba refused to believe the truth—that Dr. Dusharme was evil—perhaps she could shake Tibba's determination to go to him by frightening her with lies. Barbara would try anything to keep her friend from harm, and she was well aware what man Tibba feared the most.

"You may believe Dr. Dusharme is the one you're going to, but you're wrong," Barbara told her. "The man who calls you isn't the doctor, he's your father—he's General Meachum. He's the man who killed your mother."

Seeing Tibba blink, she leaned closer, staring into her friend's eyes. "Meachum, Meachum, Meachum!" she chanted. "General Meachum calls you. Your father means to kill you as he killed your mother."

"Not my father," Tibba whispered.

"Yes, he is. He's the one who calls you. He's General Meachum. Go to him and you'll die."

Tears welled in Tibba's eyes and rolled down her cheeks. "I'm afraid," she wailed. "I have to go but I'm scared of him."

Barbara lifted a freshly laundered handkerchief from the nightstand and handed it to Tibba. "Never mind wiping your eyes," she ordered, "tear this into strips. Now!"

At first she thought Tibba wasn't going to obey her but finally, slowly and clumsily, her friend ripped the handkerchief into four pieces. Wadding the small pieces of cloth into two balls, Barbara stuffed one into Tibba's left ear. Before she crammed the other into Tibba's right ear, she whispered, "Don't forget who he really is. General Meachum. Your father."

She wasn't sure if earplugs would help. Even if Tibba couldn't hear the summoning, her friend might still try to get away and go to the doctor. While Barbara was deciding what to do, she noticed her boots, missing earlier, were back, neatly set on the floor beside the wardrobe. Leaving Tibba on the bed, she hurried to the wardrobe, opened it, and found that not only had her gown been cleaned and returned but also the red petticoat. She felt the hem—the two coins were still inside!

Not that money was any use if they couldn't get away from Dr. Dusharme's house. She turned to look at Tibba who'd risen and was standing uncertainly beside the bed. The fear and confusion on her friend's face struck at her heart, but she knew that, cruel as it was, lying to Tibba about General Meachum was the only way to keep her safe.

Dr. Dusharme, Barbara was sure, was as evil at heart as the general. He meant them all ill. A dreadful word echoed in her mind. *Zombies.*

Barbara grimaced. The doctor had already sapped Tibba's will with drugs until she behaved much like the men Mimba called the walking dead.

She urged Tibba back onto the bed, gently forcing her to lie down. Keeping a close watch on her friend, Barbara put on her own clothes, then dashed across the hall, removed Tibba's clothes from her wardrobe and ran back to find Tibba on her feet again.

Showing her the clothes, Barbara persuaded her to change into them. She hoped that, if Tibba wore nothing that belonged to the doctor, his spell might be lessened. Also, both gowns were dark and less likely to be noticed in the dark than white dresses. Since there was no lock on the door, she forced a chair under the knob so no one could gain entry unexpectedly.

For the rest of the afternoon, she stayed close to Tibba's side, periodically removing one of the earplugs and whispering, "It's your father calling you—don't go!"

Near sunset the drums finally ceased. Minutes later someone tapped on the door. Barbara hurried to it. About to remove the chair, she decided the person couldn't be Mimba because it wasn't yet dark. Yvette?

"Don't disturb us, Yvette," she said in a low tone, speaking French. "Tibba is sleeping on my bed and I'm not hungry—perhaps I will be later. I'll let you know."

She held her breath, waiting. What if Dr. Dusharme himself stood outside the door?

"Very well," Yvette said, her voice muffled by the wood paneling. Barbara eased out her breath, thankful for the reprieve.

Sooner or later the doctor would come for Tibba. The only reason Barbara could think of why he hadn't already was because he must believe the drug in the lunch drink had stupified Tibba beyond obedience. She prayed Mimba would arrive first.

The room was dim with evening shadows when the next knock came, a soft, hesitant rap. Barbara went to the door. "Who is it?" she asked fearfully.

"Mimba." The whisper could scarcely be heard.

Barbara removed the chair and opened the door.

"Is doctor wait for her," Mimba said in a low tone, jerking her head toward Tibba who'd followed Barbara to the door. "Is her go to him."

"No," Barbara said. "I won't let her. She's my friend; she comes with us."

Mimba shrugged. "Us try." Untying the black sash around her waist, she looped it twice around Tibba's wrist and tied the two free ends around Barbara's wrist. "Is only way her stay with us," she muttered. "Is you keep her quiet."

Barbara removed one of the earplugs and whispered into Tibba's ear, "Mimba will help us get away from General Meachum. But you mustn't make any noise or your father might hear and stop us."

Mimba led them into the room next to Barbara's, then outside through the French doors. Here, the shrubbery grew close to the house and, concealed by the greenery, they crept through the gathering darkness. Every other minute Barbara expected the zombie troops to appear, but when they'd gone far enough so the house was hidden from view, she relaxed a trifle.

After struggling for some time through jungle-like growth, she followed Mimba up a rocky incline. From the top she saw lights glittering below and heard the faint sound of the surf. Mimba turned her back to the sound, facing away from the ocean, and pushed aside the low branches of a tree to reveal a pit descending into pitch darkness.

287

Barbara swallowed. "We go down there?"

"Is us go down to sea caves," Mimba said. "Must take care. Hold rope. Very steep." She pressed a small cloth sack into Barbara's hand. "Salt fe you. Fe give walking dead."

Barbara had all but forgotten Mimba telling her about putting salt on the tongues of the walking dead to free them from the zombie spell. "I wouldn't know how to use it," she protested.

"Is you take anyway." Mimba started down steps carved into the stone. Barbara shoved the sack into a pocket, then removed one of Tibba's earplugs, leaving it out. "We're climbing down into a cave," she said. "There are steep steps and a rope to hold onto. You go first."

Though Tibba hadn't struggled against following her, she'd made no move on her own and she didn't now. Barbara was forced to push her ahead. She groped for the rope and placed Tibba's hand on it.

"Remember, the steps are steep," she warned. "Be careful."

Tibba stumbled on the first step and Barbara steadied her until she regained her balance. Slowly, hesitantly, Tibba began to descend. Barbara, still tied to her at the wrist, came close behind, whispering to her, encouraging her. Her worry that Tibba would fall helped to ease her own fear of descending into the dark unknown. Still, she couldn't help wondering apprehensively what awaited them below.

Trevor's in the sea cave, she told herself. Trevor needs my help. I'm the only hope he has. If I don't save him . . .

She couldn't bear to finish the thought, to dwell on what might happen to Trevor if she wasn't successful—on what might happen to them all if Dr. Dusharme captured them. She prayed it wasn't too late to rescue Trevor from whatever horrible fate the doctor planned for him.

At last the steps ended and they stood on the level. Barbara stifled a scream when someone grasped her arm in the dark, belatedly realizing it was Mimba.

"Listen," Mimba whispered.

But Barbara had already heard the dread beat of the drums begin again, magnified by the rocky walls surrounding them. Tibba heard the drums, too, and strained toward their throbbing, only the sash tying her wrist to Barbara's keeping her with them. As Barbara fumbled to replace Tibba's earplug she realized the dark was no longer absolute. Somewhere ahead lights shone, casting a dim gleam to guide them.

"Drums mean doctor is come," Mimba whispered. "Hurry!"

They half-ran along the floor of the rocky tunnel, careless of noise since the throbbing drums smothered all other sound. The tunnel widened, the light grew brighter. Mimba halted just short of where the tunnel widened into a cave.

"Is us go inside cave. You go that way," Mimba pointed to the left, "me go other way. Keep close to wall."

Barbara nodded as she stared into a cave large as a double parlor with a high, arched roof. The muted sound of the surf crashing against the far wall made her realize it truly was a sea cave. Water trickled in from tiny openings along that wall, ran along the floor, and disappeared through an unseen drain hole.

In the center twelve Negro men squatted in a circle around flaming torches, two of them beating drums. Dr. Dusharme stood on a marble pedestal outside the circle, his side to the entrance. As she watched, he raised a black flute to his lips and began to play.

At the first of the notes Tibba jerked and lunged toward the doctor. Taken by surprise, Barbara barely managed to keep her balance. She dragged Tibba back, pinned her against the tunnel wall with her hip and removed one earplug long enough to whisper, "It's your father playing the flute. Your father. General Meachum."

But where was Trevor? He was nowhere in sight. She'd have to enter the cave and look for him. Mimba had already vanished inside. Though afraid they had little chance of remaining undiscovered, Barbara knew she couldn't turn back. If she did, Trevor was doomed. Taking a deep beath, she grasped Tibba's hand and eased through the cave entrance, inching along the left wall with her friend in tow.

She was directly in back of the doctor when she saw Trevor lying on the cave's rocky floor at the foot of the pedestal Dr. Dusharme stood on. The sight of Trevor's hands crossed over his chest terrified her. He couldn't be dead!

Abandoning caution, she rushed toward him, forgetting she was tied to Tibba. The sash tugged hard at her wrist and the knot gave. Intent on Trevor, Barbara scarcely noticed when the sash slipped from her wrist. She dropped to her knees beside him, frantically feeling for a pulse. No reassuring throb met her searching fingers, nor could she hear a heartbeat when she put an ear to his chest.

His face and hands were cool. Too cool? She slapped his cheeks, shook him. He didn't respond.

On his pedestal above her, the doctor continued to play the flute, the shrill notes rising above the drums in a melody that commanded rather than coaxed. Trevor stirred. Sat up.

Barbara's heart lifted until she saw his dull eyes and blank expression. His face turned toward the doctor. Putting a hand to each of Trevor's cheeks, she forced him to look at her instead. Despair struck deep within her when she realized he didn't see her. He started to rise and she knew he meant to join the circle of Negro men. The circle of zombies.

It was then she remembered the salt. Would it work? She had nothing else to try. Getting to her feet, she yanked the cloth sack from her pocket, opened the drawstring, and took a pinch of salt in her fingers. Before Trevor could move away from her, she rubbed the salt onto his lips, forcing a few grains between them.

For a long moment nothing happened and her heart sank. He'd begun to turn away from her when she saw him blink. Then he licked his lips. Hoping against hope, she offered him more salt, feeling the warm wetness of his tongue with hopeful joy as he lapped the grains from her fingers.

"More," he rasped hoarsely, and she poured salt into his cupped hand. He swallowed it all, then took the sack from her.

The flute stopped.

Barbara looked up at the doctor, certain she'd been discovered. He wasn't looking at her.

"Welcome Tibba," he said. "You are late."

Barbara's hand flew to her mouth. The black sash dangling from her wrist, Tibba stood just inside the circle of zombies, staring at Dr. Dusharme. Barbara turned back to Trevor but, to her dismay, he was already striding away, heading for the circle. She'd failed to save him and she'd lost Tibba as well.

There was nothing more she could do.

Numbly she watched Trevor march to the circle and enter it. He touched the lips of one of the men, then repeated the gesture with the next. It wasn't until he reached the third that she realized what he was doing. Evidently Mimba understood at the same time for, as Barbara stood stunned, she rushed across the cave and plunged into the circle, rubbing salt onto the lips of one of the zombies playing a drum. After a moment the drummer faltered and stopped. Mimba fed him more salt. He dropped his drum and toppled over.

"Free!" Mimba shrieked. "Is my man Cuffee free at last!"

"Stop, you fools!" Dr. Dusharme leaped from the pedestal and strode to the circle. "You're destroying them." A dagger gleamed in his hand. Ignoring Mimba, he lunged at Trevor.

Barbara screamed.

Tibba grabbed one of the torches from the holder and swung it at the doctor, striking him across the back of the head. He sprawled onto the floor. Tibba stood over him with the blazing torch in her hand until Barbara reached her and pulled her away. The torch fell onto Dr. Dusharme, setting his clothes on fire.

Before Barbara could decide what to do, one of the zombies who'd been given salt fell over on top of the doctor and the torch and lay unmoving. Flames licked up around him.

Keeping an arm around Tibba's waist, Barbara backed away from the blaze. She found Mimba kneeling beside her husband's dead body and the three women huddled together until Trevor finished feeding salt to the last of the zombies and stumbled over to them.

"Is good you didn't really die," Mimba told him. "Else the salt make you dead man already again like my man."

"No, I wasn't dead," Trevor said. "I knew everything that was going on but I couldn't help myself. That bastard fed me some drug that paralyzed my will and made me do whatever he said." He glanced at the fallen bodies. "They *are* dead, aren't they?"

"My man die two years ago," Mimba said. "Us bury him. Is doctor dig up my man, make him walking dead. Now my man and him spirit at peace. All them others, is doctor dig them corpses up, too. Doctor, is him burn in hell, just like him burn now."

Tibba, her face turned to Barbara's shoulder, shuddered with sobs. Barbara took out the ear-plugs.

"You saved us, Tibba," she said. "You saved everyone."

The weeping Tibba didn't reply.

"We'd best get out of here," Trevor said.

Dawn was graying the sky when they stumbled into the small settlement of Montego Bay, exhausted. The first person they met was a man walking along the shore. To Barbara's astonishment, she recognized Captain Prevorst, who she'd thought had drowned.

The grounded blockade runner, he told them, had stayed together through the night and when the sea calmed in the morning every man aboard had been taken to shore. Even their belongings had been saved.

Since Captain Prevorst believed all three of them had drowned in the night's stormy seas, he hadn't searched long for them.

"I sincerely regret that I didn't persist," he finished. "I didn't believe anyone could survive those waves."

"We were lucky enough to be washed ashore," Trevor said. He didn't mention Dr. Dusharme or anything else that had happened. Barbara didn't blame him—she wanted nothing more than to forget the doctor and his hideous practices as quickly as she could.

Captain Prevorst knew of a British ship bound for Canada that was due to take on cargo at the town dock in two days. While they were talking to him, Mimba went off and found a one-room cabin for them to stay in.

Though the beds were no more than reed mats, they dropped onto them gratefully and slept all through the day. When Barbara woke near sunset, Mimba was gone, Trevor was sitting up on his mat, and Tibba was still asleep.

"I gave Mimba money to get food for us," Trevor said, rising to his feet. He reached a hand to help her up. "How do you feel?"

"I'm fine," Barbara assured him. "I had only one dose of the doctor's laudanum."

"There was more than laudanum in what he gave me." Trevor's tone was grim.

"Tibba was drugged, too," she said. "I don't know what the doctor planned for her but—" She grimaced, her words trailing off.

Trevor drew her closer. "Thanks to you, we survived, that's what matters."

"It was Mimba's doing. Without her—" Again Barbara stopped, shuddering.

Trevor held her against him, his strength comforting her. "It's over," he said. "We're safe."

The door swung open and they quickly separated. "Is me fetch good breadkind, good fruit," Mimba said cheerfully as she entered the cabin.

After the three of them had eaten, Barbara tried to wake Tibba. Though her friend opened her eyes, she didn't try to sit up until Barbara assisted her.

"Tibba," Barbara said, "we're out of danger. Dr. Dusharme is dead."

"Him," Tibba mumbled.

After a moment Barbara remembered the deception she'd practiced to save Tibba and bit her lip in chagrin. Tibba had believed her all too well.

"Your father's gone," she said carefully. "We're on the island of Jamaica and General Meachum isn't here: He's back in his West Virginia valley."

"*He's* dead," Tibba whispered. "I killed him."

"The doctor's dead," Barbara repeated.

Tibba stared at her. *"Him."*

"Tibba, we're all safe," Trevor put in. "In a few days we'll be aboard a ship sailing to Canada."

Slowly Tibba turned her head to look at him. "Safe?" she whispered.

Trevor smiled reassuringly. "Safe."

Tibba's haunted expression didn't change as she glanced around the cottage. She shrank away when she saw Mimba.

"Mimba's our friend," Barbara said. "Come, have something to eat."

Tibba didn't move. In the end, Barbara had to help her to her feet, help her wash, and hand-feed her. As soon as she was finished eating, Tibba curled up on the mat, closed her eyes, and was soon asleep again.

Barbara fretted, aware whatever drug the doctor had given Tibba was still affecting her. She hovered over her friend for the rest of the evening until Mimba intervened.

"Is me watch over her," Mimba insisted. "Is you go fe walk with your man." She pointed to the door that Trevor had just closed behind him after leaving the cabin.

Barbara started to protest that Trevor wasn't her man but Mimba shook her head. "Is her sleep, don't need no one. Is him need you. Go."

She *would* like to get out of the cabin for a little while, Barbara decided. Perhaps the sea wind might blow some of the cobwebs from her mind.

Tibba would be safe enough with Mimba watching over her.

The island's balmy air embraced Barbara as she stepped through the door, a fragrant breeze teasing her hair and caressing her face. The sun had disappeared, leaving a thin line of red tinting the horizon clouds in the darkening sky as she strolled barefoot toward the shoreline where lazy waves washed onto the sand.

A lone figure stood silhouetted against the sky. Trevor. For a moment her step faltered. No matter what Mimba might think, he wasn't her man and never would be. And yet she was drawn to him by a magic far more potent than any drug ever invented.

When she reached his side she stopped and gazed at the dark water where, in the distance, the lights of passing ships twinkled. From the greenery behind the cabin a variety of frogs croaked and whistled a welcome to the night.

They stood for a time in a silence that would have been companionable if his nearness hadn't stirred her pulses so.

"This night seems like a beautiful dream," he said at last.

"After a ghastly nightmare," she said.

He put his hands on her shoulders, turning her to face him. "You'll have no more nightmares if I can help it."

She pulled away from him while she still could. If he kissed her she was lost. "Let's walk along the shore," she suggested.

He took her hand as they walked away from the

lights of the town and she relished the feel of his strong fingers enclosing hers.

"Going barefoot makes me feel like a boy again," he said.

She smiled, imagining him as a child, carefree and headstrong, running through summer days as though they'd never end, taking charge of games played with his friends, testing his own courage to the limit. "I'm sure you were quite a handful for your parents," she murmured.

He laughed. "I was so much of a problem that my mother used to say if I'd been her first child, I'd have been her only child. Luckily for them, my sisters were born before me."

"What are your sisters' names?"

"Rachel and Naomi. My mother, being a minister's daughter, was Biblical-minded—even to *my* middle name. Trevor was her maiden name. Rachel married an Englishman and lives in London. Naomi and her husband are settled near Sacramento, in California. After my father was killed at Shiloh, my mother sailed off to join them." He half-smiled. "Her farewell words to me were, 'Now you remember to behave yourself.'"

"And have you?"

"I leave the verdict up to you."

"I'm not sure you even know what the word behave means."

He laughed, released her hand and draped an arm over her shoulders, drawing her closer to his side. "Do you mind so very much?"

She didn't answer immediately, wishing to conceal the sudden breathlessness caused by his casual embrace. Because he'd shared details of his past with her, she felt closer to him than she ever had before. She glanced at the moon rising over the water and sighed. If only they could go on walking like this forever, along sand licked by a warm sea, his arm around her and no causes to separate them.

"I'll have you know I can be very proper when the occasion calls for such unnatural behavior," he told her. "What I do is imitate my mother's father. He was a good man but so eminently respectable that I doubt he ever went barefoot once he passed boyhood. I'm afraid I often drove the poor man to despair of my salvation."

"My mother's father was a farmer and quite jolly, as I recall," she said. "Though by the time I knew him, he never went barefoot."

"Yet here we are, the two of us with wet sand oozing between our toes. How can anyone not relish the feeling?"

She laughed. "I wouldn't miss it for anything."

A big rock blocked their path and they stopped. Trevor rolled up his trouser legs to his knees, saying, "We can wade around it."

Without hesitating, she lifted her skirts above the water and followed him into the shallows. When they rounded the point and waded back to shore, she saw they were in a small, secluded cove with another point extending into the sea just beyond where they stood. The moon cast silver rays along the water, illuminating the sandy beach.

"I've never seen anything more beautiful," she said, turning her face up to the moon.

"I have," he murmured, drawing her into his arms. "You."

Chapter 18

Trevor longed to go on gazing at Barbara's lovely face glowing in the moonlight; he'd never have his fill of looking at her. But the age-old urge thrumming in his blood, the overwhelming need for a woman, was too strong to be resisted.

His need was not for just any woman but for this particular woman, this stubborn Yankee he hadn't been able to banish from his heart. He'd wanted her from the moment he first touched her. He not only desired her physically but in every way a man could want a woman, not merely for the moment but for as long as life lasted. And beyond.

Only yesterday he'd believed he was about to die at the hands of that mad devil of a doctor. So close a brush with death had triggered a wild urge to celebrate life's wonders, and he yearned to savor the most wonderful of all with the woman who stood only a breath away.

Beyond doubt, she was the right woman. Their isolation, the soft air, the lazy rhythm of the sea caressing the sand, and the sweet fragrance of exotic night blooms assured him this was the right time and the right place. At long last.

Gathering her into his arms, he murmured, "Snow Bird, my love, my love."

She melted against him as he kissed her and the feel of her soft curves fired his blood. There was nothing coy about the way she welcomed his caresses; she wasn't afraid to let him know she wanted him. She was as honest as she was beautiful, a combination he found unusual and irresistible. His lovely Snow Bird was excitingly unique, unlike any woman he'd ever known.

Before her eager responses took him beyond thought he vowed to make the night as magical for her as it would be for him, a time not only of love and passion but of wonder. Only God knew what lay ahead for either of them but no matter what might come between them, this night together would never be forgotten. . . .

Exactly as she'd known would happen, Barbara had no will to resist the moment Trevor's lips touched hers. But she didn't care, she was where she belonged, in his arms.

She'd come frighteningly close to losing him beyond recall. How could she have lived without ever again feeing his strong body against hers and the sweet agony of his lips on hers? They'd been meant to come together from the beginning and she knew their time was now, here on this tropical island where the sea embraced the sand gently and, sometimes, with wild passion.

With him she'd discovered passion and was now

discovering it all over again. Passion simmered within her, heating her blood and melting her bones. Tonight he was hers and she was his.

My love, he'd called her, and she cradled his words in her heart, treasuring them. There'd never been a man like him; for her there never would be one again.

My love. The words turned every kiss into a promise, a promise to be fulfilled this night. With his lips on hers, how could she think about tomorrow? Time didn't matter, nothing mattered but the two of them, together in the moonlight.

His scent, male and enticing, mingled with the night-blooming island fragrance, the silk of his hair under her fingers, and the tantalizing brush of his beard intoxicated her until she could no longer think. She wanted more, she needed more.

"Ishmael," she murmured, "oh, Ishmael . . ."

As if aware her whisper of the name was an invitation she was too bemused to make, he eased her onto the sand. Moments later his hands, then his lips, found her bared breasts, making her moan in pleasure. Soon they lay flesh to flesh and the entrancing sensation of his warm skin touching hers made her wish she could purr like a cat.

His lips and tongue caressed her into rapturous need. "Please," she whispered, "oh, please . . ." Though unsure of exactly what she begged for, she knew she wanted all a man could give to a woman and she wanted it now, from this man and no other. Never any other.

"My love," he said once more, his voice hoarse with passion, and rose above her.

His hardness pushed gently inside her moist softness. He moved slowly, hesitantly, making her writhe under him, eager for more, but he refused to hurry. She gasped for breath, on fire with need. She wrapped her arms around him, then her legs, feverishly urging him closer, deeper.

He groaned and plunged into her. Instinctively she matched his rhythmic thrusts, crying out in wonderment as throbbing waves of ecstasy thrilled through her, taking her out of herself and uniting her with him.

He cuddled her to him afterwards. With her head on his chest she listened contentedly to the even beat of his heart. Eventually, though, she was reminded of the horrible time in the cave when she wasn't sure whether she heard his heart beat or not.

She raised her head to look at him. "In the cave," she said, "I thought . . ." She couldn't go on.

"I knew you were there," he told her, "but I couldn't break through the drug-induced paralysis to reach you. Not until you put the salt on my lips."

"Mimba admitted she got the salt from a medicine man of her own people and that he'd put 'secret roots' in the salt. Heaven only knows what I gave you."

"The important thing is it worked."

"Thank God! The doctor told me you were dead from a serious head injury. I couldn't believe him but I didn't know for sure what was wrong with you."

"I recall hitting my head on a rock when I dived into the sea after you when you were swept overboard. I hit it hard enough to make me dizzy when I finally reached shore and stood on my feet, hard enough to make me pass out on the sand. But the injury wasn't serious."

"Dr. Dusharme lied to me from the beginning," she said. "I believed him at first but then I had a strange dream, a warning dream. I was a chickadee in a strange tree. White Deer was in it and a fox . . ." She paused and smiled. "I just remembered that when we were aboard the ship I compared Captain Prevorst to a fox, so I guess he must have been the fox. There was an eagle . . ."

"Never mind your dreams. You're what I want and you're too far away." He pulled her down, shifting her at the same time so she lay on top of him. "That's better."

Everything fled from her mind except the glorious sensation of his body beneath hers and the warm insistence of his kiss. Excitement caught at her as his hands slid down her spine to the swell of her hips, pressing her closer.

Words rose in her throat, words of love, but she caught them back, uncertain how to express her deepest feelings and afraid, as well. All she finally murmured was, "Ishmael . . ."

He'd never cared much for his middle name but the way she said it, with the huskiness of passion in her voice, sent a thrill through him. He wanted her again. Would he ever stop wanting her?

"Snow Bird," he whispered into her ear, "make love to me." For a long moment she didn't move and he was afraid he'd confused her or that she was too shy to begin. Then she cupped his face between her hands and kissed him, her tongue slipping between his lips to taste him and seduce him with erotic promises.

Her response to his lovemaking the first time had been beyond his wildest dreams. He knew she'd never lain with a man before him and yet her eagerness and her innocent demands had been far more arousing than any art practiced by the most experienced courtesan.

She'd given herself to him with such sweet passion that he vowed if he had anything to say about it she'd never lie with another man—only with him.

Her hands caressed him, sliding along his chest, his stomach, then hesitating until he groaned in frustrated anticipation. Her fingers crept down slowly, slowly. He held his breath, waiting. At last she touched his hardness, feeling him with such a delicate yet intimate touch that he thought he'd die of pleasure.

Unable to wait any longer, he raised her hips and fitted her over him, entering her, capturing her delighted moan when he kissed her. He was where he belonged, he'd never been more certain of anything in his life. He was hers as much as she was his. He was a part of her and the joy of giving and taking was theirs to share.

Even after the frenzied rapture had peaked, he was reluctant to release her from his embrace. He wanted to hold her in his arms and never let her go. Eventually, though, he felt the grittiness of sand under his hand as he caressed the curve of her hip.

"Let's bathe in the sea," he said.

Hand in hand they walked into the shallows, going deeper and deeper until the water rose to her waist. She pulled away and ducked under, emerged dripping, turned her face up to the moon, and smiled. Noticing how the moonlight gleamed on the tiny droplets and on her smooth skin, he felt struck dumb by her beauty.

She glanced at him and said accusingly, "You're not washing." Before he could move, she scooped water with her hands, laughing as she splashed him.

The splashing escalated into a water fight like those he used to have in the past with other boys when they skinny-dipped in the creeks running into the James.

But she was no boy. As he wrestled with her playfully, he found, somewhat to his astonishment, that he wanted her again. Gripping her by the waist he raised her high, then slid her down the length of his body until her feet once more touched bottom.

Holding her close, he said, "Do you have any idea what you do to me?"

Her smile was impish. "I'm finding out."

He grinned at her, appreciation of her sense of humor mingling with his desire. What a prize she was!

He ran his thumb over her taut nipple and heard her quick intake of breath. "Did I ever tell you that in every way you're the loveliest woman in the world?" he asked.

She placed her hands flat on his chest, her fingers tangling in his chest hair. "I never before thought of men as beautiful, but *you* are." She whispered the words so softly he could scarcely hear her.

He hugged her, aware that every touch bound them closer, bound them with invisible ties that he wished would never break. In possessing her, he'd become possessed. If only this night would go on forever. It would not, could not, but he refused to think of tomorrow. . . .

She didn't want the night to end. How could she bear not to be in his arms? To share him with others? If only she could devise some moonlight magic to make their time together everlasting and keep the world away.

Hand in hand again, they waded toward shore but didn't quite reach the beach. Locked in each other's arms, they fell at the waterline and made love in the lapping waves.

Barbara dressed slowly, her skin tingling from the salt and sand and from the memory of Trevor's caresses. Though she had no idea what time it was—nor did she really care—she suspected it was near dawn. She knew he watched her but the idea of him seeing her unclad no longer made her shy.

"Tired, Snow Bird?" he asked when she fastened the last button and held out her hand to him.

She didn't feel tired, she felt remarkably alive. "No, what I am is happy," she said. "If I truly were a bird I'd burst into song."

"Yes, happy." His voice was tinged with sadness and his grip on her hand tightened. "This night will live with me until the day I die."

His words echoed in her mind. *Until the day I die.* But you're alive! she wanted to shout. We're alive! Why talk about dying when we've years ahead of us? Instead, she sighed. Years, yes, but would they spend them together? She feared the answer.

They walked back to Montego Bay in silence, the sky lightening as they neared the docks. Barbara noticed a ship steaming into the bay and she tensed. Was it the British ship, arriving a day early?

"It's still too dark to see if she's flying the Union Jack," Trevor commented, his thoughts obviously similar to hers.

The knowledge of what was ahead for them once they left Jamaica flooded through her, washing aside her happy memories of the night and forcing her to taste the bitter truth beneath. The man she'd shared the most wonderful hours of her life with would soon be forcing her to betray her beliefs—and her country.

She pulled her hand from his.

He gripped her arm, stopping her. "Barbara, you don't know how much I wish—" He paused, looking not at her but toward the inbound ship. Finally he shook his head and let her go.

He didn't need to say anything more. She understood what hadn't been said. He regretted what lay ahead, the betrayal that would necessarily divide them beyond hope. God knows she did too. But if he truly loved her wouldn't he release her from her promise to help him free the Reb prisoners from Johnson Island? Or, better still, give up his ill-advised plan?

There was nothing she could say or do to change the future. Wrapped in despair, she stood beside him watching the ship sail closer and closer.

"I'm not fighting to keep slavery," he said abruptly. "I fully admit slavery demeans both slave and master. I've never owned another human being and I never will."

"But I saw—" She broke off. "You had Negro servants in your townhouse."

"My mother freed all the servants after my father died. I pay the ones who work for me." He sighed. "For me it was simple, but for the South the slavery issue is more complex than you Yankees understand."

You Yankees. The phrase stabbed at her heart, reminding her they were enemies.

"My great-grandfather started a bank in Richmond's early days," Trevor went on, "and my grandfather, then my father, continued in the banking business. Because my family didn't own a plantation they had no need for slaves to work in the fields. While we did own house servants, they were relatively few. It created no problems when my mother freed them and then hired those who wished to continue to work for us.

"Plantation owners feel quite differently. Many are convinced they'd be ruined if they lost their slaves—and they may be right. But that isn't why most of them are fighting this war, either." Trevor turned to her and placed his hands on her shoulders.

"Try to imagine," he asked, "how you Northerners would feel if we insisted on forcing unwanted laws down your throats. We in the South are fighting against just such a violation of our rights. We're fighting for our right not to be dictated to, our right to determine what's best for us ourselves rather than suffering the injustice of Northern bias. Can you understand what I'm saying?"

Barbara stared at him in the gray predawn light. What he was saying hadn't been in the abolitionist tracts she'd read, though she vaguely recalled her father saying, before he left to join the medical corps, that it was unfortunate there were so many hotheads on both sides because, if men had been more reasonable, the problems might have been worked out in negotiation rather than by going to war.

She could understand Trevor's views but she couldn't agree with him.

"You can't deny slavery is still an unsolved problem," she said, "a shameful problem. But slavery aside, I believe the union of the states made us a country where everyone must abide by the same laws."

His smile was sad. "A stubborn Yankee, aren't you?"

She swallowed, but the lump in her throat remained, making it difficult to speak. "No more stubborn than you Rebs."

His grip tightened. "You made me a promise."

"Yes." She could hardly force the word out.

"See that you remember it." He dropped his

310

hands from her shoulders. "You go on back to the cabin. I'll wait for the ship to dock." Without another word he turned and strode away from her.

With tears streaming down her face unheeded, Barbara stumbled toward the cabin.

Later, their removal to the British ship, *Golden Lion*, Mimba's mournful farewell, and the good wishes of Captain Prevorst all passed in a blur for Barbara. In the tiny cabin allotted to her and Tibba, she sat listlessly on the lower bunk beside her friend until sheer exhaustion made her climb into the upper berth where she fell into an uneasy sleep.

She woke to Tibba's screams and a pounding at the door.

"What's wrong?" Trevor called above Tibba's cries and shoved open the door.

By then Barbara was on her knees beside the lower berth, trying to calm Tibba, who shrank away at her touch.

"Let me try," he said, easing down beside her. He grasped Tibba's hands in his. "Stop that noise!" he ordered. "You know you're perfectly safe with me."

As Tibba's screams of fear subsided into agitated sobbing, Trevor gathered her into his arms, patting her back and speaking soothingly. "There, there, everything's all right. I'm here and I won't let you be harmed."

Barbara sat back on her heels watching Tibba cry on his shoulder, ashamed of her feeling that she, not Tibba, belonged in his arms.

"He's not dead," Tibba wailed when she could speak. "He was here in the cabin, coming after me."

"Dr. Dusharme is most assuredly dead." Trevor's voice was firm as he settled her back onto the bunk. "You had a bad dream."

"Not the doctor. *Him.*" Fear edged Tibba's voice and she grasped at Trevor's hand.

"She means her father," Barbara explained. "General Meachum."

Trevor glanced from Tibba to her and then refocused on Tibba. "Though I doubt that he's dead," he told Tibba, "General Meachum is certainly not aboard the *Golden Lion*. You've been dreaming."

"She told me he was here." Tibba gazed accusingly at Barbara.

"Tibba, I lied to save you," Barbara said apologetically. "You were under the doctor's influence and wouldn't believe he meant you ill. I had to keep you from answering his call and the only way I could think of to do that was to frighten you into believing the doctor was really your father. I'm sorry you're still upset but at the time I didn't know what else to do."

Trevor, holding Tibba's hand between his, frowned at Barbara. "Apparently you scared the poor girl out of her wits."

She glared at him. "Her wits! I was at my wit's end and did the best I could."

He turned back to Tibba. "Listen to me," he ordered. "Your father is not aboard this ship. He was not in Jamaica with us. And I'll do the best I can to prevent him from ever coming anywhere near you again."

Tibba gazed up at him, her dark eyes wide. "Will you?" she breathed.

He smiled down at her and patted her cheek. "You can trust me."

Jealousy cast a dart that pierced Barbara's heart. They didn't have to look so soulfully at one another! And why must he touch Tibba like that?

"You can trust Barbara, too," Trevor went on. "She's your friend. What she told you on the island might have been ill-advised but she meant it for the best."

Anger intermingled with Barbara's jealousy. He hadn't been with them, he didn't know how desperate the situation was at the time. What else *could* she have said or done to keep Tibba safe?

Tibba glanced at Barbara and winced. "She doesn't look like my friend, she looks mad enough to take a knife to me."

Accused by two of the people who mattered most to her, and upset by her own jealousy, Barbara was too stricken to defend herself. She jumped to her feet and marched from the cabin only to be humiliated moments later when Trevor came after her with her shoes in his hand.

"There's a time and place to go barefoot," he said with a half-smile.

"Not anymore! Not ever again!" Shoes in her hand, she flung herself away from him.

When she'd managed to calm herself, Barbara returned to the cabin to make peace, if she could, with Tibba.

Tibba was quite willing to forgive. "I realize it

must have been a terrible time for you," she said, "with both me and Trevor depending on you to rescue us."

Trevor. Tibba had always called him the captain before. Barbara took a deep breath and vowed not to allow herself to be jealous. Despite what had happened between them in the cove, she had no claim on Trevor and never would have.

"I *was* afraid," she acknowledged. "Otherwise I never would have lied to you. The last thing in the world I want to do is hurt you."

But, though the schism between them was mended, or at least papered over, she felt a certain coolness in Tibba. Barbara did her best to avoid Trevor as much as possible and was quite successful. It hurt, though, to notice Trevor paying more attention to Tibba than he ever had before.

Tibba was pretty, there was no denying that. Judging from the behavior of the British sailors—officers and men alike—she was a woman that men noticed. The sailors might be attentive to Barbara but they gaped after Tibba.

An unexpected passenger boarded when they stopped in Bermuda—Harrison Chambers. Barbara greeted him with enthusiasm, grateful to have someone she could talk to, someone to take her mind off Trevor.

She didn't tell Harrison about her promise to Trevor. That promise was a secret she could reveal to no one. Trevor hadn't yet been specific about the way in which she was to help him free the Johnson Island prisoners but she had to admit she harbored a sympathy for prisoners of war—even Rebs. Not that she'd ever tell Trevor and not that it would excuse her for betraying her cause.

"When we reach Canada," Harrison said during one of their walks on deck, "I'm hoping to get in touch with what you Yanks call 'Copperheads.' Do you know the term?"

Barbara nodded. "Snakes," she said, grimacing. "Snakes who strike without warning, just like real copperheads. Their poison weakens the Union forces."

"In Canada I hope to interview a man privy to Copperhead councils."

She gave him a sharp glance. "I don't envy you. An out and out Reb is preferable to those who seek to damage us from within. Or don't you agree?"

Harrison tugged at his mustache. "As I see it, I'm a neutral observer."

"Aren't you sometimes tempted to favor one side or the other?"

"If I did, I would never admit it. Otherwise I'd have difficulty passing freely through the battle lines and reporting the news from both sides."

She compressed her lips in exasperation. Even though he was an Englishman, how could he not prefer the Union side?

Harrison smiled thinly. "I see you don't agree with my stand. Try to think of it this way—how could my reporting be unbiased if I favored either the Union or the Confederate cause?"

"I suppose you must stay neutral but I don't understand how you possibly can."

"Shall we then speak of more mutually agree-

315

able topics? American authors, perhaps? I confess myself amazed at their scribblings." Harrison launched into a discussion of Herman Melville as compared to Sir Walter Scott.

Only later, back in the cabin, did she remember his words about interviewing someone about Copperhead plans. In Canada. Where Trevor was taking her. Was there a conspiracy brewing between the Copperheads and the Rebs? Barbara drew in her breath. Back in Ohio she'd heard rumors that Jefferson Davis had a secret emissary in Canada. What if it were true? What if Trevor's real mission wasn't to free the prisoners on Johnson's Island for use in Southern battlefields, but to provide men for a surprise invasion of the North?

A shiver ran along Barbara's spine. It could be true! Ohio, Illinois, and Indiana were full of Copperheads who'd be able to wreak untold damage, clearing the way for a Reb incursion from Canada, spearheaded by the freed soldiers from Johnson's Island.

Trevor needed her help in arranging the escape of the prisoners. She'd given her word that she would help. But that was before she'd realized what might really be the Confederate plan. In such a case how could she possibly keep her word?

Barbara's eyes widened as she realized that she might, by the careful use of duplicity, be the only person in the world who could save her country.

Chapter 19

Trevor clenched his fists as he watched Chambers standing beside Barbara at the ship's rail. Standing too damn close! From the expression on her face, she found whatever the journalist was saying extremely fascinating. Or was she fascinated by Chambers himself?

Tibba, clinging to Trevor's arm, said tartly, "How cozy they look."

He didn't trust himself to answer without cursing so he said nothing. Though he liked Tibba well enough, he regretted having to escort her every time she came on deck. He'd had little choice in the matter after he'd been forced to rescue her from the unwelcome advances of one of the sailors. Because of her race, many of the British tars regarded poor Tibba as fair game. A shame. In her way she was as much of a lady as Barbara.

Tibba was damned attractive but other women left him cold—Barbara was the only woman he wanted. He glowered at her as, oblivious, she smiled up at Chambers. He could understand why she avoided him, but why in hell must she be so friendly with Chambers?

"I thought you and Barbara were—" Tibba paused and shrugged. "You know."

He'd thought so too. At least for one night. If it weren't for this damned mission . . . He sighed. What lay ahead of him in Canada was far more important than himself or his own desires. The fate of the Confederacy might well depend on him.

"Don't you agree that the polite thing to do would be to wish Mr. Chambers a good morning?" Tibba's voice held an odd combination of wistfulness and anger.

Trevor had no interest in being polite to the bastard, but Tibba tugged him toward the rail. He would have resisted, but Barbara's presence drew him in her direction like a magnet.

Tibba sidled up behind the couple. "Why if it isn't Mr. Chambers! No doubt you're finding much to admire about Miss Thackery." Her mocking tone startled Trevor. He noticed that Barbara also seemed taken aback.

Not Chambers. Capturing Tibba's hand, he bowed and said suavely, "Rarely do I find two such lovely women traveling together. I consider myself—what is that interesting expression you Americans use?—oh, yes, 'shot through with luck.'"

Luck wouldn't be the ammunition I'd use on you, Trevor thought sourly, watching Chambers do his best to charm Tibba.

"Hello, Trevor." Barbara spoke quietly.

He had to touch her. Unable to stop himself, he gripped her hand, bringing it to his lips, watching her face as he did. Her lips parted as though he were kissing them instead of her fingers and a piercing shaft of need transfixed him. He fought the impulse to pull her into his arms and to hell with everyone and everything.

Barbara drew her hand away. "Tibba tells me you've been very kind to her."

"*Someone* has to protect her from overamorous sailors."

"Yes, of course. Although none of them has bothered me."

He scowled. "Chambers makes damn sure you're never alone on deck."

"He's been very courteous."

Trevor snorted. "I doubt courtesy is all he has in mind."

Barbara raised her chin. "I'll have you know we've been discussing the war. Harrison's most knowledgeable."

"Amazing! I wasn't aware he'd done any fighting. Which side is he on? Or does he switch back and forth hoping to end up with the winner?"

She ignored the sarcasm. "Harrison takes an overview. Something a soldier in the lines can't do. I've learned a great deal."

Harrison. He resented the name coming from her lips. That son of a bitch of a journalist was trespassing on his territory—Barbara belonged to him.

"Must you scowl so?" she asked.

Couldn't she see he was in agony? He reached for her hand again but she drew back against the rail.

"It's over between us," she whispered. "Over forever. You know why."

His hand dropped to his side. Over forever. He knew she meant what she said, knew that because of her integrity and loyalty to what she believed in it could be no other way. Yet that didn't ease his need for her, a need that would never again be satisfied. He had no choice but to carry out his assignment even though in doing so he doomed himself to the hell of a life without her. Heartsick, he turned from her to Tibba.

He caught Chambers whispering something to Tibba that brought a flush to her cheeks. She shook her head but her languishing gaze, fixed on Chamber's face, told a different story.

Trevor regarded the journalist carefully before touching Tibba's arm. "Shall we go on?" he asked.

"Yes," Tibba said breathlessly. "Oh, yes, let's."

"Trading secrets?" he asked her lightly when they'd walked on.

"Mr. Chambers was being silly." Tibba didn't look at him as she spoke.

Silly? Trevor didn't think so. Nor did he believe she thought so. This exchange, plus Tibba's insistence on speaking to the journalist in the first place, made Trevor all but certain there was something between the pair. An attraction. He hoped Tibba knew what she was doing. Chambers struck him as a man who was very conscious of his position as an English gentleman. If Chambers thought of marriage he might consider Barbara as a possible wife but not Tibba. Because of her color, he'd not be interested in more than a brief fling with someone like her.

Tibba deserved better.

The notion of Barbara as Chamber's wife twisted like a knife in Trevor's gut. Never!

As the days passed, Tibba's increasing coolness toward her upset Barbara more and more until she finally couldn't bear the strain.

On the evening before they were to dock at Halifax, she confronted Tibba as they were getting ready to retire.

"What's wrong between us?" she asked. "Are you still angry because I lied to you about your father?"

Tibba glanced at her, then away. "No, I reckon you did what you had to."

"Then what *is* wrong? You treat me like a stranger."

"Maybe that's because you don't act like a friend." Tibba's voice was sullen.

Taken aback, Barbara stared at her. "What do you mean?"

Tibba glared at her. "Making up to Harrison all the time, that's what I mean. You're breaking Trevor's heart."

"I don't admit I'm 'making up' to Harrison. But why this sudden concern for Trevor?"

"He's in love with you."

Barbara tried to tamp down her rising anger. "I

beg to differ. If he were truly in love with me, he never would have—" She broke off, aware she mustn't reveal too much about what lay ahead to Tibba. Or to anyone. "He would have behaved differently," she ended lamely.

"Don't you feel anything at all for Trevor?" Tibba asked.

Barbara's anger burst through. "I don't care to talk about it! Besides, I don't think you're telling me what's really bothering you."

Tibba eyed her accusingly. "You know. You *must* know."

The truth flooded through Barbara, washing away her anger. Harrison. She'd been so wrapped up in her own misery over Trevor and so grateful for the distraction of talking to Harrison that she'd forgotten how Tibba felt about the Englishman.

She reached a hand toward her friend. "I'm sorry. I've been selfish to monopolize Harrison's time when he means nothing to me. Or me to him. Oh, Tibba, please forgive me. I didn't mean to hurt you."

Tibba didn't take her hand and after a moment, Barbara dropped it to her side.

"He doesn't mean anything to me, either." Tibba's words weren't convincing. "If he prefers your company, it's nothing to me."

"That's not the way of it. The poor man's had no choice but to escort me around the deck. I'm sure he'd much rather be with you."

Tibba shook her head slowly back and forth. "He doesn't want me. If he did he'd seek my company no matter what."

Barbara bit her lip. How could she convince Tibba there was nothing between her and Harrison? Because there wasn't. True, he often paid her compliments but it was second nature for him to sweet-talk women and she'd paid no attention to it.

"I love Trevor," she said at last, deciding she had to tell as much of the truth as possible, "but we can never be together. He's a Reb, I'm a Yankee, and we just don't agree on anything. I'll never love another man as I do him but we can't—" She broke off, tears in her eyes. She groped for a handkerchief, trying not to give way and failing. "I'm so miserable," she wailed.

Tibba's arms closed around her and she wept on her friend's shoulder. Tibba cried too. Later, as they mopped their eyes, Tibba smiled at Barbara.

"I won't be so foolish again," she said. "Deep down I know you'll always be my friend. While Harrison—" Tibba sighed. "No matter what I feel for him I know he's someone I'll never be able to trust."

Barbara didn't ask why because she thought she understood. Harrison was a bit too glib, too ready to say what he thought a person wanted to hear. Unlike Trevor. She trusted Trevor. But trust had no power to heal what divided them.

Once the ship docked in Halifax, Trevor lost no time in taking passage for himself and the two women on a side-wheeler whose route was across the Gulf of St. Lawrence and on up the river to

323

Toronto, where he was to meet with his Confederate coconspirators. To his annoyance, Chambers caught the same boat.

The second day aboard the boat, Chambers surprised the hell out of him by offering an apology.

"Sorry, old man, I had no idea how things were. Miss Meachum told me only yesterday about your understanding with Miss Thackery. I've been called all sorts of names but never a poacher—no hard feelings, I hope." He held out his hand.

Trevor shook it. An understanding with Barbara? Not to his knowledge. But if it kept Chambers away from her, he was more than willing to go along with the lie that Tibba, for some reason of her own, had told.

"No hard feelings," he agreed.

"Good show." Chambers glanced around. "Doesn't seem likely anyone can overhear us." He lowered his voice. "I'm traveling to Toronto to meet a man your Miss Thackery would no doubt refer to as 'one of those vile snakes.' In other words, a Copperhead. Since Toronto also appears to be your destination, I can't help wondering if you intend to meet Confederate sympathizers in an attempt to plan some sort of Northern offensive."

"I can't discuss my reasons." Trevor's tone was curt.

"I quite understand, old man. Far be it from me to attempt to unseal your lips. Because I owe you some sort of recompense, I'll go even further and promise not to put my speculations into print until after the Rebs take action, whatever it may be." Chambers twisted his mustache. "That doesn't mean I won't try to discover what's going on."

"I can't stop you from nosing around." Trevor did his best to keep his voice neutral. Though he didn't care for Chambers, it was decent of the man to hold up on writing his story—no use to antagonize him by showing contempt.

"I believe we understand one another," Chambers said. "Good day."

As he watched the journalist walk away, an idea came to Trevor. Since Chambers already suspected something was to happen, why not use him in his plans?

Barbara's presence on Johnson Island was absolutely essential to the Confederate scheme, but it was obviously impossible for Trevor to personally escort her and Tibba to Sandusky. He'd been worrying about getting them there safely. Now he decided it would cause little comment if the Englishman escorted Tibba and Barbara to Ohio, with the added bonus of people assuming Chambers had helped them get away from Richmond. And Chambers, if appealed to as a gentleman needed to protect the ladies, wouldn't tumble to the fact he was being rushed away from Toronto as quickly as possible.

Trevor smiled thinly. After the meeting in Toronto he'd approach Chambers. His smile faded. He'd also have to give Barbara her final instructions and he didn't look forward to that briefing. It hurt to see her and not be able to touch her—the session would be painful in every way.

The closer it came to their parting, the harder it was to admit to himself that he was sending her away from him forever. She still avoided him and he had to allow it. What would he gain by forcing her to speak to him?

That evening they sailed from the St. Lawrence River into Lake Erie. Standing by the rail looking at the tag end of the sunset—the red horizon clouds—Trevor was startled when Barbara came up to him.

"I hoped Tibba might be with you," she said. "Have you seen her? She missed dinner."

"I haven't had so much as a glimpse of Tibba all day," he said, fighting to keep his hands off Barbara. She wore a shawl over her head and shoulders against the evening chill, hiding her hair and her gown. Nothing, though, could ever completely hide her beauty. He desperately wanted to touch her, if only to run his fingers along her lips.

"I can't imagine where Tibba is," Barbara said.

Trevor could. "Have you seen Chambers?" he asked.

"Yes, he was at dinner. Didn't you notice?"

Now that she mentioned it, he did recall seeing the journalist then, if briefly.

Barbara bit her lip. "I'm so worried. Would you please help me look for her?"

She ought to know he'd be willing to try to swim across Lake Erie if she asked.

"I'll be happy to help," he said. "Perhaps we should begin with your cabin—she may have returned while you were out." Trevor offered his arm and a thrill shot along his nerves when he felt her fingers on his sleeve.

If Tibba wasn't in the cabin he'd be tempted to close himself and Barbara inside. His groin tightened as he imagined making love to her. Would she resist? He thought of her ardent response in the cove and hastened his step, hoping she wanted him as much as he wanted her. He was half-crazed with his need for her.

When they reached the cabin he paused, his back to the door. Unable to wait any longer, he bent and brushed his lips over hers. For one sweet breath she leaned to him, then she drew back.

"Trevor, no!"

The cabin door swung open to reveal Tibba. "I thought I heard someone," she said.

"I've been looking all over for you," Barbara told her. "It worried me when you missed dinner."

Tibba blinked and her hand went to her mouth. "I'm sorry if I caused you anxiety," she said after a moment. "I was helping a sick woman care for her child."

Tibba's lying, Trevor thought, watching her and noting her glowing face. She's been with a man. Recalling how brief an appearance Chambers had made at dinner, he decided they'd been together and Chambers had brought food back to his cabin for her. In his opinion a rendezvous with Chambers was a mistake for Tibba, but it was none of his business what she chose to do.

"You must be starved," Barbara said.

"No, no. The woman gave me something to eat."

Barbara glanced at Trevor. "Thank you for your help," she said formally. Dismissively.

He bowed. "The pleasure was mine. I'm delighted that you found Tibba safe, after all."

It was just as well Tibba had been in the cabin, he told himself as he strode away, because otherwise I might have done something I'd regret.

Not force Barbara, no, never. But seduce her into forgetting they were enemies, seduce her with kisses and caresses until she begged him to make love to her—yes, he was capable of that. Seducing her would have been wrong, a violation, and he knew it, yet he doubted he could have stopped himself if they'd been alone together.

He was a man who'd always prided himself on his control of any situation, but where she was concerned pride goeth before a fall. His vaunted self-will was worth nothing in her presence; he was damn well besotted with her. . . .

Barbara sat uneasily on the tearoom's round-bottomed chair. Instead of looking at Trevor, seated across the small table from her, she watched herself fiddle with her cup.

"More tea?" he asked.

She shook her head. She didn't want anything from him, not even this cup of tea. They'd arrived in Toronto yesterday morning and, on the way to the hotel, he'd pointed out this tearoom and told her to meet him there at two the following day. Alone. She'd done so. It was now two-thirty.

"Do you understand what you're to do?" he

asked after another glance around the almost empty room. No one was sitting anywhere near them.

"I understand."

"Please repeat what I've told you."

She moistened her lips with a sip of tea before complying. "I'm to bring a letter that's supposedly from my father to the Johnson Island commandant, Major York. The letter explains that my father appreciated being helped by Southern women when in Libby and wishes me to reciprocate. He asks that I be allowed to bring food and medicines in to the Rebel prisoners. When I have the chance to do so, I'm to slip a note from you to a Reb prisoner, one Colonel Picard."

"Very good. And you will do this?"

Barbara swallowed. "I promised, didn't I?"

He nodded. "What will you do if you're unable to pass the note on?"

"I'll find Colonel Picard and tell him that the attack to free the prisoners is scheduled for November 10th and will be by land."

"I think you'll be able to deliver the note. I've been told Major York is an army friend of your father's. Do you know him?"

"I've never met the major but I recognize the name from Papa's letters." With an effort she kept her voice even and her tone neutral, refusing to allow her angry despair to creep into her words.

"Fine. Tomorrow morning you and Tibba will leave Toronto in the company of Mr. Chambers. He'll escort you to Sandusky and see that you have proper accommodations."

329

Since no reply was required, she said nothing and a silence fell.

"Barbara." Trevor stretched his hand across the table and clasped her fingers.

She caught her breath, tensing.

"I wish we didn't have to part like this," he said.

"There's no choice."

"There's always a choice!" His voice rose. "How can you forget what we shared in that cove? God knows I can't."

Despite her best intentions, tears blurred her vision. "I haven't said I'd forget."

"Then don't make this a final parting. Tell me we'll meet again."

Blinking to keep back the tears, she shook her head. "I never want to see you again." Pain tinged her words. She tugged at her hand, trying to get away before she broke down and wept for all they were losing.

"Do you hate me that much?"

Hate him? She couldn't.

"After all," he went on, smiling one-sidedly, "the Bible exhorts you to love thine enemy."

Tibba had reminded her of the same verse. The trouble was she *did* love him. Otherwise her heart wouldn't be breaking.

With his free hand Trevor dropped money onto the table, then rose and pulled her to her feet. Looking intently into her eyes, he said, "It doesn't matter what you tell me; I'm not easily discouraged. When this war is over I'll come and find you, Snow Bird, wherever you are, and we'll start from there. Start over."

He bent his head and kissed her, a tender, searching kiss that warmed her from head to toe. Cupping her face between his hands, he murmured, "It's not goodbye, it's till we meet again."

Before she could find any words, he turned and strode from the tearoom. Barbara sighed and walked slowly toward the door. When Trevor learned of her betrayal, and he was bound to, she was certain he'd change his mind. War or no war, he'd never want to see her again. . . .

After the bright flowers and the pleasant weather of Jamaica, the North seemed chillier than Barbara remembered. Unlike Canada where the trees were mostly bare, in Ohio the autumn leaves still clung to their branches, providing a blaze of color—but no warmth. Barbara's wool shawl cut the chill of the lake wind but her heart felt as cold as winter as she walked off the boat onto Johnson Island on the last day of October.

The island, three miles north of Sandusky and a half mile south of the Marblehead Peninsula, lay in the protected waters of Sandusky Bay and the prison had been built on the island's southeastern end. The island's remaining trees—many had been cut for firewood—clustered near several large two-story buildings outside the stockade.

After reading the letter Barbara had sent him, a letter purporting to be from her father, Major York had arranged for her visit and was at the dock to meet her. He was shorter than her father and quite stout.

"My dear Miss Thackery," he said, as they walked toward the stockade. "I can't tell you what a pleasure this is. Your father's not only my good friend but a fine man, yes, indeed. I was delighted to hear he'd been released from Libby Prison."

"It's kind of you to allow me to come here," she said, unable to simply blurt out what she meant to tell him.

"I thought you might like to have a cup of coffee in my office before we go inside the stockade," he said, steering her toward one of the frame buildings under the trees.

"That's kind of you, sir," she said hastily, "but if you don't mind I really would like to deliver the food I've brought for the prisoners first." She nodded toward the satchel Major York was carrying for her.

"I trust you won't be insulted if I glance inside your bag. Regulations, you know."

"I'd be surprised if you didn't check what I've brought, Major."

While he examined the contents of the bag, she gazed at the Stars and Stripes flying above the stockade palings of the stockade. It was good to see her country's flag again, good to be home and yet . . . She bit her lip, vowing she would not allow so much as one thought of Trevor to cross her mind.

As Major York escorted her through the guarded entrance of the stockade, the sentries shot her curious glances. Once inside, she found herself facing two long rows of barracks.

"We've more than three thousand Confederate

prisoners housed here at the moment," the major told her. He pointed out the exercise yards and the sentry boxes. "We try to treat the men as well as possible, considering they're enemies. This first building here is for officers. It's not possible for you to go inside but I'll ask the guard to bring out a few of the men and you can entrust them with the food. After this, perhaps it would be best if you visited only those men confined to the hospital."

Barbara nodded, feeling unutterably depressed by the drab buildings, the muddy ground between them, and the oppressive stench of human waste. Was this any better than Libby? Being inside these prison walls made her skin creep.

She mustered up a smile when two armed guards escorted four Reb officers toward where she stood with Major York.

"Halt!" one guard ordered. "'Tenshun!"

The heavily bearded Rebs obeyed. Barbara disliked seeming to stare at them, so she kept her eyes on the major. "Would it be all right if I asked their names?" she said.

As soon as the words were out of her mouth she realized that she meant to go ahead with what she'd promised Trevor she'd do, meant to betray her country instead of revealing the plot to Major York as she'd secretly planned. Somehow she just couldn't break her promise to Trevor.

She hated herself.

"Call out your name and rank," Major York ordered.

The Reb faces blurred as tears pricked her eyes.

"Captain Linden."

"Major Quindlen."

"Colonel Picard."

The officer she was to deliver the note to! Barbara quickly blinked away the tears so she could get a good look at Colonel Picard.

"General Meachum."

For a moment the last man's name didn't register with Barbara because she was concentrating on Colonel Picard. Then she realized what she'd heard. She stared at the fourth prisoner in shocked dismay.

General Meachum's hate-filled black eyes drilled into hers.

Barbara gasped and grabbed hold of Major York's arm. "Please," she begged, "take me out of here!"

Chapter 20

In the commandant's office, Major York hovered over Barbara who was huddled in a chair. "I blame myself," he said. "A prison compound is no place for a lady."

By exerting all her will, she managed to pull herself together enough to speak. "No, no, what happened wasn't your fault. I—" Her voice faltered and she couldn't go on, she couldn't bring herself to explain her intense hatred and fear of General Meachum.

"Your father meant well," the major said, "and you're a courageous young lady to attempt to carry out his wish to befriend our prisoners. Still, I'm not surprised the confrontation with the grimness of prison life overwhelmed you."

As he went on about the tender sensibilities of gently reared women, it finally struck Barbara that Major York had no idea what had upset her—he didn't connect her near collapse with General Meachum's presence. After all, how could he? He knew nothing of what had happened to her in the past few months.

At last fate had caught up with the general. If any man belonged inside a prison stockade, he did. And if she had anything to do with the matter, that's where he'd remain. Setting a madman like the general free would be a crime. A crime she didn't intend to commit. Even though it meant betraying Trevor.

Barbara took a deep breath, her mind made up. "Major, I have a confession to make."

Without mentioning Trevor, she explained the bargain she'd made with Confederate authorities—the release of her father for her cooperation in freeing Reb prisoners. "I was to pass a note to Colonel Picard," she finished, "but I find I can't go through with it, even though I'm breaking my promise." Reaching into her pocket, she produced the note.

Major York, his face mirroring his astonishment, unfolded the paper and read it. "On the tenth of the month, it says here," he commented. "A land assault." He banged a fist on his desk. "If this is true, you may be sure we'll be ready for them."

Barbara started to rise, thankful her part was over and done with. All she wanted now was to get as far away from General Meachum as possible.

"Just a minute, young lady," the major said. "Give me a few minutes to think this through." He steepled his fingers and tapped them against his chin.

Barbara sank back, tensing again as she waited

for him to speak. What now? Was she to be punished for her near traitorous role?

At last the major refolded the note and brandished it at her. "If this isn't delivered the Rebs may discover you haven't carried out your mission and change their plans to a different date. Are you game enough to spend another hour or two on the island, Miss Thackery? The arrangements I must make will take some time."

Though Barbara quailed inwardly, she said, "I'll do whatever you believe is necessary."

"I can see you're your father's daughter." He smiled his approval. "Luckily I still have your food satchel for you to use. Here's my plan . . ."

An hour later, Barbara was escorted by guards to the prison hospital where Dr. Woodbridge met her at the door. "Greetings, Miss Thackery," he said, smiling. "Major York tells me you wish to distribute food to my patients."

Judging by his face, he seemed a kind and patient man, Barbara thought as she summoned up a return smile. "Yes, Doctor. I trust you'll tell me what men most need the bread, rolls, butter, and cheese I've brought."

The doctor sighed. "I fear they all do. The rations here, even for the sick, are far from generous. I'll do my best to help you mete out the food fairly."

She discovered there were thirty-five patients, most suffering from pneumonia or typhoid fever. By walling off her emotions, she was able to pass among the gaunt-faced, hollow-eyed soldiers without breaking down. Since she'd divided the bread loaves into chunks, she was able to offer a portion of food to each of the thirty-five. Their feeble attempts to smile and their inarticulate gratitude tugged at her heart.

"You've been a godsend to my patients, Miss Thackery," Dr. Woodbridge told her after they left the ward rooms. "Not merely by bringing the food but in delivering it yourself. These poor men treasure the sight of a woman. Your being young and attractive is an added bonus. I thank you for your thoughtfulness."

Guilt settled over her like a cloud. This was none of her doing; she felt like an imposter. What had begun as a Confederate plot had been altered by the major to a Union counterplot and, though she was a key figure in both, she hadn't really come to Johnson Island because she wished to help the prisoners.

If the sight of the sick men haunted her forever it was no more than she deserved. How could she have lived in Sandusky all those years and given no thought to the suffering of the Johnson Island prisoners?

"I wish I could do more," she told the doctor, meaning every word. Though she doubted Major York would allow her to return to the island, she'd find some way to send food to the men in the hospital and in the stockade as well.

As the doctor escorted her to the entry where her guard waited, the door opened and two men, prisoners, stepped inside.

"Picard and Knowles reporting for orderly duty," Colonel Picard announced.

Barbara swallowed. Plastering a smile on her face that she hoped didn't look as fake as it felt, she walked up to the colonel. "I'm Miss Thackery, Colonel," she said, holding out her hand. "I believe I saw you by your barracks."

For a long moment Colonel Picard stared from her hand to her face as if he couldn't believe she was actually inviting him to touch her. Recovering himself, he took her hand and bowed over it, managing to conceal his surprise when she slid the note into his palm.

"I do hope you'll take good care of the sick men," she said as she stepped back. "They need it."

The colonel nodded. "We do our best. I'm honored to have met you, Miss Thackery."

Her smile now felt more like a grimace but she kept it in place until she was outside the hospital. By the time the major saw her aboard the boat for Sandusky she was past making any effort to talk. After the unexpected and frightening sight of General Meachum and the tension of carrying out the major's plan, all she wanted to do was reach her room in the boarding house, crawl into bed, and pull the covers over her head.

Perhaps she should feel proud that she hadn't betrayed her country, instead guilt hovered at her shoulder. She'd changed her mind, not because of high principles but because she'd been confronted with Meachum and found she could be no part of any plan that set him free. Whatever the reason, the result was the same—she'd broken her promise to Trevor.

When the ferry docked, she hurried along Sandusky's familiar streets. This had been her home once, but today she felt like a stranger here. Was it because she no longer had a home?

When she reached the boarding house, Mrs. Edwards, the landlady, met her at the door. "You have a gentleman waiting for you in the parlor," Mrs. Edwards said.

Though she knew Trevor didn't dare be seen in Sandusky, Barbara's heart lifted. Perhaps he'd come in disguise. Her fatigue forgotten, she rushed across the entry and stepped inside the parlor.

Reverend Hargreaves rose from the green brocaded chair with the claw feet and advanced with his hands held out to her. "My dear child," he said, "how grateful I am that God has returned you to us unharmed."

She couldn't prevent him from capturing one of her hands and clasping it between his but she refused to smile at the man who'd driven her from Sandusky. Greeting him coolly, she pulled her hand away and asked after his wife, keeping her words politely formal.

"Alas, my poor afflicted helpmeet has passed on into the chambers of the Lord," he said.

"I'm sorry." Was she? All Barbara could feel inside was a great weariness.

"Perhaps you could call at another time," she said. "I fear I'm too exhausted to be able to converse with you or anyone just now."

"You'll change your mind when you hear I've brought you a letter from your father," he assured

340

her. "Addressed to me, since he didn't know when you'd be home. Shall I read you the—?"

"No, don't read it, give it to me, please." Barbara held out her hand.

Annoyance creased his face as he fumbled in a pocket but he gave her the letter. "You've no need to remain in a boarding house," he said. "Your room at home is just as you left it."

Barbara stared at him, aghast. Was he actually proposing she move back into his house? Even if his wife had still been alive she wouldn't dream of such a thing. Since he'd become a widower, it made his invitation sickening to her.

"Your house ceased being mine months ago." Her distaste etched the words in acid. "I appreciate you bringing me my father's letter but I feel it's best if we don't meet again."

He drew himself up. "The Bible warns of the peril awaiting those with ungrateful hearts. Without my guidance, I'm afraid you're in danger of falling into wicked ways and will suffer dire consequences."

Anger overcame her attempt to remain polite. "You know very well why I won't ever live in your house again. God knows the truth as well and in the end He, not you, will determine who, if anyone, is punished. Good day, sir." She turned on her heel, marched from the parlor, and up the stairs to the room she shared with Tibba.

Tibba wasn't there and Barbara was just as glad. After her harrowing hours on Johnson Island, encountering Reverend Hargreaves in the parlor and being invited back to live with him had been the final straw. At the moment she didn't want to see or talk to another soul.

She took off her shoes and propped herself on the bed before looking at her father's letter. Just as she'd thought, it was addressed to her and not to Reverend Hargreaves. As far as she was concerned, the minister had no right to open it. He'd forfeited any rights he might have had as a guardian on the night she left his house.

No matter, she had the letter. And her father, thank God, was no longer imprisoned.

"My dear daughter," he wrote, "I hope this reaches you. Mail, as everything else in these uncertain times, is chancy. Self-reliant and courageous as you are, I assume you'll return to Sandusky unscathed. Besides, Captain Sandoe assures me he intends to look after you as he would his sister. I suspect, though, his feelings for you are quite different than brotherly.

"He may be a Reb, but the captain is a fine man, Barbara. He not only obtained my release from Libby on the 13th of September, but enlisted the aid of Miss Van Lew in finding suitable quarters and care for me."

Barbara paused, biting her lip. September 13th? But that was *before* Trevor had forced her into the agreement to help him free the prisoners on Johnson's Island. He'd arranged her father's freedom without her promise to cooperate in the Rebel plot. Her father had been out of Libby days before Trevor coerced her into promising to help the Rebs.

Conflicting emotions whirled in her head. It

342

was such a shock to discover her father's release hadn't depended on her agreement with Trevor that she wasn't sure whether she was angry or grateful. Bemused, she returned to the letter.

"I doubt you'd recognize me these days," he wrote, "for my hair has turned quite white—'The Yankee Eagle,' the guards at Libby called me."

The eagle in her dream! It had been her father, warning her about Dr. Dusharme. She now knew who the deer, the fox, and the eagle represented. But who had been the hawk battling to save her from the monstrous flower that had threatened to engulf her?

Barbara half-smiled. Trevor. She knew, oh, yes, she'd always known deep inside that Trevor would somehow rescue her from every danger.

"I don't quite know how to tell you my most recent news," her father wrote. "While I was imprisoned, a Richmond widow, Mrs. Appleton, came daily to Libby to do what she could for the ill among us, the enemies who'd killed her husband. I met her because I wasn't well for a time—my old malaria flaring up from lack of quinine. In any case, she was so kind and devoted I must confess that I, like many another sick Yankee prisoners, lost my heart to her.

"When I was released, I sent a message to her, not really believing she could possibly reciprocate my tender feelings. It was one of the happiest moments of my life when she came to me and confessed that she'd never been able to get me out of her mind. I love her in a different way than I loved your mother, Barbara, but I love her very much. When this war is finally over, we'll marry.

"That isn't all. I won't be returning to Ohio. The North has suffered losses, dear ones who'll never return, but the South has suffered far more. The end of the war will see a broken land and a broken people. I'm needed here, my dear, as I've never been needed anywhere else. I feel it's my duty to remain in Virginia and help heal the wounds of war. I hope and pray you'll want to join me here for I miss you, my darling girl. Your devoted father."

Barbara dropped the letter onto the bed as she tried to come to terms with its contents. Her father meant to marry this Mrs. Appleton? A Confederate! Somehow she'd never expected him to remarry and certainly he'd never before given her reason to believe he wasn't coming back to Ohio.

He'd asked her to write him in care of Mrs. Appleton. Was he staying with her? Living in her house? What was she like? Barbara tried to imagine what kind of a woman her father would fall in love with. Kind and devoted, he'd called her. She must be that, and more, to not only be able to forgive the enemies who'd killed her husband but to nurse sick and wounded Union prisoners. Obviously the Widow Appleton was an extraordinary woman.

Since Barbara hardly remembered her mother, she didn't believe her father should remain true to the memory of a woman she'd never really known. On the other hand, this letter made her wonder how well she knew her father. While she wished him to be happy, she couldn't help but feel he was

344

deserting her, even though he'd invited her to return to Richmond after the war and live with him. No, with them. But if she did, wouldn't she be intruding? Besides, there was Tibba to consider. Tibba hadn't liked living in Richmond. Even when the War had been won and slavery no longer existed, would the people of Virginia treat Tibba any differently?

Once this Johnson Island plot is over and done with Tibba and I must talk seriously about the future, Barbara told herself.

Now that she'd warned Major York, the Confederate plot was doomed—the prisoners would remain where they were, behind the stockade. What would Trevor do after his attack on the prison was defeated? Return to Richmond? Probably. Unless he was captured in the fighting. Or worse . . .

She shook her head, unable to bear the thought of Trevor in danger. She had to keep believing nothing bad would happen to him.

Exhausted by the day's upsets and her worries, Barbara dozed off, falling into a deep sleep. When she woke the room was in darkness and she heard rain beating against the windows. Where is Tibba? she wondered as she swung her feet over the side of the bed and groped for the match case so she could light the kerosene lamp. She was adjusting the burning wick when Tibba came into the room.

Before Barbara could ask any questions, Tibba said, "I've been downstairs talking to Mrs. Edwards. Hurry, or you'll miss supper."

As she tidied her hair and smoothed the wrinkles

345

from her gown, Barbara noticed how flushed Tibba was. "You're not getting a fever, are you?" she asked, concerned.

Tibba laughed. "I've never felt better in my entire life." She lifted her arms and, humming a waltz, twirled around the room. "Life is wonderful!" she exclaimed, grasping Barbara's hands and pulling her into the dance.

Though bewildered by Tibba's excitement, Barbara humored her by taking several turns about the room before stepping back. "Didn't you say supper was being served?" she asked.

"Who needs to eat?" Tibba asked, her eyes dreamy.

Barbara frowned. Tibba's behavior was decidedly odd. "Where have you been all afternoon?" she asked.

"In another world," Tibba said. "I found a music store that has a harp for sale and the man allowed me to play it."

Barbara took Tibba's arm. "Other world or not, we're going down to supper."

All through the meal Barbara tried to come up with a painless method of telling Tibba that her father was a prisoner on Johnson Island. At last she concluded there was no painless way and made up her mind to remain quiet. Why did Tibba need to be frightened when General Meachum was safely behind a fourteen-foot high stockade with armed guards in sentry boxes watching every move the prisoners made? Even if a Reb should manage to scale the stockade wall without being shot and reach the lake without anyone from the garrison spotting him, he'd face the half-mile of water separating the island from the shore. This time of year even a good swimmer might falter in Lake Erie's chilly waters.

She'd about convinced herself escape was impossible when she remembered that Trevor had done the impossible just a few months ago. He'd never told her the details of his escape—why hadn't she asked him? If he'd gotten away from the island, then the general might be able to. Barbara shuddered at the thought.

Tibba must be told.

She put it off until they were undressing for bed, then blurted out the bad news all at once. "Your father's a prisoner on Johnson Island. I saw him there today."

Tibba gasped, the becoming flush draining from her cheeks. "God help me! He'll escape and come after me, I know he will."

Barbara sought to reassure her by listing the many safeguards but when she finished Tibba shook her head. "Trevor got away from there, didn't he? My father will, too. If he saw you he'll suspect I'm with you and he'll come for me." She hugged herself, shivering. "What can I do, oh, dear God, what can I do?"

It took Barbara over an hour to calm Tibba enough to get her to try to sleep. After that she lay awake for some time trying to calm herself. She heard a church bell toll midnight before she finally slept.

When she woke in the morning Tibba was gone, her carpetbag with her. Alarmed, Barbara dressed hastily and hurried downstairs. Tibba wasn't in the house.

"Why, no, I didn't see Miss Meachum leave," Mrs. Edwards said when asked.

Now truly upset, Barbara didn't now where to turn next. If Harrison were in town she'd ask him to help her search for Tibba but she knew he'd left on the early morning train for Cleveland to interview Copperheads. He'd said he wouldn't be back for at least three days.

Where could Tibba be? Barbara's only consolation was that the rain had ended so at least her friend wasn't wandering about cold and wet.

She had no appetite for breakfast but she forced herself to eat before she left the boarding house to go to the music store. Though she doubted Tibba was there, she had to be sure.

"No, miss," the proprietor said. "I haven't seen any woman like you describe. Not today. Not yesterday, either, not in my store."

"She played your harp," Barbara persisted.

"Miss, I don't have a harp on the premises. Not enough demand for them in these parts."

His shop had always been the only music store in Sandusky and Barbara hadn't seen another as she walked through town. She asked him anyway.

"Not enough business for two music stores," the proprietor told her. "Mine's all there is."

Barbara thanked him and left, more upset than ever. He hadn't been lying, she was sure. But that meant Tibba had been. Why?

Since she could hardly stop each person on the street to ask if they'd seen a woman of Tibba's description and didn't have any idea what else to do, Barbara walked slowly back to the boarding house, hoping against hope Tibba would have returned when she got there.

Tibba wasn't at Mrs. Edwards's. The landlady, though, had a message for Barbara.

"A young lad brought the note," Mrs. Edwards said. "He told me a man paid him a penny to deliver it here."

A man? What man? Alarmed by what might have happened to Tibba, Barbara opened the paper and scanned the contents. To her surprise it wasn't from Tibba, nor about Tibba. According to the note, Major York wished her presence on Johnson Island regarding a matter of great importance and would send Lieutenant Tabler to escort her there at four that afternoon.

Her first impulse was to decline to go. With Tibba missing, how could she? Besides, she never wanted to set foot on Johnson Island again. But as she thought it over she realized the major must need her on the island for a good reason, one he'd been too wary to put onto paper. It was her duty to obey his request.

She fretted her way through the day, fearful for Tibba and apprehensive about having to return to Johnson Island. By four she was waiting in the parlor with her bonnet and shawl ready. Lieutenant Tabler, a young man who looked no older than herself, arrived fifteen minutes late. Though his blonde mustache and beard were neatly trimmed, she thought his blue uniform rather ill-fitting.

349

His name wasn't familiar but she thought she'd seen him before—no doubt on the island.

"Ready, miss?" he asked.

She tied on her bonnet, took up her shawl, and then nodded. "Did we meet yesterday?" she asked as they walked down the boarding house steps.

"No, miss."

On the way to the docks she asked other questions, hoping he'd indicate in some way she was being summoned by the major, but the lieutenant's answers, though polite, were confined to yes, no, and don't know.

Rather than one of the stern-wheeler ferries serving the various nearby islands, the boat he led her to was no larger than a fishing tug—in fact, that's what it resembled.

When she gave the lieutenant an inquiring look, he said, "Major York don't want you seen."

About to ask why, she frowned, struck by something familiar in his voice now that he'd spoken more than two words at a time. She'd be willing to swear she'd heard him speak to her before today. But if not on the island, where could it have been? And why hadn't he mentioned a former meeting? Could it be he'd forgotten it?

"Right this way, miss." Lieutenant Tabler urged her up the rough plank serving as a gangway.

Unable to place where or when she'd come in contact with him before, she shrugged and boarded the tug, though the question still nagged at her.

The boat cast off immediately, the sailor who'd

released the lines from the dock posts leaping aboard at the last moment.

"You'd best duck inside the cabin, miss," the lieutenant suggested. "So's they can't see you."

She stared at him, more and more certain she knew him, yet she couldn't place where they'd met. Maybe he'd grown a beard in the meantime? Beard. The word reverberated in her mind and suddenly she knew. She'd last seen him in West Virginia—he was the man she'd thought too young to grow a beard.

"Beardless!" she gasped. Pointing her finger at him, she demanded, "What are you doing in a Union uniform?"

"Lem's wearing the uniform because it fit him the best," a man's voice said from inside the open door of the cabin, a voice that froze the very blood in her veins.

"Do come in, my dear," General Meachum said. "We have time for a cozy chat before we reach our rendezvous."

Barbara started to back away from the door but found Beardless behind her blocking her retreat. She glanced desperately toward the rail, at the widening gap between the boat and the dock and saw another of Meachum's Raiders—Redbeard—grinning at her and knew the boat must be entirely manned by his men. She was trapped.

"Will you walk into my cabin," the general asked, "or will you be dragged in?"

Chapter 21

As the tug churned steadily away from the pier, Barbara gave one last frantic look around her. She saw no dock workers and, though there were other boats in the bay, none was close enough for those aboard to hear a call for help. Meachum's Raiders manned the tug, giving her no one to turn to. Since she refused to be dragged ignominiously inside, she took a deep breath and walked into the tiny cabin.

In a protective wall holder, a lantern burned dimly, its glass chimney smudged with soot. A bunk hugged the back wall with a built-in commode beside it. To her left was a table attached to the side wall. Finally she had to look at the man sitting on a chair, one arm resting on the table as he methodically pricked its battered wooden top with a horn-handled hunting knife.

Tasting fear's bitterness on her tongue, Barbara fought to control her terror. Since she'd last seen him behind the stockade, General Meachum had shaved off his beard, leaving only the thin mustache he'd sported when he captured her the first time. His face, always gaunt, verged on the skeletal now, giving him even more of a snakelike appearance.

"Do sit down, Barbara," he said, smiling as he gestured to the chair across the table from him. "I can't tell you how pleased I am to see you."

She seated herself stiffly, saying nothing, so frightened she was unsure she could speak if she tried. Although she struggled not to watch the point of his knife rise and fall, entering the wood each time with a dull snick, the sharp blade inexorably drew her gaze.

"Do you know why you're here, my dear?" he asked.

She managed a shake of her head, looking neither at him nor the bunk at the back of the cabin, her hands twisting together in her lap as the horrors of her captivity in his valley plantation roiled in her mind.

"I see by your face you fear the worst." The words were laced with amusement. "Who knows, you may be right. For the present, though, I shall take care that no one harms so much as one hair of your head since you, my dear, are my ticket to freedom."

Ticket to freedom. Someone else had said that to her. Who? When? Where? Slowly her mind began to clear. Trevor had been the first to call her a ticket to freedom. In the boxcar. Trevor had frightened her in the beginning but he hadn't really harmed her. General Meachum was a very different kind of man.

She forced one word from her paralyzed throat. "How?"

"It's very simple. Didn't you read the note before you passed it to Picard?"

"No." It was the truth. She knew of the note's contents both from Trevor and from Major York but she had no intention of revealing that.

The general shook his head. "Such nobility of character. It wouldn't have mattered if you had read it because the note was in code—or so I learned from Picard who was foolish enough to trust me."

Barbara drew in her breath. Code! Major York hadn't mentioned the possibility. Had he even considered code?

"A simple enough code," the general said. "The first number was to be the date of the invasion and, if the note said by land, the attack would come by sea—or vice versa."

Not the tenth of this month, then, but the first, she thought. The first—today! And by sea.

Without meaning to, she stared at the general and whispered, "Today."

He smiled. "Excellent, my dear. Somewhere beyond the confines of Sandusky Bay, the invasion boat awaits. The Confederate plan is to approach the *USS Michigan* tonight in their boat, swarm aboard under cover of darkness, capture the crew, and take control of the gunboat, the only armed vessel on Lake Erie.

"They will then liberate the Johnson Island prisoners, arm them, and stage an invasion of the North by land and sea, aided and abetted by local Copperheads, thus diverting Grant's troops from Virginia and giving Lee a chance to regroup."

The Rebel plot seemed clear enough but

Barbara couldn't quite understand what role General Meachum meant to play. "But you've escaped from the island ahead of time," she said.

"I've never been accused of being a fool," he told her. "It's a desperate plot, the last gasp of a dying South—I knew the plan was doomed from the moment Picard broached it. For one thing, I doubt a single Copperhead will be willing to fight for his so-called beliefs. But in the plot, I saw my chance, so last night I put my own plan into action. Prisoners are allowed to make their own furniture so for weeks my men have been separately fashioning pieces of a raft under the guise of table tops and quietly slipping them through the four-inch gaps between the pales on the lake side of the stockade, slipping them to one of our men working as an orderly at the hospital.

"Last night we dressed Lem in the Yankee uniform we've been hiding and he marched four of us through the gate pretending he was taking us to the hospital. The other three managed to scale the stockade under cover of darkness. We met by the shore where the raft pieces were concealed, lashed them together and paddled for the mainland. There would have been little point to this daring escape without the raid planned for the first of November. Some, if not all of us, would have been quickly recaptured."

He paused and she mulled over what he'd told her. "I thought you believed the Confederate plot was doomed," she said.

"As it is. But the planners, according to Picard, are aboard a Canadian vessel resembling a blockade runner. In other words, a boat built for speed.

We wouldn't get far enough fast enough with this plodding tug since we dare sail only by daylight. Jack's the one man among us who knows anything about boats—and he can't navigate at night. Once our escape's made public and the theft of the tug's discovered, the *Michigan* would blast us out of the water as soon as it got light.

"Fortunately, Jack does have enough skill to get us to the Reb boat before nightfall." He smiled at her. "That's where you come in. I like my revenge but I wouldn't have bothered with you at this time if Picard hadn't let slip who was leading the incursion. Once I learned Sandoe was commanding, you became a necessity. Sandoe's already risked his neck for you; you're his weak spot. Using you as hostage, I'll soon have control of his boat. My men will have no trouble forcing the sailors to return to Canada before dawn—and there we'll be safe."

"But you—you're betraying your own side!"

With a vicious jerk he stabbed the knife point deeply into the table. "Didn't they repudiate *me?* Those who cross me eventually regret it."

The fear that had ebbed while she listened to his tale of escape returned full force, fear as much for Trevor as for herself. He meant to kill Trevor, she was certain, even if he didn't have to gain control of the boat. What could she do? Was there any way to scuttle his evil scheme?

As if divining her thoughts, General Meachum yanked the knife from the wood and thrust the point toward her. "This is to insure your cooperation," he said.

A quiver of terror ran along her spine as she

recalled how he'd used another knife to slash her clothes from her and how, as she lay helplessly tied to the bed, she'd expected him to use the knife on her. She remembered Tibba mentioning the valley graveyard where the general's other women victims lay, and she shuddered.

The general laughed. "This time there'll be no escape, my dear. At least not for you and the redoubtable captain. I'm a man who never forgets an insult or an injury. Never. I also mean to keep what belongs to me. I assume my daughter came with you to Sandusky. I haven't time to retrieve her now but I'll find her someday if I have to track her to the ends of the earth—and she knows it, doesn't she?"

When Barbara said nothing, he jabbed the knife point into the tabletop again. "Answer me!"

She jumped. "I—I suppose so."

"Tibba's as obstinate as her mother. Soft as silk on the surface but with an iron heart. And devious, too, but perhaps she gets that from me. I wanted a son but that New Orleans bitch defied me even there. Women are never to be trusted. You, for instance, are sitting there planning how to outwit me."

Anger sizzled inside her, burning away some of her fear. How she loathed this man! She refused to give up and submit numbly to whatever horrible fate he had planned for her. She'd fight against him to the end.

"Jack's got her spotted, sir," Lem called in through the open door. "Says he's sure 'tis the right boat."

The general thrust the knife into a sheath on his

belt and rose. He pulled her to her feet and shoved her in front of him from the cabin, her arm twisted painfully behind her back.

Dead ahead Barbara saw a two-masted boat, sails furled, silhouetted against the evening sky. Smoke curled from her stack.

"Flying the Stars and Stripes," the general noted. "Sandoe evidently pays attention to details."

"What if she ain't the right boat, sir?" Lem asked.

"No harm done—they won't know who we are. Wave the lantern and give her a hail. Say we need help."

An answering shout came from the bigger boat. "Can't help. Stand aside!"

"Tell them Colonel Picard wishes to come aboard," the general ordered. Lem obeyed.

After a few moment's delay came the answer. "Stand to port and cut your engine."

"Got him!" General Meachum's voice rang with triumph.

Barbara knew she must warn Trevor here and now but before she could draw breath to shout, she felt the cold blade of the horn-handled knife prick her throat.

"I wouldn't try it," the general whispered into her ear, the words as chilling as a snake's hiss.

When the tug had pulled alongside the boat, Barbara heard Trevor's voice from the deck above. "Train your guns on him until I see his face."

"A careful man," the general murmured to her. "But not careful enough. In his place I would have rammed and sunk the tug rather than take any risk."

Barbara swallowed, feeling the knife's pressure against her throat. He was as cold-blooded as the snake he reminded her of.

"Picard here," General Meachum barked in a disguised voice. "Bastards winged me. Need help."

Lanterns bobbed at the bigger boat's rail but failed to cast enough light to illuminate the deck of the tug. "We're dropping you a ladder," Trevor's voice called from above.

"That you, Sandoe?" the general barked. "For God's sake, man come down and help me aboard."

Don't do it, Barbara prayed.

Muttered conversation above, then Trevor said, "I'm sending down a sling. Have someone help you into it and we'll pull you up."

"Hurry!" The general turned to Lem and said, sotto voce, "Gag her."

His knife never left her throat as Lem stuffed a smelly, vile-tasting rag into her mouth, then shoved another over her lips and tied it behind her head.

Barbara gagged, trying desperately not to vomit for she feared she'd choke to death if she did.

A webbed sling inched down until it touched the deck of the tug. The general hooked an arm around her neck and yanked her down into the sling with him so she was seated on his lap. Her struggle to breathe against the pressure of his arm left her without strength to fight. Slowly the sling rose up the hull and over the rail into the light of the lanterns.

"Damned if he ain't got a woman with him!" a man cried.

As General Meachum leaped from the sling with his arm still locked around her throat, Barbara, numb with terror, saw the shock in Trevor's eyes.

The general put his back to the rail. "See the knife, Sandoe? Have your men throw down their arms. If anyone makes a wrong move, she dies."

For a long moment no one spoke. She held her breath.

"Do as he says, men." Trevor's voice was strained.

She heard metal hitting the deck as the boat's crew obeyed.

"What the hell is this, Meachum?" Trevor demanded. "We're all on the same side."

"Send a ladder down to my men on the tug."

Evidently no one moved to obey quickly enough for the general because Barbara felt the knife point prick the swell of her breast. Her moan of pain and fear was muffled by the gag.

"Good God, Meachum, I'm doing everything you ask!" Trevor cried.

General Meachum waited until his Raiders stood on the deck before speaking. "I'm taking over the invasion, Sandoe. My men are going to pick up those guns and if anything happens while they're at it . . ." He let the words trail off.

"You don't know the invasion plan," Trevor protested.

"Picard told me."

"All right, anything you say. Just let her go." She could hear the desperation in Trevor's voice.

"Not quite yet."

All of a sudden Barbara realized what the general planned. She was sure he meant to shoot Trevor, to kill him in front of her. She must stop him—but how?

Her father's voice rang in her head. "Some men try to take advantage of girls," he'd warned. "Don't let them. Women aren't as strong as men but they can learn to fight in their own way." She reviewed the simple methods he'd taught her and found one possibility that might work. If the general's knife didn't kill her first.

She raised her foot and stomped hard with the heel of her boot on his toes. When he lurched involuntarily, his arm relaxed slightly, giving her enough leverage to lower her head, then abruptly ram it upward so the top of her skull hit him under the chin.

He staggered backward, his grip loosening, and she slid free and flung herself sideways, rolling onto the deck, seeing stars from the blow to her head. Men shouted and swore. By the time her vision cleared she saw to her horror that Meachum had a gun in his hand and that Trevor, flinging himself toward her, didn't notice.

She screamed but the sound was muffled by the gag. Meachum shot. Trevor jumped back. Had he been hit? Meachum aimed again, more carefully. But Trevor was up and over the rail before he pulled the trigger the second time. Meachum raced to the rail.

"No sign of him," he muttered. "I know I hit the bastard." He turned to Lem. "How about the tug? Can he swim to it?"

Lem, looking over the opposite rail, said, "I scuttled her like Jack showed me afore we climbed up. She's a goner, half sunk already."

"Good. Then Sandoe's a goner as well. Jack, you go to the bridge and make sure the man up there routes us to Canada." He gestured toward Barbara. "Lem, you take her inside the cabin and tie her to the bunk."

Barbara knew Trevor was an excellent swimmer but they were miles from shore and he was wounded as well. He'd drown in the cold November lake. Her will to resist gone, her head throbbing with pain, she wept as Lem led her away. The discomfort of sobbing with a gag in place made her reach up and untie the cloth and spit out the rag before they reached the cabin.

"I don't like doing this, miss," Lem muttered as he wrapped a rope around her wrists. "I purely don't like it and that's the truth."

But he tied her anyway. Not to the bunk, though, she realized after he left her alone. What he'd done was bind her ankles together and tie her wrists together in front of her. A faint hope flickered inside Barbara. She couldn't possibly get away from Meachum, but there might be a chance to free herself before he came into the cabin. God knows she'd prefer to be free when she finally had to face him.

A lantern burned in a fixed holder on the commode next to the bunk. She maneuvered and struggled for what seemed hours before she finally squirmed into a position where she was able to raise her wrists above the lamp chimney in the hope she could burn through the rope. But as she was doing so she noticed one of the metal hasps on the lamp holder was broken off, leaving on a sharp edge. Even better!

The rope at her wrists took some time to saw through and after that her numb fingers fumbled at the knots for long minutes before she freed her ankles. She stood up and staggered around the cabin searching for a weapon while the circulation returned to her feet. She found a small wooden chest and opened it. To her disappointment nothing she could use for a weapon was inside, just sailor's rough winter garb.

She'd taken another turn around the room before she saw how she might possibly elude the general, at least for a while.

Yanking off her clothes hurriedly, every second expecting him to slam the door open, she flung on thick woolen pants, a long-sleeved sweater and tucked her hair up under a stocking cap. In the dark her boots wouldn't be noticeable as a woman's under the rolled-up legs of the pants. She stowed her clothes inside the chest and, after pulling a pair of knit gloves over her hands, she eased open the door and peered out.

Men strode back and forth on deck but she didn't see the general. She slipped free of the cabin, carefully closed the door behind her, and sidled along the cabin's outside wall, keeping in the shadows until she found a stack of kegs. She weighed the chances of being caught hiding behind the kegs against being caught in the open and opted for hiding. She'd no sooner settled herself than a flare burst in the sky, showering its cold green light over the boat and the water.

Barbara gasped. A large boat stood off the stern, a boat with a familiar outline. She'd seen the *USS Michigan* anchored in Sandusky Bay often enough to recognize the gunboat.

The flare dimmed and went out, leaving the darkness more profound than before to her dazzled eyes. Almost immediately flame spurted from where she'd seen the *Michigan*, and a shell exploded to the port of her boat, all but deafening her. They were being fired on! This boat had no mounted cannons like the gunboat so they were helpless. What could General Meachum do?

Barbara cowered behind the kegs as men raced along the deck, shouting. She feared Meachum would never give up, that he'd sooner see his boat at the bottom of Lake Erie than surrender.

Another flare lit up the sky and in its glare she saw the general not more than five or six feet away from her, waving his pistol as he snapped orders at two of the boat's crewmen. Another shell exploded close by.

Without giving herself time to think what might happen to her once she was discovered, Barbara rose and shoved the top keg, tipping it until the keg fell onto the deck. The noise of its rolling was concealed by the echoes of the shellburst and General Meachum didn't spot the keg before it slammed into his legs, knocking him against the rail. The pistol flew from his hand and one of the sailors scooped it up. Without hesitation he fired pointblank at the general, once, twice, three times.

With no more emotion than if the sailor had shot a venemous copperhead, Barbara watched the

364

general slide onto the deck and lie unmoving, blood stains spreading across the front of his jacket.

"Meachum's dead!" the sailor shouted. "The bastard's dead. Run up the white flag! Stop the engines or we'll be blown to hell."

Barbara was still crouched behind the remaining kegs when Union sailors boarded the boat and it was some time before one of them found her and discovered, to his amazement, that she was a woman.

At Mrs. Edwards's boarding house, Barbara gazed listlessly up from her pillow at Tibba who was seated on the edge of the bed frowning down at her.

"You can't lie in bed forever," Tibba scolded. "The sun's out and Harrison's waiting in the parlor to take us for a drive."

"I don't want to go."

"You *have* to. The doctor said there's nothing wrong with you so if you don't get up right now I'm going to drag you out of that bed and dress you by force—see if I don't!" She took hold of Barbara's wrist and pulled.

Deciding that Tibba might make good her threat, Barbara sighed, sat up and swung her legs over the edge of the bed. She didn't care if the sun shone or not, didn't care whether she ate or not, didn't care about anything. But even in her misery over Trevor, she realized she'd been causing Tibba a lot of unnecessary work carrying trays of food up and down stairs, food she scarcely touched.

Four days had passed since that horrible night on the lake when the *Michigan* captured the invasion boat. Barbara had learned that the reason the *Michigan* had hunted down the Canadian boat so quickly was because Harrison had returned to the boarding house with Tibba soon after Barbara left with the false Lieutenant Tabler.

After Tibba queried Mrs. Edwards and learned about the note, she persuaded Harrison to go to the docks with her. A couple of angry fishermen stood on the pier watching the tug sail off and Harrison learned from them the boat had been stolen.

Other dockhands had noticed a Union officer escort a young woman aboard the tug. Tibba immediately suspected General Meachum had escaped, and had kidnapped Barbara and stolen the tug. She finally convinced Harrison, and he hired a boat and carried the news to Major York at the prison. The major, already aware the general and his men had escaped, notified the commanding officer of the *Michigan*.

The result was that the gunboat set off in pursuit of the tug, discovered it foundering, and caught sight of the invasion boat when they sent up flares. They had then fired the shots across the stern as a warning to stop and be boarded.

In effect, Harrison and Tibba had saved Barbara's life.

The least I can do, she told herself as she dressed, is please them by going for a drive. It isn't their fault they don't understand that nothing matters to me, not without Trevor.

In the carriage, she sat between Harrison and Tibba while he drove.

"Though I realize how ghastly it must have been for you," Harrison said to Barbara, "Tibba was vastly relieved when you assured her you'd seen General Meachum die with your very own eyes. She was weeping and shaking all over when she routed me from my bed at the hotel early on November 1st, insisting I must take her to Cleveland with me or her father would find her and kill her."

So that was where Tibba had fled, Barbara thought. She'd not considered the possibility at the time.

"It was hours before I could persuade her to return to the boardinghouse," Harrison went on, "only to find *you* gone."

"It's over and *he's* dead and gone," Tibba said. "Please let's not talk about him."

Tears stung Barbara's eyes. Trevor was dead and gone, too. Caught up in her grief, she didn't notice which road Harrison took until she found herself looking at the pine grove along the lake where White Deer's village once stood. Immediately she was overwhelmed with awful memories of the night the village burned.

"No!" she cried. "No, not this way. Turn around!"

Harrison turned back without question.

"So many dead," Barbara whispered brokenly. "The good as well as the evil."

Holding the reins with one hand, Harrison patted her shoulder. "A few of us in-betweeners are still among the living," he said.

His attempt at humor, weak though it was, reminded her she hadn't been invited on the drive so they could watch her weep. Barbara blocked off her mind as best she could and descended into numbness. When the carriage passed familiar scenes of her childhood, she felt nothing. She couldn't even pretend interest in what she saw.

On the way back to the boarding house, Harrison stopped at the dry goods store while Tibba ran in and bought embroidery floss for Mrs. Edwards.

"Will you meet me at the bandstand in the park tomorrow morning at ten?" Harrison asked Barbara abruptly. "Leave Tibba behind. I have an important matter I must discuss with you alone."

Startled from her apathy, she stared at him.

"*Very* important," he insisted.

"Why, yes, I suppose I can." She spoke uncertainly, wondering what he could possibly wish to discuss with her.

In the morning, Barbara slipped from the house while Tibba was practicing scales on the parlor piano. Once Mrs. Edwards had learned Tibba played the harp, she'd taken it upon herself to teach Tibba the piano.

The day was sunny and crisp, with a hint of frost in the air, the kind of late autumn morning that Barbara once loved. Today, though, it might as well have been the dead of winter for all she cared about the weather. The park was nearly deserted this early on a weekday and no one besides Harrison was anywhere near the bandstand.

He took both her hands in greeting and led her up to sit on the top step of the gazebolike structure.

When he satisfied himself she was comfortable and not too chilly, he shook his head at her.

"Do you intend to wear the black of mourning both inside and out for the rest of your life?" he demanded.

Barbara was taken aback. "I believe what I do is my own business," she said finally.

"Not if it makes you ill. I realize you were more than fond of Trevor but you mustn't go on like this. Tibba tells me your father plans to marry a Richmond widow and remain in the South. What will *you* do?"

Barbara had no answer. She didn't know what she meant to do.

"Now that her father's dead, Tibba can claim his holdings in West Virginia—she's his only legitimate child. She plans to go back home. Will you go with her?" Harrison asked.

No! Even though the general was no more, Barbara never wanted to enter that terrible valley again. She shook her head.

"I thought as much." Harrison smiled slightly and tugged his mustache. "Why not sail for England with me?"

"England? With you?" she echoed, not believing her ears.

"We'd marry first, of course, everything proper and aboveboard."

Barbara was dumbfounded. Was Harrison actually proposing marriage?

He held up a hand. "Don't answer immediately. Think over my proposal very carefully. The mater's been after me to choose a wife and I know my family would take to you immediately, unlike—" He broke off and cleared his throat. "What I mean to say is, you and I would get on well, don't you think? I really am very fond of you." Again he held up his hand. "No, don't say a word until you've weighed all the possibilities and considered all the choices. Meanwhile, this will be our secret."

Needing to be alone, Barbara firmly refused his offer to escort her back to the boardinghouse. She walked through the fallen leaves, absently scuffling them with her boots as she'd used to do as a child, her thoughts bleak. Tibba would be leaving, going home to West Virginia. Harrison would soon sail for London. And her father wasn't returning to Ohio. She'd be alone here. Unless she accepted Harrison's proposal.

She'd never love any man except Trevor, so if she ever did marry, liking the man would be the best she could hope for.

She did like Harrison. And England would be a new country, a place she'd never been, a land with no memories for her, happy or unhappy. She'd be starting anew.

Did she really have any other choice except to marry him?

Chapter 22

Tibba wasn't at the boardinghouse when Barbara returned, but she came into the bedroom about an hour later. Barbara, sitting in the rocker by the window, staring down at the brown lifelessness of the sideyard garden, had just decided that she couldn't possibly marry Harrison. After Trevor, how could she bear any other man's touch? No, she wouldn't marry Harrison—she'd never marry.

She greeted Tibba absently, but her friend didn't respond. Marching to the wardrobe, Tibba removed her carpetbag from its depths, set the bag on the bed, and opened it.

Barbara, jolted from her preoccupation with her own problems, rose. "Tibba?"

Tibba, flinging her clothes into the bag willynilly, didn't so much as glance at her.

Barbara walked to the bed and laid a hand on her friend's arm. "Tibba, what's wrong?"

Tibba flung off her hand. "As if you didn't know!"

About to insist she didn't, Barbara paused, recalling that Tibba had behaved this way before—when they were aboard the boat bound for Canada, after Harrison boarded at Bermuda. She stared at Tibba, remembering how her friend had disappeared for hours on the boat, explaining later that she'd been helping a mother care for a child.

Just a few days ago Tibba had lied to her about spending hours in the music store, playing a harp. Had she lied on the boat, as well? Was it possible she'd been with Harrison both those times? Thinking about how Tibba had danced about the room, giddy with happiness, saying she was in another world, Barbara nodded to herself. She knew the incandescent joy of those other worlds, for she'd visited one herself. With Trevor.

"You're in love with Harrison, aren't you?" she asked.

Tibba whirled to face her. "No! I hate him!" Her chin quivered. "And you—" Sobs choked her as tears ran down her cheeks. Words spewed incoherently from her between the sobs. " . . . made love to me . . . his family . . . not good enough . . . you instead . . ."

Anger flowed into Barbara as the realization of Harrison's perfidy became clear. He must have been making love to Tibba for weeks, making believe he loved her as she so clearly loved him. Yet when it came to marriage, suddenly Tibba wasn't good enough—his family wouldn't approve. He'd given that much away at the bandstand when he'd proposed marriage to her.

"How dare he!" Barbara cried. She took hold of Tibba's shoulders and shook her. "Where is he? Where is that deceiving, heartless excuse for a man?"

Tibba stopped crying abruptly and stared at Barbara. "I thought you were going to marry him."

"Never! What I intend to do is give him a piece of my mind."

"When I left him he was going back to the hotel."

Barbara turned Tibba and pressed her down until she sat on the bed. "You stay here. Don't you dare leave before I get back. Promise?"

Tibba hesitated, then nodded.

At the hotel, Barbara asked the desk clerk to send a message to Mr. Chambers to meet her in the lobby. When he hurried into the room she was standing in an alcove by the front window, as far removed as possible from the few men sitting and smoking their cigars. She turned on him the minute he came up to her.

"You don't deserve a sweet girl like Tibba." Anger and distaste tinged her voice. "What kind of a man are you to seduce a girl who's in love with you and then reject her so callously? If this is how Englishmen behave, thank God I live in America."

Harrison glanced over his shoulder uneasily. "Please, Barbara, this is no place—"

"I don't care if the entire world discovers how despicable you are." She narrowed her eyes. "I've heard the word cad but I never before met a man the description fit. Now I have. You, sir, are one. A cad. To satisfy your own selfish pleasures you've broken Tibba's heart."

Harrison grasped her arm, propelled her across the lobby and out the entrance of the hotel. At first she thought he only meant to get rid of her, but then he began walking her briskly along the street.

"I don't wish to go anywhere with you," she said coldly, extricating herself.

He tugged at his mustache. "To be fair you should hear my side. I have one, you know. But I don't wash my linen in public. A hotel lobby is no place for a private conversation. Will you hear me out?"

She didn't want to spend a moment longer with him, but it was true she hadn't allowed him to say a word in his defense. Not that anything he could say would change her mind about his devious, badly blemished character.

"Well?" she demanded.

"Shall we turn down this side street where it isn't so busy?"

She complied.

"Do you realize I love Tibba?" he asked.

She gave a ladylike snort. "Considering your recent underhanded behavior, how can you expect me to believe that?"

"Tibba's unique, she's wonderful, I've never met anyone like her before and I don't expect to again. But she *is* part Negro. That doesn't matter to me. I'd take her to England with me; I'd even marry her if it weren't for the fact Mater would be extremely distraught. She could never tolerate Negro blood in the family."

"By Mater I take it you mean your mother. Strange, I thought you were a grown man, one who made his own decisions."

"You don't understand—"

"Oh, I think I do. You say you love Tibba but you really don't or no one could keep you two apart." She stopped and faced him. "In time I might be able to forgive you for proposing marriage to me without telling me about you and Tibba, but I can never forgive you for your callous behavior toward her. You're a man of no principles, Harrison Chambers, as well as cravenly. I despise you and I sincerely hope I never have to see you again." She turned from him, crossed the street, and marched off.

Tibba was waiting in the bedroom. "What did he say?" she demanded when Barbara came in.

"He claims he loves you and blames his mother. If that's so, he's a coward and you deserve better." Barbara nodded toward the half-packed carpetbag. "Where were you going?"

"To West Virginia."

"Do you really want to go—" About to say home, Barbara substituted, "There?"

Tibba bit her lip. "I don't know what I want to do."

Barbara gave her a sad smile. "That makes two of us."

"I have nowhere else to go," Tibba said. "Will you come with me?"

Barbara shook her head. "I couldn't live in that

valley. Not after—" She broke off. "But you're very kind to invite me."

Tibba sighed. "You and I, we both found love. Wouldn't we be better off if we hadn't? Once you've discovered what love is, the world looks so bleak without it."

Tibba's words reminded Barbara of John Donne's poem:

> The day breaks not: it is my heart
> Because that you and I must part . . .

She'd always known that she and Trevor must part but never, she thought sadly, had she believed it would be death that separated them.

After the evening meal, Tibba lingered in the parlor to play the piano. Because of her ability with the harp, she'd progressed quickly and had learned a few simple tunes. Barbara moved restlessly from the piano to the bookcase, aimlessly reading the titles to herself.

Moby Dick. She started to reach for the book. No. If she so much as read the first line, her heart would break all over again. Her Ishmael was gone forever.

When the door knocker banged, she started, then called to Mrs. Edwards, busy in the kitchen, saying she'd answer the door.

Harrison Chambers stood on the porch.

"What do *you* want?" she demanded.

"I've come to see Tibba."

She didn't move to let him pass. "I don't think—"

He grasped her arms, lifted her, and set her

aside, saying, "You've made your point. Nevertheless, I mean to come in."

Unable to stop him, Barbara followed Harrison
into the parlor. Tibba swung around on the piano
stool to stare at him, one hand flying to her mouth.

"Please have the courtesy to leave us," Harrison
said to Barbara, his tone formal.

She climbed the stairs slowly, unsure she was
doing the right thing in deserting her friend,
fearing that no matter what he'd come to say,
Tibba would only be hurt.

Later, when she heard Tibba dragging up the
steps, she was sure that was exactly what had
happened. Trying to dredge up comforting words,
she waited for the door to open. Tibba walked in,
her face blank, and stood dazedly in the center of
the room.

"Barbara," she said, "I don't know what to do."
Her voice was toneless. "He—he asked me to
marry him."

Barbara's mouth dropped open.

Tibba sank on the bed. "I'm so stunned that my
mind's in bits and pieces."

"Did you accept?" Barbara asked.

"I told him I had to think about it and I'd let
him know in the morning." Tibba held out a hand
to Barbara. "If I marry him he'll take me home to
England, to his family, and they don't want me.
They'll make my life miserable."

"Apparently *he* wants you. That's enough to
start with." Barbara was surprised to find herself
arguing for Harrison. "Or don't you love him that
much?"

Tibba blinked. "I love him so much I feel like I'll die without him. But I'm afraid to trust him."

Barbara couldn't blame her for that. She wouldn't trust Harrison any farther than she could see him. "I can't tell you what to do," she said.

Tibba smiled, her face taking on animation. "He *does* love me. Maybe that's the only important thing."

Two days later, Barbara stood beside Tibba in Judge O'Hara's chambers as he pronounced Tibba and Harrison man and wife. Tibba, wearing a new midnight blue gown with a fashionable hoop and a blue hat, smiled radiantly at her new husband before he kissed her.

Hugging Tibba, Barbara said, "Be happy." Turning to Harrison, she looked up at him sternly. "I hope you realize that you're a very fortunate man."

He smiled wryly. "Shot through with luck, as I believe I once said."

"See that you remember it."

He bent and kissed her cheek. "I have the feeling that even though you'll be an ocean away you don't intend to let me forget it." He put an arm around Tibba. "And I promise I won't."

Watching them leave the room, tears filled Barbara's eyes, tears of joy for her friend, but of loss too. Tibba would be leaving on the noon train and once she and Harrison had settled what to do about the Meachum estate in West Virginia, they'd be sailing for England.

Then she'd be truly alone.

*   *   *

In the afternoon Barbara, dressed in her warmest clothes, left the boardinghouse and strode briskly toward the town limits, going east, having decided she had to come to terms with the past before she did anything else.

To begin with, she'd visit the site of the burned Chippewa village. She'd never truly mourned White Deer in the Indian fashion and she planned to do that today. After a time she passed the mill and the siding where Trevor had forced her into the boxcar last summer. Even then, enemies that they were, sparks had flown between them. She sighed and hurried on.

Soon she reached the pine grove where she found the few charred logs that were all that remained of the village. The fall rains had washed away the scent of burnt wood, but for a moment the dreadful odor of burnt flesh came to her in memory, and she cloosed her eyes, grimacing. Coming here was even more difficult than she'd expected.

Since she had no way of knowing where Running Otter had buried his wife, Barbara walked slowly along the trail to the beach, absently listening to the chickadees calling from the pines. About here, she told herself, Trevor had stopped her and they'd gone the rest of the way together. And here at the water line she'd found White Deer's poor maimed body.

Choking back tears, Barbara knelt on the sand.

"May your spirit roam free and happy in the After-land," she prayed. "May you live forever in the land beyond the Sky Path of stars. Great Spirit, Kitchi Manitou, God, hear my plea and grant White Deer eternal peace."

Some time later she rose and wandered east along the damp sand of the water line, her eyes blurred with tears. Tears of mourning not only for White Deer but for the man she loved as well. Trevor and she had walked hand in hand along another, warmer beach where they'd found a world of their own. . . .

On and on she walked, oblivious to her surroundings, smiling now and then as she relived every moment of that magic night.

"Snow Bird."

For a moment she thought she'd imagined the call, that it was part of her reverie. But when it came again, this time in the Chippewa tongue, she looked quickly around. An old Indian stood near the pines, his hand raised.

"Running Otter?" she asked, almost certain it was he.

He strode toward her, moving with the vigor of a younger man and she saw she'd been right. She ran to him and threw her arms around him.

Running Otter hugged her in return. "The chickadees told me you were coming," he said. "You are welcome in my lodge."

Relieved that he'd forgiven her for what she couldn't help—her white skin—she smiled at him. "I'm so glad to see you. I feared you'd left the lake completely."

He shrugged. "These pines have always sheltered us. This is our home. Where else would we go?"

She followed him into the pines and along a

nearly invisible trail, the scent of woodsmoke now meaning only the warmth of a hearth fire.

"A stranger lies ill in my lodge," he said. "I've done what I could for him and so he lives. Yet he isn't well. It may be you will know better than I how to cure him. Perhaps that's why the chickadees called you, their sister, here."

"I have no medicines," she protested.

"All the same, you may cure him."

Barbara gazed inquiringly at him but he said no more. She'd forgotten how enigmatic the Chippewas could be. She doubted she could do anything for the ill stranger that Running Otter hadn't already done but, for whatever reason, the old man was giving her little choice. She'd have to try.

The new Chippewa village looked much like the old one—eight small shacks with bark roofs huddling under the shelter of the pines. Near the lodges, animal skins dried on crude stretching frames and she saw a tiny bark structure where she knew the men purified themselves in ritual steam baths. Smoke seeped from the roof vent holes in the centers of the lodges.

Running Otter lifted aside the deer hide covering the opening to his lodge and gestured for her to enter the smoke-tinged gloom. After she was inside it took her eyes a few moments to adjust to the dimmer light. A dark-haired man wrapped in a blanket lay by the fire on a deerskin-covered reed mat. The old Chippewa nodded toward him, then, to her dismay, turned and left the lodge, leaving her alone with the sick stranger.

Barbara approached the man hesitantly. His face was turned away from her, toward the fire. Was he asleep? If so, should she disturb him? Sleep was as healing as anything she could do for him. As quietly as she could, she edged closer. With some surprise she noticed his skin was not only too pale for an Indian's, but that he had a full beard. Chippewas didn't have much facial hair. Knowing Running Otter's hatred of white men following White Deer's death, she'd never expected him to befriend one.

What should she do? Barbara stood for a few minutes undecided. At last she sank to her knees beside the man and bent over him to look at his face, still turned from her. She drew in her breath. "No!" she whispered, certain she must be hallucinating.

The sound roused him and he turned his head, his eyes opening. Brown eyes. Trevor's eyes. He smiled. "I knew you'd come," he said. "It's what kept me alive."

Unable to speak, Barbara pressed her cheek to his, her hands gripping his shoulders fiercely. His arms wrapped around her and they clung to one another, faces wet with tears—his and hers.

When she finally sat back on her heels, she clasped one of his hands between hers, reluctant to let go of him. "I thought you'd drowned," she said. "After the general shot you, I couldn't believe you had a chance."

Trevor turned his head as far as he could toward her and she saw the nearly healed gash running along the side of his head. "His bullet creased my

382

skull. I knew I didn't stand a chance unless I jumped overboard. I hated to leave you behind but what use would I be to you dead?"

"I was rescued when your boat surrendered to the *Michigan* after General Meachum was killed."

"So the world's finally rid of him. High time."

She pressed his hand to her cheek. "I still can't quite believe you're really here with me."

"You can thank the *Michigan*. The light from the flares she set off saved my life by not only showing me the shoreline but a floating life ring from the scuttled tug."

"And when you reached shore Running Otter found you."

"I was pretty far gone by then. Past reason. When I saw him bending over me all I could say was 'Snow Bird.'"

She kissed his palm. "That was enough."

"So here I am in enemy territory once again," he said ruefully.

"You're safe enough in this lodge—especially since everyone believes Trevor Sandoe is dead. When you're feeling better we'll find a way to get back to Richmond."

His hand escaped hers, slid around to her nape and pulled her down until her lips met his. The kiss was gentle, loving. "I can hardly wait until I'm feeling better," he murmured. "You don't mind living in the South and consorting with enemies?"

"The war won't last forever. Besides, I've been consorting with one particular enemy for quite some time."

"We can't let such a scandalous situation continue. It looks as though you'll have to marry me." His hand tightened on her nape. "You will, won't you?"

His words thrilled through her. "General Grant himself couldn't stop me," she said tremulously and kissed him again.

A while later she laid her head on his chest, the faint but steady beat of his heart the most precious sound in the world to her. She smiled a little, remembering how they'd met and how furious she'd been with him.

"Do you know," she asked, "that when you held me prisoner in the boxcar I vowed to get even with you for the way you treated me?"

"And a true revenge it's been!"

Not understanding, she raised her head to look at him.

He stroked her cheek with gentle fingers. "Snow Bird, meeting you changed my life. You made me fall in love with you and I'll never be the same. But I've learned that love is the best and the sweetest revenge of all."

Below: the village of Castleton from Peveril Castle. Right: the Crescent, Buxton.

- THE -
PEAK DISTRICT

Simon Kirwan

MYRIAD

Left: the Old Hall Hotel, Buxton, is reputed to be the oldest hotel in England. It occupies the site of the former townhouse of Bess of Hardwick and her husband the Earl of Shrewsbury. Mary Queen of Scots was held here as a "house prisoner" in 1573.

Below left: the Devonshire Royal Hospital, Buxton was originally a stable block for the horses of spa visitors. It is now part of the University of Derby.

Right: Pavilion Gardens, Buxton, home to the impressive concert hall known as the Octagon and the adjoining Paxton Suite.

Above: the historic Holme Bridge dates from 1664 and spans the river Wye at Bakewell.

Right: the famous Bakewell pudding, and its close cousin the Bakewell tart, originated in this little town.

Above: St Giles' Church, Great Longstone. The twin villages of Great and Little Longstone are just east of Hassop.

Left: Holy Trinity church, Ashford-in-the-Water, two miles north-west of Bakewell on the river Wye.

Right: the 17th and 18th century stone cottages of Litton are clustered around the village green with its stocks and ancient cross.

Below right: Tideswell, one of the Peak District's most ancient settlements.

Below: the imposing Hassop Hall is located in the tiny village of Hassop, three miles north of the market town of Bakewell.

Four miles south-east of Buxton, the village of Chelmorton is the highest village in Derbyshire.

Left: the church of St Lawrence, Eyam. The church contains many artefacts dating back to 1665 when Eyam became known as "the plague village", when the village rector, William Mompesson, persuaded the inhabitants to quarantine the area in order to prevent the plague spreading to neighbouring villages.

Right: the churchyard of St Lawrence is the resting place for many of the plague victims. Among those buried here is William Mompesson's wife, Catherine.

Left and above: beautiful Monsal Dale and the viaduct which carried the Midland railway over the river Wye.

Right: the tiny hamlet of Upperdale is situated amidst some of the finest limestone scenery in the Peak District.

Left: often referred to as "the Palace of the Peaks", Chatsworth is a treasure house of art and antiques. It is the creation of the first Duke of Devonshire who, between 1686-1707, remodelled the original house and turned it into a fabulous Palladian mansion. The gardens were designed by Lancelot "Capability" Brown and Joseph Paxton.

Right: the grand Stable Block at Chatsworth.

Left and right: the romantic and mysterious Haddon Hall is situated next to the river Wye just south of Bakewell.

It is one of the finest medieval and Tudor houses in England and has been the home of the Manners family, the Dukes of Rutland, since 1567. The air of romance that lingers around the house is in part due to the legend that in 1558 Lady Dorothy Vernon eloped from the house on horseback with Sir John Manners. This inspired the 1927 film *Dorothy Vernon of Haddon Hall*, starring Mary Pickford.

Today Haddon Hall is famous for its gardens and its terraced rose plantings are a great favourite with visitors.

Left and above: the imposing edges fringing the Peak District are at their most spectacular north of Bakewell where Froggatt's Edge, Curbar Edge and Baslow Edge join in a breathtaking sequence overlooking the valley of the river Derwent and the villages of Curbar and Calver.

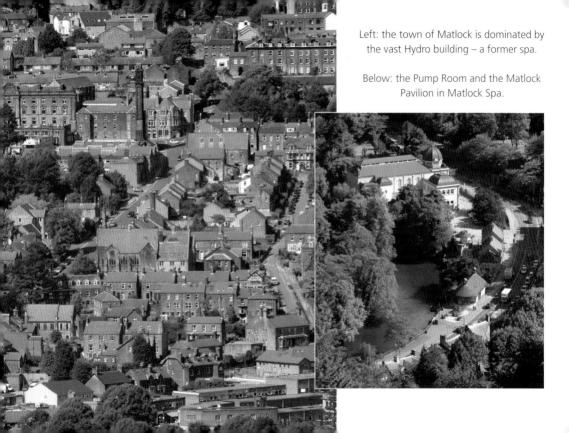

Left: the town of Matlock is dominated by the vast Hydro building – a former spa.

Below: the Pump Room and the Matlock Pavilion in Matlock Spa.

Left: Cromford Mill. Constructed by Sir Richard Arkwright in 1783 this is now at the centre of the Derwent Valley Mills World Heritage Site, which also includes Smedley's Mill at Lea Bridge and the Silk Mill at Derby.

Right: Black Rock, an outcrop of gritstone sculpted by the wind and rain, hangs high above the historic town of Cromford.

Left and above: the spectacular limestone scenery of Dovedale with its steep-sided valleys and exposed crags.

Right: Ilam Hall and the distinctive Alpine-style village of Ilam were built by industrialist Jesse Watts-Russell.

Above and right: Ashbourne, situated at the southern tip of Derbyshire, near the Staffordshire border, is an attractive market town. The splendid stone building in Church Street housed the original Queen Elizabeth Grammar School which was established in 1585.

Left and right: the Roaches form one of the most impressive and dramatic outcrops of the Western Peaks and provide a challenge to climbers. Many classic routes have been established and some of these have been given colourful names such as "Valkyrie", "the Sloth" and "the Swan". On reaching the summit there are spectacular views of Tittesworth Reservoir and the town of Leek in neighbouring Staffordshire. Hen Cloud, right, is a separate southern extremity of the Roaches and overlooks the hamlet of Upper Hulme.

Left: Castleton, situated at the western end of the broad Hope Valley, where the dark gritstone Peaks of the north give way to the white limestone Peaks of the south, is one of the most popular destinations in the Peak District.

Right: Peveril Castle is perched high above Cavedale, overlooking Castleton. The castle was built in 1080 by William Peverel, one of William the Conqueror's most trusted allies. The sheer sides of Cavedale made the castle impregnable; its role was to defend the royal hunting grounds and the local leadmining industry.

Mam Tor is formed from an unstable mix of sandstone and shale. The entire hill is gradually slipping into the valley giving the peak the nickname of the "shivering mountain".

Below: from Castleton there is an enjoyable 6.5 mile (10km) walk that takes in Lose Hill and Winnats Pass.

Right: the busy market town of Chapel-en-le-Frith stands 776ft (237m) above sea level between Stockport and Buxton. Church Brow is a steep, cobbled street leading down from Market Street to the High Street, lined with quaint stone cottages. The Peak Forest Tramway once passed through the town and linked Bugsworth Canal Basin, at the head of the Peak Forest Canal, to the limestone quarries at Dove Holes Dale.

Above: Old Glossop is situated in the far north-west of Derbyshire, just outside the boundaries of the Peak District National Park.

Left: Doctor's Gate, a bleak spot which by legend is named after John Talbot, vicar of Glossop, who built this track to link Sheffield and Glossop.

Right: Kinder Downfall. The windswept 15 mile wide plateau of Kinder Scout is a desolate mix of wind and ice-shattered boulders, peat bogs and deep trenches called "groughs". Kinder Downfall is on the north-western edge of Kinder Scout where much of the plateau's water gathers to drop 98ft (30m) on to the land below.

Above: the Pennine Way, Britain's first long-distance footpath close to its start at the little village of Edale. The path continues for 250 miles northwards.

Right: the surreal, almost lunar landscapes of Over Owler Tor and Higger Tor are located south-east of Hathersage and the Derwent valley. They are thought to have been the inspiration for parts of Charlotte Brontë's famous novel *Jane Eyre*.

Left and right: Stanage Edge, lying on the western moors with views over the Derwent valley, is the largest and most impressive of the Peaks' gritstone edges and is visible from far down in the Hope Valley. The entire edge is approximately 3.5 miles long from its northern tip to the southern point near the Cowper Stone. It is an ideal spot for climbing and is within easy reach of Sheffield. A paved packhorse route ran along the top of Stanage Edge and its path can still be traced.

Thorpe Cloud Hill, with its distinctive conical summit, sits above the village of Thorpe. The hill stands guard over the southern entrance to Dovedale.